BEST SERVED ICY

ALSO BY JAY FITZPATRICK
Fear Itself

BEST SERVED ICY

Revenge is a Dish Best Served Icy

JAY FITZPATRICK

Hard Pressed Publishing
New York

Hard Pressed Publishing
Copyright © 2015 Jay Fitzpatrick
All rights reserved.
ISBN-13: 9780692275412
ISBN-10: 069227541X
Library of Congress Control Number: 2016908376
Hard Pressed, Southampton, NY

For
Thomas J Dean III
Tommy
To Absent Friends

*"And this is good old Boston,
The home of the bean and the cod.
Where the Lowell's speak only to the Cabot's
and the Cabot's speak Yiddish, by God."*

Ellen B

St. Michelle, MD

The four-foot wide catwalk seemed to float on the water. Ten-inch diameter wood pilings, supporting the wood deck, led the way to the deep-water dock some twenty-five yards out onto Bone Creek. The former Vice President walked from his house, across the manicured lawn, down three steps, and onto the catwalk. He walked slowly, guided by a runway of soft deck lights, towards the dock and his refuge. When he reached the end, he noticed that the moon was full, and the tide was high. It was beautiful and breathtaking. The night was chilly but the water steamed as it cooled after the warm summer day. He reached his hand into his jacket and removed a Montecristo Cuban cigar, cut the cap with his wedge cutter and lit the cigar with a Dunhill Gold Apex lighter. A gift from Al Talal bin al Saud, a Saudi business associate and a member of the Saudi royal family.

Veteran Secret Service agent Bob Porter and his newly assigned partner, agent-in-training, Cynthia Taylor, watched the former Vice President's nocturnal ritual from the guard shack located towards the front of the house, a little back from the main road. Taylor was excited to be assigned such an important posting and just happy to be out of the Federal Law Enforcement Training Center (FLETC) in Glynco, Georgia. Agent Porter, however, felt watching over a former Vice President demeaning and a waste of time. Hopefully, in a few weeks, he would rotate back to Washington and the real action. He was assigned this downgrade, by the former President, for what he,

Porter, felt a minor blunder. He was given direct orders from the President's chief of staff, to admit the mayor of New York City and his three guests directly into the Oval Office. He knew he should have followed Secret Service procedure and had them searched, but they were escorted by a senior Secret Service agent. Porter was not about to interfere or argue with a direct order from the chief of staff or with an agent who outranked him. What happened next was a donnybrook. So bad that the President had him reassigned the next day. The chief of staff denied giving him the order.

President Hilton was now out of office. One of the men that Porter let in the Oval Office was now the President of the United States. Porter hoped that would be his ticket back to Washington.

The former Vice President didn't even rate Secret Service protection past six months, but with terrorism and fear still part of the American psyche, somehow strings were pulled to extend the security detail. When Agents Porter and Taylor saw the flame from the lighter, Agent Porter said, "Ok. I am going to make my round. You hold the fort."

Agent Taylor nodded as Potter walked down towards the house and started his clockwise circumnavigation. As he was walking away he pressed his collar mic and added, "If Dodger moves before I get to him, let me know."

Dodger was the Secret Service code name for the former Vice President and not because he was a baseball fan.

Puffing on his cigar Dodger looked west towards Washington, and although forty-five miles distant, he could see the glow of the city in the night sky. While he was contemplating his glory days, his power, his wars, his lies, his lies about his lies, and the money he made from it all, he failed to notice a slight downward movement from the starboard side of the dock. Silently up the swim ladder came a single black form. Wearing a full body dive skin and hood, the black form moved swiftly up behind the former Vice President. The Vice President felt a hand cover his mouth, and his knees buckle. He dropped his cigar on the deck and tried to scream, but nothing came out. He was then forced backward into a sitting position, onto what felt like a lap. A quick forward movement and he and the black form gently and quietly rocked forward into Bone Creek and blackness. Not a ripple. Not a sound. In just under six seconds Dodger was gone.

Agent Taylor, who, for the last minute, had been diligently doing everything but actually watching Dodger, turned to see that he was now gone. She pressed her collar mic and said to Agent Porter, "Dodgers moved off the dock. He must be headed back to the house. I've lost visual." She thought to herself; *that was a quick smoke.*

At the same moment, Agent Porter came in view of the dock and catwalk, pressed his mic and said, "If he went back to the house he must have run. I don't see him at all. Get on the horn and call in a code one. Stay put and stay alert."

A code one was just a heads up to the Secret Service central station duty officer in DC that there is an issue that is being investigated. Porter, closer to the house, ran to the door, entered and did a quick search. He then went to Dodgers bedroom and gently knocked and asked Willow, the Vice President's wife code name, if her husband had come back in. After a negative reply, he then entered the bedroom uninvited and searched the master bath. The house, as he suspected, was empty. With Willow now screaming behind him, Porter raced out the back door, across the lawn, down the three steps to the catwalk and twenty-five yards out to the dock. As he ran, he pushed his collar mic button and told Agent Taylor to call in a code three.

The fact that he bypassed code two and went directly to code three was not lost on Taylor. She knew something awful has happened to the former Vice President, and that probably something awful was going to happen to her.

When Porter got to the dock, he saw the half smoked cigar still smoldering on the deck. Dodger never wasted a cigar and always flicked it into the water when he was through. At the same instant, he saw the wet footprints coming from the swim ladder and across the deck. Dodger was gone. Regardless if Dodger entered the water voluntarily, had another heart attack and fell in or was assisted in, Dodger was gone. Potter knew he would not be going back to DC. He would be lucky to spend the rest of his career chasing counterfeit twenties in Fairbanks.

CHAPTER 1

ST. MICHELLE, MD

About an hour and a half from Washington, across the Chesapeake Bay Bridge, or less than 30 minutes by helicopter, is the eastern shore of Maryland and the waterside village of St. Michelle. St. Michelle had begun to lure VIPs who, some old-timers say, could propel their village into the realm of something like the Hamptons. Realistically, it was more akin to Sag Harbor. One VIP is the former Vice President; another is his old friend the former Secretary of Defense. These VIP's, especially the former Vice President, were not welcomed by most of the village residents, except real estate agents, contractors, and tax assessors.

With helicopters coming and going to and from the former Vice President's residence, most of the village locals knew something bad or good, depending on one's politics, had happened to the former Vice President. The Secret Service tried to put a lid on it but with local police and fire and rescue called in to help, the word spread. There was also a great amount of activity in and around the water with coast guard and police boats looking for something. Harbor Master, Captain Bruce Robertson, right out of central casting, white beard and all, heard radio traffic indicating that Dodger, whom he assumed was the former Vice President, fell off his dock and drowned. If that were the case, he knew exactly where and when Dodger would wash up. That is if they find Dodger before the Maryland blue crabs do.

In the heart of the village, just down Peach Street, sits the Crab Trap Restaurant overlooking Two Mile Harbor and the marinas. Mostly under 40-foot sloops and 30-foot Grady-White fishing boats filled the marinas. The Crab Trap owner, an eccentric old-timer named Antoinette Tennille, but her friends call her Toni, suffered from what the locals called "Old-Timers" decided there was money to be made because of all the activity, and she knew just how to make it. Knowing the town would soon be packed with agents, reporters and curious tourists, she decided to introduce a new lunch-time special. She never liked the mean old former Vice President. She thought him a scary ghoul and a mean old bastard who never left a tip.

Her partner, who by chance was the harbor master, happened to be having lunch at the Crab Trap, and Toni called to him over the counter, and for the benefit of her patrons said, "Say, Captain Bruce, where would you guess a body drowned in Bone Creek would wash up?"

Captain Bruce pretended to ponder the question while local diners stopped eating and talking to listen. "I'm pretty sure this time of year, with the moon full and the tide high, Blackwalnut Cove just at Stillman Island Pt. where the Chesapeake and Bone Creek conflux, would be my guess," said the captain in his best New Hampshire 'Ayuh' accent.

"That's a pretty exact guess captain, even for the harbor master," replied Toni.

"It would be, had it not happened twenty years ago. Similar time of the year and weather and about the same starting point. The only difference is it was a good woman drowned, not a bad man. Don't think the tides and current would care much, though," answered Captain Bruce.

"How long would it take a body to get there?" asked Toni.

"Suppose about a week," concluded Captain Bruce.

Sitting among the locals was Ron Todd, a reporter for the *New York Post*. He was a top investigative reporter, and got a good tip to get to St. Michelle, for what could be a huge story. Todd got his start in journalism at 16 as a copy boy at the *Chattanooga Times*. He has written for *The Washington Post*, *The New York Times*, and *The Boston Globe*, and was the first director of computer-assisted reporting for the *Associated Press*. He taught investigative reporting at the University of Maryland, Northwestern University, and Boston University. He was in his mid-fifties, below average height, with red hair and a full beard. He looked like a short Viking. His instincts told him there was more to this story than meets the eye. He needed to find some locals who could be his eyes.

Turning to a grubby looking older man at the next table, who appeared to be a local, Todd asked, "If you don't mind my asking, who are those two characters?"

"Don't mind at all young fella. The dandy with the white beard is the harbor master and co-owner of this here Crab Trap, Captain Bruce. The woman behind the counter asking the questions is the co-owner and proprietor of the Crab Trap, Toni Tennille."

"I can't believe my luck. The Captain and Tennille right here in St. Michelle," said Todd.

"What was that young fella?"

"Nothing. I was just thinking out loud," replied Ron.

The next Day, the *New York Post* front page headline read:

Former Vice President, Slam-Dunked
by Ron Todd

Richard Rumson the 47th. Vice President of the United States, while on his dock in the tony town of St. Michelle, MD., apparently had a heart attack, fell into the water and drowned. The Vice Presidents Secret Service protection unit…

Excerpts to an earlier *Post* article:

"Rarely has a U.S. Vice President been so wrong about so much at the expense of so many."
Few figures in American political and business history are held in lower regard than the former Vice President …

Afterward, in the kitchen, Toni instructed her crab men to trap around Blackwalnut Cove and also to keep an eye out for anything other than crabs. The new money making scheme, Toni decided, would be an old Crab Trap favorite but with a twist. It would be her basic crab chowder which included: crab, potato, corn and some other ingredients, but she would add to that; Cholula Hot Sauce, cayenne pepper with Vincent's Hot Tomato Sauce instead of his traditional cream sauce. She thought the red color would add to the mystery. Additionally, she would harvest the crabs from Blackwalnut Cove, to legitimize it. Toni wanted the chowder to be more than hot; she wanted it to be, like its inspiration, mean. She added a little Carolina Reaper chili pepper to take it up a notch.

At closing time, she prepared the menu blackboard for tomorrow's lunch special and thought of what she would call her newly invented crab chowder. She decided it would be too crass name it after the former Vice President. With chalk in her hand, she started to write, Shock and Awl crab chowder. No, that was the other guy. She grabbed some newspaper to erase the lunch board and then she saw it. Right on the front page of the rag.

"That's it. That's the ticket. How appropriate, Slam Dunk Crab Chowder," she said aloud but to no one.

CHAPTER 2

St. Michelle, MD

Secret Service Agents Porter and Taylor had been through the grind of telling the story over a dozen times to a dozen different people. Secret Service, Special Agent in Charge (SAC) Robert Scales, from the DC office, was now on the scene and in charge. Together they reviewed the beefed up home security camera tape over and over again. One camera, on the house façade, pointed towards the dock, caught the whole event. It showed Dodger lighting up and enjoying his Cuban. It showed the terrorist, kidnapper, murderer or whoever, coming out of the water and taking Dodger down and over the side. What was certain, from the tape, is that the black form was that of a well-defined person. The form looked and moved like a Special Forces operative but without a weapon, fins, or breathing apparatus. What the tape shows is that they both went in the water and didn't come up, at least not in camera range. It's possible that a small AUV (Autonomous Underwater Vehicle) could have been under the dock and used to spirit them away to a rendezvous with a larger surface boat and on to escape. Since no breathing apparatus was applied to Dodger before they went in, in all probability the operator had no intention of keeping Dodger alive. Hell, with Dodger's bad heart he probably croaked before his Cuban hit the deck.

SAC Scales, on direction from above, made it clear to his entire team, federal and local, "This is a drowning, and that's the way it will be released. We suspect the Vice President went out on his dock for a smoke, had a heart attack, fell in the water, and drowned. We will, of course, await the autopsy and coroner's report for the final verdict, and we will have that shortly after we locate the body."

Secret Service Agents Porter and Taylors job, only job, was to protect Dodger, and they failed miserably. Even if Agent Taylor had had eye contact with Dodger when it went down, nothing would have changed. Neither was in a position to stop the event. The only thing that would have changed is going to a code five immediately, which may have blocked an escape.

It has been almost two days now with no one claiming responsibility or demanding a ransom. It now has gone, for the benefit of the public, from a rescue operation to a recovery mission.

With Harbor Master Captain Bruce Robertson's assistance, the recovery focused around points leading towards Stillman Island Pt. The Captain would not steer them directly to Blackwalnut Cove until his partner harvested more crabs. For Captain Bruce, when it came to finding Dodger's drowned body, business came before pleasure, and business was good.

The Captain was becoming pretty popular as one of the few locals assisting the Feds. Even that pesky *Post* reporter was pressing him and Toni for some inside information. "Well," said the Captain to Todd, "I might just give you something I heard, but it will cost you and your rag. My picture on the front page and a boat load of cash. Fame and fortune are but little payment for what I know."

CHAPTER 3

WASHINGTON, DC

Back in Washington, FBI Director Raymond Riley entered the President of the United States office. "Morning Sarge, are you ready?"

"Were waiting on you Captain," replied the President.

President Thomas Dean Burk and FBI Director Raymond Riley have a long history and have been through a couple of wars together, one in a far off country, and another closer to home. In the far off war, Riley had been Captain Riley, commanding officer of Golf Company 2nd Battalion 7th Marines. Burk had been Sergeant Burk 2nd platoon leader. President Burk sometimes addressed Riley by his former title Captain while FBI Director Riley would sometimes refer to the President as Sarge.

In the war closer to home, Burk took command, and together they fought evil, won, and Burk was propelled from darkness into POTUS and Riley, then NYC Police Commissioner, into Director of the Federal Bureau of Investigation.

Also in the office was Secret Service Director Christian Bounty. The three of them were thick as thieves, but that's another and earlier story.

President Burk, an outsider with no political experience, was swept into office less than two years ago. He and his team implemented radical changes to Congress, defense, taxation, and transparency. They introduced a whole slew of other important "Live and Let Live" campaign platform ideas and just plain common sense. The country was at peace within and without. Radical

Islam terrorist groups were not promoted, tolerated or televised. They were not bombed or captured. They were simply hunted, internationally and at home by small US Special Forces Teams and killed. No reporters were embedded, no press conferences held, and no information leaked. They would not get free press from the Americans, or use America for exposing their propaganda. Their Facebook and Twitter accounts were hacked or taken down. Social Media was no longer a communication tool for terrorists.

What FBI Director Riley, Secret Service Director Bounty and President Burk were meeting for, was to discuss the former Vice President's murder. SSD Bounty had been in close contact with SAC Scales and knew, from the camera tape, that the Vice President was murdered. They also suspected why and whom. For now, they wanted to keep all that a secret.

The old Dodger had been out of office for over nine years but was still appearing on Sunday TV shows, to lie and defend his policies and his reputation. That, they thought, is what got the old sod killed. The son of a bitch just couldn't keep his mouth shut. He had to keep reminding the country what he did and how he got away with it. Dodger and his partners in crime lied to the American people. They told us Sadam and Iraq were involved in 9-11. They told us Sadam and Iraq had WMD and were going to use them against us. They lied and when confronted about the lies, they lied again. They then led our country to the worst financial meltdown ever, but unlike Dodger, they had the decency to keep quiet about the past and stay under the radar. Not Dodger. He had to keep opening his pie hole, so it seemed someone finally decided to serve him his just desserts.

Burk, Riley, and Bounty were not meeting to find Dodger's killer. They knew who did it. They were meeting to discuss who might be next and what, if anything, to do about it. Burk and Riley play by the rules. Their rules. And their rules said it's OK if bad people, who did bad things to our country, get their just desserts. It seems, at least with Dodger, his just desserts may have been a bit overdue. But sometimes "Revenge, like dessert, is best served cold." Or, as in this case, best served icy.

CHAPTER 4

EVERYWHERE

Israel Colburn was a Southie. Born in 1949 in the predominantly Irish community of South Boston. His da was Irish, and his mother was Jewish. He had wavy jet black hair and amazing turquoise eyes. As a young student at St. Brigid's grade school he excelled at art and sports, both of which, unfortunately, were not offered at St. Brigid's, so to compensate, he became a daydreamer. He was an altar boy and a basic good kid except when he wasn't.

One school day, after assisting at noon mass, he hung up his surplice and cassock and joined four of his friends for a joy ride in one of the friend's father's car. They hit a parked car, were identified, and reported to the police. Since they were all under thirteen and the boy's father didn't press charges, dealing out punishment, fell to St. Brigid's. The punishment was severe. All five boys were suspended for a week. To Israel's parents, this was devastating. The cat and nine tail, a leather strap, was administered by his da, and his mother grounded him for a month. But all was soon forgotten, and Israel finally graduated.

On to Cathedral High School, across the tracks on Union Parks Street, Israel now almost 6' tall, 160 lbs., was handsome, tough but again, in with the wrong crowd. Cathedral High was all about academics and science. They had sports but no artistic program. Israel's grades dropped, and he began getting into fights. He was, however, a good kid and wanted to do good. He and a few of his new friends started protecting less able kids from bullies. Israel was doing this because of his dislike for bullies. His friends, however, had ulterior motives. They were collecting protection money from the bullied. When the school found out they were running a protection racket, they invited Israel and his friends to leave. This turned out to be a godsend, as Israel was enrolled in South Boston High School. A public high school, South Boston offered art, mechanical drawing, wood shop, and print shop in addition to the required classes. Israel was in heaven, and his grades shot up.

He graduated in 1966 and immediately joined the Marines with his mother's signature as he was only 17. He signed up for a four-year hitch. After graduating from Paris Island, Israel received his MOS, Military Occupational Specialty. Because he joined for four years, he had his pick of specialties, and he choose tanks. He proceeded to train as an M1A1 tank crewman.

By March 1967, he was six months into his Vietnam tour, as a Sergeant and tank commander attached to the 7th Marines. Tanks, especially the 50-ton behemoth, M-48 Patton medium battle tank, and Vietnam didn't go well together. The tank tracks got stuck in the rice paddies or broke-up in the hills. Where most of the ground support was needed, the tanks couldn't go. Not a lot of roads in I Corp, and the ones traversable were constantly mined. Sergeant Israel Colburn met Captain Raymond Riley and Sergeant Tommy Burk while accompanying Golf Company 2/7 on a search and destroy mission in Duc Phu. Captain Riley learned fast to keep the tank anchored and bring the enemy to the tank and its 105 mm main battle gun, and 50 and 30 cal. machine guns. He positioned Sergeant Colburn's tank with Sergeant Burk's platoon as security. Captain Riley headed the rest of the company, the hammer, towards the anvil. It worked over and over again, so well, that while other companies stayed clear of tanks, Golf 2/7 requested tank commander Sergeant Colburn, his tank and crew be permanently attached. They worked well together, and after just a few operations they got the routine down pat. They were inseparable but since Burk and Colburn were both Sergeants, Captain Riley and Sergeant Burk began calling Sergeant Colburn by his Initials, IC. Less confusion. They got their wish to work together, but soon, something bigger would tear them apart. Something no one saw coming.

Towards the end of May, things started heating up about 4500 miles away in the Sinai Desert. The Six Day War was about to begin with the State of Israel fighting for its life against its Arab neighbors, Egypt, Jordan, Syria, Iraq, and Lebanon. These main Arab countries were supported by Algeria, Kuwait, Libya, Morocco, Pakistan, Saudi Arabia, Sudan, Tunisia and the PLO. They were all gearing up for a big battle, and it all started over water. At least that was the proverbial straw. The United States was worried and sent the 6th Fleet into the Mediterranean as support for Israel. The 7th Marines, in Vietnam, were put on standby to be pulled out of Vietnam to aid Israel if needed. Not wanting to wait, Sergeant Israel Colburn requested through his chain of command that he be immediately op/coned to the IDF, the Israel Defense Forces. He was, after all, a half Jew and what better learning experience for a USMC tank commander than being in what could be the biggest tank battle since WWII.

No one thought Sergeant Coburn's offer to embed with the IDF as a tank commander, would be accepted or even considered. But somehow it got shoved up the chain of command, to the commanding officer of the 7th. Marines, Colonel Haffey, who took it to General Westmoreland. Westmoreland to McNamara. McNamara to Israeli Major-General Ariel Sharon and the next thing Sergeant Israel Colburn knew, he was on a jet plane to Israel.

During the run-up to the Six-Day War, the Americans unexpectedly rebuffed Israeli requests for military aid and approval for an Israeli preemptive attack on Egypt. The United States, bogged down in Vietnam and facing domestic opposition to that war, was loathe to become embroiled in a second front. Rather than get involved militarily, the Americans aggressively pursued diplomatic solutions and sought to cobble together an international regatta to challenge the Egyptian blockade of Israeli shipping in the Straits of Tiran, a campaign that ultimately failed. But while the U.S. continued to refuse to aid Israel militarily, the American opposition to unilateral Israeli action began to soften at the beginning of June 1967.

General Westmoreland and Secretary of Defence McNamara, felt they could spare at least one man. If he survived, the US could learn a hell of a lot about our allies and how they fought their enemies. On June 1st, 1967

Sergeant Israel Colburn arrived in Israel and was assigned to the 8th Armored Brigade, led by Colonel Albert Mandler. Sergeant Colburn was assigned to an M-48 Patton Medium Battle Tank, the same type of tank he commanded in Vietnam. He was introduced to his new crew, by his platoon leader Lieutenant Uzi Gur: Corporal Doug Lamm, driver; Private Jeremiah Levy, gunner; and Private Benny Morris, loader. Two of the crew spoke Hebrew, one Arabic, but all three spoke English.

Attempting to mimic a British accent, Corporal Lamm said: "What brings a Yank across the pond to fight our war?" Privates Levy and Morris knew Lamm was an instigator and a needle and waited to see how the Yank would react to his dig. Sergeant Colburn seemed to ponder the question then said, "To paraphrase the great Marine "Chesty" Puller; 'They are in front of us, behind us, and we are flanked on both sides by an enemy that outnumbers us 15:1. They can't get away from us now!'" The three crew members thought that was hilarious, and under the current circumstances that seemed to ease the tension. Sergeant Colburn then added "And after I help you with your business, this Irish Catholic Jew is going to Northern Ireland to fight the Paras. I don't like bullies, wherever they are."

They quickly accepted Colburn as part of the crew and got busy learning how to work together. The IDF and the 8th Armored Brigade had their way of doing things, and Colburn had his. After all, Sergeant Colburn was the only tank commander in Alpha Company to have been in combat. During the few days they trained together, the crew went from skeptical to respectful. There were four tanks in Colburn's 1st tank platoon, led by Lieutenant Uzi Gur, and three more platoons in his Alpha Company. Also, and as support, there was a headquarters and maintenance company led by Captain Ezar Bitton. There were four companies in the 8th Armored Brigade, all led by Colonel Albert Mandler.

Many fronts were going to happen at the same time with many different units going up against many different enemies. Sergeant Colburn's war would only be where the 8th Armored Brigade would go, only where his Alpha Company would go, and only where his 1st.tank platoon would go. But more to the point, his war would be what he saw from his tank, a tunnel view out his small, narrow, viewport. Corporal Lamm was painting Colburn's initials, in large white letters, on the tank sides. "Why initials and why my initials IC?" asked Colburn.

"From what I have been told, it's company SOP. All tanks will take on the initials of their commander, so we can identify each other without giving the tanks names," Lamm said.

"Why in English and not Hebrew?

"Because most of our enemies can't read English. We are now Tank IC," Lamm replied.

Sergeant Colburn's and Tank IC's war started on the morning of June 9, as Israeli jets began carrying out dozens of sorties against Syrian positions from Mount Hermon to Tawfiq, using rockets salvaged from captured Egyptian stocks. The airstrikes knocked out artillery batteries and storehouses and forced transport columns off the roads. The Syrians suffered heavy casualties and a drop in morale, with a number of senior officers and troops deserting. The attacks also provided time as Israeli forces cleared paths through Syrian minefields; however, the airstrikes did not seriously damage the Syrians' bunkers and trench systems, and the bulk of Syrian forces on the Golan remained in their positions.

About two hours after the airstrikes began, the 8th Armored Brigade, led by Colonel Albert Mandler, advanced into the Golan Heights from Givat HaEm. Its advance was spearheaded by Engineering Corps's sappers and eight bulldozers, which cleared away barbed wire and mines. As they advanced, the force came under fire, and five bulldozers were immediately hit. The Israeli tanks, with their maneuverability sharply reduced by the terrain, advanced slowly under fire toward the fortified village of Sir al-Dib, with their ultimate objective being the fortress at Qala. Israeli casualties steadily mounted. Part of the attacking force, including Colburn's 1st platoon, lost its way and emerged opposite of Za'ura, a redoubt manned by Syrian reservists. 1st platoon immediately lost two tanks. Sergeant Colburn's Tank IC and the other remaining 1st platoon tank were ordered to pull back. Colburn disregarded the order and pushed forward with Tank UG, Commanded by Lieutenant Uzi Gur, right behind.

Unknown to Colburn and his crew, two Syrian T-54, Russian-made, main battle tanks, had apparently been waiting in ambush at a distance of roughly 600 yards away, the same direction that, what was left of 1st platoon, were turning. At this distance, easily within its capability, the T-54 fired at Colburn, but its infamous high-velocity 100mm shell, the type that had destroyed so many IDF tanks and vehicles later in the war, went high and was not even close. Colburn's gunner, Private Jeremiah Levy, only 18 years old, responded almost instantly with a round that struck the T-54 huge angled glasis, or front plate, but the shot, a non-armor-piercing high explosive (HE) shell, had no effect. Ricocheting off the armor, it shot skyward and exploded harmlessly. Colburn's Patton had been loaded mostly with an HE only because Alpha Company Commander, Captain Ezar Bitton, had been expecting urban targets, such as buildings, personnel, and light anti-tank guns. "AP!" Colburn shouted to his loader Benny, which meant an armor-piercing shell would be next. Colburn and his crew then felt a concussion or thud on the turret. It was never known if this shot came from the Syrian T-54, or from some other anti-tank weapon. In any case, no serious damage was done, probably a lucky glancing impact. In the next instant, Jeremiah aimed and fired a second time, just as the monster was moving forward and raising up over a pile of rubble. The Patton's 105mm AP round penetrated the T-54's underbelly, apparently striking the ammo well and resulting in a tremendous explosion that blew its turret loose. With near certainty, the entire Syrian crew was killed. Now the momentum seemed to be changing, and Captain Ezar Bitton had to support what was left of 1st Platoon or stall. He got on the horn to 2nd platoons Lieutenant Kaplan, "Follow that crazy son of a bitch Colburn, but keep your intervals and watch your flanks."

As Colburn moved forward, there was no time to examine their "trophy." A battle was raging, and the 1st platoon's Patton's continued down the road, passing the lifeless and burning T-54. Tough fighting still lay ahead, as RPG bazooka type rockets and machine-gun fire came from slits in the bunkers on both sides of the road. Colburn said out loud but to no one "Into the valley of death rode the 600." With the situation critical, Colonel Mandler ordered simultaneous assaults on Za'ura and Qala. Heavy and confused fighting followed, with Israeli and Syrian tanks struggling around obstacles and firing at extremely short ranges. The second Syrian T-54 came at Colburn's flank and fired. The HE round hit his side plates and exploded. "Douggie, turn and ram him before he can reload," Colburn yelled to his driver Corporal Doug Lamm. The Patton slammed into the Syrian T-54 with such impact that the T-54 up sided, and its starboard tracks started to spin in the air. Colburn ordered Douggie to pull back just as Lt. Kaplan yelled "Fire!" An AP round hit the Syrian T-54 side skirt and went right through the armor plates before it exploded.

With no more Syrian tanks in site, 1st and 2nd platoons opened the hatches, and the commanders turned their Browning 50 Cal. Machine guns on the bunkers. Six 50's all firing at the same time can do a lot of damage. Syrian troops, now without tank support, began running for their lives. The 50's tore them up.

Colonel Mandler recalled that "the Syrians fought well and bloodied us. We beat them only by crushing them under our treads and by blasting them with our cannons and 50's at very short range, from 100 to 500 meters."

The first three Israeli tanks, of Alpha 2/8 to enter Qala were stopped by a Syrian bazooka team, and a relief column of seven Syrian tanks arrived to repel the attackers. The Israelis took heavy fire from the houses, but could not turn back, as other forces were advancing behind them, and they were on a narrow path with mines on either side. Alpha 2/8 now with Lt. Kaplan in the lead, tore head on into the Syrian tanks. Colburn flanked him and came up on his port side. Both tanks fired on the run. Kaplan was broadsided by an RPG, disabled but not dead. Colburn joined the last surviving tank of 2/8, and together they took on the seven Syrian tanks. They each took one Syrian tank out. The fighting was close and near run, but the Syrian's lost the advantage. Tank UG, Commanded by Lieutenant Uzi Gur, got hit, and Colburn went to his defense. Colburn stayed with the wounded tank, continued to pound the Syrian's and took out another T-54. He could have retreated to safety, but that was not Colburn. He would not leave a wounded buddy. The Israelis continued pressing forward and called for air support. A pair of Israeli jets destroyed two of the Syrian tanks, and the remainder withdrew.

The surviving defenders of Qala retreated after their commander was killed. Meanwhile, Za'ura fell in an Israeli assault, and the Israelis also captured the 'Ein Fit fortress.

The next day, June 10th, the 8th Brigade's tanks moved south from Qala, advancing six miles to Wasit under heavy artillery and tank bombardment. At Banaias in the north, Syrian mortar batteries opened fire on advancing Israeli forces only after Golani Brigade sappers cleared a path through a minefield, killing sixteen Israeli soldiers and wounding four.

Israel had completed its final offensive in the Golan Heights, and a ceasefire was signed the day after. Israel had seized the Gaza Strip, the Sinai Peninsula, the West Bank of the Jordan River (including East Jerusalem), and the Golan Heights. Overall, Israel's territory grew by a factor of three, including about one million Arabs placed under Israel's direct control in the newly captured territories. Israel's strategic depth grew to at least 300 kilometers in the south, 60 kilometers in the east, and 20 kilometers of extremely rugged terrain in the north, a security asset that would prove useful in the Yom Kippur War six years later.

Sergeant Israel Colburn became the only active American servicemen to have participated in tank warfare on this scale. Although he and his crew all sustained wounds, the IDF did not give medals for wounds. They did, however, award Sergeant Israel Colburn their second highest award. The Medal of Courage, which his company and platoon commanders, and especially his crew, all agreed he deserved.

He was awarded the medal by General Ariel Sharon. Colburn was introduced to Sharon by his Company Commander, Captain Ezar Bitton, as Sergeant Israel Colburn. "We call him Icy," said Captain Bitton. When Sharon asked why you call him by his initials instead of his name, Captain Bitton said, "No General, not IC, Icy. The men and I have seen Israel Colburn in combat, and he has ice cold blood running through his veins. We now call him 'Icy,' because he's cold and fearless in battle, not for his initials."

Sergeant Israel Colburn didn't go back to Vietnam after the end of the Six Day war but instead finished his hitch training young tank commanders in

Camp Pendleton, CA. When his enlistment was up, he headed off to Northern Ireland, then Angola, Laos, Afghanistan, Central America and anywhere bullies and bad people wanted to instill their will on the weak.

CHAPTER 5

St. Michelle, MD

"**W**hat are you guys doing back so early and is that all the crabs you got?" asked Toni Tennille of her crab men, as they appeared in the kitchen.

"We were crabbing Blackwalnut Cove like you told us, but about a half hour ago, some Secret Service types told us to skedaddle."

Captain Bruce, who had been in the back room monitoring his VHF marine radio, came into the kitchen and announced, "They found Dodger, or I should say what's left of him just where I said they would, Blackwalnut Cove. The crabs tore him up pretty bad."

The Captain and Tennille looked at each trying to decide if this was good news or bad. Toni asked, "Do you think there will still be a demand for our Slam Dunk Crab Chowder when word gets out?"

"Toni," said Captain Bruce, "I think when the customers come to the realization that they may have actually been eating the crabs, in our Slam Dunk Crab Chowder, that had actually eaten the former Vice President, they are going to throw-up. I think we had a good run, but it's time for the Slam Dunk Crab Chowder to take a dunk."

Toni walked out of the kitchen and into the dining room. She took the blackboard eraser and with one swipe, Slam Dunk Crab Chowder, like the Vice President, disappeared.

New York Post Reporter Ron Todd, listened carefully to what the Captain and Tennille had to say and decided to pry them for more details, but he would have to agree to the Captain's terms first.

Back in Blackwalnut Cove, Secret Service, FBI and Homeland agents were stumbling all over themselves, trying to rope off the crime scene. Local and state police and the Coast Guard was charged with keeping the reporters in boats and choppers at bay. Captain Bruce continued to monitor the radio and wondered to himself, *Crime scene. Do they think the crabs did it?*

Secret Service SAC Bob Scales bent over Dodgers body. It was face up with the waist and legs still under a foot or so of water, but the chest and head were above water and propped against a mud flat. Out of Dodgers open mouth, like a scene from the Blue Lagoon, a Hermit Crab crawled out, dropped into the water, and disappeared. Dodger's eyes, cheeks and lips were gone, and his chest was open and void. What was left inside were his white ribs and some muscle, tendons and tissue but all the organs were gone, as were the Maryland blue crabs. An FBI photographer backed off so SAC Scales could get a better look. Inside the chest cavity was something Scales was hoping to find. A small round piece of metal and a long cord. It was there. The crabs hadn't taken it, the former Vice President's pacemaker. They would get a positive identification from prints, from what fingers remained, dental and DNA later, but for now, the Washington University Hospital name stamped on the pacemaker was a pretty positive ID.

SAC Scales pulled out his secure phone, pushed #1 and a second later his boss was on the phone.

"What have you got Bob?" asked Secret Service Director Bounty.

"We got him," said Scales.

"What's he look like?"

"Bad," said Scales.

"OK, box him up and get him to Bethesda and keep a lid on it as much as possible. I don't want to see pictures of the old sod on *CNN* tonight."

"What do you want to do with the two assigned agents that fucked up, Porter and Taylor?" asked Scales.

Scales heard Bounty repeat his question to someone, perhaps the President, and then Director Bounty came back on and said, "Promote them."

CHAPTER 6

WASHINGTON, DC

The President, FBI Director Ray Riley, and Secret Service Director Christian Bounty walked out of the Oval Office, some thirty feet, to the Cabinet Room. The President entered, and his entire Cabinet plus some staff and aids stood until the President seated himself in the Presidents chair at the center of the oval table. Directly across from President Burk was Vice President Claire Hilton, the daughter of the former President. Claire Hilton and Tommy Burk ran a good, clean campaign, to sweep them, with landslide numbers, into the White House. Their "Live and Let Live" party, Tommy's hero status, Claire's youth, enthusiasm, and break-away from her mother's politics was uniting the country. To the President's right was his Secretary of State Matt Walsh. To the President's left sat his Secretary of Defense Ed Stanton. His friend and supporter, Secretary of the Treasury Michael Bloomfield, sat across the table directly to the right of the Vice President. His trusted Riley, Bounty and his boyhood friend and Chief of Staff Bill Nicholas, sat against the window directly behind the President. They had a lot on their plate to discuss today, but the President started with an announcement.

"I just received word that they found former Vice President Richard Rumson. As you all know, and as we suspected, he drowned, after falling into the water, from his dock. His body is now in route to Bethesda Naval Hospital for an autopsy. There is no reason to suspect foul play. Let us bow our heads for a moment of prayer."

They all did, but from behind, the President could feel the bowed eyes of Riley and Bounty burning into his back. *The President is holding back the truth from his cabinet. Never a good thing,* they thought.

The Cabinet meeting lasted about an hour, and then the President, Ray Riley, Chris Bounty and Bill Nicholas walked back to the Oval Office. The White House Press Secretary, Kelly Sullivan Burk, who was also the President's wife and the country's First Lady, joined them. Kelly was the reporter who tried to bring Tommy Burk down before the election and before she learned the truth and joined his side. The four of them were now thick as thieves, and his Chief of Staff Bill Nicholas, although a boyhood friend, was clueless but was about to be read in. They all sat down on the chairs and sofa around the coffee table, and the President said, "Kelly, make sure your press brief keeps to the official story. I know some reporter is going to dig, but for now, we hold the line."

"What are you saying Mr. President?" asked Bill Nicholas.

"Oh right, you haven't heard the latest. Dodger was pushed into the water. No heart attack. No fall. He did drown, though."

"Dodger?"

"Sorry, Dodger was the Secret Service handle for the former Vice President."

"But that's not what we're telling the press and the American people. And not what you just told your Cabinet?" asked Nicholas.

"Correct. Chris, why don't you read Bill in?"

"We have security camera tape showing an operative coming out of the water, securing Dodger from the back, and both of them entering the water. No mask. No breathing apparatus. No boat, water sled or submersible. No ransom demands. No one has claimed responsibility," said Chris Bounty.

"Look, Bill; we think this is a revenge killing. We are not 100% sure yet so we want to play it close to the vest," added the President.

"I know this guy was bad, with Iraq, WMD and all the lies and money he made because of it all, but why now? He's been out of office for almost ten years," asked Nicholas.

"This guy was bad. The worst. And a lot of people hated him, and a lot of people are going to be happy he's gone. As for why now? Have you heard the expression "Revenge is a dessert best served cold"? When the public finds out, and they will, a lot of people are going to be ecstatic that that lying, self-serving, son of a bitch got what was coming to him. Especially when he thought he skated and got away with it," said the President.

"It sounds like you agree with them," said Nicholas.

The President and his three close associates all looked at one another and then the President added, "If you don't agree Chief of Staff Nicholas, you better tell me now."

CHAPTER 7

CAMBRIDGE, MA

After Vietnam, the Six Day War, and Pendleton CA., Israel Colburn traveled to Northern Ireland during the Troubles. He no longer commanded tanks, but every Marine was a basic rifleman first. He helped the IRA in their fight against the Paras and the Ulster Volunteer Force. He then went on as a mercenary to Pakistan, Rhodesia, Cambodia, Lebanon, Laos, Angola, and El Salvador. He fought against China in the Vietnam-China war.

No longer called a mercenary, now called a contractor, he went to Afghanistan to fight the Russians and to Nicaragua to help the Contras. All along the way his credentials were checked out and verified. There were a lot of contractors, aka mercenaries, available from Korea and the French and American Vietnams. You first got hooked up thru SOF, *Soldier of Fortune* Magazine but after that and all through his wars, his creds were checked. Israel Colburn's creds checked out better than most, and his nom de guerre Icy followed him around the world. After all, everyone who fought with or against him said he had ice water running through his veins. Icy was cold. He was cold in battle and cold to anyone who had never been in battle.

He fought the good fight, made a few enemies, a lot of friends, and a lot of money. He had wounds, broken bones, and a reputation of ice cold fearlessness and cunning. But he always protected the old, women, and kids, regardless of what side they were on. Colburn was now in his early sixty's but still handsome at six foot, with wavy jet black hair and amazing turquoise eyes. But he was now beaten up, tired and ready to come home.

Israel Colburn became a partner in the Cambridge law firm of Beston Servienti and Colburn. His clients knew there was no Beston or Servienti, just Colburn and his assistant, Mary Weeks. They didn't get any walk-ins; they weren't listed in the phone book; they had no website, Twitter or Facebook accounts. They were strictly referral. Beston Servienti and Colburn, known to the trade as Best Served Cold, didn't handle litigation. Their international clientele came to Beston Servienti and Colburn seeking one thing and one thing only. Revenge. Best Served Cold don't litigate, they eliminate.

CHAPTER 8

HEDGEHAMPTON, NY

The Tuesday *New* York *Post* front page headline read:

Globalwide's Albert Mazola, Underwater
by Ron Todd and Tom Sweeney
Albert Mazola, the single most corrupt subprime mortgage lender in America, was found drowned this morning, in the swimming pool of his Hedgehampton estate.
The estate groundskeeper ...

Excerpts to an earlier *Post* article:

At the beginning of the financial crisis, there was Albert Mazola...
Few figures in American business history are held in lower regard than the former Globalwide's chief executive, whose perpetual tan and penchant for French cuffs made him a lightning rod for critics who vilified him as the symbol of the subprime mortgage crisis...

The day before the *Post* story broke, Hedgehampton village Detective Gregg Keghlian was the second police officer on the scene. He directed Patrol Officer Suzanne Petty, first on the scene, to rope off an even larger crime scene. Why take chances?

"Tell me exactly what went down from when you got the call," said Detective Keghlian.

"From the time I got the call to the scene, five minutes tops. The estate groundskeeper," Officer Petty looked down at her notes to check the name, "Charley Beacon, said he was walking the property as he did every morning and found his employer Albert Mazola's nude and face down in the bottom of the pool. He did not attempt a rescue because he assumed he was dead."

"So no one has touched the body?"

"Affirmative."

"So how do we know it's Mr. Mazola, and how do we know he's dead?" asked Detective Keghlian.

"I've been here almost ten minutes, and Mr. Beacon has been here maybe 10 minutes before me. The body has not moved, for what twenty minutes and no air bubbles. So unless Mr. Mazola is pretending to be Harry Houdini, I think it's safe to assume he's dead. As to how Mr. Beacon can identify Mr. Mazola's nude body from the rear, you'll have to ask him. He is right over there by the pool house, and he is pretty shaken up."

"I will," said Detective Keghlian, "but first let's get some photos started. I'll call the medical examiner and the state police dive team to help get the body out. By the way, you did a good job but don't repeat that last part of your report to the chief. He won't appreciate it." *Nobody likes a smart ass*, he thought to himself.

Hedgehampton Village Police Chief Thomas Drumming and Mayor Mark Early arrived at the scene together and walked towards Detective Keghlian, who was standing by the pool. They both looked into the pool, and the chief said, "Tell me exactly what went down from when you got the call, and why is the body still in the pool?"

Detective Keghlian recapped Patrol Officer Petty's report, leaving out the smart ass comment and added that he just got off the phone with coroner's office and the state police.

Two more village patrol cars arrived and began assisting securing the property and knocking on neighbors doors. Properties in the estate section were typically 3-5 acres. Mazola's property was about 8 acres, so neighbors were few and far between.

It took a half hour for the medical examiner and state police to arrive, and the two state police divers were suiting up. A reporter, known to the chief, and some curious passersby, started to gather at the entrance gates. The chief gave the OK for the reporter to come on in.

Then things got interesting. A black helicopter with big FBI letters on the side started circling. Two black Chevy Suburban's pulled into the driveway, and two FBI agents got out. The chopper landed on the lawn north of the tennis court, and two agents got out. Mayor Early, Chief Drumming, and Detective Keghlian, the coroner, and divers all knew instantly their world was about to change.

Assistant Director in Charge of the New York City office, Michael Hoar, recently promoted, and Special Agent in Charge Harold Shaw walked over to the men who looked to be in charge, showed their creds and introduced themselves. Two other FBI agents came from the driveway, stood to the side, but were not introduced. ADC Hoar looked at one of his agents, then looked at the reporter. The reporter had his press cred lanyard around his neck and a phone to his ear. The agent then moved directly to the reporter, gently grasped the reporters arm, and led him outside the security tape. Things now got tense.

"Chief, mayor, detective," said ADC Hoar, "We are officially going to assist you on this case, but you will coordinate everything directly through us. Is that clear?" The chief, mayor and detective all nodded and seemed relieved that the FBI was not moving in but only assisting. Tensions seemed to ease somewhat. *But what could be the FBI interest, in this case,* thought the chief.

Two hours later a Hertz rental car drove up to Mazola's driveway gate and *NY Post* reporter Ron Todd got out. Another tip had mysteriously come his way. He walked over to the only person who looked like a local reporter and said, "Are you Tom Sweeney with *The Hedgehampton Press?*"

Tom Sweeney grew up in Hedgehampton, an incorporated village in the town of Southampton, graduated Hedgehampton High School and majored in journalism from Stony Brook, Southampton Campus. A real hometown boy. He was just over six feet tall, with dusty blond hair. He just turned twenty-five and has been with *The Hedgehampton Press* for three years not including two years of internship. He was good looking, hardworking and proving to be a good, aggressive reporter. Tom knew Hedgehampton and everyone in it. Exactly what Todd needed. Just like his local St. Michelle insiders, Captain, and Tennille. Todd always said *you can get knee high in July a lot faster if you have an ear of local corn.*

"I am. And you're Ron Todd with the *Post?*"

"Correct." they shook hands, and Todd continued, "Your paper and mine decided to cooperate on this story so let's hear what you've got so far.

"Whoa!" said Sweeney. "I got the word from my boss to cooperate with you, but what I want to know is why?"

"The why, my young friend, is because a co-byline with me in the *NY Post,* won't hurt your career."

"That I understand and appreciate. But why do you want to work with me or anyone for that matter? I have followed your work and even studied you in journalism school. You're good, but you always work alone."

"That my boy is the past. It's a different world, and I have a feeling I need some local help on this one. So fill me in now with what you've got, and I will fill you in on what I have over dinner tonight, on me. Deal?"

"Deal," said Sweeney. "Mazola drowned. I presume you know that, or you wouldn't be here. I know the chief and the mayor pretty well and was about to be briefed, off the record. Then the FBI showed up, and I was escorted off the property. I saw Mazola's nude body in the bottom of the pool and even got a picture of it on my phone. I heard them say the ETD, estimated time of death, to be around 2 a.m. this morning. On a hunch, I started calling some of the popular restaurants here in the village and bingo! He dined with friends at Le Steak on Main Street. He left alone but his waiter, disappointed in his tip, saw him chat up an attractive twenty-something outside. They left together in Mazola's Bentley."

"What time was that?"

"1 a.m.," said Sweeney.

Deputy Medical Examiner Paul Mellon, M.D., left Mazola's estate about an hour ago, to take the body back to the office of the Suffolk County Medical

Examiner Department in Hauppauge. Detective Keghlian and Special Agent in Charge Harold Shaw were let into the house by the caretaker, Charley Beacon, and proceeded to go room to room looking for clues. The beds had not been slept in, and the kitchen was spotless. It appeared Mazola had not come into the house since the housekeeper left. So where was he before he took his swim? They decided to start backtracking.

The chief had left right after the Medical Examiner arrived to see if he could get copies of the home security camera tape from the security firm. Experience told him the security tape would be stored on the security firm's server or in its cloud. When the chief arrived at the security firm's central station, he was told the FBI had already confiscated the tapes, and no copies were available.

"No copies at the house?" asked the chief.

"No. Everything is recorded here and stored on our server. No hard copies exist."

So much for the FBI assisting, thought the chief.

Chief Drumming called Detective Keghlian and asked to speak with FBI ADC Hoar, only to be told he had boarded the chopper right after the chief had left, but that SAC Shaw was here with him.

"Put him on the phone," said the chief.

"Yes, chief," said SAC Shaw.

"You picked up the home security camera tape?"

"Yes. ADC Hoar did."

"Can we get a copy or see them?"

"Sorry chief, we should have let you see them, but the ADC wanted to see them. We had to send them to the city. They reviewed them, and it shows him coming home, stripping, diving in and appearing to hit his head on the bottom and drowning. I will try and get you a copy."

"Yea you do that. Put the detective back on." The chief had dispensed with pleasantries.

"Detective, we're through playing nice with these guys, Give them nothing. Got it!"

"Got it."

The chief called Mayor Early and filled him in on the confiscated tape, his talk with SAC Shaw and his instructions to Detective Keghlian. The mayor ran a tight village, and he didn't suffer fools and didn't like the FBI moving in.

"I agree chief but without those tapes, we have nothing unless we get a witness or something back from the autopsy. After the FBI leave, why don't you drain the pool and then we can have our forensic people take a look at the pool sides and bottom for blood or tissue. If he hit his head on the pool surface, there will be blood or tissue on the gunite pool deck or bulkhead or marble dust on his head. We need to wait for the autopsy results, but call forensics and give them a heads up," suggested Mayor Early.

CHAPTER 9

WASHINGTON, DC

President Burk, FBI Director Riley and Press Secretary Sullivan sat around the Oval Office coffee table waiting for ADC Michael Hoar, who was due in from Hedgehampton any moment.

"Should I get Bill Nicholas?" asked Kelly.

"I think from his last response; we should keep him clean on this matter. I trust him, but it may get dirty. We may need someone untainted in-house.

The President's Secretary, Noreen Ward, knocked and stuck her head into the office.

"ADC Hoar is here, Mr. President."

"Thank you, Noreen. Send him in please."

ADC Hoar was involved in a plot to incriminate and finally kill Presidential Candidate Thomas Dean Burk, in Dallas. Thank God he didn't succeed but not for lack of trying. He, his boss FBI Director Miller, and President Hilton were outgunned. Literally. Hoar was arrested by the Dallas Police Department but would not talk. Not a word. Riley thought him a real trooper and thought he deserved a second chance. After all, he was following orders, kept his mouth shut, and was a former Marine. President Burk had former President Hilton, then heading the Hilton Commission, to supposedly investigate and head off suspicion regarding the assassination of Presidential Candidate John Fitzhugh Kearney, subpoena Hoar back to Washington. FBI Director Riley, true to his word after Hoar was cleared, promoted Hoar to

FBI Assistant Director in Charge of the New York Office. *Keep your enemies closer.*

"Good evening, Director Hoar. Good to see you again. You know everyone. Have a seat," said the President.

Hoar knew this was his second chance, and he was going to make the most of it. His initial relationship with all three in the room admittedly was not righteous. He intended to be part of this team if they would have him.

"Mr. President, boss, Press Secretary Sullivan; Semper Fi," said Hoar as he set down next to Riley across from the President and Press Secretary Sullivan.

Hoar, Burk, and Riley were all Marines together many years ago in a faraway war. Kelly Sullivan was included in the strictly Marine to Marine greeting "Semper Fi", (Always Faithful) not just because she married into it but because she deserved it.

"What do the tapes from Mazola's home security cameras tell us?" asked Director Riley.

"Just as we suspected Boss. He came home at 1:32 a.m. He was with a very young, very hot, blond Asian. By the time they left the car under the porte-cochere and the pool camera picked them up, they had their clothes off. In the pool, they went. Some hugging and kissing then the blond climbed out the deep end ladder and Mozilla was right behind her. *No bum intended,* he thought to himself. She turned and with her palm struck his forehead with tremendous force as if she had a sledgehammer. His head snapped back, and his brain must have bounced inside. He lost consciousness and slid down the ladder into the pool. She watched as he sank to the bottom. Air bubbles were visible on the water surface. She stayed another five minutes and then started picking up her clothes and getting dressed. She went back to the pool and checked on him. Satisfied he drowned, she went back to the car where the front camera picked her up. She walked down the driveway, was picked up again by the gate camera, turned down the street and disappeared.

We checked all the neighbors' cameras and picked her up again heading towards the village. Another gate camera picked her up getting into a black Suburban. Plates and driver obscured, heading towards the village, and then we lost her. The village police department doesn't have many proprietary cameras, so we had to rely on private residences and businesses."

"Thanks, Michael. You have the tapes with you?"

"Affirmative. The locals are pissed that we took the tapes, and they are now pulling back."

"They'll get over it. Without the tapes, all they will be able to confirm is an accidental drowning. Bumped his head he did. Anything else?" asked Riley.

"SAC Shaw backtracked Mazola to a village restaurant where he had dinner and drinks with some friends. They all left separately. We know the blond stalked Mazola and made her play as he left the restaurant. We have a waiter who witnessed it, but we are the only ones that have proof she actually went home with him," said Hoar.

"OK," said the President, "Kelly, we should stay out of this and defer all comments to the local authorities. Unlike Dodger, we have no connection to Mazola. All the locals can say is he came home after dinner and drinks, stripped, went for a swim, hit his head, and drowned. End of story."

"He's not going to stop you know," said Riley.

"I know. We can stop him but should we? These are bad people he's targeting who had it coming to them in spades, but I am afraid if the public finds out the truth, they will start rooting for him and turn it into a reality show," said the President.

"Someone is going to put it together, and then what do we do," replied Riley.

"That *NY Post* reporter Ron Todd, who was snooping around St. Michelle, is now snooping around Hedgehampton," added Hoar.

"That's not good. Let's let it go a bit longer and see if he put it together or the next one on the list turns up. Or maybe I should have said goes down," said the President.

"Let's hope none of us are on his list," cautioned Kelly.

CHAPTER 10

HEDGEHAMPTON, NY

Hedgehampton Press reporter Sweeney and *NY Post*, reporter Todd, met for dinner at the same restaurant where Mazola and his friends dined the night before he drowned.

"I got a chance to speak with Detective Keghlian a couple of hours ago, and he is very tight lipped. I did get out of him, off the record, that the FBI has turned hostile and neither he nor the chief had seen any home surveillance tapes yet. They, the FBI, say the tapes show Mazola coming home a bit tipsy, stripping, diving into the pool, hitting his head, and not coming up. An accidental drowning," said *Hedgehampton Press* reporter, Tom Sweeney.

"If that's the case why not release the tapes?" asked Ron Todd of *The NY Post*.

"It's obvious isn't it? The tapes show something different, and the FBI doesn't want the police and therefore the public to know what really happened. Now I have given you my end what have you got?" asked Sweeney.

"The short story is, I believe, a serial killer's out there. Some sort of a modern day Jill the Ripper. Only now she is killing notorious bad guys instead of innocent prostitutes, and our government wants to keep it quiet. The big difference is that the public instead of becoming enraged may actually cheer her on. If nothing else it should force some of these bad guys to go underground."

"You covered the former Vice President's drowning in St. Michelle. Are you saying that was not a drowning?"

"Oh, he drowned alright. He just didn't fall in. He was pushed."

"How do you know?"

"I have a contact down in St. Michelle who listened in on some early VHF traffic and saw the tape. The scuttlebutt is that it was a woman," said Todd.

"You haven't reported that yet. Why?"

"Because I, we, only have a footing in with the Vice President's murder. Now we need to build the foundation, and this Mazola drowning is a building block to that foundation."

"But we don't know for sure without the tapes," said Sweeney.

"So we need to get the tapes and the autopsy report."

"Why the autopsy report?"

"To see if Mazola hit his head on the pool, or hit his head on a hammer. You and I need to talk to Detective Keghlian."

"The chief has put a lid on everything, and I don't think we will get too much from Detective Keghlian."

"Well, let's talk to him, and see if we can pop the lid and open a new friend. The enemy of my enemy and all that."

The next day, Tom Sweeney called Ron Todd to tell him he had a meeting set for 11 a.m. with Detective Keghlian at the Hedgehampton Police Station. Todd preferred a more discreet location but decided to take what they could get. Detective Keghlian was waiting for them in a small interview room. After introductions, they set down on metal chairs around a metal table. One wall had a mirror which Todd suspected was a two-way mirror, and the room was probably wired for A/V. He guessed the chief would be on the other side watching and listening. Todd looked at Sweeney and glanced at the mirror. Sweeney nodded he understood.

"OK. What's the *Post* and the *Press* have to tell me that I don't already know?" asked Detective Keghlian.

Before they entered the police station, they agreed that Sweeney would start off, and Todd would wait until the time was right to jump in. Then they would push buttons and see what opened.

"We think there is more to this than a drowning, and we think you agree."

Detective Keghlian just sat there stoned faced and did not reply.

Sweeney took this as a cue to continue. "There is no reason for the FBI to be involved. A former businessman drowns in his pool. Controversial scum bag yea but not exactly a federal case."

"Look, this is an ongoing investigation, and there are things I just can't talk about," said Detective Keghlian.

"You know about the restaurant and the blond outside. Right?" asked Sweeney.

"Right."

Now Todd decided to jump in with a little speculation. "What you don't know is, she went home with him. You don't know she went swimming with him, and you don't know what happened in the pool. You don't know when she left or where she went. You don't know any of this because the FBI not only confiscated Mazola's surveillance tapes but those of his neighbors and any other tapes from commercial businesses. The village surveillance tapes are far and few between and picked up nothing."

With that, the door opened, and Chief Drumming came in, pulled up a chair next to Detective Keghlian, sat down and said, "OK fellas. What do you know that we don't know?" He didn't wait for an answer. "If you're holding back evidence or information we are going to go from persons having a conversation to persons of interest real fast."

"No need for threats chief. I believe we can help each other. Look, something big is going on. You know it, and we know it. The FBI is withholding information and evidence from the police and the media," said Todd.

"Maybe it's as simple as they say. He dove in, hit his head, and drowned," offered Detective Keghlian.

"You mean as simple as the Vice President also drowning?" asked Todd.

"I've heard scuttlebutt about that. The word is his Secret Service detail pushed him in," said the chief with a wink and a smirk.

"He was pushed alright but not by the Secret Service. At least not his personal detail," said Todd.

"All right, you got my attention. What do you know that we don't?"

"I know a lot more than you, the media, and the public knows. For starters, they also withheld the home security tapes from the locals and state police. Just like they are doing here. Something big is happening, and the government doesn't want us to know about it. But two very bad, hated guys have drowned, and I bet you a nickel, very soon, another very bad person will go down," said Todd.

"Are you thinking Roswell, UFO's and Aliens?" suggested Detective Keghlian.

The chief looked like he was going to smack Detective Keghlian, but let it go.

"Detective, you're not too far off. But what I am thinking is worse. A hell of a lot worse."

CHAPTER 11

CAMBRIDGE, MA

In the middle of liberalism, just blocks from Harvard Square, on a quiet street, sits the office of Beston Servienti and Colburn. It is on Harvard Street, less than a quarter mile to the River Charles and terrific running paths all along the river. The office shares a beautiful brick colonial commercial building with other but separate law firms. Beston Servienti and Colburn was the smallest space at just under 2000 sf, but very nicely appointed. A reception area and a separate office for his assistant office manager, Mary Weeks. One office each for Beston, Servienti, and Colburn. Colburn's office had a shower and a large library conference room, with a wonderful wood burning fireplace for those cold Boston winters. They also had security in the office. Under Coburn's desk sat a 120 lb. black and silver German Shepherd named Natasha, who religiously guarded Colburn, Weeks and the office. Colburn had had Natasha since she was a puppy. She was now five years old.

The other law firms in the building all seemed to keep to themselves, but they couldn't help but notice that Beston and Servienti were never there nor were there ever any clients. Rumor had it that Beston Servienti and Colburn were a "White Shoe" firm with very few and very private clients. In other words, the attorneys go to the client the clients never come to the attorney. Israel Colburn and his assistant-office manager, Mary Weeks, did nothing to dissuade that rumor.

It had been a bad winter for Boston. The most snow ever recorded, 108 inches beating the 95-96 record by half an inch. Spring was lovely, and by July, it was hot and humid. Colburn's type of weather. Today it was in the 90's, and he had just finished a 10k run along the river when his cell phone rang.

He answered, "Yes, Mary." Not because he had caller ID, which he did, but because Mary was the only person, who had his number.

"He called," she said.

Colburn didn't need to ask who or why and wouldn't. He assumed they, NSA, were monitoring his calls on his non-encrypted smartphone. Besides it could wait till he got back to the office.

"See you in ten," he said. And touched off.

Back in the office, he showered and was sitting behind his desk when Mary Weeks knocked, came in and said, "He wants to talk."

"What was his tone?"

"As usual, but with a slight edge. Do you want me to get him now?"

"No. I'll call him myself."

Colburn picked up his Satellite Blackphone. A new Android-centric operating system called Privat OS. It comes with built-in industrial grade encryption that protects IMs, voice, video, and chat. There is, for good reason, a big demand for commercially available encrypted smartphones, impervious to the data demands of spy agencies and cyber criminals worldwide. Colburn owns stock in the company. The man who answered Coburn's call, Dmitri Vova, had a thick Russian accent but spoke perfect English. Colburn met him in Afghanistan while fighting with the Sunni Mujahedeen against the Russians and Russian-led Democratic Republic of Afghanistan forces. It was 1980, and he met Vova in Kunar province. Vova was a young lieutenant in Spetsnaz, Russian Special Forces. A Russian tank company came into the valley. Colburn was leading a Mujahedeen anti-tank team, and when they met it was not pretty. The fighting went on for two days and in the end, four Russians tanks were afire, and six prisoners were taken. The Mujahedeen planned to execute them, but Colburn suggested a trade. Through back channels Colburn reached out to the Russian Kunar

Province headquarters commander and arranged for a prisoner swap. Twelve Mujahedeen for the six Russians.

Two Russian Mi-24 Hind attack helicopters landed while two more held back behind the mountain range. Close but quiet. Besides the pilot and co-pilot each of the two forward helicopters held six prisoners and two Russian Spetsnaz Special Forces soldiers. Lieutenant Vova met with Coburn, and the Mujahedeen leader and made the switch. When the Mujahedeen leader, Mohammed al-Zawahiri, saw the soldiers were Spetsnaz, he gave a subtle nod to one of his lieutenants. Spetsnaz was feared and hated for their cruelty. Colburn noticed some Mujahedeen rocket teams on the move and suspected a double-cross. He alerted Vova and Vova reacted in lighting speed although it seemed like slow motion. He got his team and recovered prisoners boarded and called in the two hidden Hind helicopters. The Hinds found the Mujahedeen rocket teams and hacked them to pieces with their 12.7 mm Yakushev-Borzov Yak-B Gatling guns. Colburn, his Mujahedeen loyalty now blown, raced with Vova and boarded the first Hind. They made it safely out, and Colburn never returned to fight against the Russians. At least not in Afghanistan. Vova helped get Colburn out of Afghanistan, and the two remained, if not friends, comrades. Vova, as thanks to Colburn for saving his life, souvenired Colburn his leather gloves. All he had really. Vova later sent back a Spetsnaz unit to find and decimate what was left of Colburn's old Mujahedeen team.

Vova was a short solidly built man, with penetrating black eyes that could see right through you. Vova was now a Colonel in the FSB, Federal Security Service, successor to the KGB.

Colburn touched speaker then speed-dialed #1.

"Good morning, Icy. So nice of you to call back."

"I am in your employ and serve at your pleasure Vova," answered Colburn.

Natasha, under Colburn's desk, gave off a long low guttural growl. The pack was threatened.

In hearing Natasha growl, Vova said, "I see I still have the same carnivorous effect on your wolf."

Colburn didn't take the bait and waited for Vova to continue.

"I am afraid, my dear Icy, our desserts, although served properly, don't seem to be having the desired effect we hoped."

Natasha's growl continued, and Colburn made no attempt to quiet her. He felt the same way about Vova, but would internalize his urge to growl, at least for now. He would chorus with Natasha later to defend their territory and rally their pack together. Natasha went to her Da's credenza, behind his desk, stood on her hind legs and removed one of Vova's gloves and started chewing and shaking it in a wild frenzy.

Vova was not a man you wanted to cross or disappoint. He was, however, a man with a plan and Colburn was like minded. Colburn knew why he hated these bad people on the terminate list. They were bullies; men, and in some cases women, who did very bad things to good people and got away with it. Colburn would have, and even intended to, dispatch many of these same characters when time permitted, but why not get paid to do it? Vova claimed his reasons were honorable and aligned with Coburn's, but Colburn didn't believe him. Vova was like the bad kids Colburn grew up with. Always an ulterior motive but Colburn knew it and accepted it. A little chaos never hurts. Besides, Vova paid quite well to dispatch these bad people. A million dollars each, plus expenses. Colburn visualized putting Vova's name on the list. He and Natasha would do that termination for free.

Colburn answered, "The FBI, hell with President Burk's authority, is holding back releasing the truth. In fact, Burk has the FBI sequestering evidence. I think he figured out what we are up to and wants to keep it out of the media until he can figure out a way to deal with it and us."

"Burk can't suppress it for long. We need the country to get on board with this scheme and take it to the next level. When they do, we will see every Wall Street crook, dishonest businessman, immoral minister, crooked cop, shady lawyer and two-faced politician, running for the sewers. Especially when we plant bounties on their heads," puffed Vova.

"I've given, a certain reporter, some leads. He'll connect the dots and break the true story soon," said Colburn.

"Well, I don't think we can wait. You need to do one termination that can leave no mistake that bad guys are finally getting their just desserts. I want you to move up a name from our deck of cards. I want you do play the race card and soon. It's got to be big and loud. You saw what happened to your country after the King Brothers incidents, and that Brown kid in Ferguson."

There. He said it again, thought Colburn. *"Your country."*

"The Brown kid yea, but the King Brothers? I think I missed that one," said Colburn.

"You don't remember Martin and Rodney and what happened after? The Blacks will tear your country apart. They will riot, loot and set fire to every city. Your President will have to release the truth to keep the peace," said Vova.

"Let me do the third name on the list as planned before we go to the race card. I will make sure this one will break the story wide open," said Colburn.

"OK. But don't disappoint me. Do it fast my little Mick Jew; *it sounded like McJew,* or I may have to reconsider our relationship."

The line went dead, and Natasha came over to her Da for a neck rub. "Yes girl, I don't like that son of a bitch either."

CHAPTER 12

San Francisco, CA

The former House Speaker, only the second woman to have served as the House Speaker, Paula Vitelli, was home and in her element. A member of the Democratic Party, Vitelli represented California's 13th congressional district, which consists of four-fifths of the city and county of San Francisco. She, along with the other three congressional leaders, was removed from power by President Burk on his first day in office.

President Burk, meeting with all four during his first day in the office said, "You know why I asked you here this morning. You all started out, I am sure, idealistic with good intentions, but somehow you lost your way. For the last sixteen years – but primarily the last eight with you four as leaders – you prevented Congress from functioning as intended. The American people have paid the price. Instead of consensus, we got confrontation. Instead of teamwork, we got no work. Pork barrel bills, special interest lobbyists, and term limit rejections have corrupted you, and Congress and I intend to end it all today. I have promised the American people that I would get our dysfunctional Congress functioning. The only way I know how to do that is to remove all four of you from leadership roles. You may remain in Congress, but you will not chair or sit on any important committees. Or you can resign your seat. I have already met with your replacements and said resolution has already been presented and accepted unanimously by your peers. But more importantly, they have the full support of the American people and their President. I wish I could say that it has been a pleasure, but it hasn't."

They did not expect this. Vitelli's lips began to quiver; Tweed grabbed his chest, and Bonner began to weep. Only McDonnell sat there stoic and resigned. The president stood and as he was walking out he turned back and said, "Do it. Do it by noon, and don't fuck with me."

Some say Mrs. Vitelli was nothing but a gangster; a "capo di tutti capi," which is all she ever wanted to be. She illegally enriched herself at the expense of others; she's a bully; she has no capability whatsoever of considering any viewpoint save her own, but that's OK because she believes she is without sin. Her image as a caring, grandmotherly public servant is nothing more than a facade for a ruling-class diva whose power rests in backroom deal-making and hypocrisy. She has an absolute hatred for the Republican Party. She would like to be seen as a champion of ethics reform and has used the issue as a central campaign message. Her activities in Congress suggest that the only corruption she is interested in talking about is what she can gin up about Republicans.

Why only Vitelli was on the termination list and not the other three was quite simple. Bonner and McDonnell were obstructionists, but not inherently bad men. Tweed was as evil and as hated as Vitelli but was on his death bed. Why bother? Even out of a leadership position, like former Vice President Rumson, Vitelli could not keep her mouth shut. The truth is that most Americans just hated Paula Vitelli, hated how she forced The Affordable Health Care Act down their throats.

A summary by a Notre Dame University engineer condensed the Affordable Health Care Act bill into four simple sentences:

1. In order to insure the uninsured, we first have to un-insure the insured.
2. Next, we require the newly uninsured to be re-insured.
3. To re-insure the newly uninsured, they are required to pay extra charges to be re-insured.
4. The extra charges are required so that the original insured, who became uninsured, and then became re-insured, can pay enough extra

so that the original uninsured can be insured so that it will be 'free-of-charge' to them.

As humorous as it sounds every last word is absolutely TRUE!

Kim Ly, meaning golden lion in Vietnamese, received the call from Colburn three days ago and arrived at San Francisco International Airport, from Hanoi, yesterday. It was a long flight, and she should have been tired. She wasn't. She hopped in a cab and headed for the Radisson Hotel at Fisherman's Wharf. After checking in, she went for a run. Down Bay Street to Golden State Park, up and over the Golden Gate Bridge to Sausalito. She stopped 8 miles later in front of Scoma's Sausalito, a wonderful waterfront restaurant on Bridgeway. She hardly broke a sweat. Kim Ly is a beautiful 25-year-old Vietnamese former commando in the Vietnam People's Ground Forces. From her backpack, she pulled out a pair of shorts to put on over her Nike running capris and a clean white dri-fit top. With her New Balance 920 Trail running shoes, she looked like a typical tourist out for lunch; only she was beautiful and exotic. She had almond shaped eyes, a lithe, hard 178cm body, and long black hair in a ponytail. Colburn watched her enter and rose from the table as she approached. "Xin chào Kim Ly," said Colburn to which Kim Ly replied, "Xin chào Mr. Colburn."

The waiter seated Kim Ly, took their drink order, and left. Their table was by the window with a wonderful view of San Francisco Bay and Alcatraz. Their conversation was interrupted by the drinks, two iced teas, and lunch. Kim Ly ordered Wellfleet oysters and a Dungeness crab salad sandwich and Colburn, a crab cake burger.

Kim Ly was an asset Colburn used twice recently and with fantastic results. He hoped she was available, and as luck would have it, she was.

"We need to move fast. Tomorrow would be good. The mark, Paula Vitelli, is at her Pacific Ave house but will be leaving for Washington the day after tomorrow," said Colburn.

Showing no emotion after hearing the name of one of the most powerful people in the country, Kim Ly said, "Please tell me exactly what you want me to do."

"Tomorrow evening, at 7 p.m., she will be speaking at the Loews Regency Hotel. She will arrive at the hotel at 5:30 p.m. accompanied by her driver and a bodyguard. The driver will stay with the car in front of the hotel, but the bodyguard will accompany her to her courtesy PH suite. There she will relax and prepare for the speech. She will leave the suite to mingle and for photo ops at 6:30 p.m. Between 5:30 and 6:30 you need to liberate her, completely sterile, except for what she is wearing, from the suite. No fuss, no bother, and no witnesses. Her bodyguard is a former Ranger and retired SFPD. You don't want to deal with him. Get him out of the suite."

Kim Ly sat there stone faced. No notes. No questions. Colburn handed her a small brown shopping bag from Bloomingdale's cosmetic department.

"Here is everything you will need. Chloroform to knock her out and the syringe has medication to keep her out. Get her out of the suite and back to this safe house on Eddy Street. The address is in the bag. A false identity including a Photoshop picture are part of her new legend, and it is up to you to make her look like the photo. When she is ready, inject her with Alprazolam. It has time release capabilities which will keep her in, what will appear, a stupor. Her speech, if she can speak at all will be slurred. She will eventually lose control of her body functions. She will not be able to communicate and will slowly become comatose. Drop her off near the emergency entrance of St. Francis Hospital after you have injected her with the Alprazolam. The antiarrhythmic drugs, Paradoxical, Sotalol, and Timolol, used to treat arrhythmias, will produce lethal ventricular arrhythmias and significant changes in blood levels of potassium and magnesium, and then it will stop the heart. Cardiac arrest. The Paradoxical will begin its destruction about 12 hours after administered. The syringes are all marked, and do her between her toes.

Kim Ly smiled softly as she realized the injections will work even if they pump her stomach, or she releases her bowels. Either would preclude oral or anal ingestion.

"But why this way," asked Kim Ly, "What did she do to deserve to die like this?"

"She has done nothing. For the last 16 years in Congress, she has done nothing."

"It will be done as you direct, Mr. Colburn," said Kim Ly.

CHAPTER 13

SAN FRANCISCO, CA

After lunch Colburn went directly to the airport and Kim Ly took a cab back to her hotel.

Paula Vitelli may have been out of a leadership position, but she was still in demand. Tonight she was the guest speaker at the Loews Regency Hotel, formally the Mandarin Oriental, which comprises 11 floors atop a 48-floor high-rise on Sansome Street in the Financial District. The speech was about the success of the Affordable Health Care Act and her role in making it happen. Sponsored by the Sierra Club and Moveon.org, 5,000 guests were paying $25,000 each or $100,000 for a table. It was sold out. Vitelli was to receive $250,000 plus dinner for her 20-minute speech and private meetings with several big donors.

She was driven from her home to the Loews Regency by her two-man security detail which consisted of a black Suburban, driver and personal bodyguard, former SFPD Detective Kirk White. A suite was provided by the hotel, and she was whisked past reception and went directly up to her room. Detective White preceded Vitelli into the suite and did a quick room check. The hotel phone rang, and she answered it.

'Ms. Vitelli?"

"Yes."

"Ms. Vitelli, I am Betty Short the assistant hotel manager, and I would like to welcome you."

Ms. Vitelli didn't respond.

Ms. Short continued, "I am in the event hall and although the Teleprompter is working the speech content seems a bit mixed up. Could you send someone down to make sure it is correct?"

Again Ms. Vitelli didn't respond. She just hung up.

Kim Ly, in the suite floor business office, also hung up the service phone and waited. She thought Vitelli very rude. She hoped Vitelli would send White to check out the Teleprompter but as General Patton said, "Make your plans to fit the circumstances."

"Kirk, please go down and make sure the Teleprompters are working and everything is perfect. Some idiot thinks something is wrong. You know what I like, and I just don't trust the hotel staff," said Vitelli.

"I will if you promise to lock the door and stay put," responded Detective White.

She smiled, nodded, and closed the door. He waited till he heard the top lock click then headed for the elevator.

Kim Ly blended well at the Loews Regency, with many of the former Mandarin Oriental staff kept on, especially as a member of the housekeeping staff, and especially with the proper uniform, equipment, and attitude. The plan she discussed over lunch with Colburn was anything but typical. In fact, it was logistically and technically to the extreme but when successfully completed, would be another arrow in her quiver. Kim Ly had to kidnap Vitelli from her hotel room; get her away unnoticed and into a safe house; change her identity and give her a new legend; medicate her into a stupor; get her admitted to a hospital and have her expire. Piece of cake.

Earlier, Kim Ly had chatted up, at Café Med, a local coffee house across the street from the Lowes Regency, a young woman named Lisa Benson, who held a housekeeping position in that very hotel. Kim Ly got all the inside information she needed, and Ms. Benson was rewarded with a strong sedative. She would be asleep for several hours. Not unusual for coffee shop patrons in this neighborhood. Kim Ly put on her ultra-thin transparent latex surgical gloves, crossed the street and entered the employee entrance and faced her first hurdle. An elderly security guard.

"Good afternoon young lady. Haven't seen you here before," said the guard.

"Good afternoon to you Officer Malone," said Kim Ly. *Smiling and flirting as only she could.* "My name is Sue Li and Mrs. Audrey in Human Resources, asked me to come in as an emergency replacement for Lisa Benson, and she said to tell you all my paperwork and ID would be down shortly. I am to get ready for my shift and then report to my supervisor, Mrs. Tu. Mrs. Audrey said you were her best officer and could sign me in and direct me to the locker room."

Officer Malone wasn't the best hotel security officer by any stretch. He even forgot to wear his name tag, but she had him from Officer Malone. She was so attractive, knew his name and all about Lisa, Mrs. Audrey, and Mrs. Tu. All's good.

"Is Lisa OK?"

"It is nothing serious. Just a doctor's appointment she couldn't reschedule. I have her locker key card. We're about the same size, so it works out perfectly."

"Well then just sign in here and then head down the corridor and make a left into the locker room."

"Can I bring my car in and park it in the employee level?"

"Sure, just enter off Battery Street and follow the employee signs down to the lower level. Take the service elevator back up here to Level B-2."

"Mrs. Audrey was right. She said you were good looking."

Officer Malone was not good looking, but that made his day. Kim Ly was happy Officer Malone was so easy. She preferred not to kill him. She knew that in a few hours he would be in the hot seat with the FBI and SFPD, not to mention Mrs. Audrey. Officer Malone may have had a good day, but his night would be hell.

Kim Ly brought her white Kia rental car down and took the service elevator back up to B-2. She found the locker room and Lisa's locker, changed into Lisa's uniform, which included her name tag and master room pass key. The only personal items she took were her wallet and car keys. She commandeered a housekeeping cart, checked the room roster to find Ms. Vitelli's room, and headed to the service elevator. She landed on the top VIP floor, went to the business office, and made the call to Vitelli's room. The few hotel personnel she encountered, acknowledged her but did not approach. She was too beautiful to be a housekeeper, but she dressed the part and had the right attitude, so…

She watched Vitelli's bodyguard leave the room and enter the elevator. She wheeled her cart over to Vitelli's door and paused to listen. She decided not to knock but just go for surprise. She inserted the pass key card, which deactivated both door locks and quietly entered. She doubled locked the door again. If the bodyguard came back, his room key would only deactivate the bottom lock. She heard Vitelli moving around in another part of the suite. Vitelli came back into the foyer. She was wearing a lavender-colored Armani suit, with lavender pumps, dyed to match, and Tahitian pearls. "Why are you back? What's wrong?" asked Vitelli, thinking Kirk had returned so soon.

Kim Ly came out from behind the paneled French doors.

"Ms. Vitelli, I have something for you," said Kim Ly.

Vitelli said, "Why are you in my room and why are you talking to me." It wasn't so much a question as it was a statement.

Kim Ly's hands came from behind her back revealing a white hand towel. She seemed to be offering it to Vitelli. Vitelli, a quick study, knew immediately something was wrong and backed away. Kim Ly pursued her, but Vitelli was fast for an old gal and managed to topple a table and lamp into Kim Ly's path. The table top smashed into Kim Ly's shin and momentarily stunned her. Kim Ly deferred the pain, sidestepped the table, and was on Vitelli in a flash. Vitelli kicked Kim Ly in the same shin but Kim Ly countered with a sharp jab to Vitelli's cheek, and it was over in an instant. Vitelli hit the floor like a 100 lb. sack of sand. Kim Ly still administered the chloroform soaked hand towel as insurance. She removed Vitelli's shoe and inserted the syringe, containing a sedative, through her pantyhose and into the flesh between her toes. Kim Ly opened the door, brought in her cleaning cart, and relocked both locks. She opened the large center dirty linen container and carefully lifted and placed Vitelli down and inside. She picked up the table and lamp and replaced them in the exact same spot as shown by the carpet indents. She picked up Vitelli's shoe, the hand towel and added it to the dirty linen catch. She placed the syringe in the cart's trash bin.

The whole matter took less than two minutes, and Kim Ly and the now half-full cleaning cart were out the door and into the corridor. She just closed the door, and the single lock engaged. She wheeled the cart to the service elevator pressed the down button and waited. It came quickly, and she pressed Level B-4, employee parking, some 52 floors down and hoped for an express. She got a local and a stern looking woman bearing the name tag Mrs. Audrey got on.

Mrs. Audrey prided herself in knowing all of her staff and certainly she would remember someone as attractive as this person standing in front of her. The door closed, and the descent continued. Mrs. Audrey was about to question the employee when she noticed Lisa Benson's name tag on this Asian person who was most certainly not Lisa Benson.

"Where's Lisa?" she asked.

Kim Ly knowing she was busted and remembered an appropriate saying, *"Everything is falling apart according to plan,"* opened the dirty linen top and said, "Lisa is in here."

The ridiculous statement was compounded by Mrs. Audrey stepping over to the cart and looking in, "What is she doing in the basket?"

Kim Ly was out of time and out of cleverness, so she decided to implement KISS. *Keep It Simple Stupid.* She cracked the heel of her hand onto the back of Mrs. Audrey's skull, the momentum of which carried Mrs. Audrey into the dirty linen basket with Ms. Vitelli. She replaced the top and again hoped for an express. Finally, the elevator door opened to level B-4, and she and her cart exited towards her car.

Kim Ly had purposely parked in a congested section with her car trunk towards the wall. She wheeled the cart between the cars, which provided privacy, popped the car trunk and pulled Vitelli out past Mrs. Audrey and let Mrs. Audrey sink to the bottom. She lifted the sedated Vitelli into the trunk and closed it. She checked Mrs. Audrey's pulse, which was strong and then tossed some clean towels over her body and closed the dirty linen top. She got in her car and drove up the ramp, out of the garage and onto Battery Street, south on Battery Street, across Market to Ecker Street and left onto Jessie Street. She drove down into a covered garage that had no camera surveillance. The garage was small and empty except for her switch car. She made the switch including the Congresswoman and changed out of her housekeeping uniform. She drove the rented black Toyota up and out onto Market Street, west on Market to Turk Street then Evenworth to Eddy Street. All told, just a little over 1 mile.

The safe house was right across the street from the Tenderloin District Police Station in an area called Little Saigon. She pulled into the building through an electronic gate into a secluded spot behind the building. The building was a series of apartments with no other tenant than Kim Ly. She parked and lifted Ms. Vitelli over her shoulder and headed for the service lift. She made it to the safe house, safe and sound. By now, she thought, Kirk White would have returned to the room and discovered Ms. Vitelli gone. He would call down to the driver and verify that she was not with him, and they would both begin a search. Kim Ly figured they would now be in a panic mode and about to 911 the SFPD and the Secret Service in Washington.

For the next few days and nights, Lisa Benson, Mr. Kirk White, Mrs. Audrey and Officer Malone would experience a "Quality of Life" adjustment which they could never have expected nor believed possible. They would become witnesses, then suspects, then celebrities and finally, with the exception of White, would just be considered clowns for being so easily duped.

CHAPTER 14

WASHINGTON, DC

"Bounty," answered Secret Service Director Christian Bounty after one ring of his cell phone.

"Hey, chief, Pfeiffer here. We got a situation," said Chuck Pfeiffer, Bounty's SAC San Francisco.

"Make my day Chuck."

"Congresswoman Vitelli is missing. She was here at the Loews Regency, to give a speech tonight then she just disappeared. I got a call from Kirk White, retired SFPD, her local security. I am with him now at the hotel," said Pfeiffer.

"Oh shit," said Bounty.

"Yea, oh shit is right. We are keeping it tight and saying she just had a senior moment and wandered off but…"

"But what? What's White got to say?"

"He said they arrived in the hotel PH Suite on the 48th floor around 5:45 p.m. for a 7 p.m. speech in the ballroom on the 38th floor. White was with her as they checked in. Their driver waited with the car. A call came into the room from the assistant hotel manager. Something about a Teleprompter problem and requested someone come down and help straighten it out. White went down but waited outside till Vitelli double locked the door. He was down and back in 10 minutes. He knew something was wrong as soon as he got to the ballroom. There was no assistant manager and no Teleprompter problem. He raced back up. The door was locked, but he had the extra key card and let himself in. Nothing! She was gone. Nothing out of place and her purse was on her dresser. Her purse had her room key card in it along with her house keys and ID. He called the driver and nada. The driver did a quick search outside, and White checked the halls, business rooms, and checked back in the ballroom, bar, restaurant, and lobby. Nothing. He called the hotel manager, who said the assistant manager was off tonight, then she alerted security. He called SFPD, and the search was on. He called me as a heads up.

"Oh shit," said Bounty again. "What's White's gut say?"

"The bogus call and Teleprompter bullshit kind of tells the story, but he also smelled something."

"Don't tell me," said Bounty.

"Yea. Something sweet-smelling, and it wasn't her perfume."

"Chloroform?"

"Yea."

"Keep me posted," said Bounty and touched off.

"Oh shit," thought Bounty.

It was late when FBI Director Riley got the call from Bounty and arranged an immediate meeting with the President. He then contacted his Assistant Director, SAC Hoar, to get the local San Francisco office on it if they weren't already. Riley and Bounty arrived at the same time and were buzzed into the Oval Office by the President's secretary Noreen Ward. Press Secretary Kelly Sullivan and the President were already seated across from the couch waiting for Riley and Bounty.

"Bad?" asked the President.

FBI Director Riley deferred to Secret Service Director Bounty.

"Yes, sir. Bad. Very bad."

Bounty relayed the information as he had received it from SAC Pfeiffer and then added,

"On the way over, SAC Pfeiffer called with an update. He, Vitelli's body-guard, Kirk White, and hotel security, independent of the SFPD, found Mrs. Elisabeth Audrey, the hotel Director of Human Resources, unconscious and dumped in a cleaning cart in the hotel employee parking garage. The employee entrance security guard, Officer Malone, is telling a story about a walk-in housekeeping substitute, by the name Sue Li, who said she was approved by Mrs. Audrey to replace temporarily one Lisa Benson, who reported in sick. Then Lisa Benson showed up and said she was chatting in the Café Med coffee shop, with a very inquisitive Asian woman and the next thing she knew she was being shoved awake by a waiter wanting the table."

"You have tape?" asked Riley.

"Agent Pfeiffer says they got it all on tape. The hotel has cameras everywhere. They got this Sue Li going in and out of the coffee shop across the street from the hotel, entering the hotel, in the hallways, dressed as a cleaning lady, and in the elevator both coming to and leaving the hotel. We even got her going to her car, a white four-door Kia and the car leaving the hotel, but to get where she went after leaving the hotel, we need to widen the search and bring SFPD into the loop," said Bounty.

Riley looked at President Burk and got the nod. "Do it, and get me her photo."

Bounty's phone instant message sound alerted him of a message. He pulled out his phone, read the message, and forwarded it to those present.

"Check your messages. You now have a photo of Sue Li," said Bounty.

"She beautiful, even in that housekeeping getup," said Kelly.

"Beautiful, cunning and dangerous," added the President.

"Let me get out of here and get a BOLO (Be On the Look Out) out and get SFPD moving," said Bounty as he hopped up and off the couch.

Riley yelled at Bounty as he was moving out the door, "Get the Capitol police on high alert and have them notify all members of Congress, here and in their districts, that Vitelli is missing."

FBI Director Riley, Press Secretary Kelly Sullivan, and President Burk sat quietly for a moment after Secret Service Director Bounty left the room.

Kelly broke the ice, "Look. First former Vice President Rumson and then Globalwide's Albert Mazola, two bad guys die mysteriously, to say the least. Both could be just a coincidence but now the former Speaker of the House Vitelli? If she somehow ends up dead, were going to have a bingo. I have been getting calls, emails and questions since Dodger went overboard. If Vitelli winds up dead, they are going to want answers from you Mr. President, and if it's another water incident, the press is going to make it Biblical."

"It won't be water," murmured the President.

"What was that Thomas Dean Burk?" asked Kelly, more as a wife than press secretary.

The President knew he was in for it now.

"You and your den of thieves have been keeping me, not to mention the American people, in the dark, from the start. I have been covering up as best I can, but not only do you and your gang know who's doing these crimes you are, for some reason, covering for him or her. Now I find out you not only know Vitelli is dead but how she died," said Kelly.

The President looked at Riley, who was looking down at his shoes. Riley didn't want to get between the President and his wife but knew things were about to be said that could not be put back in the bottle. Kelly Sullivan was nobody's fool, and she deserved the truth. He just wondered whether the President would tell the truth.

"Kelly, we have not kept you completely in the dark. You know the former VP and Mazola were murdered. We just felt-feel that the timing is-was not right for the public to know the truth at least not from us. We thought that NY Post reporter, Todd, would put it together, but he hasn't. yet."

"I understand all that. What I want to know is why? Why you know, and why you are covering it up?" responded Kelly.

"Since Dodger went in the water we have been all over this. FBI, Secret Service, Homeland, NSA, CIA. We know who is pulling the trigger, who is paying for it and why," said the President.

"Jesus Tommy, you're scaring me," said Kelly.

The President continued, "What they are trying to do is make the killing of bad people, who did bad things to good people, a good thing. You have listened to Fox, CNN, the newspapers and social media. People are applauding not only the deaths of the former VP and Mazola but the way they died. If the public finds out that someone or some vigilante group is actually murdering these scum bags, then the people will want to watch it live on a reality show. *The Assassin* will replace *The Apprentice*. This will go viral, and copycats will start killing everyone who has ever done anything wrong or bad. Hell, Congress could be decimated. Local politicians will be lynched. Main Street and Wall Street billionaires will be thrown out of the temple and stoned. I'm not covering this up because I want to. I am covering it up to stop Americans from seeking revenge on all the bad people, and God knows America has spawned a lot of bad people."

Kelly took this in and said, "OK, Mr. President, I get it. But how do you know that Vitelli is dead? And how do you know how she died? Bounty, your Secret Service Director just left here, and he doesn't know. Or maybe he's a really good actor," said Kelly.

"First of all, I don't know she's dead. But I strongly suspect she is, and we will hear something very soon. As to how she will die, it seems the killer themes his marks. Dodger, for his famous WMD "Slam Dunk" remark, ended up getting slammed dunked in the Potomac. Globalwide's Albert Mazola, the prime mover in the housing collapse with homes and mortgages being "Underwater" was found dead underwater in his home pool.

No Vitelli won't show up in a water incident, like those two, unless she was some sort of closet Otis Redding fan. She'll get trampled in a gay rights parade or shot by an illegal, sheltering in her Sanctuary City, or some such themed event," said the President.

"Mr. President, you are awfully glib about this. I am barely OK with the demise of the former Vice President and Mazola, but Vitelli is the former Speaker and is a current elected member of Congress. You, we, need to get in front of this. You need to get the "OHP" speech out and soon," said Kelly.

"You're right. Get something going. Set up something outlining our official position, then send out a press release. Tomorrow, at my meeting with the Prime Minister of Pakistan, during the Q&A, I will give the "Our Hearts and Prayers" speech."

"OK, sounds like a plan, weak but a plan. I'll take what you said at face value for now, but you also alluded to the fact that you knew who was behind all this. Who is pulling the trigger?" asked Kelly.

"Kelly, "Revenge is a Dessert Best Served Cold," or in this case "Best Served Icy,"" answered the President.

"So you're not going to tell me who's behind these murders?" asked Kelly.

"I just did," responded the President.

FBI Director Riley kept his eyes averted, but thought to himself; *The President has told the truth. He just didn't tell the whole truth.*

CHAPTER 15

SAN FRANCISCO, CA

Ron Todd of the *NY Post* and *Hedgehampton Press* reporter Tom Sweeney arrived together at San Francisco International Airport aboard a non-stop Delta Flight. The flight was crowded, but they managed aisle seats across from each other.

Just 12 hours earlier, after Todd received a tip from his anonymous source about Congresswoman Vitelli's disappearance from the hotel, he called Sweeney, and they decided to get to San Francisco right away. Todd made the flight arrangements, and Sweeney took the Hampton Jitney to the airport connection and a cab to LaGuardia Airport. By the time they met at Delta boarding, Vitelli's disappearance rumors were swarming, and Sweeney was glad Todd's anonymous source came through again. As soon as they landed, Todd was working his phone as they both pushed forward through the crowd and raced for the Avis car rental bus. Todd touched off as they boarded the bus and gave Sweeney the latest.

"She is still missing, but my source in the SFPD said everything is looking like a kidnapping. They found the hotel personnel director unconscious and dumped in a cleaning cart in the parking garage. The employee entrance security guard is telling a story about a beautiful Asian walk-in housekeeping substitute. Then an employee showed up and said she was chatting in a coffee shop with a very inquisitive Asian woman who drugged her. Apparently the hotel has cameras everywhere. They got tape of this Asian woman going in and out of the coffee shop across the street from the hotel, entering the hotel on foot, and then later driving in. They got tape of her in the hallways, dressed as a cleaning lady, in the elevator, and both going to and from the hotel. They even got her going to her car, a white four-door Kia and tape of the car leaving the hotel."

"Oh shit," said Sweeney as they ran off the bus to the rental counter.

They got to their car, a brand new red Ford Mustang, tossed their overnights in the back seat. Todd jumped in behind the wheel and started the engine while Sweeney started punching the hotel name into the Mustang's navigation system.

"They got a BOLO out on the car and the Asian women?" asked Sweeney.

"Yea," he handed Sweeney his phone. "Got a name, too. Sue Li and a photo, see?"

"An alias no doubt, but even from the vid cap, you can see she's a looker. Could this be the same gal that did Mazola?" asked Sweeney.

"Oh, this is gonna be good. I can feel it," said Todd.

"Anyone claimed responsibility or a ransom demand?"

"Where the fuck have you been Sweeney? Get your fucking head out of your ass. This is the Triple Crown, first former Vice President Rumson, then Globalwide's Mazola, now Vitelli. There will be no one claiming responsibility. No ransom note. We should be checking the hospitals instead of wasting time at the hotel. I bet you a nickel she's dead. Hell, we should be checking the fucking morgue. Turn on the radio, and let's see what's on the news."

When they arrived at the Lowes Regency, it was still a crime scene. There were still tons of cameras and spot reporters doing their live shots and no place to park. Todd pulled over by a fire hydrant jumped out, grabbed something out of his overnight, placed it on his dash and yelled to Sweeney to get moving. Sweeney jumped out, crossed the front of the car and raced to catch up with Todd. He just caught the writing on the metal sign Todd put on his dashboard. *FBI/GOV/NY/PRESS.*

While Sweeney and Todd were in the air, the SFPD, Secret Service and FBI investigating Ms. Vitelli's disappearance had taken it from a missing person to a kidnapping. Since she is a federal employee, it has become a federal offense. The Secret Service and the FBI were quivering over who would take the lead, but since it is now officially a kidnapping, the FBI won.

The Eddy Street safe house Colburn had set up for Kim Ly was directly across from the Tenderloin District Police Station. The apartment he chose was on the third floor in the back. Kim Ly placed the still unconscious Vitelli in a leather chair and turned on some music. She went to the kitchen for a glass of water, came back out, then splashed some of Vitelli's face.

"Ms. Vitelli … Ms. Vitelli wake up," said Kim Ly.

Vitelli began to shake her head and seemed to be coming off her sedatives.

"Ms. Vitelli, can you hear me? Wake up."

"Yes, I think so. I'm not sure. What happened?" asked Vitelli.

"You had a fall and hit your head, but you are all right now. We need to fix your hair and change your clothes. Then I will get you back to your room in time for your speech."

She looked down at her blood stained and wrinkled Armani suit and seemed not to be able to comprehend how she got so disheveled.

"Yes, but who are you? Where is Kirk?" asked Vitelli.

"I am the hotel nurse, and Kirk asked me to attend to you, and he is waiting for us in your room."

"What is this room? Are we in the hotel infirmary?"

"We are. Now let's get you out of these clothes and into something clean shall we?"

Kim Ly could easily put Ms. Vitelli out with more sedatives or with a well-placed pressure point squeeze, but it would be so much easier changing clothes with Ms. Vitelli awake and helping. After relieving Ms. Vitelli of her jewelry, Armani suit, and shoes, Kim Ly removed Ms. Vitelli's new ensemble from a generic plastic suit bag that was hanging in the closet.

"Ahhh," screamed Vitelli. "I am not wearing that. I wouldn't be caught dead it that. Is this some kind of a joke? I want to see Kirk right now."

"This is just to get you back to your room. Kirk has already retrieved a new Armani suit, blouse, and shoes from your home closet and has them waiting for you in your room. We can't have anyone in the hallways see you in those old dirty clothes? Now can we?"

Vitelli continued to resist, but with Kim Ly guiding her, she was finally re-suited in a lovely Evan Picone two button, green and black pant suit from Sears. Once that was done, Kim Ly applied pressure to Ms. Vitelli's shoulder collar bone, and Ms. Vitelli again blacked out. Kim Ly carried her to the bathroom and propped her up on a four leg high back stool, tilted the stool and her head back over the sink, and carefully applied towels to her suit collar to protect it. She then proceeded to wash off all of Ms. Vitelli's makeup. Then she soaked her hair and began to cut it short but neat. Kim Ly applied the red hair coloring and followed the instructions. She towel dried her hair then blew it dry. When dyed and styled, she took Ms. Vitelli back to the leather chair and slipped a pair of frumpy black pumps on her feet, some cheap jewelry, and a $29.95 Aldo handbag from JC Penny, containing her new identity. Kim Ly held up alongside Ms. Vitelli's face, the new Michigan driver's license supplied by Colburn. The likeness was remarkable. Ms. Vitelli, former speaker of the House and still one of the most powerful people in the United States, was now just plain old Ms. Ilse Koch of Dearborn, Michigan.

A few minutes later, Ms. Vitelli started to stir and began to slowly regain consciousness. She barely was able to recognize, what appeared to be, an outrageous looking woman in a horrible looking outfit sitting directly in front of her. She stood, and so did the woman. It only took a matter of seconds before she realized she was looking at herself in front of a full-length mirror. She screamed and fell back into the chair. It didn't take long for Ms. Vitelli to regain her composure and typical nasty demeanor. Kim Ly walked up beside the mirror and said, "Quite a change wouldn't you say?" Vitelli's eyes narrowed, and her left philtrum below her nose began to tremble. She looked Kim Ly in the eye and said, "You bitch. Do you have any idea of who I am, and what we are going to do to you?"

Kim Ly bent closer to Ms. Vitelli and frowned. She appeared almost sympathetic but then with her right hand swung and punched Ms. Vitelli square in the face. Vitelli's head snapped back, her nose and eye became instantly red, and blood started flowing from her nose. To Kim Ly's complete surprise, Ms. Vitelli, instead of collapsing, struck out with her right hand slashing her fingernails across Kim Ly's face. Not bad for a septuagenarian. Vitelli jumped up and was about to try a run for the door but was stopped when she was lifted off her feet from behind and roughly introduced to a rear choke hold. She lost consciousness and dropped to the floor. Kim Ly looked in the mirror and was horrified at what she saw. From above her left eye to her chin, four long ugly streaks were oozing blood. Her face. Her beautiful face. She had gone in one second, from Kim Ly, Asian beauty, to looking like Bruce Lee, Asian killer. She went into the bathroom and poured some cold water onto a towel and dabbed her face. She looked at the blood on the towel and then into the vanity mirror hoping to see the scratches gone, but she only saw them getting puffier with more blood oozing out. She knew she should put ice on her face but could not drive with an icepack, and she could not afford the time to sit home and recuperate. It was getting dark, and she needed to get moving. In the medicine cabinet, there was, fortuitously, a styptic pencil which she applied to stop the bleeding.

"Bitch! I'll show her bitch," cried, Kim Ly.

She grabbed Vitelli and put her in a borrowed food market shopping cart, along with her pocketbook. She then reached for the Bloomies bag for the last Syringe containing the time released Alprazolam. She removed Vitelli's left shoe and stuck her in the base of her big toe and injected the Alprazolam. She replaced Vitelli's shoe and wheeled her out of the apartment, into the elevator and down to the ground level. She wheeled the cart out of the safe house back door and locked the door. She would not be returning. She placed Vitelli in the passenger seat, belted her in and wiped the blood from Vitelli's face. Vitelli's nose continued to bleed.

Kim Ly drove from behind the apartment building to the gate, it automatically opened. She drove out and turned down Eddy Street while the gate closed behind her. Kim Ly drove down Eddy Street to Taylor Street and north on Taylor to Pine Street, west on Pine to Hyde Street and St. Francis Memorial Hospital, less than six blocks away. She drove around the block to the emergency entrance on Bush Street. Kim Ly skidded to a sharp stop in front of the emergency entrance, jumped out and ran inside screaming that she had a mugging victim in her car that needed immediate attention. An emergency response crew, pushing a gurney, rushed out with Kim Ly to the car.

"What happened to her?" asked the chief nurse.

"It was an attempted mugging. She was struggling with the mugger when I drove by and jumped out to help," said Kim Ly.

"Do you know her?" asked the nurse.

"No. I was driving home from work, and I saw the struggle. I guess I scared him off. I looked for a policeman, and when I couldn't find one I put her in my car and brought her here. I live around the corner."

They were now wheeling Vitelli into the emergency entrance when the nurse said, "You can't leave your car there you need to move it. We're having a busy night."

"I'll move it now."

"What happened to your face?"

"Must have gotten in the way of the mugger's hand."

"After you move the car come back in, and we'll fix you up."

"No thanks. It's just a scratch. I'll put some antiseptics on it and ice it down when I get home."

"Your call, but what you did was a good thing. What's your name?"

"Sue Li and I will come back later to check on her," said Kim Ly.

Kim Ly got in her car and headed back to her hotel room at the Radisson Hotel at Fisherman's Wharf. She was glad to be rid of Vitelli and had no intention of returning to St. Francis Memorial.

CHAPTER 16

CAMBRIDGE, MA - MOSCOW, ME

Israel Colburn was back in Cambridge in his office, Beston Servienti and Colburn, on Harvard Street. Mary Weeks, his office manager, was off for the weekend, but his 120 lb. German Shepherd, Natasha, who religiously guarded Colburn was under his desk. Colburn just finished some internet banking and remote home monitoring, signed off, and shut his computer down.

"Ok Tosh girl, let's you and Da get this show on the road."

Natasha leaped up off the floor artfully avoiding the desktop and her Da's legs. They were a pack and Da, how Colburn addressed himself when talking to Natasha, was her leader, her Alpha. Each pack has a leader, an individual who is dominant over all pack members, even a pack of just two. In wolf society, this individual is called the "Alpha." This is the member who makes the decisions, who must be obeyed, who must be protected.

Natasha understood over one hundred words and commands and answered to four different names: Natasha, Tosh, Girl and Good Girl. Natasha would die for her Da. Natasha would kill for her Da. Natasha would protect Mary Weeks, but Mary did not live with them and was not part of their pack. There was another human that she and Da would occasionally welcome into the pack. Da called him Sarge and Sarge called her Da; Icy. She loved Sarge and considered him pack. An equal. Sarge did not live with them but sometimes joined them at the special place. But not that much lately.

Today they were going north to the cabin, the special place. She knew they were going because Da had told her they were going. Da had been telling her this since he got back from his trip. He was only gone a week but to Natasha, it might as well have been a year.

"Want to go to the cabin girl?" her Da would say. *Go, cabin, girl,* is what Natasha heard.

She knew he would want a response, and she would not disappoint. She would run to the door, circle a few times, then sit on her hind legs, pant her tongue and maintain direct, unflinching eye contact with her Da, then she would smile.

Yea Da, I want, thought Natasha with a tilt of her head and a low guttural moan.

Colburn had his black Range Rover parked on Harvard Street directly in front of the office, an occurrence to be appreciated for sure. It was late Friday afternoon and professionals, teachers and professors were gone for the weekend. Cambridge was a college town, and students didn't have cars. Colburn grabbed a light overnight bag and his old black leather two handle Crouch and Fitzgerald briefcase and opened the door. Natasha followed him out without a leash. She never needed one. Simple commands from Colburn were all that was needed.

"Vedette Tosh," commanded Colburn.

Da wants me to scout the area and make sure it is safe, thought Natasha.

She pushed past Colburn looking left, right, and forward as she bounded down the steps to the Range Rover, circled the truck sniffing and looking until she was sure it was safe. She then sat by the passenger door and waited. Silent and still as a vedette until her Da came down to join her.

A couple of young female students walking by, stopped to not only admire the shepherd's size and beauty but also to marvel at the performance. Natasha did not consider them a threat to the pack.

"Beautiful dog, sir. What's his name? Is he friendly? May I pet him?" asked one of the students.

"She is a beautiful dog. Her name is Natasha, and she is friendly to nice people. Are you a nice person?" asked Colburn.

"Yes, I think so," replied the young student.

"Then bend down and slowly put your hand out. She has senses that you can't imagine. She will be able to tell whether you're nice or not. When she comes over, she will either let you pet the top of her head, or she will take your arm off. Your call."

The student did not hesitate at the dare and bent down and slowly raised her hand.

Da wants me to do the licky kiss face thing, thought Natasha.

"Say hello, Natasha," commanded Colburn.

Natasha walked straight towards the student, sniffed her hand and rubbed her head into the student's outstretched hand. The student scratched Natasha's head and ears and brought her other hand up to scratch Natasha's chin. Natasha groaned in ecstasy.

"I guess she knows a good person when she sees one," said the student.

As if on cue, Natasha placed her huge front left leg up upon the students shoulder and started licking and kissing her. The student, her friend, and another passerby all seemed to enjoy the encounter, and murmurs of "oohs and aahs" could be heard.

"Wow," said Colburn. "Never saw her take to anyone like that before. You must be a very special person."

Natasha backed off and returned to the Range Rover door.

The young student was beaming.

"Thank you and goodbye Natasha. You are a good, smart girl," she said, as she and her friend continued down the street.

Colburn heard her say, to her friend in passing, "German Shepherds are the most intelligent and intuitive dogs, you know."

Colburn opened the passenger door, and Natasha jumped in. He then crossed in the rear of the Rover, lifted the tailgate and tossed in his briefcase and overnight, continued on and hopped into the driver's seat.

"Well girl, another convert," said Colburn.

Natasha, who had been looking straight ahead, turned directly towards her Da and nodded in agreement.

"Too bad she wasn't ten years older, I could have had a date. You're what they call a 'Chick Magnet,'" said Colburn.

Da happy. Natasha happy. Pack happy, thought Natasha.

The cabin was in Maine two miles north of a town with the peculiar name of Moscow. The Town of Moscow's western boundaries are Wyman Lake and the Kennebec River. The scenic Benedict Arnold Trail, named for Arnold, after his unsuccessful attempt, to capture Canada before he became a traitor, winds northward through Moscow on its way to Quebec. In September 1775, early in the American Revolutionary War, Colonel Benedict Arnold led a force of 1,100 Continental Army troops on an expedition from Cambridge, Massachusetts to the gates of Quebec City. The invasion failed, but passing back through Moscow, one of his men, Johnathan Colburn remained. He married and had six children.

In 1804, Isaac Temple and his family came up the Kennebec and built the first sawmill in Moscow. The lumber from which, Johnathan Colburn built a two room cabin by the lake two miles north of a small town of Bakerstown.

In November of 1812, a petition was signed to try to incorporate the town. The town had gone by the name of Bakerstown, but by this time, there was a Bakerstown in Southern Maine (now the town of Poland). The name of Northfield also appears on the petition but was crossed out. There was a Northfield in Washington County. The town was finally given the name Moscow, named after the Russian city that was burned in 1812 to dislodge the French.

Colburn and Natasha drove out of Cambridge around 3 p.m. and took 95 north towards Portland to Waterville, then 201 north to Bingham, then to the small town of Moscow. A little over 200 miles start to finish. The cabin was two miles north of Moscow. The drive was pleasant with moderate to light traffic. The radio was on, and they were listening to Sirius 50's doo-wop station. Natasha would join Colburn and howl when one of their favorite songs came on, especially when the lead or first tenor did the falsetto parts. They arrived in Bingham around 7 p.m. and stopped at Jimmy's Market for supplies and gas. The owner, Jimmy, would be sure to alert everyone in Bingham and Moscow that the mercenary and his wolf were heading to the cabin. Jimmy and the other locals did not know for sure that Colburn was a mercenary or even a soldier, for that matter. He just looked the part. Quiet, strong, a black Range Rover, and a dog that looked like a Timber Wolf. He was polite. Always respectful with "yes sir this and yes sir that". It's what people wanted to think, and so the legend grew.

They then drove on through Moscow and on to the cabin. The cabin was a real log cabin. Colburn bought the place five years ago and refurbished it himself along with Sarge and his apprentice Natasha. Therapy-pure and simple. He had done the research and knew the property's history although the realtor who sold him the property didn't. Colburn didn't feel it necessary to inform him.

The cabin sat on twelve acres and bordered the lake to the west and two thousand acres of reserve north, east, and west, all in the shadow of Wolf Mountain. The nearest neighbors were in Moscow two miles distant. The 650 sf, cabin was one level with two sections, a front section, and back. The front was a combination kitchen/dining room and library. While the back had the main bedroom, guest bedroom, and a bath. In the wall separating the library and the main bedroom was a double-sided open fireplace. The cabin, despite its isolation, had all the creature comforts, hot and cold running water, propane gas stove, and solar, and wind generated DC power which was then converted to AC. No TV but they did have direct satellite internet connection. It even had a flushing toilet, hot shower, and a dishwasher. From the outside Johnathan Colburn, his ancestor, might have recognized the place, but from the inside, it might as well have been something from outer space.

They drove down the quarter mile dirt driveway to the cabin. Since it was dark and Colburn didn't want to miss the main turnoff, he turned on the Range Rovers navigation system and was told by a very proper British voice through the speaker system, "You have arrived."

"Ok Tosh, it seems we have arrived," said Colburn mimicking the British announcer's accent.

Natasha, with her strong left front leg and paw, reached across and pulled away the door release. She pushed her body against the door and out she jumped. She turned and shoved her shoulder against the door and slammed it shut. She was not taught to do these things, she just instinctively figured it out, originally, to Coburn's surprise and wonderment, but that all ceased to amaze him long ago.

"Vedette Tosh," commanded Colburn.

Natasha charged the cabin and slowly and methodically circled sniffing and listening all the way. She stopped several times no doubt recalling recent animal presence, human or otherwise. At the side window and again at the front door she sat down and stared directly where the human scent was the strongest. Colburn was not too alarmed because the real estate agent who sold him the property was also a caretaker and would periodically stop by to check on things. Had any explosives been detected Natasha would have reacted much differently. It was a redundant exercise because he had GoPro motion detector monitors inside and out with a smartphone alert app.

Colburn grabbed the bags and briefcase and headed for the cabin door.

"Good girl! Let's go in and get the fire started."

Da safe, Natasha safe, Pack safe.

He unlocked the double dead bolts and opened the door. Natasha sprang through the door and did another interior vedette without being asked. It was dark and cold, so Colburn turned on the lights and went to the fireplace and opened the flu. He primed the flu by rolling up some paper and lit it to create a draft before lighting the tented logs, kindling, and paper. The paper, kindling and hardwoods caught immediately, and in seconds, they had a blazing fire and immediate heat. Moscow was a bit cooler than Cambridge. Colburn went to the utility closet and turned on the water and gas lines. He then went to the kitchen area and turned on the refrigerator. He unpacked the groceries, which included a bag of ice, two T-bone steaks, potatoes, string beans, butter and things for breakfast. Natasha watched intently, especially when the steaks came out.

"Do you want to have a steak tonight with your Da, Natasha girl?" asked Colburn.

This was too much for Natasha to take. She jumped up and started licking her Da, all the while not losing eye contact with the steaks. Colburn took a bottle of champagne from the cupboard and placed it into the bag of ice. He peeled the potatoes, cut the string beans, and put them on to boil. Off the kitchen were French doors that led to a small cantilevered deck, holding two Adirondack chairs, a small table and a gas barbecue mounted on the railing. The deck faced the lake, which was about a hundred yards down a steep slope from the cabin. The view was spectacular and refreshing. He turned the gas grill low, covered it, and let it heat up. He would put the steaks on in about twenty minutes to give the potatoes and string beans a chance to cook.

From his briefcase, he removed his Satellite Blackphone, cellphone and two paperback novels he intended to read, *The Crossing* by Michael Connelly and *The Promise* by Robert Crais. He read one of Crais's previous novels *Suspect*, which was about LAPD cop, Scott James, and his new partner Maggie. Maggie was a German Shepherd, who survived three tours in Iraq and Afghanistan sniffing explosives before losing her handler to an IED. The interaction between the two new partners helped Colburn understand his relationship with Natasha. He had read the book aloud to Natasha, as they sat by the fire a few years ago and would do the same with *The Promise* tonight. Colburn and Natasha enjoyed reading much more than watching TV. Colburn was quite sure Natasha not only enjoyed the story but began to think like Maggie. He would observe Natasha's behavior after they finished reading *Suspect* and could swear she was channeling Maggie. Colburn knew Natasha instinctively believed that she was part of a pack but also wanted to believe that Crais's novel was getting through. Natasha and her Da, she never knew anything else.

Colburn picked up his Satellite Blackphone, hit a selected speed dial number and waited for the connection.

"Yes, Icy," answered Kim Ly.

Hmm. What happened to Mr. Colburn?

"Is it done?" asked Colburn.

"Yes. She was appropriated, detained, repersonalized, infused and deposited. All without incident," said Kim Ly.

"When will it break?"

"The establishment was very busy. A lot of people waiting for tables. So unless some good samaritan canceled, I would suspect she is still waiting in line. Tomorrow morning 9 a.m. your time, would be my guess."

"Where are you?" asked Colburn.

"On my way home," replied Kim Ly.

"Your money will be deposited tonight," said Colburn and touched off.

Funny. My GPS tracks your phone to Jackson Mississippi. On your way home to Vietnam through Jackson, Mississippi? thought Colburn.

Colburn had his banker wire the money into Kim Ly's account, then put the steaks on. He and Natasha stayed on the deck while the steaks cooked.

Natasha smelled him first, then offered a low growl. Colburn turned to the direction Natasha was looking.

"I see him too girl."

It was the same little boy who was following them on their previous walks through the woods. Natasha was leery, but not overly concerned. Colburn thought the boy reminded him of himself at about the same age, inquisitive, daring and clandestine. From the deck, Colburn waved at the boy. The boy came out from behind a tree and walked slowly up the hill towards the cabin. Natasha's ears were straight up and rotated left and right searching for danger. Her eyes and nose were fixed on the boy, but she did not see, smell, or hear a threat. The boy looked somewhere around eleven years old but didn't seem upset or scared for having just been busted.

"What are you doing out there in the woods alone? It's getting dark and kind of chilly. What's your name?" asked Colburn.

"Timmy. Timmy Logan," answered the boy.

"Timmy, I'm Israel Colburn, and this is Natasha. Now that were formally introduced, why don't you come on up and we can talk by the fire."

"Is it true what they say about you and your wolf, I mean your dog, I mean Natasha?" asked Timmy.

"Don't know. What do they say?"

"That your dog is a Timber Wolf and that you are a mercenary soldier," said Timmy.

"Natasha is a German Shepherd, and I was once a soldier, so I guess they are right. Why don't you come up so I can at least drive you home?"

"No thank you, sir. I know these woods and can be home in 30 minutes. Nice to meet you and Natasha. I'll come back again. Is that ok?"

"Sure. Anytime and it was nice meeting you too," said Colburn.

The boy dissolved back into the trees and was gone. Natasha stayed fixed on his movements even though Colburn could no longer see him.

That was interesting, thought Colburn.

"Let's get something to eat girl. Want your steak like usual. Charred and rare?" Colburn asked as he took a sip of champagne.

I would prefer it uncooked, thought Natasha but she knew Da liked his cooked and enjoyed the ritual. *Da happy, Natasha happy, Pack happy.*

Colburn put Natasha's steak, bone and all, on a paper plate and set it on the deck. Natasha remained seated on her haunches fixated until Colburn gave the command.

"Have at it girl," said Colburn, and Natasha did just that.

Colburn retired to the kitchen with his steak and added the potatoes, string beans, butter and salt and pepper. It hit the spot. Natasha was still on the deck when he finished, but her steak was long gone. She was now eating the bone marrow; then she would grind, clean and sharpen her fangs and teeth on the bone. After dinner, they sat by the fire and began reading *The Promise.*

Around midnight wolves howling was heard by several Moscow residents. They said it seemed to be coming from the direction of Mr. Colburn's cabin. It was a sweet, eerie sound almost like a chorus singing in harmony. The Moscow residents also heard, from atop of Wolf Mountain, howls in replies. It went on for half an hour, two packs searching for each other. The howling got closer together then stopped. There had been some recent wolf sightings and reports of wolves coming closer and closer to Moscow. The town's mayor heard the howling and made a note to check with Mr. Colburn next opportunity.

CHAPTER 17

SAN FRANCISCO, CA

At the Lowes Regency Hotel, Ron Todd and Tom Sweeney meet with their SFPD source, Detective Stan Marcus.

"The FBI brought us in officially because they needed our street cameras. The big shits would never have otherwise, and you know they don't seem to be all over this one," said Marcus.

"I think I know why," said Todd.

"Did you review the street tape?" asked Sweeney.

Marcus kept looking at Todd and answered "Yea. I reviewed the tape from the surveillance cameras. So did the FBI and the SS. The cameras tracked her white Kia across Market to Ecker and then we lost her. None of our other surveillance cameras on adjacent streets picked her up again, so she either stashed Vitelli somewhere in that area, switched cars, or slipped through somehow," said Marcus.

"You run the plates?" asked Sweeney.

This time, Detective Marcus looked at Sweeney and said. "No, we didn't think to do that. Yes, we ran the plates! A rental car from Hertz at the airport. FBI checked it out and got a bogus ID and credit card, but we got video of Miss Saigon coming and going."

"What about private business surveillance cameras around Ecker Street? You know, banks, stores, that kind of thing," asked Todd.

"There were none, or they were broken," said Marcus.

"She didn't stash Vitelli there or slip through. She switched cars. You think we can get a look at the surveillance tapes?" asked Todd.

"The FBI is sitting on them so I would say the chances of a reporter seeing them are pretty slim," said Marcus.

"Then let's head over to Ecker Street, and see what we can see," said Todd.

When they got to Ecker Street, just a few blocks from the hotel, they parked, got out, and started to look around.

"We got cameras at the end of Ecker Street and all over 1st Street," said Marcus.

"Let's split up and look for underground parking without surveillance cameras," said Todd.

After about twenty minutes, Sweeney found the car in a private garage on Jessie Street. He called Todd, and Todd rounded up Marcus.

There sat a white four-door, Kia, clean as a whistle.

"Let me call this in," said Marcus.

"Why don't you call it into the FBI as a favor and get us a look-see at the tape," suggested Todd.

Detective Marcus did as suggested, and the FBI, as a favor, let them review all the surveillance tape.

Sweeney picked it up first. A black Toyota exiting Jessie Street about 15 minutes after the surveillance cameras lost the white Kia.

"Ok now's the hard part. She turned left on 1st Street, and she could be heading anywhere," said Marcus.

"You called Sue Li, Miss Saigon. Is she Vietnamese?" asked Sweeney.

"According to FBI facial analysis, she is. But the name Sue Li isn't registering with the face. In fact, no name is registering with her face, and she left no prints," said Marcus.

"Don't you have a neighborhood near here called Little Saigon?" asked Sweeney.

Detective Marcus was starting to warm to Sweeney and looked at him this time and answered his question with a bit more respect. "We do. It's in the Tenderloin district and real close."

"I bet if we look at surveillance cameras from here to there we will pick her up," said Sweeney.

"Now I know why I brought you," said Todd.

It was a pretty easy trail to follow, but where it ended was not so pretty.

"Oh for Christ's sake! Right across the street from the Tenderloin Police Station. You have got to be shitting me," said Marcus.

The Feds were watching the tapes with them, and now everyone in the room starting getting excited. They left together, this time in Detective Marcus's unmarked black Ford Crown Vic with black wheels. They were heading to the Tenderloin district only blocks away. The FBI were in two black Suburban's right behind.

The parking gate to the apartment building was locked, so they went to the buildings front door and rang the bell. They rang all the bells. No answer. FBI agent Don Mead got on his phone to either get a court order to break in or get an OK to break in as a matter of life and death. He ordered one of his agents, along with Detective Marcus and Sweeney tagging along, to go across the street to the police station and look at the station's surveillance tape. There was, hanging from the station wall, not one, but three cameras, one of which was pointed directly at the apartment building.

FBI Agent Mead got permission over the phone to break in. A metal ram was produced, and the door and most of the door frame came down after just one swing. In the frenzy of the break-in, Todd was somehow allowed to accompany the FBI into the apartment building. The SFPD was mandated to assume exterior security. While the three remaining FBI agents started searching the ground floor, Todd headed up to the third floor and by chance, luck, instinct or a combination of all three, the first door he opened was the one in the back. He knew immediately he was in the room where Sue Li held Vitelli. He felt it, smelled it, then saw it. Sue Li made no attempt to conceal or destroy any evidence. He pulled out his cell phone and started taking photos. Vitelli's clothes were on the floor. Blood all over a chair. A Bloomingdale's bag and a Sears's clothing bag started to tell a story, but in the bathroom, it all came together.

Todd ran out of the apartment and down the steps. To keep good relations with the FBI, he yelled to Agent Mead, "Third floor rear."

Todd ran across the street to the police station just as Detective Marcus and Sweeney were coming out.

"We got her driving in yesterday and coming back out last night. She had a passenger. We couldn't get a facial, but it didn't look like Vitelli. Could be a possible accomplice. We accessed three of our proprietary surveillance cameras on Jones and Pine Streets. We saw her turn onto Hyde but lost her," reported Detective Marcus.

"What's around there?" asked Todd.

"St. Francis Memorial Hospital," replied Marcus.

"Let's go see St. Francis and I bet her passenger had short red hair," said Todd.

"That's a bingo," replied Sweeney.

CHAPTER 18

SAN FRANCISCO, CA

The next day *New York Post* front page headline read:

Paula Vitelli - Death by Obamacare

by Ron Todd and Tom Sweeney

Congresswoman Paula Vitelli was found dead of cardiac arrest in the emergency ward at St. Francis Memorial Sloan Hospital on Bush Street near the Tenderloin District of San Francisco.

First reports stated that Ms. Vitelli was not recognized by hospital staff and was in fact admitted to the emergency ward as one Ms. Ilse Koch of Dearborn, Michigan.

"She had short red hair and was wearing an Evan Picone two button, green and black pant suit from Sears. She had bruises on her face and looked nothing like Ms. Vitelli. She had, among other documents, a Michigan driver's license and an Obamacare medical insurance card (the new healthcare plan named after former President Hilton's Secretary of Health and Human Services, Barack Albert Obama) issued by a Michigan Affordable Health Care provider. Unfortunately, the Obamacare provider, United Healthcare, had a very high deductible, and although initial emergency care was administered, further test and admittance to the hospital were delayed because payments were declined by the provider. No next of kin could not be reached," said Mildred Hemming, a hospital spokesperson.

Ms. Vitelli aka Ilse Koch was discovered deceased in the emergency room hallway twelve hours after she was admitted. Several physicians and nurses remembered seeing her in the hallway, and one remembered trying to converse with Ms. Vitelli. She was said to be very emotional and excited. She kept telling everyone who passed; she was someone important and that she deserved a private room. She kept insisting the nurse stole her Armani suit, but then she would start to stammer, convulse and pass in and out of consciousness.

Not until SFPD Detective Stan Marcus began his preliminary investigation including running fingerprints, was Ms. Vitelli's true identity discovered. When the mistaken identity was discovered, the death by natural causes became a probable abduction and homicide. Ms. Vitelli's body was immediately transferred to San Francisco Medical Examiner's Office. Chief Medical Examiner, Omi Kelly, Chief of Forensic Pathologist for the City and County of San Francisco, stated cause of death to be cardiac arrest but would not elaborate what caused the heart attack. She further stated that had timely proactive procedures and medication been administered, Ms. Vitelli could have survived.

Paula Vitelli was reported missing Wednesday by her aide when she failed to appear as the guest speaker at the Loews Regency Hotel. The speech was about the success of the Affordable Health Care Act and her role in making it happen. Foul play was originally not suspected because she was so well loved in the community, and she had been suffering from early stages of Alzheimer's. It was originally thought she had wandered out of her hotel room and would turn up shortly.

Ms. Vitelli was the 53rd. Speaker of the United States House of Representatives. A Democrat, she was the second woman to lead a major political party in either house of Congress and became the second female Speaker of the House on January 4, 2011. She had represented California's 13th District.

How Ms. Vitelli became Ms. Ilse Koch of Dearborn, Michigan and how and why Ms. Vitelli was abducted from the Loews Regency Hotel and wound up dead in St. Francis Memorial Sloan Hospital is the story that we will unfold to you, shortly. But we can tell you the kidnapper is one Sue Li, a 25 to 30 year old Vietnamese with severe scratches across her face. Sue Li is probably an alias. She is dangerous, ruthless and on the run.

SFPD Detective Stanly Marcus has been the catalyst in leading the investigation. We, along with Detective Marcus, are on the trail of the kidnapper and murderer.

But there may be a bigger picture unfolding. Tom Sweeney of the *Hedgehampton Press*, yours truly, Ron Todd of the *NY Post*, and a very reliable inside source, working together, are on the trail of the assassin. Is something rotten in Washington? Are they stonewalling and withholding critical information linking the deaths of Former Vice President Richard Rumson, Globalwide's Albert Mazola and now the former Speaker of the House Paula Vitelli? I suggest, my dear informed readers that a conspiracy may exist at the highest level of government to withhold, suppress and cover up a bigger plot.

Our preliminary investigation differs from what the official FBI position and I...

CHAPTER 19

WASHINGTON, DC

The President was up early and in the Oval Office. He, FBI Director Riley, and Secret Service Director Bounty had been out and back from an early morning 10k run. They had changed and were having coffee, the President a Diet Coke, when Press Secretary Kelly Sullivan came in.

"Busted," said Kelly.

"Yea. We just got a heads up from the *NY Post* owner Rupert Murdoch, but haven't seen anything in print. You have a copy of the *Post* story?" asked the President.

"I do. And it's not pretty." Kelly passed copies to the President, Riley, and Bounty.

Everyone knew since yesterday morning, that former speaker Ms. Vitelli was dead. The reports they were getting, as the investigation proceeded, was that she had also been kidnapped.

But now the *NY Post* was putting it all out there in print with pictures.

"Paula Vitelli -Death by Obamacare."

"The crime scene is a hospital, and the murder weapon is Obamacare. But this reporter, Todd, and his partner Sweeney were saying the government, at the highest level, was withholding critical information linking the deaths of former Vice President Richard Rumson, Globalwide's Albert Mazola and now the former Speaker of the House Paula Vitelli. And suggesting a conspiracy and cover up. Not good," said Kelly.

"Kelly, get me this Ron Todd from the *Post* on the phone then have Bill convene, in the Cabinet Room, as many of my Cabinet members that are available. Set up a televised address to the nation for 9 p.m. this evening," said the President.

It was 7:30 a.m. in New York and Todd was finishing up a phone call with Detective Marcus in San Francisco when his phone flashed another incoming call. The caller ID read, 'The White House.'

"Got to take this, Stan. I'll get back to you." And touched the icon to accept the incoming call.

"Todd here."

"Please hold for the President," said the White House operator.

"Mr. Todd. Tommy Burk here, and thanks for taking my call," said the President.

"Yes, Mr. President. What can I do for you sir?" asked Todd.

"I think you have already done it, but you might want to hear what I have to say before you go forward," said the President.

"I am not exactly sure what it is you think I've done Mr. President, but of course, I am more than anxious to hear what you have to say," said Todd. For all his years as a reporter Todd understood words and the way they were used. Because of that, he learned, when under questioning, to structure one's answer to mirror the question. The President was of the same mindset.

"If I may read your words Mr. Todd: *"But there may be a bigger picture unfolding. Tom Sweeney of the Hedgehampton Press, yours truly, Ron Todd of the NY Post, and a very reliable inside source, working together, are on the trail of the assassin. Is something rotten in Washington? Are they stonewalling and withholding critical information linking the deaths of former Vice President, Richard Rumson, Globalwide's Albert Mazola and now the former Speaker of the House Paula Vitelli? I suggest, my dear informed readers that a conspiracy may exist at the highest level of government, to withhold, suppress and cover up a bigger plot."* That's what you have already done for me, Mr. Todd, and this is what I have to say to you. We hoped you would have figured it out after Mazola drowned. I think you did, but you just weren't ready to release it. We, too, had it figured out by then but were hoping you would put it out first. We would look a little less of a conspirator that way. Unfortunately, neither of us did, and Ms. Vitelli is dead because of it. It is a shame, but her demise was probably in the works regardless. Did you ever wonder why or how you were tipped off before each murder? Did you ever think that you're "inside source" might be the assassin? That you were being played, Mr. Todd?"

Todd was momentarily shaken. After the first tip, he checked his source as best he could, and he seemed to check out. Dangerously so. He would get phone calls and tips which proved to be reliable and accurate. Todd was led to believe by his source, that he was on the fringes of government.

"With all due respect Mr. President, if there is someone or some group out there, vengeance killing people, why keep it quiet?"

"We couldn't prove it till after Mazola, and were getting ready to release what we had, but we were afraid it would turn into a free for all with good guys going after bad guys. It's not one person but a group with a mission and ideology. That mission is to kill bad guys or at least their definition of bad guys. Bad guys that did bad things to our country and got away with it. Their ideology is to create a lynch mob mentality of copycats, to start hunting down crooked politicians, shady lawyers, Wall Street crooks and corrupt business-men. We think that this is a group operating outside the United States with the intention of creating chaos throughout our country. Your article this morning seems to be pointing a finger at us," said the President.

"Do you think this is the end? Do you think there will be more ven-geance killings?" asked Todd.

"I certainly hope it is the end. You have given them what they want. You connected the dots, and bad guys and bad girls, throughout the country, should be pretty scared. It now depends on how your readers, how the coun-try reacts. Are they going to say OK, enough is enough or are they going to want more blood? I am not telling you to stop your story or investigation, but if you continue to lead it in my direction, you will be heading down the wrong path and falling into their hands. You work with us on this, and we will work with you," said the President.

"What exactly does that mean?" asked Todd.

"Come to Washington tomorrow morning and I will tell you," said the President.

"Can I bring my partner Tom Sweeney?"

"Yes, of course. I'll bring mine."

FBI Director Riley and Secret Service Director Bounty listened to the conversation via a silent speaker connection. The President filled Kelly in and arranged for passes for Todd and Sweeney for tomorrow morning. He then got up and left for the Cabinet Room around the corner from the Oval Office, with Riley, Bounty and Sullivan in tow.

CHAPTER 20

MOSCOW, ME

Colburn and Natasha had a full day planned. They decided to take a long hike in the woods up to the top of Wolf Mountain. After the hike, come back to the cabin and do some reading. Later have an early dinner, then get ready to head back to Cambridge the next day. But first, breakfast.

"What do you feel like girl? Something to eat? Some fried eggs, sausage and home fries? Sound good?" asked Colburn.

Natasha cocked her head and listened to what her Da was saying. What she understood was; *girl, eat, good.* What she saw was her Da pulling out a cooking skillet and opening the refrigerator door. What she heard and saw made her lick her lips. *Pack hungry. Pack hunt. Pack eat.*

While breakfast cooked, under the watchful eye of Natasha, Colburn pulled up a satellite link on his Blackphone and got *FOX and Friends.* His Sat. Blackphone brought him live streaming video of Steve Darcy finishing up a breaking story. Colburn just caught the end. Something about a *Post* article by Ron Todd incriminating the White House. He quickly hit *CNN* and got New Day 8 a.m. slot, with Peter Caine in the middle of a live phone interview with *NY Post* reporter Ron Todd.

"It sounds like you're changing your story, and the ink hasn't had time to dry?" asked Caine.

"No. That's not what I am saying," answered Todd.

"OK. But I want to make sure I understand you correctly."

"I said there may be a bigger picture unfolding and that we are on the trail of the assassin," said Todd.

"Who is this assassin Sue Li, and where is she?" asked Caine.

"We have a name and a photo. More details will be released soon. What I asked, in my article, is if Washington was stonewalling and withholding critical information linking the deaths of former Vice President Richard Rumson, Globalwide's Albert Mazola and now the former Speaker of the House Paula Vitelli," said Todd.

"What about your closing affirmation and I quote, "I suggest, my dear informed readers, that a conspiracy may exist at the highest level of government to withhold, suppress and cover up a bigger plot." Do you stand by that statement?" asked Caine.

"Yes I do stand by it, but as it turns out it may not be our government," replied Todd.

Colburn touched off from the interview and pulled up the morning's *Post* article by Todd and Sweeney and read it over the Blackphone screen.

OK. The story's out. Vova got what he wanted. Now we'll see how the country reacts. But I'm through with it. I'm out, thought Colburn.

"Come on girl, let's have some breakfast."

After they had finished eating and cleaning up, Colburn put on a light jacket and grabbed a small backpack, containing his phones, some water, snacks and his M1911 Colt 45 Automatic with two extended clips. With one round in the chamber and the extended magazine he had 12 hollow point rounds instead of the standard 8 rounds. He had 23 rounds including the extra clip. He was an expert shot but had no intention of shooting animals although the Colt 45 would stop a bear. The 45 cal. hollow point ammunition is one of the most effective self-defense loads used today. The hollow cavity in a hollow point allows the round to expand and deform upon impact. This expansion and deformity create a large wound channel throughout a soft target, creating more damage. More importantly, when hollow point ammunition expands it rapidly loses speed and slows greatly inside a soft target. This works to prevent the round from over penetrating an attacker and striking someone else.

"OK girl, let's have some fun."

The hike up and back from Wolf Mountain was about 14.5 k or 9 miles. Not that far, but with half of the hike up and the other half down, muscles not often used would be put to the test. Natasha kept looking backward as if something or someone was following.

"You feel it too girl?" asked Colburn.

Natasha looked down the mountain, then turned to catch up with her Da. *Pack safe.*

Two hours later they were on the top of the mountain, in a small clearing. Colburn was looking for it but Natasha found it first. She alerted then went down on her belly and stalked towards a fallen tree.

"Found it girl? Yea you did, didn't you? Good girl."

Da happy, Natasha happy, Pack happy.

There under a fallen tree was a wolves den. Colburn and Natasha didn't approach it closer than a few feet, but all the signs were there and recently. He gauged from the ground disturbance, six wolfs. An adult mated pair and four offspring two to three years old. Natasha was hoping she would recognize a familiar scent, and she did.

Colburn and Natasha sensed something wrong almost simultaneously. His hair went up on the back of his neck and Natasha's ears alerted and started to rotate. They were being watched.

Threat to Da, Threat to Natasha, Threat to Pack, thought Natasha.

Natasha turned, went down on her belly and stalked. She sprang up and charged another 20 feet to the wood line and went to ground again. Colburn cautiously followed. She sprang again into the wood line and alerted but did not attack. Colburn approached, and behind a tree hiding, was the young boy from yesterday.

"Well Timmy didn't think we would meet you up here."

"Neither did I, sir. I was just out for a hike and well…," said Timmy as he let it kind of roll off.

Colburn knew this was not an accidental meeting but had to hand it to the kid. He and Natasha sensed he had been tracking them for 3 miles.

Colburn showed Timmy the wolves den and then they moved away as to not contaminate the site.

"Timmy, it's not a good idea coming up here by yourself with the wolves and all," said Colburn.

"I never come this far up. I only did because I wanted to follow you and Natasha," answered Timmy.

Out of his backpack, Colburn pulled two small bottles of water and a cup. He gave Timmy one bottle, and he and Natasha shared the other. They joked around a bit about their accidental encounter and headed back down the mountain to the cabin. As they walked, Timmy opened up about himself and his family as did Colburn about his life. A little under two hours later and some sore downhill muscles, they reached the cabin.

"Why don't you come up for some hot tea or soda?" asked Colburn.

As it was starting to get late in the afternoon, Timmy begged off and said goodbye. Colburn told him they would be leaving tomorrow for Boston. They shook hands and Timmy patted Natasha on the head said goodbye. Natasha ran after him and rubbed against his legs. She accepted one more pat on her head then ran back to her Da. And just like before, Timmy melted into the woods and was gone. Natasha followed him with her eyes, nose, and ears.

"OK, girl. That was interesting, and it looks like you made another friend. At least we had a good work out and found where our friends live. I am up for a fire and a hot bath and something to eat. How about you girl?"

Fire good, bath bad, eat good, thought Natasha.

Just as they were about to enter the cabin, they both froze. A sound. Distant but familiar. Colburn knew the sound, and it was out of place and could be bad. Natasha heard the sound and was alerted. Anyone who has been in combat looks skyward when the sound first becomes apparent and usually in the wrong direction. Not Colburn. Not Natasha. They looked north, and the sound got louder. A helicopter was coming in low and fast. At first a spec, then Colburn was able to identify it as non-military. A silver seven-passenger Mercedes-Benz EC145 helicopter was about to land in a clearing towards the east of the property. Whoever was coming to visit had power and money.

They were coming in uninvited but not flying a warbird but a state of the art, 8 million dollar luxury Mercedes Airbus helicopter.

It could be either of two people; either had the means to find him. One he loathed; the other he loved. Natasha stood alert and didn't even flinch at the noise and the wind the helicopter generated. The chopper touched down, and both side doors opened, and six men jumped out using the skids as steps. Colburn knew immediately it wasn't Dmitri Vova. Four men fanned out covering strategic points of the property. The pilot and co-pilot stayed aboard and shut her down. The two remaining men ducked under the rotor blades and approached Colburn. Natasha stood ready to attack, defend or stand down as her Da commanded.

"Stand down girl. It's OK. It's Sarge," said Colburn.

Natasha looked, sniffed and cocked her head but was still not sure nor ready to stand down. As the two men approached, still twenty yards away, one split off to the side, the other bent down and said, "Natasha girl. It's me, Sarge. Come say hello you big beautiful girl."

"Go girl. Say hello to Sarge," said Colburn.

Natasha leaped forward and charged towards the man she knew as Sarge. The other man started to make a move, but the Sarge motioned for him to stop. Natasha threw herself upon Sarge and almost knocked him over. Hugs and kisses followed from both.

"It's been too long girl," said Sarge.

Pack together, thought Natasha.

Sarge and Natasha walked towards Colburn and the cabin. Natasha resumed her position next to her Da, sitting facing Sarge.

"Been a while Icy," said Sarge.

"What took you so long? Thought I would hear from you a while ago?" replied Icy.

Sarge approached with his hand out. Normally Natasha would have taken it off, but Sarge was not a threat. They shook hands. Just two old friends who, when they were young, had each other's back in combat. ("Greater love hath no man than to lay down his life for a friend") No man hug was required. None expected. When they were together, they would often revert to their former titles.

"Come on in Sarge. I'll put some tea on, and you can tell me to what I owe this honor," said Icy.

The three of them went inside, and Icy immediately started building a fire. When he had it just right, he lit it, and in less than a minute, warmth, light and the smell of burning hardwood filled the cabin.

"Tea, coffee, beer or something stronger?" asked Icy.

"Its 5 p.m. somewhere, as they say, so why not a glass of Champagne. Knowing you, you will be well stocked," suggested Sarge. Icy took a bottle of Veuve-Clicquot Brute from the refrigerator, gently popped the cork and poured some into two Waterford Champagne flutes. It was a just cabin true, but...

After the pleasantries had been dispensed with, Sarge got down to the reason for his visit. They were seated in two upholstered vintage wingback chairs each facing the fire, anchoring opposite ends of a brass fender.

Natasha lay between them. *Pack together, Pack happy, Pack safe.*

"Is it over?" asked Sarge.

Icy thought before he answered, "It is. At least for me it is. He has a list. He contracted me to dispatch those on the list until the media figured it out and broke the story. The *Post* piece this morning did just that."

"Does this Sue Li work for you?"

"Yes but that's an alias. Her real name is Kim Ly. She is in the Vietnam People's Army, and she is in Special Forces. She also did Rumson and Mazola, and she works for me."

"Will he stop now?" asked Sarge.

"He's betting good people will take to the streets and take it to the next level all by themselves. He wants chaos, anarchy, madness. Anywhere he can get it," replied Icy.

"Why did you do it?" asked Sarge.

"I did it for the money. I did it because it's what I do. I did it because they deserved it. Why did you let me? Why didn't you try to stop me?" asked Icy.

There was no tension in posture or speech. Natasha would have sensed it.

"They all deserved what they got. I suspected after Dodger got it, you were probably involved, but after Mazola, I knew for sure. I suspected Vova, and I suspected his reasons. I don't think the American people will react in the way he hopes," said Sarge.

"If they don't, he won't stop. He will play the next person on the list," said Icy.

"Do you know who that is?" asked Sarge.

"I do," said Icy.

They were only together for just one hour before Sarge had to leave. He made a big fuss over Natasha, and she reciprocated. All three walked out together and said their final goodbyes. Sarge walked to the helicopter and picked up his security on the way. The helicopter started up, and the six men boarded. The rotors picked up speed as the noise increased. It rose up, put its nose down, gained forward speed and lifted off. The noise and wind were terrific and very familiar. At least to Colburn. Then it was quiet. Just like always. Only this time Colburn did not have to 'Continue Mission.' Colburn and Natasha headed back into the cabin. To the fire, warmth, dinner and a good book.

"OK girl. Yea I miss him too. How about some dinner?" asked Colburn.

Natasha seemed sad but perked up at the mention of dinner. They had done a long hike today and with all the excitement they were both starved.

"How about we have some pasta with spicy hot sauce," suggested Colburn.

Natasha tilted her head but showed little excitement for Da's pasta with spicy hot sauce. She knew the game and played along. She laid down and pretended to be sad. It always worked.

"No? You don't want to share my pasta? Don't you like my cooking? Is it because I'm not Italian?"

Natasha groaned as only she could. *Wait for it. Wait for it,* she thought.

"OK then. You'll just have to settle for my leftover steak," said Colburn.

With the mention of steak, Natasha was up, circling, down again and singing arrrrr…

Colburn took hamburger meat that was previously stewed with onions, from the refrigerator, put it in a saucepan, added the Vincent's Hot Tomato Sauce, some cayenne pepper and Cholula Hot Sauce, stirred it, heated it, and poured it over a bowl of cooked pasta shells. A meal in a minute. From the refrigerator, he pulled out his leftover steak, still on the bone, and put it out on the deck for Natasha.

Natasha happy. Natasha stopped eating and concentrated her senses on movement in the tree line. She alerted which signaled Colburn. Colburn joined her on the deck.

"What do you got girl?"

It was starting to get dark. Whatever light there was, came from the cabin and the low full moon. Colburn followed Natasha's gaze but could see nothing. He looked a little to the left of where Natasha was looking; an old military trick called averted vision, and he saw it. There was Timmy Logan, and he was moving away from the cabin towards his home.

He must have hidden when the helicopter came in, thought Colburn.

Not a threat, thought Natasha.

"I wonder what he saw girl?" said Colburn.

Natasha went back to her steak and Colburn to his hot spicy pasta.

"Tonight we'll chorus about it and see if our mountain friends will join us."

Da good, Natasha good, Pack good, thought Natasha.

By the time Timmy made it back home to Moscow, it was almost 9 p.m. and dark. He had gotten completely lost and turned around and sheltered in place for a while when he thought he was being stalked. He lost his footing and fell a couple of times. He was not at his best. Maybe it was the helicopter that troubled him or maybe it was the man he saw getting off it. Mr. Logan, Timmy's father, heard him come in. He, as town mayor, had several town officials over to his house including Police Chief Jim Pruitt from Bingham and the Pastor Jerry Buffer of Moscow's Trinity Baptist Church. They were in his living room discussing the strange events from last night and the helicopter they heard and saw earlier in the afternoon. They also had their Dish satellite tuned into NBC local affiliate WSCH channel 6, to hear the President's 9 p.m. live address to the country regarding the recent string of revenge killings. As dutiful town fathers, they wanted to make sure no citizens of Moscow would fall to a similar fate.

"Where have you been young man?" asked Timmy's father. Timmy tried unsuccessfully to navigate through the living room to the stairs to his bedroom. The others in the room were betwixt and between trying to watch and listen to the President's opening remarks and at the same time consumed by the alarming sight of a disheveled Timmy Logan.

"Ladies and Gentlemen, the President of the United States," announced the Sergeant at Arms.

Although usually the sight of an angel, Timmy now looked anything but. His jeans were dirty and ripped. His blond hair was matted with sweat and streaked with blood from a nasty cut on his forehead. His shirt and shoes were muddy.

"Stop right there young man. Answer me boy. Where have you been, and what in God's name happened to you?" demanded his father.

"Good evening. In the last few weeks, three great Americans were murdered. Two have served this great nation, and one helped build it. They were taken from family and friends who loved them deeply. Former Vice President Richard Rumson, Mr. Albert Mazola, CEO of Globalwide and Ms. Paula Vitelli, former Speaker of the House. Each of whom served their fellow citizens in their respective way and all of them were part of our American family.

"What a crock of shit," said Police Chief Pruitt, adding solemnly "No disrespect intended pastor."

"None taken. But it sounds to me like President Burk's Addresses to the Nation, on keeping the American people safe, is going to be a Heifer Dust speech," replied the pastor. His euphemism for Bull Shit.

"What did you say?" asked Mr. Logan looking away from his son and back towards the chief and pastor.

"No! Not you. We were talking about the President," said the chief.

Tonight, I want to talk with you about this tragedy, the broader threat of terrorism, and how we can keep our country safe.

Swinging back to Timmy, his father continued, "Answer me, boy. Where you up in the north woods again? Up by that cabin with the crazy mercenary and his wolf?"

The others all turned their attention from the TV to the more interesting drama unfolding right before their eyes and ears. Timmy was a good kid. Adventurist and spirited but a good kid who always told the truth. As he saw it.

"Dad I was just out in the woods tracking a deer when I heard a helicopter. I went further into the woods, and the helicopter noise got louder. Before I knew it I was near a cabin, and the helicopter was landing," said Timmy.

"You saw the helicopter?" asked his father.

"Yes," answered Timmy.

"Who roughed you up, son? Was it that crazy man and his wolf?" asked the chief.

"No sir. When the helicopter took off again, I got a little spooked. I tried to run home, but I got a little disoriented and fell a couple of times," said Timmy.

The FBI is still gathering the facts about what happened in St. Michelle, Hedgehampton and San Francisco, but here is what we know. The victims were brutally murdered by organizations with Islamic jihadi affiliations. This was an act of terrorism, designed to kill innocent people...

"You saw the helicopter land?" asked his father.

"Yes sir," said Timmy.

"Was it an Army helicopter? Marine helicopter? What happened?

"I don't think they were Marines. Six men got out dressed in suits, and one man came to the cabin. I was hiding in the trees when I saw Natasha charge the man," said Timmy.

"Who's Natasha? Did a woman attack someone?" asked the chief.

"Oh no, sir. His dog's name is Natasha, and she knew the man, and they were friends. Then the three of them went into the cabin together while the other men stood guard outside. That's why I couldn't leave. They would have spotted me," said Timmy.

"The man in the cabin, was he that mercenary soldier Colburn?"

"Yes, sir. But he is not a soldier anymore. He's just a nice guy," said Timmy.

"Who was the other man? What did he look like?" asked the chief.

Our nation has been at war with terrorists since al Qaeda killed nearly 3,000 Americans on 9/11. In the process, we've hardened our defenses -- from airports to financial centers, to other critical infrastructure. Intelligence and law enforcement agencies have disrupted countless plots here and overseas and worked around the clock to keep us safe. Our military and counterterrorism professionals have relentlessly pursued terrorist networks overseas -- disrupting safe havens in several different countries, killing Osama bin Laden, and decimating al Qaeda's leadership...

Timmy looked away from Chief Pruitt, towards the TV as the President was speaking.

"Answer the chief. Look at me Timmy. Answer the chief," scolded Mr. Logan.

Timmy looked away from the TV and looked at Chief Pruitt.

"Who was the other man? What did he look like?" asked the chief again.

Now Mr. Logan, Chief Pruitt and Pastor Buffer and the other town officials all were focused directly on Timmy.

Timmy turned away and again looked at the TV and then nodded.

They all turned in unison to see what Timmy was nodding at.

"The President? The man who you saw looked like the President?" asked his father.

"No," said Timmy, "The man I saw was the President."

Over the last few years, however, the terrorist threat has evolved into a new phase. As we've become better at preventing complex, multifaceted attacks like 9/11, terrorists turned to less complicated acts of violence like the mass shootings that are all too common in our society. It is this type of attack that we saw at Fort Hood in 2009; in Chattanooga a few year; and lately in San Bernardino. And as groups like ISIL grow stronger amidst the chaos of war in Iraq and then Syria, and as the Internet erases the distance between countries, we see growing efforts by terrorists to poison the minds of people like the Boston Marathon bombers and the San Bernardino killers.

Now, here at home, we have to work together to address the challenge. There are several steps that Congress should take right away.

To begin with, Congress should act to make sure no one on a no-fly list can buy a gun. What could be the argument for allowing a terrorist suspect to buy a semi-automatic weapon? This is a matter of national security. We also need to make it harder for people to buy powerful assault weapons like the ones that were used in San Bernardino. I know there are some who reject any gun safety measures. But the fact is that our intelligence and law enforcement agencies -- no matter how effective they are -- cannot identify every would-be mass shooter, whether that individual is motivated by ISIL or some other hateful ideology. What we can do -- and must do -- is make it harder for them to kill.

Everyone was still looking at Timmy except Pastor Buffer, who was back to looking at the TV, and having a one-way conversation with the President.

"Excuse me, Mr. President. Two of these people were killed by water. The other by Obamacare. Not assault weapons. Are we going to ban assault water? We certainly don't need to ban Obamacare; it will soon implode on its failed self," said Pastor Buffer.

"What's wrong with you Pastor? Didn't you just hear what Timmy just said? The President of these United States just flew secretly to Moscow," said the chief.

Next, we should put in place stronger screening for those who come to America without a visa so that we can take a hard look at whether they've traveled to war zones. And we're working with members of both parties in Congress to do exactly that.

Finally, if Congress believes, as I do, that we are at war with ISIL, it should go ahead and vote to authorize the continued use of military force against these terrorists. For over a year, I have ordered our military to take thousands of airstrikes against ISIL targets. I think it's time for Congress to vote to demonstrate that the American people are united and committed, to this fight....

"Does that mean he intends to bomb St. Michelle, Hedgehampton and San Francisco?" asked Pastor Buffer. Still fixated on the TV.

"St. Michelle and Hedgehampton no. San Francisco possibly. Anyway, this whole speech sounds so familiar. Didn't President Hilton use it? They just seem to switch out mass murder locations and recycle the same speech," added Chief Pruitt.

My fellow Americans, these are the steps that we can take together to defeat the terrorist threat. Let me now say a word about what we should not do.

We should not be drawn once more into a long and costly ground war in Iraq or Syria. That's what groups like ISIL want. They know they can't defeat us on the battlefield. ISIL fighters were part of the insurgency that we faced in Iraq, but they also know that if we occupy foreign lands, they can maintain insurgencies for years, killing thousands of our troops, draining our resources, and using our presence to draw new recruits.

The strategy that we are using now -- airstrikes, Special Forces, and working with local forces who are fighting to regain control of their country -- that is how we'll achieve a more sustainable victory. And it won't require us sending a new generation of Americans overseas to fight and die for another decade on foreign soil. Here's what else we cannot do. We cannot turn against one another by letting this fight be defined as a war between America and Islam. That, too, is what groups like ISIL want. ISIL does not speak for Islam. They are thugs and killers, part of a cult of death, and they account for a tiny fraction of more than a billion Muslims around the world -- including millions of patriotic Muslim Americans who reject their hateful ideology. Moreover, the vast majority of terrorist victims around the world are Muslim. If we're to succeed in defeating terrorism, we must enlist Muslim communities as some of our strongest allies, rather than push them away through suspicion and hate.

That does not mean denying the fact that an extremist ideology has spread within some Muslim communities. This is a real problem that Muslims must confront, without excuse. Muslim leaders, here and around the globe have to continue working with us to decisively and unequivocally reject the hateful ideology that groups like ISIL and al Qaeda promote. They speak out against not just acts of violence, but also those interpretations of Islam that are incompatible with the values of religious tolerance, mutual respect, and human dignity.

Just as it is the responsibility of Muslims around the world to root out misguided ideas that lead to radicalization, it is the responsibility of all Americans -- of every faith -- to reject discrimination. It is our responsibility to reject religious tests on who we admit into this country. It's our responsibility to reject proposals that Muslim Americans should somehow be treated differently, because when we travel down that road, we lose. That kind of divisiveness, that betrayal of our values plays into the hands of groups like ISIL. Muslim Americans are our friends, and our neighbors, our co-workers, our sports heroes -- and, yes, they are our men and women in uniform who are willing to die in defense of our country. We have to remember that.

My fellow Americans, I am confident we will succeed in this mission because we are on the right side of history. We were founded upon a belief in human dignity -- that no matter who you are, or where you come from, or what you look like, or what religion you practice, you are equal in the eyes of God and equal in the eyes of the law. We will hunt down these murderers here or wherever they hide. Rest assured we will find and prosecute the murderers of Former Vice President Richard Rumson, Mr. Albert Mazola, CEO of Globalwide and Ms. Paula Vitelli, former Speaker of the House.

Even in this political season, even as we properly debate what steps I and future Presidents must take to keep our country safe, let's make sure we never forget what makes us exceptional. Let's not forget that freedom is more powerful than fear; that we have always met challenges -- whether war or depression, natural disasters or terrorist attacks -- by coming together around our common ideals as one nation, as one people. So long as we stay true to that tradition, I have no doubt America will prevail.
Thank you. God bless you, and may God bless the United States of America."

If the President's speech mystified the group, Timmy's revelation astonished them. They were trying to digest both the speech and the inquest. By the head shaking and pruned up faces, the consensus seemed to be bewilderment and skepticism on both counts. Police Chief Pruitt was the first to speak out.

"I think the President is smoking dope. Is he trying to tell us that ISIL is coming over here and murdering a former dick head Vice President? Excuse me, pastor. A corrupt mortgage broker and a former Speaker of the House? And this hurts America how? And Timmy telling us a story that the President of the United States of America visited Peter the Wolf, here today, in good old Moscow Maine?"

"Whoa chief. Let's slow down here. Say what you want about the President's speech but Timmy ain't been raised no fool or liar."

"Amen to that," added Pastor Buffer.

The chief started to back pedal when Timmy heard it. Timmy held up his hand for quiet. His dad turned off the TV. Timmy headed for the front door with the town fathers in tow. Once outside it was clear what they were hearing. The moon was full and high, and the howls were coming from near the lake in the direction of the cabin. Beautiful, eerie and haunting. Like the other night. Almost like a chorus in harmony. Then from the top of Wolf Mountain came a reply. Stronger. A larger chorus but just as haunting. Closer and closer they seem to be coming together until at last they seemed to be singing as one pack. The hypotonic trance was broken when the local town dogs started to get in on the act; then it just seemed to unravel into a parody of Pongo and the Great Dane during a scene from Disney's *One Hundred and One Dalmatians*.

Back inside and with Timmy off upstairs to bed. Mayor Logan said, "Chief, tomorrow morning before that Colburn fellow and his wolf leave, you should arrest him."

"On what charges?" asked the chief.

"I don't know, but call the FBI or Homeland Security. Tell them something fishy is going on out in these woods. Helicopters, wolfs, ISIL, the President. Hell, I don't know, but something is going on here in Moscow. You can be sure of that."

CHAPTER 21

WASHINGTON, DC

The next morning, after his usual 10k run, President Burk was in the Oval Office with FBI Director Riley, Secret Service Director Bounty and Press Secretary Sullivan discussing last night's speech, when his Chief of Staff Bill Nicholas came in to join them.

"We were just discussing last night's speech, Bill. What are you hearing?" asked the President.

"The response from your Cabinet was supportive, as you would expect. I was expecting more backlash from the other side of the aisle, but so far it's not happened. California Governor Criss, and Senator Frankenbaum are upset about lumping Vitelli with Rumson and Mazola and that her murder is being associated with the Affordable Health Care Act. A state senator from Long Island, Paul Valla is yelling about Hedgehampton getting a reputation as a playground for the rich and disgusting. Rumson representatives are furious about the way the Vice President has been portrayed in the media and want you to dissociate him from the Vitelli and Mazola. Other than that, the calls and emails we're getting seem to point towards apathy over the murders. The gist of which is "They got what they deserved," said Chief of Staff Nicholas.

Press Secretary Sullivan picked up, "The media thinks you're blowing the ISIL connection to the murders out of proportion, but are saying, off the record, that newspaper sales and TV news programs have experienced a huge spike. Feedback from Main Street and Wall Street is they don't seem to care, and the market is still up. I think the speech was necessary, and now we move on. If there are no more high profile revenge murders, we'll be fine but…"

The President took it all in and said, "We know there is a list of at least five more names. If this *NY Post* article doesn't get the reaction they want, they will play the race card. The next one on the list is the Reverend Jeremiah Johnson. If anything happens to him, all hell will break loose. 'Blacks React - Whites Refrain.' If we stop the assassin from getting Reverend Johnson, we stop a nationwide black uprising. If we stop the assassin from getting Reverend Johnson, we get the assassin. If we get the assassin, we get the fingerprints of ISIL and who is behind them."

"With all due respect Mr. President, how did we take the leap from murder, by a nostalgic serial killer, to murder by ISIL and whoever is pushing their buttons? Where did we get a list and race card?" asked Chief of Staff Nicholas.

"Bill. Some things we had to keep under wraps. Now it's out, we can tell you what we know. You listened to the speech, but the background is this. We know who ran the operations. A contractor named Icy. We suspected, and he confirmed, who is behind it and why. Demetri Vova, a Colonel in FSB. Russia Federal Security Service, successor to the KGB. Among other things, he is in charge of international chaos, and he's the 'customer agent' ISIL calls when they need help. He funds, uses and supports ISIL. He is a nasty piece of work. He works for Vladimir Vladimirovich Putin. President of Russia. We get him, and we get Putin. We get Putin and ISIL loses an important ally and benefactor," said the President.

"OK. I get it. But who is this guy IC and how did you know it was him in the first place and how can we trust him?" asked Nicholas.

The President looked at FBI Director Riley, and Riley answered. "Icy is Israel Colburn. Former Marine in Vietnam back in '67, former CIA, former mercenary and now a private contractor. We go back a ways, but that's another story. I would trust him with my life, and the President does too. As nasty a piece of work as this Vova guy is, he fears only two men. Putin and Icy."

"What does IC stand for? His initials?" asked Nicholas.

"Originally yes. But as the story goes, he was shot during the Six Day War, and when the medics tried to stop the blood pouring out of his shoulder, it was ice cold. They had to cauterize the wound to warm the blood for it to coagulate. He was so brave and cold in battle; well, you can imagine what happened when the medic's story about him having ice cold blood flowing through his veins started to spread. His nom de guerre from then on was Icy."

"I thought you said he was a US Marine. What's he doing fighting for Israel in '67 when you said he was in Vietnam in '67?" asked Nicholas.

Chief of Staff Nicholas knows his history, thought Press Secretary Sullivan.

"As Ray said, that's another story," said the President.

"Sounds like the most interesting man in the world," added Nicholas.

President Burk and FBI Director Riley just looked at each other and smiled.

The briefing soon broke up after lunch, with Secret Service Director Bounty and Chief of Staff Bill Nicholas leaving the Office. Now, just the President, FBI Director Riley and Press Secretary Sullivan remained in the Oval Office. Noreen Ward, the President's secretary came in and said that Mr. Todd and Mr. Sweeney were here.

"Noreen ask the steward to bring in some fresh coffee and some Diet Coke. Give us five minutes and then show them in," said the President. Then both he and Riley hit the two Oval Office johns.

Noreen Ward entered, followed by Mr. Todd and Mr. Sweeney. FBI Director Riley, President Burk and the steward, with a tray of coffee, tea and Diet Coke, all enter the Oval Office through different doors at the same time.

Almost like a Chinese puzzle, thought Kelly Sullivan.

"Gentlemen, thank you for coming. He walked over and shook hands with both and introduced FBI Director Ray Riley and Press Secretary Kelly Sullivan. Coffee, tea and Diet Coke were poured, and popped, then they sat down on the couch and chairs around the coffee table with Sweeney and Todd on the other couch.

"How was your flight?" asked the President.

"Jet Blue. What can I say? Not like the old days on the Eastern Shuttle. Didn't need a reservation then, paid cash on board, flights every half hour and free bagel and coffee," said Todd.

"Yea. Back in the day," said Riley.

"What times your flight back?"

"Open."

"OK. Let's get on with it so you can head back early or see the sights. First, what did you think about the speech Mr. Sweeney?" asked the President.

Amazed, but not intimidated, to be sitting in the Oval Office with the President of the United States and the FBI Director, Tom Sweeney of the *Hedgehampton Press* said, "Mr. President, Abraham Lincoln once said "I am a firm believer in the people. If given the truth, they can be depended upon to meet any national crisis. The great point is to bring them the real facts.""

Todd looked over at Sweeney with surprise. He would have never led off with that, but there you are.

"And what you heard last night did not appear to be truth and facts?" asked the President.

"Mr. President we have been on the trail of a crazed Navy Seal wannabe in St. Michelle, a blond bombshell swimming coach in Hedgehampton and Bruce Lee's sister in San Francisco. How has this morphed to murders organized by Islamic jihadi? Terrorism? Not selling guns to anyone on the no-fly list? What did Todd and I miss?"

FBI Director Riley looked like he was going to tear Sweeney a new one while Todd looked like he just found his Woodward.

"Fair enough," said the President. "You only know, from last night's speech, what we know for sure and could truthfully and factually tell the American people. We now know who is orchestrating these murders, and it's not for revenge as it appears. It is to produce and bring to the United States another form of terrorism. It's just another weapon in their arsenal. They flew planes filled with innocents into our buildings. They have tried to burn our country to the ground. They had set bogus dirty bombs in our cities just to create fear and panic. They have incited lone wolf attacks, cyber-attacks and now revenge-attacks. They want to entitle next-door neighbors to turn on each other over some past encounter, incite lynch mobs to have instant justice with a politician or businessman who they dislike or who may have misspoken. To date, it hasn't worked, and we may be in for another round. We now know Russia and ISIL are plotting together, more revenge killings, and we know who is next on the list."

"How do you know Russia and ISIL are involved, and where did you get this list?" asked Todd.

FBI Director Riley picked up. "We now know who coordinated the murders here in the United Stated and why. The guy who set the murders up. The guy who hired the so-called crazed Navy Seal wannabe, the blond bombshell swimming coach and Bruce Lee's sister. We now know Sui Li, Bruce Lee's sister, is actually Kim Ly, a Vietnamese Special Forces operative and the actual assassin of all three; Rumson, Mazola, and Vitelli. Her boss is our source, and he's out of it and has given up his boss. We'll deal with him later. His boss, the one who is paying for it and orchestrating it, is Demetri Vova, a Colonel in FSB, Russia Federal Security Service, and successor to the KGB. He's in charge of international chaos. He funds, uses and supports ISIL. He is a very nasty piece of work. He works for Vladimir Vladimirovich Putin. President of Russia. We get him, and we get Putin. We get Putin we get Russia, and it all stops."

"We will work with you both if you let us. But keep on with your investigation," said the President.

"OK. Good start. We'll work with you. But whose next on the list?" asked Todd.

"The next one on the list is the Reverend Jeremiah Johnson. He's in Chicago now, and we got him blanketed. But it may or may not go down. Hold it close for now," said Riley.

"Ok, we'll work with you, but we won't hide the truth. When we find something we'll share it with you, but if you try to suppress it, we'll get it out even if we have to leak it," said Todd.

"Fair enough, said Riley. He then looked at the President then back to Sweeney and in his best Sollozzo voice from the *Godfather* scene where

Sollozzo releases Tom Hagan said, "Good...then you can go...I don't like violence. I'm a businessman, and blood is a big expense."

Sweeney stared at the FBI Director for a few seconds then turned to Todd for support or explanation. Todd just shook his head and gave Sweeney a 'what the fuck' expression.

The President and Riley had a habit of channeling different actors from the *Godfather* and *Goodfellas*. Usually between themselves. Kelly thought it was childish, but she knew both Riley and her husband, the President, were just little boys at heart. Knowing Riley was pulling Sweeney's leg, the President tried to defuse the awkward moment.

"Now you can head back to New York or have a private tour of the White House. Or if there is anything else I can offer you?" asked the President.

Sweeney was hoping for a private tour of the White House but Todd said instead, "Sorry Mr. President, We'll have to take a raincheck. We're heading from here straight to a town with the strange name of Moscow, Maine."

President Burk and FBI Director Riley looked at one another, and Todd caught it.

"Why? What's up there?" asked Riley.

"Just something out last night on the *UPI* wire. A local TV news program reporting on some strange occurrence. They're saying something suspicious happened out in the woods. A helicopter coming and going, men in suits, wolf packs. All kinds of crazy stuff," said Todd.

Again Todd saw it. The President and Riley looking nefariously at each other.

"One more thing," asked Sweeney as they were getting up to leave. "Why the Russians? Why are they doing this?"

The President recovered quickly, thought for a moment, then said, "The best way I can answer that is to recall for you what Winston Churchill said, which I believe is as germane today as it was seventy-five years ago. "I cannot forecast to you the action of Russia. It is a riddle, wrapped in a mystery, inside an enigma.""

As Todd and Sweeney were leaving by one door. Secret Service Director Bounty came in the other and joined The President. Riley and Sullivan were still sitting around the coffee table.

"Busted again," said Riley.

"Those two are sharp, and what was that Sollozzo bit about?" asked the President.

"What?" asked Riley.

"What did I miss?" asked Bounty.

"We filled Sweeney and Todd in, and they agreed to work with us. To a point. But somehow they found out about Moscow, and it caught us off guard. I think Todd noticed it. I know he saw it," said Riley.

The President buzzed his secretary Noreen, "Please get me Colburn on the phone."

FBI Director Riley got on the phone to his NYC ADC Hoar to check out what Todd had told them about Moscow.

They continued to discuss the ramifications of being busted when Noreen buzzed back that she had Mr. Colburn on the phone.

"Icy. I got you on speaker with Kelly, the Captain, and Secret Service Director Bounty. Glad I caught you. Where are you?"

"We're out on a hike now. We'll have a late lunch, then start packing up, and take off back to Cambridge later this afternoon. Why? What's up?" asked Colburn.

"It seems we have a bit of a problem. The helicopter was spotted and so were we, although I don't know specifics. We're checking."

"The town is small and nosey. A local kid, snooping in the woods might have seen us, but I don't think he'll say much. Besides, who's going to believe it?" asked Colburn.

"Did you watch the speech last night?" asked the President.

"Don't have a TV. You got security on Reverend Johnson?" asked Colburn.

"Buttoned up tight in Chicago," said Riley.

Silence.

"Are you still there Icy?" asked the President.

"Chicago?" asked Colburn. His mind was churning.

"Why? What's wrong?" asked Riley.

"Who's in Jackson Mississippi? Any black rebel rousers?" asked Colburn.

Director Riley said, "Hold on a sec." And got on the phone to his Jackson Mississippi field office. After a minute he touched off, turned back, and said, "The Reverend Ali Shabazz. I say he qualifies."

"Oh shit. I think my contractor might have gone freelance, and my former employer might have gone off script. Get your people on Shabazz, and do it fast. We've been played. I've got to get to Jackson right away," said Colburn.

"What are you driving?" asked Riley.

"A black Range Rover."

Riley jumped up with the phone in his hand and got his Jackson, Mississippi field office back on the line. He gave them their marching orders about Shabazz then called the FBI office in Bangor. Riley was transferred to FBI Bangor Special Agent in Charge Rob Ceretti. "Agent Ceretti, this is Director Riley in Washington. Get a chopper immediately over to Moscow, Maine, and intercept a black Range Rover heading south through Moscow. ETA about 60minutes. His name is Israel Colburn. He's armed and a VIP, so show all due respect and professional courtesy. Get him and his dog, Natasha, to Bangor International ASAP. Our LZ. Clear the way for him to board. Absolutely no interference. Bring another agent to take his Range Rover back to Cambridge. His cell is 809 674 2526. It will be on, and you can track him. Understand?" asked Riley.

"Understood," replied SAC Ceretti.

"Icy. Start towards Cambridge when you're ready. Someone will intercept you on the way and chopper you to Bangor International then a jet to Jackson, Mississippi. Keep your cell on so we can track you," said Riley.

"What about Natasha?" asked Colburn.

"Take her with you to Jackson, or she can come stay with me till you get back. Your call," said the President.

CHAPTER 22

Moscow, ME - Jackson, MS

Colburn quickly closed down the house, set the security system, and locked up. He tossed his briefcase and overnight in the back of the Range Rover, and opened the door for Natasha. She got in; he got in, and Colburn started the engine and headed out the drive to the road. It was almost 5 p.m. when Colburn got on the road to Moscow. The blacktop was slick, and he hit a low fog as he came down the mountain towards Moscow two miles away. Chief Pruitt had one of his deputy's stationed north of his driveway as a heads up for the reception party waiting in Moscow. He picked up the radio mic and said. "Chief, Deputy Hinds here. You read me?"

"Six by," said the Chief.

"He just pulled out onto the road and is heading your way. Over."

"Copy that. Follow him in but stay back and don't spook him. When I stop him, you pull up behind. Over."

"Copy. Over and out."

Colburn and Natasha strained to see the highway even with the fog lights on. The going was slow. Hills and valleys all the way with no other traffic in sight except someone coming up on him from behind with high beams on.

"Did you call the FBI last night like you were supposed to chief?" asked Mayor Logan.

The chief's police car was off to the side of the road by Town Hall and Logan, Timmy, Pastor Buffer and a few other interested citizens were behind it. The chief was in the middle of the road.

"I did," replied the chief.

"Well are they coming?" asked Mayor Logan.

"Not sure they believed me," mumbled the chief.

After a slow ten-minute drive, Colburn and Natasha passed Temple Pond on their left and the Wyman Hydroelectric Dam on their right. A straight shot now through Moscow. But just as they got to the Moscow Elementary School on the west side of the road and Town Hall on the right, they started to see and hear people, cars, and noise. Colburn slowed down. His cell chirped then a voiced announced: "We're at your 9 o'clock."

"What is that chief?" yelled Pastor Buffer.

Pastor Buffer had to yell because all of a sudden, flashing lights, tornado strength winds and what sounded like a freight train came dropping out of the fog. Chief Pruitt, Mayor Logan, Timmy, Pastor Buffer and the rest of the citizenry, bent low, shielded their eyes and watch in amazement as a dark blue helicopter with FBI stenciled in yellow on the side door, descended into a clearing south of the elementary school.

"You still got the mojo chief," yelled Pastor Buffer.

Chief Pruitt thought to himself, *Yea I still got it.*

The chief saw Coburn's black Range Rover round the corner and he stepped out into the road to use his body, if necessary, to stop Colburn. Colburn didn't quite reach the chief but turned instead, directly into the clearing where the FBI helicopter landed. Two agents wearing blue raid jackets with FBI in yellow on the front and back had jumped out and were waiting for Colburn. Colburn stopped his Range Rover 20 yards from the helicopter, jumped out, grabbed his briefcase and overnight and started towards the agents. Natasha opened her door, jumped out, banged it closed and sprinted to her Da's side. With the rotor blades still spinning, the two agents bent low and ran towards Colburn and Natasha. Colburn came forward erect. Having flown in more helicopters that most people, he knew the blades, while still spinning, were well above his head, and was immune to decapitation.

Colburn gave Natasha the "sit" command as one of the agents went towards the road and the other came forward to greet him. FBI Agent Ceretti gave Colburn a crisp salute, and they shook hands. Natasha was thinking threat and though commanded to sit, remained on alert and closely watched and sniffed the agent. The agent was told that Colburn and Natasha were VIP's, and to get them to Bangor International, ASPC.

"Agent Ceretti sir. I'm here to escort you and Natasha to Bangor International. Are you all set?"

To the other agent off to the side, Colburn tossed his Range Rover keys, and said, "Make sure this gets back to Cambridge safe and sound. Leave the keys on top of the driver's side rear wheel. And make sure it doesn't get the boot." Referring to the infamous metal tire lock Boston uses for parking violations.

"Will do sir," replied the agent.

Agent Ceretti led Colburn and Natasha to the helicopter and got Colburn seated in the rear forward facing seat. Natasha jumped up next to him. Colburn looked out across the road and saw Timmy. He gave Timmy a nod which Timmy returned. Timmy's father looked on, a little confused. Agent Ceretti sat facing Colburn and Natasha. He put on a helmet with audio connections and spoke into the mic to the pilot.

"Let's rip." The helicopter raised off the ground a couple of feet then pointed its nose down and started forward and up. Soon it was engulfed in fog. Only the sound remained. In a few seconds, even that was gone.

This was all too much for Chief Pruitt. A salute? No handcuffs? He turned back to look at his previous admirers, and they all made the 'what happened, jester.'

Chief Pruitt, at 6'2" and 220 lbs, in his tan uniform with green piping posed an opposing figure. He was not one to be ignored. He walked over towards Coburn's Range Rover as the Agent was just opening the driver's door.

Agent Ross was new to the FBI and quite excited to be on an assignment even if it meant shuttling a VIP's car back to Cambridge. She was petite, toned, black and beautiful. She wore a black suit under her FBI raid jacket with a light blue blouse. On her feet were black, made in the USA, New

Balance 577 walkers. She carried a Sig Sauer P320 compact with a .357mm 13 round capacity, plus one on the chamber. On the flight from Bangor, SAC Ceretti filled her in and she immediately googled Colburn. She got a ton of hits. Cambridge law firm of Beston Servienti and Colburn. USMC and Vietnam. *OK. So far so good,* she thought. Then some spooky stuff started to come up. Israel Defense Force and the Ulster Volunteer Force. Pakistan, Rhodesia, Cambodia, Lebanon, Laos, Angola, El Salvador, and Vietnam again. Colburn's picture appeared, but the name was now Icy. She logged on to the FBI site and typed in Israel Colburn/Icy and got a pop-up saying; ACCESS DENIED.

"Agent, I am Jim Pruitt, Chief of Police in Bingham. I am the one who called you about this Colburn character and his wolf. Would you mind telling me what just happened?"

"Chief, I am FBI Agent Ross, and we just picked up someone, and we are taking him somewhere." *That much he saw,* she thought.

"Is he under arrest?"

"He's a person we have been directed to retrieve."

"What are you doing with his Range Rover?" asked the chief.

"Taking it back to Bangor," she lied.

This is all the chief could stand. By now he had half of Moscow looking at him expecting an arrest. Instead, he lost Colburn and his wolf and was about to lose the Range Rover.

He motioned his deputy to pull up and box in the Range Rover.

"Oh no you're not," said the chief as he slammed his shoulder against the driver's door slamming it shut.

Agent Ross now found herself in the middle of a situation. What she did next could defuse or escalate it. She saw the audience across the road and realized the chief was probably trying to impress them and show her who's in charge. But the truth of the matter is that she is an FBI agent, and that trumps a local police chief every time. She thought quickly back to what the chief had first said.

"Chief Pruitt, why do you think we're here? We got the call, and we're investigating. Colburn is going back to Bangor, and so is the Range Rover." She again opened the door and said, "You done good chief." She got in started the engine rolled down her window and yelled across the street to the assembled crowd, "Thank you all for the tip. 'See something say something,' we're going to investigate this matter, and I'm sure we will get to the bottom of it and get back to you soon."

The chief stepped away from the Range Rover, seemingly vindicated.

Agent Ross said, "Chief. Can you ask your deputy to back up so I can get on my way? By the way chief, will you be available to come down to Bangor later to assist in the investigation?" That did the trick. Chief Pruitt signaled Deputy Hinds to move out of the way, smiled and said, "Certainly Agent Ross," and handed her his card. She gave him her best smile and a little salute. He smiled and returned the salute. She pulled away with a wave and gave a thumbs up to the crowd. As she drove away, she began to relax. She was close to taking the chief down, literally, but decided to defuse the situation with the chief and that proved to be the right decision. The chief said he called us about Colburn. She should have known that and intended to find out what happened to that call.

Walking back across the road, Chief Pruitt studied the eyes of Moscow's town fathers and assembled residents. It seemed to them, at least, he retained his mojo. The chief informed them he would be working with the FBI and would keep them posted.

That night with Mayor Logan and Pastor Buffer, in Logan's living room, the chief was more forthright about what actually transpired.

"I think something is going on with the FBI. They may have responded to my call, but I think someone else might have called them."

"Who?" asked Mayor Logan.

"I think the guy Timmy saw at the cabin with Colburn. The same guy we saw on TV last night."

They all nodded just as Timmy came down the stairs.

"Well, it's been an exciting weekend. Back to go old quiet Moscow," said Pastor Buffer.

Timmy was walking to the front door and waving the others to follow. There off towards Wolf Mountain they heard it. Wolves howling. It went on for almost ten minute but howls were not joined from the cabin. Not even the local dog's chorused in.

"We've got to do something about those wolves," said Chief Pruitt.

"I think you better let them be," said Timmy.

CHAPTER 23

JACKSON, MS - ATLANTA, GA

K im Ly had to move fast. She only ever feared two men. Vova and Icy. And Icy would be coming for her soon. This she knew for certain. Demetri Vova had called her before she left for San Francisco to meet Icy for the Vitelli contract, and gave her a new contract. She knew this was against the rules, but Demetri made the rules. She worked for Icy, and in the private international contracting business, one did not have two bosses at the same time. But she knew Demetri, and he offered her twice what Icy was paying for San Francisco. Plus for this new job, she would also get to set it up. Total control. Of course, she would do Icy's San Francisco job first, then Demetri's. When Icy found out, she better be back home in Vietnam, and even there she would not be completely safe.

She had been in Jackson Mississippi a couple of days setting things up and fortunately she was staying at the Jackson Marriott, the same hotel as the Reverend Ali Shabazz. That made surveillance a bit easier. The charlatan she was, for this trip she didn't donned a new disguise other than large dark sunglasses. Her facial abrasions had healed nicely, and with make-up, all but disappeared. When Demetri gave her the job, he told her to set it up any way she wanted, but it had to be a white on black murder. It had to be big and racial. She spent her first day on the internet searching her prey and race relations in the US during the 60's. One man's name keep appearing as a protagonist towards government-sanctioned racial oppression and segregation in the

United States. Jim Crow. He was a mysterious character and elusive but not favored by southern blacks. She spent her second day following her prey and formulating a plan. Her third day would be setting it up. She had to get his schedule and the best way to get it was online.

Reverend Ali Shabazz, if nothing else, was a communicator. He communicates everything. From Facebook and Twitter to his web page. He wants everyone to know he is an important, busy guy. He let everyone know he was in Jackson, why he was there, and where he was staying. He also tweeted he was meeting friends for an early dinner today at the Chimneyville Smokehouse on High Street.

Today, the fourth day, her plan would be implemented. In a few hours actually. For her plan to work, Reverend Ali would have to walk back to his hotel from the restaurant. Five blocks. He was such a health addict nowadays that he walked everywhere. But to be sure he walked to the hotel she tweeted him, anonymously, at the restaurant, that the state capital building, a few blocks down High Street, and on the way to the hotel, was again flying the Confederate flag from the capitol dome. A slap in his face and ammunition for tomorrow's 'Black Lives Matter' rally through Jackson. The rally organizers didn't want or invite Shabazz to the rally. They knew it would become all about him, and they did not want or need the Reverend Ali Shabazz appropriating their movement. But the good reverend could not pass up an opportunity to be seen and heard. 'Black Lives Matter' was a new movement, and he intended, like it or not, to be marching at its head.

Everything was all set, and Kim Ly was getting ready to leave the hotel for the airport. She knew she was cutting it close and had to get to Atlanta for a flight to Seoul then on to Hanoi before Icy connected the dots. She would miss the event itself, but had a reliable man handling the actual job. He came highly recommended and was a professional who would not be caught alive. Kim Ly arrived at Jackson-Evers International Airport, just six miles from her hotel in downtown Jackson, and one hour before her Delta flight to Atlanta. In Atlanta, she would board her flight to Seoul and then on to her home to Vietnam. The airport was not crowded and after passing through security still had forty-five minutes before her flight. Just before her gate, gate 15 in the west concourse, she passed a Starbucks and went in to get a Cappuccino. Starbucks was crowded, but she found a space at the counter that looked out into the terminal, "Mind if I squeeze in?" asked Kim Ly to the man who was writing something in an old fashion copy book.

"By all means," said the man, as he moved his stool a little to give Kim more room.

As often the case in airport bars and coffee shops, strangers strike up innocent conversation.

'How's the Cappuccino?" asked the man.

"A bit too sweet for my taste," said Kim. "Where are you headed?"

""On my way to San Francisco. You?"

"Atlanta."

"What's in Atlanta?"

"I'm an expediter for a Boston Law firm; Beston Servienti and Colburn and I'm off to Atlanta for some meetings. You?"

"I'm a writer heading to San Francisco to do some follow up on a story."

Just then Kim's cell phone rang. She took out her phone and checked the number and said to the man, "You'll have to excuse me. I have to take this. It's my boss. She got up and started to walk away searching for a more private spot to take the call. As she walked away, he heard her say, "Yes Icy."

Kim told her boss what he wanted to hear, but she knew he could track her phone, and most likely would. When he asked where she was, she gave a vague but honest reply, "On my way home."

Writer, San Francisco, story, that's interesting, thought Kim Ly as she picked up her carry-on and said goodbye to the man. *A coincidence? Possibly but not a threat. He'll live to make it to San Francisco.*

Beston Servienti and Colburn - Icy? She is beautiful. Even the sunglasses couldn't hide that. Expediter? She should be a model or at least a spy, thought the man as he jotted some more notes into his copybook.

Unfortunately for the good reverend, by the time Colburn connected the dots in Moscow, talked with Washington, and by the time the FBI could find the reverend and react, Reverend Ali Shabazz would already be dead. They were too late. Too late for the Reverend but not too late for Kim Ly.

FBI Director Riley had Kim Ly's photo from San Francisco, BOLO out to all the major transportation hubs. Atlanta International Airport's facial recognition scan cameras picked her up entering the airport, going through customs and making her way to Korean Air in the international terminal. Colburn was alerted during his flight from Bangor to Jackson and diverted to Atlanta International. Kim Ly was allowed to proceed to the mezzanine level and gain access to the Club ATL, a private lounge for international first class travelers.

Ron Todd and Tom Sweeney never made it to Moscow to check out the suspicious stories coming from there, but instead, Todd's phone rang.

"Mr. Todd. Your regular informant is in route to the scene of another revenge murder. I am calling you in his stead. It seems another event has occurred, and if you hurry to Jackson, Mississippi, you may get the scoop."

"Who?" asked Todd.

"The Reverend Ali Shabazz."

"Who am I speaking to?" asked Todd.

The line went dead.

Secret Service Director Bounty, who never met Todd, closed his throw away cell phone, looked over at President Burk, FBI Director Riley and Press Secretary Sullivan and said, "I don't think they'll be going to Moscow."

"What?" asked Sweeney.

We're now going to Jackson Mississippi." As they searched for a flight information board, Todd filled Sweeney in.

"American's got a non-stop leaving in twenty minutes. Let's move," said Todd.

They raced across the terminal to the American counter, just in time to purchase two one way coach seats to Jackson International Airport. As they were boarding, Sweeney was searching for anything current on Shabazz. Nothing other than his tweets about his having a good fresh fried catfish with hushpuppies and coleslaw dinner at Chimneyville with friends. Followed by another tweet that he was walking to the courthouse to see if that damn rebel flag was flying again. Several local news stations in Jackson were reporting that a murder has occurred, and it's someone important whose identity is under wraps. Police are claiming the name was being withheld until notification of next of kin can be established.

Colburn touched down at Atlanta International in the back seat of a Navy T-45A Goshawk. It was an unscheduled, unprecedented landing, but when Secretary of Transportation, Bill Dougherty called and requested permission to land a Navy fighter jet on a civilian runway who's going to argue.

Colburn had said goodbye to Natasha when they landed the helicopter in Bangor and told Agent Ceretti to deliver her immediately and personally to President Burk in Washington. He told Ceretti he would hold him personally responsible if anything happened to his Natasha. There was no way Natasha could have flown in the jet, and she would have a much better time with Sarge in the White House.

FBI Special Agent in Charge Henry Hill and Agent Susan Rice, of the Atlanta office, were waiting with a car when the jet approached and stopped. The cockpit cover swung up, and the captain shut the engines down. Colburn unbuckled his harness and removed his helmet. There was no ladder available, so when the captain gave him the thumbs up, Colburn climbed out onto the port engine and hopped to the ground. He turned back to the pilot, saluted, and gave a thumbs up. The salute was returned. Colburn walked towards the two agents wearing his flight suit and carrying his blue blazer. SAC Hill and Agent Rice walked towards Colburn.

"Mr. Colburn. I'm FBI SAC Henry Hill, and this is Agent Sue Rice. We have eyes on Kim Ly, and she is in the Club ATL in the international terminal. Let's get in the car. It's a seven-minute drive, and I can fill you in."

Agent Rice got in the front with the driver and SAC Hill and Colburn got in the rear, and they started to the international terminal.

"Is she alone and has she been thoroughly checked through security?" asked Colburn as he was stripping off his flight suit.

"Yes and yes. We steered her through a body scanner and nothing registered. She has a handbag and carry-on bag. Both were x-rayed and hand searched. She checked nothing."

"You said you have eyes on her."

"Yes. Both HUMINT, Human Intelligence, and surveillance cameras inside the club."

"I want to see what she looks like right now live. Can you do that?"

SAC Hill took out his iPhone and held it so Colburn could see.

"That's her, real time. Black slacks and jacket. Sunglasses and ponytail. She is not trying to hide. Her handbag and carry-on are right there with her. She is on her second cup of coffee, made two cell phone calls, seemingly to relatives in Vietnam. We are awaiting translation, any second now. She set down about twenty minutes ago. Her flight boards in thirty minutes. She hasn't gotten up, other than to get coffee."

"I want to go in the front club entrance," said Colburn, slipping on his blazer, "You've got the weapon?" asked Colburn.

Colburn didn't want to bring his Colt 45 into the airport. Too big and too loud. SAC Hill handed him a suppressed 9mm Glock. Colburn released the magazine and pulled the slide back to check the chamber. It was empty as expected. He reinserted the magazine and released the slide chambering a round. He eased the hammer down and switched on the safety. With the suppressor attached, it was almost 12 inches.

"Seventeen rounds?" asked Colburn.

"Right," said Hill.

They pulled up in front of the terminal, and all three got out and were met by airport security and quickly guided through security, up to the mezzanine and the club front door.

"Give me your phone," said Colburn.

"You can talk and receive with it in the live feed mode. We'll use Agent Rice's phone," said SAC Hill.

The Club ATL manager and reception desk were informed by airport security, that a VIP was about to enter and would not be required to check in. He would just walk on in.

"What's the plan?" asked SAC Hill.

"My plan is I don't have a plan. I intend to get from her the information I want, then kill her," said Colburn.

Agent Rice looked at her boss and smiled at what she thought was a joke. When nothing further came from Hill or Colburn, she said, "That's a joke. Right? You're not going to shoot her in the club lounge are you?"

"No of course not. My intent is to wait till she goes into the toilet and then shoot her in the stall."

"Why do you have to kill her?" asked Agent Rice.

"Because that's what I do. I kill them now, so they can't kill me later. Any more questions Agent Rice, or can I get on with it?"

Colburn didn't wait for an answer. He checked the phone to make sure Kim Ly was still in place and went in. As the door was closing SAC Hill heard Colburn say, "Let your HUMINT know I'm coming in and what I'm going to do. Have maintenance close down the toilet after I enter. Hopefully, she'll have to go, and it will just be the two of us in there."

Once inside, Colburn walked past the lounge front desk without a challenge. His description and ETA had been previously texted to them. He grabbed a newspaper, ducked into the carry-on bag storage room, and slipped the suppressed Glock into the newspaper fold. His right hand was on the grip and with his thumb, he cocked the hammer back. The safety was on, and his thumb moved onto it while his trigger finger rested outside the trigger guard. He held the paper against his side with his pinky finger holding the fold closed. With the phone in his left hand, as though he were reading his email, he continued into the lounge steering towards to the women's toilet. He found a seat outside and watched and waited. If she didn't go to the toilet soon, he would need to sit next to her and have their discussion in public. Several seats near her were empty. A woman was heading for the toilet, and Colburn thought about stopping her, but that might cause a scene which he didn't want. Let her go in and take her chances.

Kim Ly started to stir. She placed her coffee cup on the table and grabbed her handbag. She left her Carry-on, a good sign. He followed her as the surveillance cameras picked her up from one room to the other until he had eyes on her. Colburn was certainly recognizable but with a Sports Illustrated in his face, he appeared like most of the other passengers. Kim Ly went to the women's toilet opened the door and went in. Colburn got up and followed.

He pocketed the phone. No surveillance in the toilets but the agents outside could still hear through his phone's speaker. He waited a heartbeat at the door, giving her a couple of minutes to select a stall, then he opened the door and went in.

In her stall, Kim Ly undid her belt and lowered her slacks. She lowered her panties and with some effort, reached her fingers inside her vagina and pulled a tampon, inside of which was a small six-inch long metal cylinder. She pulled up her panties and slacks and re-did her belt. She removed the cylinder from its wrapping and flushed the tampon. She took a modified hairbrush from her handbag and screwed one end of the metal cylinder into the hairbrush handle, to make a grip.

There was no one visible when Colburn entered, so Kim Ly and at least one other woman were in stalls. He selected an empty stall next to the one he sensed was occupied by Kim Ly, opened it and entered.

"I didn't know you were so interested in sports?" asked Kim Ly.

"I'm not. It was the swimsuit edition," responded Colburn.

"Will you let allow me to leave?" asked Kim Ly.

"If you tell me what I want to know, I will allow you to leave quickly," said Colburn as he stood on the toilet and prepared to fire over the partition.

In the stall to his right Colburn heard the other women hurriedly finishing her business, flushing the toilet and leaving the stall.

Kim Ly placed her finger on the cylinder firing trigger, said "Vova" and pulled the trigger. The shot sounded like a loud spit as it echoed throughout the bathroom. Colburn visibly shaken, slipped down onto the toilet into a sitting position. *She was good. Very good,* he thought. He got up, exited his stall opened hers. It was unlocked, and he saw Kim Ly sitting on the toilet with her head back, hands to her sides still holding the cylinder. Blood splattered the wall behind her head and blood dripped from a bullet hole beneath her chin. She was dead, but her body was still convulsing. Then it wasn't.

As he exited the bathroom, he passed a sign, placed in front of the door by airport security, 'Out of Order'. Two cleaning attendants, he assumed were FBI agents entered with a cleaning cart. The area outside the woman's toilet was quiet as an announcement came over the speaker for the boarding of

Korean Air flight 0036 to Seoul, Korea and Hanoi, Vietnam. It would have one less passenger.

Colburn walked toward SAC Hill and Agent Rice. He handed Hill his phone.

"It's over," said Colburn.

"Did you have to kill her?" asked Agent Rice.

He took the suppressed Glock out from inside his jacket, released the magazine and handed it to SAC Hill and said, "Sixteen."

He then pulled the slide back ejecting one round towards Agent Rice, which she caught in her right hand. "Seventeen," she said.

"Bingo," said Colburn.

CHAPTER 24

JACKSON, MS

Sweeney and Todd arrived at Jackson International Airport, grabbed their stuff and ran through the airport to the Hertz rental bus. Since getting the tip, Sweeney was on the internet, and Todd worked the phone. More information was surfacing including Todd's Jackson PD source, Detective Denning, confirming the stiff as the Reverend Ali Shabazz. He also said that it is being investigated at as a racially motivated 'Hate Crime.'

Another revenge murder thought Todd; *I wonder how this fits into President Burk's playbook.*

"Do you think the President intentionally deceived us about who was next on the list?" asked Sweeney.

"No. I think it's out of control. They lost the thread. There would be no reason for them to lie to us."

The only rental bus in sight was a National. Sweeney grabbed his bag and yelled for Todd to follow.

"This is National. I only have an Avis account," said Todd.

"I have Hertz, National, Avis, Budget, and a few others. We're in a hurry, and we must have just missed the Avis bus," said Sweeney.

"Yea. But I had made a reservation on Hertz. What if National doesn't have any cars or there's a line?" asked Todd.

"It's done! I have a National Rental App with built in GPS. It identifies my location and instantly reserves a car for me at the nearest rental location.

Which just happens to be right here in good old Jackson International Airport. All with just one click."

The bus stopped in the National lot, and Sweeney and Todd jumped off. Sweeney ran to a black Chevy Suburban, tossed his bag in the back, and Todd did the same.

"We don't need to check in for the keys and paperwork?" asked Todd.

"Where have you been Ron? Get with it. Like the ad says. 'Just choose any car on the lot.'"

Sweeney got in, started the engine and off they went. At the gate, Sweeney held up his phone, and the blue tooth reader checked them right through without even stopping.

"Sweet," said Todd.

They met Detective Denning on West Street, where the hit and run occurred. He gave Todd access to Reverend Ali's, Facebook, Twitter, and webpage. He brought them up to date on the who, why and where.

Ron Todd was the first reporter on the scene for all three of the murders; Richard Rumson, Mazola, Vitelli and now Shabazz. Admittedly, he had a little help, but he was putting two and two together back with Rumson. After the *NY Post* had released his and Sweeney's Vitelli story, everyone knew they were after an assassin and that some conspiracy existed at the highest level of government. Someone was attempting to withhold, suppress and cover up a bigger plot. After his meeting with the President, he tried to backpedal a bit during the talk show circuit. And now this. Before they went to press with the Shabazz story he had one phone call to make first. Todd was not a Washington insider but people everywhere knew and read the *NY Post* and knew him as a top investigative reporter. Todd did not want to talk with the President directly, but he had a backdoor. He didn't have her direct number, so he would try calling the White House switchboard and see what happens.

"White House," said the male operator.

"Yes. Please connect me with the Press Secretary Kelly Sullivan," said Todd.

"Are you a member of the press?"

"Yes. Ron Todd, *NY Post*."

"Mr. Todd, you must know there is a procedure for this sort of thing. May I ask what this is about?"

"I'm sorry you can't. This is for her ears only, and it's urgent I speak to her before my story deadline tonight at 10 P.M. Please get hold of her and have her call me back."

Todd left his number although he thought that was probably not necessary. In less than five minutes his phone rang.

"Mr. Todd. Kelly Sullivan here. What's so urgent?"

"I am in Jackson Mississippi. It was Reverend Ali, not Reverend Johnson," said Todd.

"That's not exactly news," said Sullivan.

"Yea. Well so much for us working together," said Todd.

"Look, Mr. Todd; We were all blindsided. Besides, I thought you were in Podunk, Maine." *A little misdirection never hurt,* she thought.

"Never got there. Received a tip from your retired assassin's surrogate, leading us to Jackson."

"What do you mean you received a tip from our retired assassin's surrogate? What's that supposed to mean?

"I think you know Mrs. Burk."

She let it go.

"So what do you have?" asked Sullivan.

"It's not pretty, and it could blow up big and bad. It seems a male copycat revenge killer did Shabazz and is on the loose. It now comes down to whether the blacks respected the Reverend Shabazz or resented him. Hell, some haters will incite to riot regardless. It's all about containment, but the story is going out."

"Here's something on good faith to show we're still working together. You'll need to get over to Atlanta International and fast," said Sullivan.

"Let me put you on speaker. Sweeney needs to hear this. OK. What's in Atlanta, or is this another miss-direction?" asked Todd.

"What's in Atlanta is your copycat killer. Only she's not a copycat. It's your Dragon Lady from San Francisco."

"Holly shit! Excuse my French. You found her? What's she doing in Atlanta?"

She blew her mind out in a stall, thought Sullivan.

"Just get over there and see FBI SAC Henry Hill. He'll fill you in."

"But the Jackson PD is investigating this as a hate crime, and they're looking for a man. They got it wrong?" asked Sweeney.

"No. They got it right, but the Dragon Lady set it up. Got to run," said Sullivan and hung up.

"I'm going to stay here and finish up with Detective Denning and check my sources. You leave now for Atlanta and find this FBI guy. Reserve me the next flight to Atlanta, and I will write the Reverend Ali story on the plane and call it in. I should be about two-three hours behind you," said Todd.

CHAPTER 25

WASHINGTON, DC

President Burk, walking a large German Shepherd inside the White House and outside on the White House lawn, received a lot of attention. The Secret Service didn't know quite what to make of it, but they received direct orders from Secret Service Director Bounty to deal with it. Essentially Natasha became the President's chief bodyguard, and she took her job seriously. Anyone walking into the Oval Office had to accept it and pretend it was normal having a German Shepherd sitting under the President's Resolute Desk. Where did the dog come from? Was President Burk sending a message? The news media couldn't get enough of it. Images became a contradiction. To his supporters, the President, with a German Shepherd, was like watching the old TV show, *The Adventures of Rin Tin Tin,* but to his detractors, it conjured up Hitler with Blondie at Wolfsschanze.

What amounted to little more than a sleep-over and a play date, was for the President and Natasha a thoroughly enjoyable reunion. President Burk was to the point of actually considering getting a dog of his own. He would have to consult his wife, Press Secretary Kelly Sullivan, first, but the harder sell would be the American public. The breed of dog you own speaks volumes. Because of his love of and experience with Natasha, he would only consider a German Shepherd. A male puppy perhaps. From the same kennel where he and Colburn got Natasha. Perhaps from the same breeder and even from Natasha's Dad and Mom. A puppy would increase their pack to four.

Before President Burk was President, back when he was just down on his luck Tommy Burk, he helped his friend Colburn find Natasha as a puppy and helped them find and build the cabin. This was before Tommy Burk helped save NYC from the Dirty Bombs and his run-in with President Hilton.

He would call his new puppy Hercules, Thor or Caesar. He could also call him Boris after Boris and Natasha, the antagonist, from the 50's TV cartoon, *Rocky and Bullwinkle*. Whatever his name, he would be known in Washington as 'The Big Dog.'

The White House Press Corp and tourists looking over the gate had a good time watching President Burk and Natasha romping around the White House front lawn, but unfortunately, it was time for business. They headed inside to the Oval Office; Natasha went under the desk and President Burk behind it. Colburn was in route from Atlanta to the White House on board United States Marine Corps aircraft, Marine Two and was due in thirty minutes.

Sarge safe, Natasha safe, Da hunting, Pack divided, thought Natasha.

President Burk heard Natasha whining under the desk and slid back in his chair and looked down. She was lying down with her head on her crossed front paws. Her eyes were sad. He reached down and grabbed her scruff and gave it a tug.

"Your Da will be here soon girl."

Natasha's head lifted and her ears perked when she heard her Sarge speak Da's name.

Da is near, thought Natasha.

The President had been meeting for the last twenty minutes with Vice President Hilton, the former President's daughter, and Secretary of the Treasury, Mike Bloomfield, former Mayor of New York and an early Tommy Burk supporter. They were discussing a new proposal to forgive college loans. The cost to the nation would be huge, but it had become a cause célèbre for the Vice President, an issue arousing widespread controversy. Student-loan debt is a big problem. The latest Federal Reserve data shows there is nearly $1.3 trillion in outstanding student-loan debt in the US. In late 2009 and early 2010, student-loan debt passed auto loans, credit cards, and home-equity lines of credit as the biggest debt burden Americans face. According to Debt.org, "The latest studies say that 70% of college graduates leave school with student loan debt that in 2014 averaged $43,000."

Realizing graduates were struggling to repay their heavy debt burdens, Vice President Hilton was proposing new plans that would allow student debt to be forgiven over time. These loan-forgiveness repayment plans were helpful, but not simple. Two of the more popular ones were Public Service Loan Forgiveness and Income-Based Repayment. Public Service Loan Forgiveness allows those working in the public sector to apply to have their loans forgiven after ten years of service, which equates to 120 payments. For those who don't work in the public sector, the Vice President created a few income-driven plans. These allow borrowers to pay 10% to 20% of their discretionary income toward their student loans, which will then be forgiven in 20 to 25 years.

But there is one big problem. The loan balance at the time of forgiveness for income-driven plans is treated as income and taxed as such. Depending on the interest rate of the loan (some Federal loans have interest of more than 7%), the income-based payments might not cover the interest that is accumulating on the debt, which would cause the payoff amount of the loan to balloon over those 25 years. Also, if someone is making income-based payments, chances are they are doing so because they cannot afford to make their regular loan payments. If that's the case, what makes the government think borrowers will be able to foot the massive tax bill at the end of 20 or 25 years?

Secretary of the Treasury Bloomfield made a hypothetical situation in which a new borrower takes out $100,000 in direct subsidized loans at a conservative 4% annual interest rate, has an annual income of $45,000, is single, lives in New York, and has no children. Under a standard repayment plan, our hypothetical borrower would have monthly payments of $1,012 for ten years. Under the Income-Based Repayment program for new borrowers, our recent graduate would have much lower monthly payments over 20 years, ranging from about $228 to $719, as his or her income increases over time.

The students and their families were obviously for these proposals. The banks and loan institutions against it because the proposals, as proposed, would put the government between them and the borrower. More importantly, forgiving student loans could put the banks and lending institutions out of business. Losing a money making product from their portfolio was not good business.

President Burk, always trying to be 'Fair and Balanced', also wants students and their families who paid their tuition from their savings or IRA's to receive a tuition refund, and here lies the rub. Student loan forgiveness and student loan refund would cost the nation close to $3 trillion, and most of it would be paid by couples who have no children or families who have children who have not attended college.

Noreen Ward knocked and stuck her head in, "Mr. Colburn is five minutes out. Mr. President."

"Claire, Mike. We're making progress. Let's meet again next week and move a step closer to helping these kids and their families."

When the Vice President and the Secretary of the Treasury left the Oval Office, President Burk got up from his desk, and Natasha followed. "Da's here girl. Ready to get Da?" On hearing her Da's name twice, Natasha started running in circles and whining. She ran to the large south-facing windows behind the President's desk and stood on her hind legs and pushed the curtains aside with her nose. She stared into the distance with her tail wagging like a ship's rudder on steroids. She heard it way off in the distance but coming closer a familiar sound.

The noisy flying thing that she and her Da were in together before her Da had to go away. Her Da is coming back to her now.

"Come on girl. Let's go out and get your Da," said the President.

Through the Oval Office doors and out to the West Wing Colonnade, then onto the South Lawn they went. Natasha running ahead, not able to contain herself, but always stopping and looking back to make sure her Sarge was in sight and safe. They could hear and now see the Marine helicopter coming down the corridor with the Jefferson Memorial behind and the Washington Monument to starboard. The helicopter continued straight ahead getting lower and louder, over the south lawn fountain to the south lawn, turning starboard just before touching down. The President stopped far enough away to be safe in case of an abort. Natasha stopped with him when he commanded, "Sit."

The forward and rear hatches opened, and the steps folded down. Secret service men exited first followed by a Marine corporal in dress blues. Then Colburn came down the steps and received and returned a salute from the Marine. Not necessary or required but out of respect. It seems Colburn's reputation had preceded him.

"Go girl. Get your Da," said the President.

Natasha was up and at full speed immediately. She charged recklessly towards her Da covering the fifty yards in under four seconds. President Burk took slightly longer. She jumped up and put her huge muscular front legs around Colburn's neck and smothered him with kisses all the time howling. Colburn wrapped his arms around Natasha's neck, and they just hugged each other. Colburn, at just under six feet tall, was looking up into Natasha's eyes. She was huge.

"Oh, I missed you too, girl. Did Sarge take good care of you?"

By now, President Burk, respectfully keeping an appropriate distance, approached. Colburn noticed the President at the same time Natasha sensed her Sarge. They broke their love fest to acknowledge Sarge. Natasha sat while Colburn and President Burk shook hands. Dog hugs are okay, but not man hugs.

"Good to see you again Icy. We missed you," said the President.

"I missed Natasha," said Colburn.

"Why don't you two take a little walk and come on in when you're caught up. I have Riley, Bounty, and Kelly in my office. We'll meet in about ten minutes. OK? We had a full run down on Atlanta from SAC Hill but want to hear your side."

"My side?"

"I didn't mean it like that. We just want it straight from the source. I also invited CIA Director John Bader and NSA Director Admiral Roger Michaels."

"Is there something you're not telling me?"

"No. But I'll fill you in after you brief us," said the President.

Ten minutes later Colburn and Natasha were let into the Oval Office by Noreen Ward. Introductions were made. Coffee, tea and Diet Cokes were served, and everyone took seats on the two couches and chairs. Natasha sat on the floor between Sarge and her Da.

Sarge safe, Da safe, Natasha safe, Pack safe.

"Israel. We would all like to hear, first hand, what happened in Atlanta," said the President. He would never address Colburn by his war name Icy, in mixed company.

"I was met after landing by SAC Henry Hill and Agent Rice. They informed me they had eyes on Kim Ly, and she was in the Club ATL in the international terminal. We got in their car and headed there. I asked if she was alone and had she been thoroughly checked through security. I was informed she was alone and thoroughly checked through security including a body scan. She had a handbag and carry-on bag. Both were x-rayed and hand searched. She checked nothing. Hill said they had eyes and surveillance cameras on her. SAC Hill gave me his phone with live A/V. I could see Kim Ly and talk to Hill at the same time. I saw her, real time, black slacks and jacket, sunglasses and ponytail. She was not trying to hide. Her handbag and carry-on were right there with her. I was told she was on her second cup of coffee, made two cell phone calls to Vietnam. She had set down about twenty minutes ago. Her flight was boarding in thirty minutes, and she hasn't gotten up to go to the toilet. I decided to go in the front club entrance and asked for a weapon. Hill gave me a suppressed 9mm Glock. I released the magazine and pulled the slide back to check the chamber. It was empty. I reinserted the magazine and released the slide chambering a round. I eased the hammer down and switched on the safety. With the suppressor attached, it was almost 12 inches. Hill confirmed Seventeen rounds. We pulled up in front of the terminal and were met by airport security and guided through security, up to the mezzanine and to the club. The Club ATL staff were all filled in, and I was given clearance to enter. I was asked if I had a plan. I said, "I intend to get the information I wanted from her and then kill her.""

CIA Director Bader interrupted by asking, "Why kill her?"

"Because that's what I do. I kill them now, so they can't kill me later. May I continue?"

Bader nodded.

"I checked the phone to make sure Kim Ly was still in place and went in and told Hill to let his HUMINT know that I was coming in and what I was going to do. I hoped she would be heading to the toilet before she boarded. I asked to have maintenance close down the toilet after I entered. I walked past the lounge front desk without being challenged; grabbed a newspaper, ducked into the carry-on bag storage room and slipped the suppressed Glock into the newspaper fold. I held the paper against my side with the phone in my left hand, as though I were reading my email. I continued into the lounge steering towards to the women's toilet. I found a seat outside and waited."

"What if she didn't go to the toilet?" asked Sullivan.

"If she didn't go to the toilet soon I would need to sit next to her and have our discussion in public. There were empty seats near her.

A woman headed for the toilet, and I let her go in. Couldn't stop her. Through the phone video, I could see Kim Ly starting to stir. She placed her coffee cup on the table and grabbed her handbag. She left her Carry-on, which was a good sign. I followed her as the surveillance cameras picked her up from one room to the other until I had eyes on her. I buried my face in a *Sports Illustrated*. Kim Ly went to the ladies room and went in. I got up and followed. I closed and pocketed the phone. No surveillance in the toilets but the agents outside could still hear me. I waited a heartbeat at the door, giving her a second to select a stall, then I opened the door and went in. There was no one visible when I entered, so Kim Ly and at least one other woman were in stalls. I selected an empty stall next to the one I sensed was occupied by Kim Ly, opened it and entered. I was immediately busted. She knew it was me and addressed me. She asked me if I would allow her to leave. I told her if she told me what I wanted to know, I would allow her to leave quickly, then I stood on the toilet and prepared to fire over the partition. I heard the other lady, in the stall to my right flush the toilet and quickly leave. Wonder what she was thinking? I heard Kim Ly say the name Vova and then a loud spit of what I recognized as a suppressed gunshot.

I thought I was in control, but this really shook me. I got up, exited my stall and opened hers. It wasn't locked. I saw Kim Ly sitting on the toilet with her head back, hands to her sides still holding a cylinder which looked like a single shot weapon. Blood was splattered on the wall behind her head, and blood dripped from a bullet hole beneath her chin. She was dead, but her body was still twitching; then it stopped. I exited the bathroom, and an out of order sign was placed in front of the door, by airport security. Two women I assumed were FBI agents dressed as cleaning attendants with a cart entered. The area outside the woman's toilet was quiet as an announcement came over the speaker for the boarding of Korean Air flight 0036 to Seoul, Korea and Hanoi, Vietnam. I walked toward SAC Hill and Agent Rice and handed him his phone. I told them it was over. They asked if I had killed her, and I said no."

"Why do you think she took her life and how did she get the gun into the airport?" asked Riley.

"Your agents, I'm sure, told you how she got the gun into the airport, so I don't need to go there. As to why she killed herself? She knew I would connect the dots and find out she was double dealing. She knew I was there to kill her. We have rules. She killed herself, I suspect because she dishonored herself by breaking the rules and deserved to die. It's an Asian thing. She took the job from Vova because that's what she does and because Vova played on her ego and probably told her that I was on the way out one way or another. That's about it. What about Todd and Sweeney. Did they go with the Shabazz story?"

"Came out this morning. Sensational as ever. Todd and Sweeney are putting the Shabazz murder with the other three, so we hope it will be more pliable. Tomorrow Todd and Sweeney will break the Atlanta story naming Kim Ly as the assassin of all four. We hope that and the fact that Shabazz was considered, by the black community, as an instigator, not the leader, will keep them calm. We're trying to homogenize the four murders as revenge murders of bad people who did bad things to the country. Exactly what Vova intended only without the reaction he intended," said the President.

Press Secretary Sullivan handed Colburn a copy of the *Post*.

New York Post front page headline read:

Reverend Ali killed by Crackers in Mississippi.
by Ron Todd and Tom Sweeney
Walking back to his hotel on East Amite Street, after an early dinner last night with associates, Reverend Ali Shabazz was struck and killed by a speeding truck. The Reverend was immediately rushed to the University of Mississippi Medical Center where he was pronounced dead. Witnesses at the scene, said the truck, later identified as a Ritz Cracker truck, did not stop. The truck was found abandoned one mile away, and a spokesperson for Ritz Crackers verified the truck was one of theirs. They also identified the driver, a recent temporary hire, as a Mr. James Crow, a white man. The police have a BOLO out for Mr. Crow. Make no mistake about it; this was no accident. It was no hit and run. It was clearly a planned hit. The Reverend Ali was murdered because of who he was and what he stood for. We have reason to believe this murder is connected to the Rumson, Mazola and Vitelli revenge murders and are on the trail of the assassin. Further information…

The *Post* continued with some background.

Albert Joseph "Ali" Shabazz, was an American black Muslim minister, civil rights activist, radio talk show host and a trusted White House adviser who, according to 60 Minutes, had become President Hiltons "go-to black Muslim leader……."
"His critics describe him as "a political radical who is to blame, in part, for the deterioration of race relations."

According to Kenny William Jr.

"Ali Shabazz has done more damage to the black cause than [segregationist Alabama Gov.] George Wallace. He has suffocated the decent black leaders in America," he says. "His transparent venal blackmail and extortion schemes taint all black leadership." Ali Shabazz was known to ...

CHAPTER 26

WASHINGTON, DC

They all waited patiently while Colburn finished reading the *NY Post* article by Todd and Sweeney. Colburn had been too distracted with being diverted to Atlanta and its aftermath to know what occurred in Jackson. He knew it was not as sensational as illustrated by Todd's piece. It seemed as if Todd was trying to incite the masses instead of defusing them, but that's what sells papers. The *NY Post* has been doing a banner business in the last couple of months.

"OK. But what happens if the Shabazz murder doesn't have the desired effect on the blacks?" said Colburn.

"Not for lack of trying. I think Todd and Sweeney have done exactly what was expected of them. They sensationalized each murder and tied them all together as 'Revenge Murders'. It's too early yet, but if we make it past tomorrow night, we're good," said Sullivan.

"I agree with Kelly. If the black community accepts Reverend Ali's murder for what it is, we think Dmitri Vova will give up his revenge murder tactic and try something new. We know he is planning something, and with whom, and he knows we're listening. He is very careful, but if we're even close to right, in what we suspect, we're in for a big surprise. I'll let NSA Director Admiral Michaels take it from here," said the President.

The Director of the National Security Agency, Admiral Roger Michaels was also Chief of Central Security Service. The National Security Agency/

Central Security Service (NSA/CSS) leads the U.S. Government in cryptology that encompasses both Signals Intelligence (SIGINT) and Information Assurance (IA) products and services, and enables Computer Network Operations (CNO) in order to gain a decision advantage for the Nation and our allies under all circumstances.

The Information Assurance mission confronts the formidable challenge of preventing foreign adversaries from gaining access to sensitive or classified national security information. The Signals Intelligence mission collects, processes, and disseminates intelligence information from foreign signals for intelligence and counterintelligence purposes and to support military operations. This Agency also enables Network Warfare operations to defeat terrorists and their organizations at home and abroad, consistent with U.S. laws and the protection of privacy and civil liberties.

Collect (including through clandestine means), process, analyze, produce, and disseminate signals intelligence information and data for foreign intelligence and counterintelligence purposes to support national and departmental missions.

Act as the National Manager for National Security Systems as established in law and policy, and in this capacity be responsible to the Secretary of Defense and the Director, National Intelligence.

Prescribe security regulations covering operating practices, including the transmission, handling, and distribution of signals intelligence and communications security material within and among the elements under control of the Director of the National Security Agency, and exercise the necessary supervisory control to ensure compliance with the regulations.

Align President Reagan's Executive Order12333 with the Intelligence Reform and Terrorism Prevention Act of 2004.

Implement additional recommendations of the 9/11 and WMD Commissions.

Further, integrate the Intelligence Community and clarify and strengthen the role of the DNI as the head of the Community.

Maintain or strengthen privacy and civil liberties protections.

"We have put a good portion of our resources into tracking Dmitri Vova and the FBS. He is a fox, but we monitor the hen house. He has been in communication with ISIL through what he thinks is secure communication. He's using pretty basic stuff like; 'End to End' encryption, 'Ephemeral Comm.' that disappears forever, immediately after being read, 'Wanding' that prohibits copy or screenshots and toss away devices, but we are always one step ahead. We were getting a lot of information but have not acted on any of it. We didn't want them to know we broke thru their encryption."

Turning back to look at the President, Colburn said, "This is all very interesting, but you said Vova is planning something new. What is it?"

The President looked at Admiral and nodded.

Admiral Michaels continued "We picked up a lot of chatter between Vova and Abu Bakr al-Baghdadi, the head of the so-called Islamic State of Iraq and the Levant (ISIL) – an al-Qaeda offshoot, but last week it all went quiet. The Russian government took measures after the extent of US electronic surveillance was revealed by the whistleblower Edward Snowden. The Federal Guard Service, a powerful body, tasked with protecting Russia's highest-ranking officials, is doing just that. Now it's very quiet.

It seems like Russia and ISIL are frantically seeking old-fashioned typewriters to embark on a low-tech OPSEC approach to communications to avoid NSA spying. The Russian government is going retro to avoid high-tech snooping by the United States government. They approved $55,000 for the purchase of new typewriters for the Federal Guard Service, along with new ink ribbons for older-model machines. They prefer the German-made Triumph-Adler, 180 model typewriter. ISIL is getting rid of all cell phones and reverting to hand written notes. They have even been running telegraph lines between towns and cities with runners to deliver and receive the telegraphed messages. We can't tap into a telegraph unless we actually splice into it, and they are guarding the lines burka and veil. They have gone low-tech, and now we need to go low-tech."

"So you've got all these high-tech toys, and Vova and Abu al-Baghdadi are communicating with tin cans and string," said Colburn.

"We don't know where Baghdadi and the other leaders like Mansour of the Taliban or Zawahiri of al-Qaeda are at the moment, but we have surveillance on all their family members and when, as they say, the rooster comes home to roost," said Admiral Michaels.

"That about sizes it up nicely," said the President.

"OK, but why are you telling me all this stuff. It must be top secret. Right? I mean I'm not part of your intelligence community. It's not as though I'm your Director of Assassinations," said Colburn.

President Burk and FBI Director Riley looked at each other. A look that was caught by Kelly Sullivan and Colburn. Colburn turned and glanced for an instant at Kelly, who was looking at him.

The President dismissed everyone but Colburn, Riley, and Kelly.

After they had left, FBI Director Riley said, "Icy. We just wanted to thank you for what you did. To let you know, we appreciate you cleaning up the mess in Atlanta."

"I'm the one that created the mess. I don't need any thanks for cleaning it up, but I appreciate the nod."

"The *New York Post* front page story about Kim Ly, by Todd and Sweeney will hit the streets tomorrow morning. Todd called me right before the meeting giving me a heads up. He said there will be follow-ups, but this will put it all together and put it to bed but not asleep," said Kelly.

"I will be sure to buy the paper tomorrow morning, but now if there is nothing more, we would really like to get back to Cambridge."

"Icy we don't get to spend much time together. I really enjoyed seeing you and Natasha. It was great to have her here if only for a short visit. We want you to stay the day. I need your and Natasha's help with a personal matter and then tonight we have a special surprise. We want you to be our guest. You and Natasha can stay in the Lincoln Bedroom, and I promise I will have you both back in Cambridge tomorrow morning with a complimentary *NY Post* for the flight," said the President.

CHAPTER 27

OLD STATE MONASTERIES, NY

Kelly loved the idea of getting a puppy and Colburn and Natasha agreed to help. Natasha was born five years previously in Salem, NY at the Old State Monasteries. Old State Monasteries is a monastic community of men and women rooted in the tradition of the European Church. Through prayer, worship, and the work of their hands, they seek to respond to the mystery of God and the Gospel's power to transform human living. Welcoming all, they seek to bridge the old with the new and to witness to the sacredness of all creation.

They also breed dogs. German Shepherd dogs.

Colburn, at the prompting of the President, called ahead and spoke with Brother Strabo, the same monk who helped them adopt Natasha. Brother Strabo remembered both Colburn and Burk, and would certainly welcome them. He asked about Natasha and Colburn said she was his best friend and companion. Yes, there was a great lawn that could accommodate Marine One. Brother Strabo said Natasha's mother, Silver Sasha, had a litter ten weeks ago but had only one puppy remained. A boy. The father, Grand Duke, was also Natasha's father.

"Hold the puppy till we get there. See you in a couple of hours," said Colburn.

It's a two-hour flight from the White House South Lawn, Aboard Marine One, to the Old State Monasteries in Salem, NY. Besides the usual crew of

Marine pilot, co-pilot, crew and crew chief, Secret Service was also aboard. President Burk, First Lady Kelly Sullivan, Israel Colburn and Natasha were the only four passengers.

"Why do you think there is only one puppy left? And a boy?" asked the President.

"Brother Strabo just said he was big. But with the same mother and father, he would be Natasha's little brother from another litter."

"Funny. But big? Wonder what he means by big?" asked Kelly.

Marine One landed in the monastery's open lawn, and the President and his three guests waited for the step ramp to be lowered to exit. The President requested a low-key visit. No Marine guard to salute when he disembarked and that the Secret Service should be invisible. All four now off the helicopter, walked towards the monastery and reception committee of one, Brother Strabo. Natasha ran past Brother Strabo towards the fenced in dog run and was immediately greeted by seven German Shepherds of different ages and sizes. Tails wagging, bodies circling and a great deal of excitement and barking.

My Pack? My Home?

President Burk, Kelly, and Colburn walked up to Brother Strabo said hello and introduced Kelly. After some pleasantries, Brother Strabo said, "Let's find Silver Sasha and re-introduce Natasha to her mom."

They turned towards the dog run, and all but one dog remained with Natasha. Natasha and the dog on the other side of the fence were completely still. Both sitting close to the fence staring at each other. No other movement.

"I think they just found each other," said Brother Strabo.

Natasha felt she was looking into her soul. She was looking at herself, as when she sometimes saw her image in pictures or the mirror. She was looking at a beautiful black and silver mirror image of herself, but it felt so different. This was not a mirror, and this was not a strange dog. This dog was familiar. This place was familiar.

I know you. I remember you. Your pack. You are my mother.

"Call Natasha, and we'll go inside for a face to face reunion," suggested Brother Strabo.

"Come girl. We're going in to meet your mom and brother," said Colburn as they all walked through the door into the kennel. Colburn could see and sense that Natasha was tense and confused. She had just found her mother, and although her memory of her first ten weeks alive would be fuzzy at best, he knew she was thinking back. *Maybe he shouldn't have brought her back,* he thought.

Brother Strabo seemed to sense Colburn and Natasha's apprehension, and said, "Mr. Colburn it will be OK. We have many family reunions, and they all seem to work out. Wait out here, and I will get Silver Sasha and bring her in to meet Natasha without the fence, and then we can all go in together and meet the puppy." He did, and Natasha's mom, Silver Sasha, greeted Natasha like the long lost daughter she was. Although five years and two more litters had gone by they still knew each other, a bond that can never be broken. After licks and hugs between men and dogs, they all went in to see Silver Sasha and Grand Duke's last remaining puppy.

Silver Sasha went to him first, then Natasha. The puppy was silver and black, but that's where the similarities ended. His ears were already standing straight up; his fur was long, and his head was almost as big as his mom's. He was very big for a ten week old and looked more like a Timber Shepherd, one-quarter Timber Wolf, and three-quarters German Shepherd. He wasn't. He was just a huge purebred German Shepherd.

"Big. Is this why he is the last to go?" asked Colburn.

"Yes. Several people were interested but this big at ten weeks. Well...," said Brother Strabo.

President Burk, who had a way with dogs and was very good and comfortable with Natasha, walked over and bent down to pet Silver Sasha and said, "Remember me, girl?"

She was very friendly and accessible and remembered Burk. He sat on the floor and petted both Silver Sasha and the puppy, finally picking the puppy up and putting it on his lap. Natasha came over and soon all three were nuzzling, licking and vying for attention from the President. Colburn walked over and joined the pack, and soon low guttural growls started that turned into howls. All five then started howling and chorusing as a pack.

Kelly looked at Brother Strabo and expected to see a shake of the head or rolled eyes, but all she saw was a smile and appreciation. He looked like he had seen this before. And he had. Five years ago. Had someone had a camera and put this on YouTube they would have been declared certifiable, but that wasn't going to happen.

Boys and their dogs thought Kelly.

Later they had a chance to meet and greet Grand Duke who when he saw the lovely Silver Sasha become quickly distracted.

They said goodbye to Silver Sasha, and she said goodbye to both her puppies and the humans. She had seen all her pups go and accepted it as a way of life. As a good thing for the puppies, a dog's life.

Kelly took care of the paperwork while the boys and Natasha bonded outside. They said goodbye to Brother Strabo, who was now joined by a host of other brothers and sisters and staff to bid farewell to the President and a very lucky puppy.

On the helicopter, it was very quiet as they began their two-hour flight back to Washington.

"Happy?" asked Colburn.

"Very. And thanks for coming. I don't think I could have done it without you and Natasha," said the President.

Natasha sat next to the large crate that contained the puppy. The puppy would need some training before he would have free reign like Natasha.

Kelly said, "OK boys. What's his name?"

This was probably the most important thing between a dog and his new owner. So personal that it is considered inappropriate for others to make suggestions. Although that did not stop some people. Besides they all believed the President had already decided on a name the moment he saw the puppy, if not before. He was a big puppy and would grow into a big German Shepherd. He was the President's dog. He would be the people's dog, and he would soon become America's dog. The name would be everything.

"So have you decided?" asked Colburn.

"Why did you call Natasha, Natasha? I mean, weren't there any good German names? You had to choose a Russian name for your German Shepherd?" asked the President.

"What? Should I have called her Helga? Heidi? Anyway, I rarely call her Natasha. It's easier and clearer to have a one syllable name. I mostly call her Tosh. Or girl. The name needs to fit the dog and vice versa. Think about it."

Natasha became very interested in the conversation. Mainly because they were taking about her, not to her.

"I have thought about it. He's not a Shiloh. That's a great name for a big Yellow Lab. He's not a Cody, Ace, Thor or Caesar. He's going to be a big German Shepherd, and he is going to have a proud German-American name."

The President got up and went to the crate, took the puppy out, and returned to his seat. Natasha followed.

Wait for it. Wait for it.

"I've decided to name him Maximillian," said President Burk.

Natasha tilted her head. Kelly said, "A bit royal. What." Colburn held up four fingers and said, "Four Syllables?"

The President held up his hand to calm the assembled and said, "Natasha, say hello to my little friend, Max."

Natasha barked her approval. Colburn smiled. And Kelly said, "Max. I like it. But if you guys are going to start howling, can you wait till after we land?"

CHAPTER 28

WASHINGTON, DC

The tires on Marine One touched down on the south lawn just after 6 p.m. It was getting dark. President Burk had to give into formalities as a crowd of tourists watched and taped the landing with their cameras and phones. The big treat was seeing the President of the United States, holding a puppy, walk down the front hatch steps followed by First Lady Kelly Sullivan Burk. When he got to the bottom, he let the puppy down and with the leash in his left hand turned and saluted the Marine guard. He, Kelly and Max then headed, in a not too direct path, towards the White House. Colburn and Natasha waited a bit before exiting the back ramp and heading obliquely towards the West Wing. The President had already given Head Groundskeeper Dale Hailey; a heads up that he may be bringing a new puppy home. Dale, who has been taking care of and training presidential dogs since 1972, was waiting to assist.

Inside the White House, the First Lady, Max, and Natasha were all happy to be off the helicopter and on solid marble. To the President and Colburn, it was just another ride in the sky. The President handed the leash to Dale, introduced them, then knelt down and said goodbye to Max.

"Icy, why don't you and Natasha head up to the Lincoln Bedroom and rest up before the dinner party. A Tux and change of clothes have been provided. Come on down around 8:15 p.m. Dale will come up at 8:00 to bring Natasha down for a play date with Max," said the President.

"Black tie? What's the dinner party about tonight? Who is it for?" asked Colburn.

"It's about a great ending to a great day. The Dragon Lady is gone. Had a great time with Natasha. Saw you again. Got Max. And we're going to have a great dinner."

"Play dates, puppies, parties. It must be good to be king," said Colburn.

"It is. At least it has been. I have many good people doing all the heavy lifting. All I do is point to where I want it all to go."

"Which reminds me. You should be distancing yourself from me, not inviting me to parties."

The President ignored Colburn's warning but knew he was right.

"You are especially going to like the guest. It's Faith Knoll, and Vanity Fair is putting on a small pre-awards award dinner for us. Faith is singing a couple of numbers and is sitting at our table," said the President.

"I'm not sure I know her."

"She is gorgeous, single, smart, and talented. She has dozens of top albums and several Grammys. She's on TV and the radio constantly, and now she is making movies. How could you not know her?"

"I don't watch TV and don't own a radio."

"Did I mention she's gorgeous?"

"How does Kelly feel about that?"

"It was her idea."

"You two aren't trying to set me up again, aren't you?"

"See you at 8:30."

The restoration of the White House by the architectural firm McKim, Mead, and White in 1902 created a more proper setting for official entertainment to occur. When the president's office moved to the newly constructed West Wing, the Neoclassical remodeling of the executive residence's stateroom gave Theodore Roosevelt a perfect venue reflecting the United States' growing power and influence around the world. While the White House underwent a complete interior reconstruction from 1948 to 1952, Harry S. Truman and Bess Truman lived at Blair House, and state dinners were held in local hotels in the nation's capital. Long banquet tables were always used in the State Dining Room before the administration of John F. Kennedy. However, these were permanently disbanded by Jacqueline Kennedy and replaced with round tables which could seat a far greater number of guests, approximately 120 to 140, in such a tight and confined space. To this day, presidents and first ladies continue to add their personal touches and flair to how they wish to entertain foreign guests of state at the White House. They have full access to the Vermeil collection of gilded candelabras and flatware, the President's house crystal pattern, as well as the priceless collection of White House china which dates from the James Monroe administration to the George W. Bush administration, for use at a state dinner.

Tonight there would be just 60 guests, and since it was not a state dinner, there would be no honor guard, no reception and no "Hail to the Chief" when the President entered the room. Instead, it resembled a large formal dinner party one would find in New York, Boston or Washington. The only difference was security. It was everywhere but nowhere. Most guests were part of the Washington establishment and had been to the White House before and knew what to expect. Including a fabulous dinner:

Dinner Menu

White House Garden Chopped Salad
Fine Herbs
White House Honey Gastrique
Tuna Tartare with Rye Crisps
Pickled Young Carrots and Mustard Oil
Spring Pea Salad
Shaved Ham and Ginger Snaps
Petite Filet with Maryland Crab Ravioli
Wild Ramp Pur'ee
Apple Strudel
Golden Raisins and Topfen
An American wine will be paired with each course.

The biggest inconveniences were the metal detectors and the collection of all cell phones, not so much for them going off but because of built in cameras. The exception were guests who were White House insiders, but all the guest mingled while wine and champagne were served and drinks were requested. A chamber orchestra played background music from the 40's, predominantly the Presidents and First Lady's favorite, Sinatra.

When Colburn was escorted into the State Dining Room, a little after 8:30, it was already crowded. Music was playing, and groups of guests were gathered here and there. It seemed like everyone knew each other because there were no singles or couples standing alone. Colburn spotted the President and First Lady talking with a small group and walked in the opposite direction. The First Lady noticed Colburn, called his name and walked over to him. She put her arm through his and guided him over to the President. Everyone became immediately interested in this handsome man with wavy jet black hair and amazing turquoise eyes, who had caught the First Lady's attention. They followed the two of them with their eyes and ears hoping to catch any clue as to who he was.

"Ah. Mr. Colburn so glad you could make it," said the President.

"Mr. President. Madam First Lady," said Colburn giving a nod of his head and a proper bow."

"May I introduce Mr. Israel Colburn? A dear and old friend of mine. Going clockwise the President said: My Chief of Staff Bill Nicholas and his wife Agnes, Michael Bloomfield and the lovely Diana Taylor, and the guest of honor, Faith Knoll."

Faith Knoll was dressed in a stunning all-white sophisticated 3/4 sleeved gown by Chado Ralph Rucci. She kept her accessories modest, wearing a simple pearl and diamond cocktail ring and stud earrings. As the President and First Lady had hoped, Colburn and Knoll's handshake seemed to linger a bit longer.

When Colburn, always the gentleman, regained his wits he added, "It is indeed an honor to meet all of you and to be invited to such a propitious event."

FBI Director Riley joined the group just as the President nodded, and a steward materialized with a tray of nine flutes filled with Cristal Champagne. When all glasses were in hand the President raised his glass, the orchestra started playing 'I Get A Kick Out Of You,' and proposed a toast. "May the friends of our youth be the companions of our old age."

Faith Knoll is an American country pop singer and actress. Born in Mobile, Alabama, she is one of the most successful country artists of all time, having sold more than 40 million records worldwide. Knoll is single and rumored to be off her on and off relationship with Yankee baseball pitcher Jimmy Hunter.

Knoll's first two albums, 'Take Me As You Will' (1994) and 'If It Matters' (1996), established her as a popular country singer; they placed a combined three number ones on Billboard's country charts and were major successes in North America. She later rose to mainstream, crossover and international fame with the release of her next two albums, Hope (1998) and Change (1999). Knoll has won six Grammy Awards, 16 Academy of Country Music Awards, 7 American Music Awards. She was named one of the "30 Most Powerful Women in America" by *Esquire Journal*. In 2009, *Billboard* named her as the No. 1 Adult Contemporary artist of the 2000 decade and also as the 39th best artist from 2007 to 2012. Faith Knoll is gorgeous, smart, and talented. She had captured the hearts of the young and old alike, from coast to coast, to become America's Sweetheart.

Israel Colburn and Faith Knoll joined the others at the table. The place cards had them sitting next to each other. They seemed interested in continuing a conversation and did so as the others gave them a little space.

"The President seemed to have taken special notice of you when he made the toast. Are you truly old friends as he suggested?" asked Knoll.

"We are. We're both Irish kids from the South and met in the Far East when we were young," said Colburn.

"I'm also Irish and from the South but I thought the President was from Philadelphia, and he mentioned something earlier about you being from Boston."

"He is, and I am. He's from South Philadelphia, South Philly, and I am from South Boston. I am what is commonly referred to as a Southie," said Colburn.

Just then the White House photographer was about to take a photograph of the couple, but Colburn reacted by putting his hand out towards the lens. The photographer hesitated and when he saw the look in Colburn's face he moved on.

"Are you protecting my privacy, Mr. Colburn?"

" I was protecting mine. Miss Knoll," said Colburn.

At that moment, the orchestra began playing 'The Way You Look Tonight.' The President said to the First Lady, "Would you do me the honor?" The First Lady smiled while the President got up and pulled out her chair. As they moved to the dance floor, he turned and said, "Our song."

Others from the table and around the room followed suit leaving Colburn with only one thing to do. He looked at Miss Knoll and said, in a thick Irish-Scottish brogue, "Are you dancing?" Without missing a beat and in her best Irish-Scottish brogue replied, "Are you asking?"

"I'm asking if you're dancing," said Colburn.

"I'm dancing," said Knoll.

Colburn stood and pulled out her chair, offered his hand, and they joined the President and First Lady on the dance floor. The orchestra soon transitioned into 'Strangers In The Night', and when they finished everyone including the orchestra took a break.

Back at the table dinner was about to be served, but first, the President excused himself and moved to the podium to welcome everyone and to introduce Miss Faith Knoll, the guest of honor.

The evening went on from there, and eventually, the President, First Lady, and Faith Knoll all made it back to the table for dinner.

"May I propose a toast, made famous by Wellingtons Calvary Regimental Officers during the Peninsular Wars. It starts,

"To the King, God bless him.

On Monday, We toast Our Men;

On Tuesday, Our Women;

On Wednesday, Our Swords;

On Thursday, Ourselves;

On Friday, Our Religion;

On Saturday, Our Wives and Sweethearts"

At which point both Riley and Colburn added in unison, "And may they never meet."

The President looked incredulously at the two culprits before proceeding. "And Sunday, To Absent Friends"

Everyone raised their glasses and drank to Absent Friends.

Later, after all, the champagne was finished, and the last dance danced, and the last song was sung, Colburn and Knoll walked out onto the South Portico and said goodnight. As they were standing facing each other Faith stumbled a bit backward and was startled by what appeared to be an aspiration. The aspiration turned out to Natasha sitting just behind Colburn's right leg. Colburn looked down and realized he was so enamored with Miss Knoll that he failed to hear Natasha arrive.

"I am sorry. I didn't know she was here" said Colburn. As he bent down to pat Natasha on the head.

"Is this the President's dog?" asked Faith.

"No. This is Natasha, and she is with me. Natasha say hello to Miss Knoll."

Natasha lifted her right front leg and extended her paw. Faith put out her hand and grasped Natasha's paw, and the two shook hands. Natasha looked over to Da to see if he wanted her to do the licky-kiss.

"That's good enough Tosh," he said.

"Natasha you are so beautiful and well mannered."

Natasha moved over closer to Faith, sat down, and was rewarded with a head scratch. She then returned to her Da's side.

"How is it you can bring Natasha to the White House?"

"The President and Natasha are old friends, and he volunteered to watch her for a day while I was off on business."

"Interesting. You'll have to tell me more sometime, but now, sadly, I must be going. I have an early engagement in the morning." She leaned over to Colburn and kissed him on his cheek and handed him a piece of paper.

Natasha, sensing her Da was nervous but not scared, remained alert but calm.

Colburn watched her leave and felt sad but rejuvenated at the same time. *It's amazing what you find when you're not looking,* he thought.

First Sarge, then Max and now this person who makes my Da nervous. The pack may be getting bigger, thought Natasha.

From around a column came the President with Max on a leash.

"Bad timing?" asked the President.

"Not at all Sarge. In fact, I would say it was perfect timing," said Colburn.

The President let Max off the lease. Natasha ran off the terrace and onto the lawn with Max right behind. They roughhoused for a while as Sarge and Icy quietly watched.

After a few minutes, Max tired and flopped down next to Natasha. Natasha looked back at her Da and Sarge standing together under the moonlight.

Da happy, Sarge happy, Max happy, Natasha happy, Pack happy.

"Well Icy, care to join the Captain and me in my office for a night cap?" asked The President.

The FBI Director Riley, aka Captain, was seated in one of three chairs positioned in front of the fireplace. A nice fire was already going as Sarge, Icy, and Natasha, with Max following, entered the Oval Office.

The Captain started to get up, but Sarge waved him down. He continued to stand.

"Captain that's not necessary," said the President.

"I know. I was just showing respect for the lady," said Riley.

Natasha, seeming to understand, went right over to the Captain pushed him back down into his chair and placed her head in his lap. She was rewarded with praises and scratches. Max tried to muzzle in, and both Natasha and the Captain accommodated him.

Sarge sat in the end chair, and Icy set in the center one. The steward entered carrying a silver tray containing two identical Waterford Diamond

Square crystal decanters, each with a silver gorget identifying one as containing Jameson Limited Reserve and the other as Bushmill Old Single Malt. Also on the tray were three Waterford Diamond 7oz straight sided crystal tumblers, three Montecristo Cuban cigars, a wedge cutter and an old engraved Zippo lighter. The steward placed the tray on a campaign table next to the President, was thanked, and dismissed. Natasha laid down, facing the fire, between her Da and Sarge. Max climbed on top of Natasha and settled in.

Sarge removed both decanter stoppers and poured one finger of Jameson's and one finger of Bushmills into each tumbler. As he was pouring he said, "I am pouring one finger of each into each glass, because of an old tale of a widely-accepted Irish-American version that Jameson is Catholic whiskey and Bushmills is Protestant whiskey. But I believe that's merely based on geography: Bushmill is from Northern Ireland, a predominantly Protestant region, and Jameson is from Cork, a Catholic country. As we have never asked nor discussed our spiritual preference, but assuming we are one or the other, I wanted to cover the all the bases."

He handed a tumbler to each and said, "To God."

Icy replied, "To God." while the Captain, either to be contrary or sincere said, "To the Queen."

All three gave a little laugh, swirled the glass, sniffed then sipped. The blending of the two whiskeys was unconventional but delicious and warming, and as intended, began a tradition which the three would continue until the three were two, then one, then none. All three reached for a cigar then Sarge put his cigar cap through a double blade guillotine cutter and cut between the cap and the shoulder and passed the cutter to Icy. He then picked up his old war Zippo and read the word he had inscribe on it over fifty years ago.

"Survivor," said Sarge.

He placed the Zippo in one hand between the thumb and first two fingers and flicked the lid open while instantaneously striking the flint wheel with his index finger. Fire! He lit his cigar and passed the Zippo to Icy, who repeated the technique as did the Captain. Vietnam was, after all, hours of boredom interrupted by moments of sheer terror. Grunts had little other entertainment. They sat, smoked and drank in quiet for several minutes while the fire crackled. Finally, Sarge said, "Marine Three will fly you to Logan International tomorrow morning. It will leave here at 7 a.m. You will be met and taken to your office. Your pistol will be on board."

"So I'm free to leave?" said Icy.

Ignoring Icy's sarcasm, the Captain said, "You know he is going to come after you. You killed his Miss Saigon, and he won't let that go."

"She was my asset. He took her from me, and if he doesn't come for me, I will go for him."

"Where did you find Kim Ly?"

You killed his Miss Saigon. Where did you find her? The Captain didn't say things lightly, thought Icy. *What does he know?*

"Are you saying I've been played?"

"I'm saying Kim Ly's cell showed calls to and from Moscow, the real one, almost a year before you used her to do the Vice President."

"Oh Chet Tiet!" said Icy.

"Yea. Вот дерьмо. And speaking of Russia, your neighbors in Moscow Maine seem to have it in for you. They made some complaints into our Bangor office and thought we arrested you," said the Captain.

"I wonder why? Do you think you can smooth it over for me? I would like to spend some time in my cabin without having the Moscow PD trying to arrest me."

Icy got up followed by Natasha and Max by default. He took his glass tumbler and tossed it into the fire. It shattered, and the whiskey exploded sort of like a Mc Molotov cocktail. He turned and started out the door. Embarrassed he stopped, turned and said, "How do we get back to the Lincoln Bedroom?"

"The steward will show you. See you tomorrow at 6:15 for breakfast," said Sarge.

Up in the Lincoln bedroom, Colburn ran through all the possibilities that Kim Ly may have found him and not the other way around. *Is it possible he could have been taken in by her beauty? Did I let my guard down? I thought Vova had turned her. Could he have owned her?* He would backtrack and find the source that first recommended her.

Lying in Lincoln's bed staring at the ceiling he thought of what Lincoln had once said about trust. *"The people when rightly and fully trusted will return the trust."*

The signs were there. She started calling me Icy, She lied when he spoke to her in Jackson, Mississippi. Colburn realized he should have trusted his instincts. Kim Ly was rightly and fully trusted, but she did not return that trust. She chose to take her life. He should have followed Regan's maxim, "Trust and Verify."

CHAPTER 29

WASHINGTON, DC - CAMBRIDGE, MA

Colburn met President Burk in the Navy Mess on the first floor of the West Wing. The President was already seated, having a Diet Coke and reading the *Washington Post*.

"Morning Icy. Sleep well?"

"I dreamt I was back in the mid-19th century."

"The Lincoln Bedroom has that effect on people. They say it's haunted. You know it used to be the President's office before the West Wing was constructed."

"Aren't we a wealth of knowledge this morning?"

"I ordered us Spanish Omelets. How's that sound?"

"Estupendo."

"Listen Icy; the Captain said those things last night because they had to be said."

"Yea. I just didn't like what I heard."

"You helped us out of a big mess. I wish there were more I could do for you," said the President.

"Hell, Natasha and I slept in the Lincoln Bedroom, helped you find Max, were introduced to, danced with, and got Faith Knoll's phone number, free dinner and breakfast and a chopper ride home. What more can a guy ask for?" said Colburn.

"There is one more thing I might be able to do."

"And what's that?"

"You'll just have to wait and see," said the President.

At 6:45 a.m. Colburn and the President met again on the West Colonnade, then walked together into the Rose Garden and onto the South Lawn. Dave Hailey, the grounds and dog keeper, came over with Natasha and Max on his lease. Marine Three was waiting its rotors spinning, and the crew chief was at the front hatch steps waiting.

"Ready?" asked the President.

"For anything," replied Colburn.

The President with Max and Colburn with Natasha walked to Marine Three. The crew chief, not in Dress Blues, saluted the President, and the President returned the salute. Colburn turned towards his old friend the President. There was not much to be said. Colburn and the President shook hands then they both bent down to say goodbye to Natasha and Max.

Colburn turned towards the steps and Natasha followed.

"Here. I almost forgot," and handed Colburn a folded copy of the morning's *NY Post*.

"Thanks, I think."

"It's not too bad once you get past the headline."

Colburn took the paper and headed up the steps. Natasha headed up the steps behind her Da. Max strained to follow, but Natasha turned and barked. Max stopped and sat down. Natasha hurried to catch up with her Da.

There were two other passengers, an Army general, and a Marine colonel. The helicopter ramp steps were pulled up, and the President and Max made a quick retreat towards the Rose Garden. Colburn and Natasha took seats and were buckled in by the crew chief. Colburn looked out the porthole and could see the President and Max in the Rose Garden. The President saluted, and Colburn returned the salute. A second later Marine Three lifted off, turned to starboard, and began its ascent. It would be a two-hour flight to Boston.

Once airborne and headed northeast, Colburn began to relax and was served coffee by the steward. Natasha was unbelted and sat on the floor next to her Da.

Da safe, Natasha safe, Pack split.

Colburn dreaded reading the *NY Post* account of the Atlanta affair with Kim Ly. He knew Todd and Sweeney would exploit it as usual to sell papers. He pulled the folded paper out from under his leg and opened it.

New York Post front page headline read:

Miss Saigon's Final Performance
by Ron Todd and Tom Sweeney
Goodnight Miss Saigon.

Revenge Murderer, Kim Ly, Commits Seppuku in Atlanta Airport.
Rather than be captured, Kim Ly committed Seppuku, aka tự vận, to die with honor rather than fall into the hands of her enemies.

We now know Kim Ly, aka Sue Li, Miss Saigon, and the Dragon Lady was a Vietnamese Special Forces operative and the actual assassin of all four Revenge Murders: former Vice President Richard Rumson, Globalwide's Mazola, former Speaker of the House Paula Vitelli and the Reverend Ali Shabazz.

While this reporter was finishing up the story, posted yesterday in the *NY Post*, about the murder of Reverend Ali Shabazz, my associate, Tom Sweeney, rushed off to Atlanta, on a tip, to find the master assassin, Miss Saigon.

We were given complete and unprecedented access to the FBI investigation and investigators. FBI Special Agent in Charge, Henry Hill laid out the entire investigation for us. They stated emphatically that our investigative reporting helped them break and solve all four cases.

Kim Ly was in the Club ATL in the international terminal of Atlanta International Airport ready to board Korean Air Flight 0036 to Seoul, Korea and Hanoi, Vietnam. Just before boarding she went to the club toilet. Agents heard her yell the name Vova and then a loud spit of what they recognized as a suppressed gunshot.

Tom Sweeney was permitted access and saw Kim Ly sitting on the toilet, fully dressed, with her head back, hands to her side still holding a cylinder which looked like a single shot weapon. Blood was splattered on the wall behind her head, and blood dripped from a bullet hole beneath her chin. She was dead. We asked SAC Hill why he thought Kim Ly took her life and how she got the gun into the airport. He said the weapon was a 6" cylinder, with a ¾" diameter. We were left to our imagination as to how she got it past security.

SAC Hill told us they suspected she killed herself because she dishonored herself by breaking the rules and deserved to die. It was an Asian thing. She took her life because the FBI was closing in on her, and she had nowhere to run, nowhere to hide, except a stall in a bathroom.

We now know that Kim Ly was the Navy Seal wannabe, who murdered Vice President Richard Rumson. She was the Blond Bombshell, who murdered Globalwide's Albert Mazola in Hedgehampton. She was the Dragon Lady, who murdered former Speaker of the House Paula Vitelli in San Francisco, and the mastermind behind the murder of the Reverend Ali Shabazz in Jackson. Kim Ly was a Vietnamese Special Forces operative and the assassin of all four. Rumson, Mazola, Vitelli and Shabazz.

What was her motive and did she act alone or was this part of the government conspiracy we alluded to previously. The answer my friends is she did not act alone, and yes, this is part of a government conspiracy, but not our government.

Vova, the name Kim Ly called out just before she shot herself, is Colonel Demetri Vova of the FSB, Russian Federal Security Service, successor to the KGB. He's in charge of international chaos. He funds, uses and supports ISIL. He is a very nasty piece of work. He works for Vladimir Vladimirovich Putin, President of Russia.

The FBI working with the NSA and CIA believe Colonel Demetri Vova orchestrated these four murders to ...

Colburn put the paper in the empty seat beside him. The Marine lieutenant colonel sitting across from Colburn asked, "War Dog?"

"No. Just a buddy."

"You serve?"

"Yes."

"Rank?"

"Sergeant."

The colonel guessed the man sitting front of him was enlisted, and by his age, he guessed Vietnam but knew he must be important to have the President escort him to the helicopter. Colburn guessed by the colonel's age that he was probably in since Bush the Father's war or possibly just after. He sensed the colonel didn't want to have further conversation with or fraternize further with the unwashed, and that suited him fine.

"If you're through with the paper, would you mind?" asked the colonel.

Colburn picked up the paper and handed it to the colonel. The colonel looked at the headlines and said, "Can you believe this? Anything to sell papers. Where do this get this stuff?"

Colburn assumed the remarks redundant, but when he looked up, he noticed the officer looking at him waiting for a response.

"I really don't know. I've been away," said Colburn.

"Where?" asked the colonel.

"Moscow."

The colonel now thinking that the enlisted man with the wolf is a CIA spook, decided not to press further.

At 9 a.m. Marine Three touched down at Boston's Logan International. The step ramp lowered, and the crew chief was the first off followed by the general, the colonel, then Colburn and Natasha. The crew chief saluted both the general and colonel and held the salute for Colburn. A black town car was waiting, which the general assumed was for him, and the colonel hoped to be invited. The crew chief retrieved Coburn's overnight and briefcase and steered Colburn to the waiting town car, where a driver held the door for them. That left the two officers wondering what to do. Colburn and Natasha jumped in, and the crew chief offered a salute which Colburn returned. Colburn was tempted to offer the officers a ride, but he always felt the greater the amount of fruit salad (medals) on their respective chest the greater the hyperbole and lies. These two were top heavy, so he just smiled, rolled up the window, and told the driver to go.

It took almost half the time to get to his office on Harvard Street as it did to get from Washington to Boston. As the town car pulled up in front of his office, Colburn was happy to see his black Range Rover parked right out front. Amazingly without a parking ticket or boot, the metal contraption that locks your car wheel until the parking fee is paid. He and Natasha got out, thanked the driver and saw the new sidewalk sign and the yellow line painted on the blacktop framing his parking space. The white sign with a P inside a circle that had a red slash through it said "No Parking Anytime Except For Vehicle Displaying DHS Permit Golf 2/7. Colburn looked at his Range Rovers windscreen and saw the DHS Golf 2/7 permit prominently displayed next to his registration and inspection stickers.

It's good to know the king.

CHAPTER 30

WASHINGTON, DC

President Burk relieved that the "Revenge Murders" seemed to over, reconvened his meeting on student loan forgiveness, with Vice President Claire Hilton and Treasury Secretary Michael Bloomfield. He had something additional on his mind, so he also invited the Secretaries of Labor and Commerce, Harry Bedrosian and Betty Taff, Attorney General William Fare, Chief of Staff Bill Nicholas and Press Secretary Kelly Sullivan Burk.

Student loan forgiveness has become a cause célèbre for the Vice President, an issue arousing widespread controversy. Student-loan debt is a big problem. The latest Federal Reserve data shows there is nearly $1.3 trillion in outstanding student-loan debt in the US. Realizing graduates were struggling to repay their heavy debt burdens, Vice President Hilton was proposing a few plans that would allow student debt to be forgiven over time. The students and their families were obviously for these proposals. The banks and loan institutions against it because as proposed, it would put the government between them and the borrower. More importantly, forgiving student loans could put the banks and lending institutions out of business. Losing a money making product from their portfolio was not good business.

The student loan forgiveness portion of the meeting was completed, with more than half of those present wondering why they were even invited. President Burk, wrapping it up looked across the table at the Vice President and said, I'll back whichever plan you and Mike decide, but I want students and their families who paid their tuition from their savings or IRA's to receive a tuition refund. Claire, you and I will need to present our case to the people, Congress, Main Street and Wall Street. It will be a $3 trillion tough sell, and I do not want singles and couples who have no children or who have children who have not attended college to participate.

That was not exactly what Vice President Hilton and Treasury Secretary Bloomfield wanted to hear, for different reasons, but at least the program could proceed.

The President stood, and started walking slowly around the oval conference table and said, "I guess the rest of you are a little curious why you were invited to a student loan forgiveness meeting. Well, you weren't. I have something important on my mind that I want to bounce off all of you first before I go to the entire Cabinet. This is a pretty big idea, and you might think I have lost it, especially after saying we need to find $3 Trillion for student loan forgiveness, but give me a chance to pitch it. OK?"

No one around the table except the President and Kelly had any idea where this was going.

"I agree with Len Leopold, the director of the Commerce Institute in New York." He took out some notes and began reading, ""America is the richest country in all of history. We have the largest economy and the largest number of millionaires and billionaires. At the same time, we lead the developed world in economic inequality. In 1965, CEO's received $20 for every dollar earned by the average worker. Today the gap is $354 to $1. These are more than cold statistics. They also tell the story of a nation in serious trouble. Runaway inequality is lacerating the fabric of our society. Here are a few of the festering wounds.

We are among the leaders in child poverty.
We lead the developed world in homelessness.
We lead the world in student debt.
We lead the world in prisoners.
We lead the world in police brutality.
We lead the world in tax evasion.

We have the world's most outrageous tax breaks for the super-rich.
We lead the world in declining public services."

Here's how I feel it plays out. The top 25 hedge fund managers in 2013 collectively took in $24.3 billion. For starters, that gives them an average income of $467,000 an hour. They make as much in one hour as the typical American makes in ten years! Their carried interest loophole reduces their taxes about $4.8 billion a year. How much is that in human terms? It's enough to hire 175,000 pre-school teachers a year or 76,000 registered nurses. Instead, it goes into the pockets of just 25 billionaires for no reason at all, except one— they want it. Both Democrats and Republicans refuse to touch the loophole. But they welcome with open arms the fat donations that come from the billionaires they are protecting. When you are the richest of the rich, America looks damn good. Your employees and servants fawn over you. Politicians and the media flock to be in your presence. You have the keys to the economic castle. You are the economic castle. You are the creator of wealth, the maker of jobs, and the winner of the toughest competition on Earth. You feel you are only getting what you richly deserve.

Meanwhile, the rest of us need and rely on our public spaces, our public services, and our public facilities. We use the schools and the roads. We need a vibrant public sector but that, too, is slipping away. In fact, the more inequality rises, the more difficult it becomes to support a public sector, as the super-rich and wealthy corporations do all they can to avoid paying their fair share.

We can see this most clearly by the decline of public sector employment. This job loss makes the delivery of every public service more difficult. It means longer lines, larger class size, and fewer infrastructure repairs. This is especially pronounced since the Wall Street-created crash.

Just last week The Panama Papers revealed an unprecedented leak of 11.5m files from the database of the world's fourth-biggest offshore law firm, Mossack Fonseca. The records were obtained from an anonymous source by the German newspaper *Süddeutsche Zeitung*, which shared them with the International Consortium of Investigative Journalists (ICIJ). The ICIJ then shared them with a large network of international partners, including the Guardian and the BBC. The documents show the myriad ways in which the rich can exploit secretive offshore tax regimes. Twelve national leaders are among 143 politicians, their families, and close associates from around the world known to have been using offshore tax havens.

The President finished circling the table and ended up back in front of his chair. He placed both hands on the chair back and said, "The Constitution is liquid. That is why we have the Bill of Rights. They are the original first ten amendments to the Constitution. The government then added another seventeen. Some of which were good and others well… One of my first acts after taking office was to disband the IRS and institute a consumption tax. The naysayers said it would fail but it has succeeded, and the naysayers will say what I am about to propose will also fail. For this country to continue to grow we need to level the playing field. We need to bring the disenfranchised to the ballpark and build a winning team where everyone benefits from a successful America."

"You sound like a socialist," said Attorney General William Fare.

"Oh, it's radical. But you couldn't be more wrong Bill. I may be sounding like a socialist, but I'm thinking like a capitalist. Ladies and Gentlemen I propose we make the United States of America, which is the greatest country in the world with a GNP of $18 Trillion, into a Corporation, one in which all citizens will be equal shareholders. Each citizen will be paid an annual dividend, which they can spend, save or reinvest."

The gasp through the room was loud and long. Everyone was looking back and forth at each other in disbelief.

"And just how does your new AMERICA INC. make its money?" asked Sectary of Commerce Betty Taff.

"By selling services. Like charging South Korea for the 30,000 troops we have stationed there. Or the 13,000 in Kuwait. Or the 50,000 in Japan. Or the 40,000 in Germany. All for their protection I may add. We start loaning money at American Express rates to countries, instead of just giving it to them. No more buying friends. We sell our technologies; satellites and weapons. How exactly the corporation makes money will be up to you and Mike to figure out. But one thing for sure. Nothing we do will today will borrow from the future of our children."

Treasury Secretary Mike Bloomfield just shook his head and closed his eyes. *Where will he stop*, he thought.

The word 'corporation' derives from *corpus*, the Latin word for body, or a "body of people." A corporation is a company or group of people authorized to act as a single entity (legally a person) and recognized as such in law. Early incorporated entities were established by charter (i.e. by an *ad hoc* act granted by a monarch or passed by a parliament or legislature). Most jurisdictions now allow the creation of new corporations through registration.

Bill Nicholas, a student of history and the Presidents Chief of Staff, said, "Excuse me, Mr. President, didn't The Act of 1871 form a corporation called THE UNITED STATES. It's was supposed this corporation, owned by foreign interests, moved in and shoved the original Constitution into a dustbin. With the Act of 1871, the original Constitution for the United States in 1788 was defaced, in effect vandalized and sabotaged when the title was capitalized and the word "for" was changed to "of" in the title.

In 1778, it read 'the Constitution for the United States of America.' Today it reads, 'THE CONSTITUTION OF THE UNITED STATES OF AMERICA.'"

"You're correct Bill, but many constitutional scholars don't subscribe to The Act of 1871. That act passed when the country was weakened and financially depleted in the aftermath of the Civil War. It was a strategic move by foreign interests (international bankers) who were intent upon gaining a stranglehold on the coffers and neck of America. Congress cut a deal with the international bankers, specifically the Rothschild's of London, to incur debt to said bankers. Because the bankers were not about to lend money to a floundering nation without serious stipulations, they devised a way to get their foot in the door of the United States. Getting rid of the IRS has severely crippled the Federal Reserve and if I had my druthers the Federal Reserve, which is neither Federal nor Reserve, would also be eliminated."

Treasury Secretary Bloomfield said, "Mr. President, let's not go there again. It was hard enough to disband the IRS and institute the Consumption

Sales Tax. I can't stomach another fight like that in your first term. Let's wait till after you're re-elected."

There were chuckles and smiles around the table.

The President continued, "Mike I agree, but that's all beside the point. I am not talking about regurgitating The Act Of 1871 and all the other nonsense that America is still owned by Britain and the Royal Family, I am simply suggesting a concept that will bring us all together. The people of the United States were never meant to be serfs, nor were they supposed to be subjects. With the victory of the North in the Civil War, the people were not supposed to be slaves. It was never the intention of the founders that the representatives of the people would so easily sacrifice the people into indentured servitude forever! The people of the United States are supposed to be free! Free to choose their destiny. They were required to follow the rules of common law, but they always were meant to remain sovereign individuals! As shareholders in America, they will continue to vote, continue to pay taxes, but will feel as though they are part of something equally. If the country succeeds, they succeed. This is not socialism its capitalism. Anyone who has ever had skin in the game knows the difference."

CHAPTER 31

CAMBRIDGE, MA

Colburn was sitting in his Cambridge office, on Harvard Street, doing office stuff and thinking about all that had happened in the last couple of months, including his encounter with Faith Knoll. He enjoyed their short time together, and he decided he would call her soon.

Another woman was on his mind now. He had gone back and checked all his records, phone registers, and contacts to see how he first heard of Kim Ly. Everything pointed to him contacting her, but how did he first hear about her? He could find nothing concrete. No email from a reliable source recommending her. No unsolicited resume. Hiring contractors today was not like back in the 60's, and 70's where you simply placed or answered an advertisement in *Soldier of Fortune* magazine. Today, because of the internet, everyone knows everyone and has complete access to information. They know who is good, reliable, and experienced. They even have a *Yelp* site for user reviews and recommendations of a contractor's performance. If you're not good and respected, you need not apply.

His Day Minder desk calendar had one entry around the time he contacted Kim Ly. When he saw the name written on the page, a chill ran up his spine. The man had just been killed in a botched mission. He was good, real good, and that should not have happened. Colburn just heard about the FUBAR (Fucked Up Beyond All Repair) through the contractor's grapevine. It was a Vova-ISIL mission, and now he would not be able to question his contact.

I, like God, do not play with dice, and we do not believe in coincidence, thought Colburn.

Just then his cell phone rang. He got up from his desk and walked to his office manager's outer office. He saw that Mary was busy on the computer and was not calling him. What was strange is that no one had his cell number except Mary and the President. He touched the answer icon.

"Hello."

"Hello, Israel. Bet you didn't think you would hear from me, and so soon," said Faith Knoll.

"Hello, Faith. No, I didn't, but I am surprised and happy to hear from you."

"I guess you're wondering how I got your number?"

"No. I have a pretty good idea who you got it from."

"I hope you won't be too upset with him."

"I promise I'll go easy on him."

"Good. Now here's why I called. I'm coming to Boston tomorrow to do a show and was hoping we could get together."

Get together. An interesting choice of words thought Colburn.

"Love to. Did I hear you correctly? You're doing a show?"

"It's a spur of the moment thing. One night only. It's the same show I have been doing, but my agent got a desperate call from Boston's Citi Performing Arts Center. It seems they are having a benefit show for Wounded Warriors and the performer, Carrie Underwood, came down with laryngitis. I am going to spend the day rehearsing with her band, and the show starts at 8 p.m. and finishes at 9:30 p.m. I would like you to be my guest."

"Dinner after?"

"Absolutely, and I don't have to be back to Nashville until Monday. I have the rest of the weekend free."

"I'll make reservations. Where is the show?"

"The Citi Performing Arts Center, on Tremont Street. Your ticket will be at the ticket booth. Got to run. See you tomorrow night."

The Citi Performing Arts Center, formally the Wang Theater, was originally the Metropolitan Theatre designed by Clarence Blackall and C. Howard

Crane. It opened for use in 1925 and seats a little more than 3,600 people. If you look in an encyclopedia for a classic 20's theater, a picture of the Metropolitan will appear. Its elegant decoration, gilded moldings, murals, scagliola and marbleized surfaces, colors, seating plan, and accouterment were all over the top. A perfect visual and acoustical venue to see and hear Faith Knoll perform her songs.

The next day Colburn arrived on time, retrieved his ticket and was escorted to his seat, center orchestra, four rows back. The theater was completely sold out.

Faith, with her orchestra and sometimes with only her acoustical guitar, captivated the audience. She did an hour set with a short intermission then finished up with a standing ovation. She came back out and did her signature song, 'Just an Alabama Girl', and received another standing ovation.

Colburn had a backstage pass and enjoyed going back and seeing all the behind the scene stuff while he waited for Faith to change.

"Well handsome, what did you think?" said Faith after finding Colburn surveying the theater from the stage.

"Wonderful. Absolutely wonderful. I heard many of those songs on the radio but never knew they were yours or that you were the singer. I just didn't know."

"I'll take it all as a compliment, and I am ready if you are."

Colburn had a car waiting to take them to Coppos in the South End. It is known for having some of the city's best pasta and fish dishes. The owner, an old Southie friend of Colburn's from when they were kids, properly seated them and made sure they were well attended. Colburn ordered a bottle of Pellegrino and suggested a bottle of Moet Chandon Rose. When the Champagne was served, they began to relax. Well almost.

The restaurant was full, and heads were turning as Faith was recognized. Boston has some pretty women, but Faith Knoll is just plain gorgeous and an A-list celebrity. Colburn was afraid someone would come over and ask to take a photo or worse just take one. He told his friend the owner when he made the reservations, who he was bringing and asked for discretion. Again, not for Faith but himself. He could not have his photograph appearing in some tabloid. He knew this might be a problem, so he made sure his name did not appear on the reservation. His friend, the owner, knew about Colburn, and had a vague idea of who he was and what he had become, and would do his best to accommodate him. Colburn had a pair of Wayfarers in his pocket just in case.

"Nervous?" asked Faith.

"Can you tell?" asked Colburn.

"I'm starving. What's good?"

"The Caesar salad is delicious. They make it right at the table with egg instead of mayonnaise, fresh romaine, garlic, Worcestershire sauce, red wine vinegar, croutons, olive oil, lemon, real anchovy, and shaved parmesan. They make it almost as good as mine," said Colburn. They ordered the Caesar salad with Faith having the Linguine Nero and Colburn the Veal Marsala.

The waiter came to the table and prepared the Caesar salads, served them and asked if they would like ground pepper. After the waiter had left, Colburn proposed a toast to, "To new friends." They clicked glasses, and Faith smiled and added, "And to those who introduce them."

Everything was going nicely, the salad was delicious, and the waiter had just taken the salad plates away. During the lull, the inevitable happened. A mother, with her two little girls, appeared and asked if they could have a picture. Faith was very generous with her celebrity status and acquiesced immediately. Colburn excused himself while the mother took out her phone and the girls stood next to Faith. After the photo, Faith said something nice to the girls as the giggled and left to become minor celebrities themselves.

Colburn took the opportunity to remind his friend, the restaurant owner, to not let anyone take a picture of him with Faith, especially a candid shot.

When Colburn returned to the table, Faith said, "Israel, you are either shy or in the witness protection program. You're going to have to get used to it. People ask for autographs and want photos of celebrities. It goes with the territory."

"Faith, I'm neither shy nor in the witness protection program. They can take all the photos of you they want; I just do not want to be in them." *This is not going to work*, thought Colburn. *People are drawn to her, and I can't even be seen with her. She has no idea how my enemy's look for weak spots.*

"If I didn't know better, I would think you were married."

Just then the entrees arrived, and Faith and Colburn decided to let it go and enjoy their dinner.

After dinner, Faith wanted to see South Boston where Colburn was born and grew up. Colburn had the driver take them across the Congress Street Bridge and into South Boston. He decided to take her to Dorchester Heights because of the history and view. Standing on top of Thomas Park, in the middle of Dorchester Heights, Colburn gave Faith a brief history of this little known but pivotal historical location, while they both enjoyed the view.

He explained to her that on March 4, 1776, troops from the Continental Army under George Washington's command occupied Dorchester Heights, a series of low hills with a commanding view of Boston and its harbor, and mounted powerful cannons there. General William Howe, the commander of the British forces occupying the city, considered contesting this act, as the cannon threatened the town and the military ships in the harbor. Admiral Shuldham, the commander of the British fleet, declared that the fleet was in danger unless the position on the heights was taken. Howe and his staff then determined to contest the occupation of the heights, and made plans for an assault, preparing to send 2,400 men under cover of darkness to attack the position. Washington notified of the British movements, increased the forces on the heights until there were nearly 6,000 men on the Dorchester lines; however, a snowstorm began late on March 5 and halted any chance of a battle for several days. By the time the storm subsided, Howe had reconsidered launching an attack, reasoning that preserving the army for battle elsewhere was of higher value than attempting to hold Boston.

On March 8, intermediaries delivered an unsigned paper informing Washington that the city would not be burned to the ground if his troops were allowed to leave unmolested. After several days of activity and several more of bad weather, the British forces departed Boston by sea on March 17 and sailed to Halifax, Nova Scotia.

"What was it like growing up with so much history?"

"You know as kids we didn't appreciate it. We knew our neighborhood was special, but this is Boston, and every neighborhood is special. History surrounds us, the Tea Party, Paul Revere's ride, Lexington, Concord, Bunker Hill and Breed's Hill. I didn't appreciate it till much later during the 60's when another war loomed over us."

"Vietnam. You went. You served. What do you think about those who didn't go? Like Jane Fonda?"

"Everybody my age did something, Faith. Some of us drank Walter Cronkite's Cool Aid and went to war, some went to Canada, some married so they could get a deferment, some used connections to get out or went to college, some had legitimate physical problems, and some pretended too, and some protested, like Jane Fonda. Many vets will disagree with my position, but I don't hate or despise any of them. We all did what we felt was correct at the time. Some are proud today for what they choose to do, and some are not, but we all did something.

I don't believe today, and I didn't believe then, that America belonged in Vietnam. I was there and fighting for the guy in front and behind me, not for America, and not for the CIA and their twisted political ideology. Hell, Ho Chi Minh loved America. He fought as our allies against the Japanese in WW II. He thought of all countries America would understand their plight and desire for freedom from the French colonist. After all, America fought for their freedom against the British. Who better than America to understand and be a friend. After the war, Ho Chi Minh wrote Vietnams Declaration of Independence in Hanoi, 2 September 1945. He used our Declaration of Independence as a template."

"All men are created equal. They are endowed by their Creator with certain inalienable rights, among these are Life, Liberty, and the pursuit of Happiness" This immortal statement was made in the Declaration of Independence of the United States of America in 1776. In a broader sense, this means: All the people on the earth are equal from birth; all the people have a right to live, to be happy and free. The Declaration of the French Revolution made in 1791 on the Rights of Man and the Citizen also states: *"All men are born free*

and with equal rights, and must always remain free and have equal rights." Those are undeniable truths.

"Truman sold him and his country down the river and gave Vietnam back to the French. And the rest, as they say, is history. Sorry to ramble but when I get started I have a hard time stopping."

"I am glad you did. I love South Boston, and I'm proud to be here with you and hear your views on the war. Both the war that started here and the one over there."

Colburn drove Faith back to her hotel, the Four Seasons, and told his driver to wait. He walked Faith to the entrance.

"Faith, I had a wonderful time tonight. The show, dinner, and your company."

She smiled and came close and kissed him on the lips.

She then said, "I want to taste yours."

"Excuse me," said Colburn. Not a prude, but confused by what Faith just said.

"I want to taste your Caesar salad to see if it is better than tonight's."

"Oh. I see. OK, well, what about tomorrow night? I have a cabin upstate and was thinking about driving up there tomorrow morning. It's a small cabin and very private. Plenty of land for hikes and a great fireplace for chilly nights. I'll make you a better salad and cook you a fantastic dinner. What do you say?"

Faith smiled and started to turn and asked, "What time?"

As Colburn walked down the steps to his waiting car, he noticed, behind the portico column, a man with a camera. Colburn approached the man with ease and a smile.

"Get any good pics?" asked Colburn.

"Yea. Who are you?" said the man with the camera.

"Rob Unger. May I see?" asked Colburn.

The man with the camera was put at ease by Colburn's manner and decided to show him the pictures he just took of Faith Knoll. Now that the camera man had the man's name, the pictures would sell for much more. *Faith Knolls Boston Lover* thought the man with the camera. He turned the camera so

Colburn could see the screen and started scrolling the pictures. Colburn had seen enough. He was in profile but recognizable. He grabbed the camera and flipped it over and released the battery cover and snapped out the memory card.

"What the fuck do you think you're doing?" said the cameraman.

Colburn handed him back the camera and dropped the memory card to the pavement and crunched it with the heel of his shoe. Satisfied it was beyond repair, he turned towards his car and left the man standing there with his mouth open. As Colburn got in the car and was driving away, he heard the man yelling something. He could only make out a few words from the man's tirade; mother something, police, and sue.

Colburn thought as he drove away, *how can I ever have a relationship with Faith? She is a celebrity, and her fans want to see her, touch her, be part of her life. They want to know her personal life, who she dates, who she loves. I live in the shadows.*

CHAPTER 32

Moscow, ME

Colburn and Natasha live in a small house on Mellen Street, just a half-mile walk to their office on Harvard Street. Since he was granted a designated parking space in front of his office, he had been keeping his Range Rover there, and just walking back and forth. He intended to pick Faith up at the hotel at noon then head north to the cabin. He decided to do his food shopping here in Cambridge before heading out for two reasons; first, there is a good Whole Foods Supermarket nearby; and second, he didn't want to be seen shopping with Faith Knoll in Bingham, too many opportunities for fans and photos.

At 9:30 a.m. Colburn and Natasha walked to the office to pick up the Range Rover. All he carried was his briefcase. His overnight was already in the office. Whole Foods was located on Beacon Street, and it would only be a five-minute drive from the office. At Whole Foods, he brought all the necessary ingredients for his Caesar salad and their main course. The manager, at Colburn's request, boxed the entire purchase in ice for the four-hour trip north. He also brought a couple of bottles of wine and champagne from the wine store next door. When he finished, he would take Beacon Street straight into Hampshire Street, merge into Pacific Ave, then across the Longfellow Bridge into downtown Boston. As he was about to approach the bridge, his cell phone rang.

It went straight to Bluetooth, and thinking it was Faith he touched "Answer." Over the speakers came a sandpaper voice.

"Icy. How are you my friend?" said Vova.

"Дерьмо," said Colburn, regretting he took the call. He pulled over to the side of the road, anticipating that he may lose his cool.

"Shit to you too, Icy."

Colburn and Natasha started growling and baring their teeth.

"How did you get this number?" He immediately regretted asking.

"Icy, please. You think only your country has an NSA? I think, my dear friend, our little game is up. It just didn't seem to catch on, but don't worry. I have another bigger, better game to play. I've also added an incentive, a new angle if you will. Are you up for it?"

"I'm done. I'm done with you, and I'm done with your games."

"Don't be such a bad sport, Icy. I think this game will be more fun. Instead of killing bad people we'll kill good people. I think this game will get us better ratings. I have a list. Want to see it?"

Natasha was foaming, and Colburn was seething.

"You'll have to play this game by yourself, Colonel."

"Oh, I don't think so. I have a substitute wanting to get in, but just remember, you're either a player or you're played."

Natasha continued to foam and snarl at the dashboard speakers, while Colburn pounded the steering wheel.

"I hear you and your wolf. It sounds like a definite Het. You know, I wish I could meet your bitch someday," said Vova.

Be careful what you wish for Vova, thought Natasha.

Colburn touched the "Hang Up" icon and was disconnected. He scrolled the phone menu and blocked Vova's number but knew Vova could unblock it if he wanted. Natasha put her head up close to Colburn's and looked him directly in his eyes as if to say she would welcome the encounter. He petted and scratched Natasha's head which seemed to help both of them calm down. He started back across the bridge and pushed the phone speed dial button and waited.

The phone started ringing, and the White House operator answered. He was put straight through to the President.

Ten minutes later, at exactly 12 noon, he pulled up in front of the Four Seasons Hotel.

Da mad, Natasha mad, Sarge mad, Pack mad.

Faith came right out the hotel door with her overnight, down the steps and to the Range Rover. The hotel doorman opened the door, and Faith got in. He then opened the back door and placed her overnight in the back seat. That was a mistake and a story he would be telling for quite a while.

Natasha protect.

After Vova's call, it was relaxing and enjoyable to be with Faith. They drove out of Boston around 12:10 p.m. and took 95 north towards Portland, to Waterville, then 201 north to Bingham, then to the small town of Moscow, a little over 200 miles start to finish and took about four hours with a pit stop. The cabin was two miles north of Moscow. During the drive, they talked about many things including the cabin's history, how Colonel Benedict Arnold led a force of Continental Army troops on an expedition from Cambridge, Massachusetts to the gates of Quebec City, how the invasion failed, and how passing back through, one of his men, Johnathan Colburn remained. He married and had six children and built the cabin. He told Faith how he, Natasha, and Tommy Burk before Tommy became President, found and renovated the cabin.

Faith talked about her early years and growing up in rural Alabama, her bad marriage, and being a born again Christian. They talked for almost three hours and never turned on the radio. As they passed out of Bingham and were coming to Moscow, Colburn told her about the town's history and how it was named. He also told her about the town people and what they thought of him and Natasha.

Da safe. Natasha safe. Pack safe. This new human is a female. I can smell her. Da likes her. She is not a threat, but she is not pack.

Sweeney and Todd were the new Woodward and Bernstein. Since everyone felt Sweeney, younger and blond resembled Woodward, aka Robert Redford that made Todd, darker, shorter and more experienced, Bernstein, aka Dustin Hoffman. Because of their reporting on the Dragon Lady Murders, they became the darlings of the media. Sweeney was getting calls from big papers around the country. No offers were coming in for Todd because everyone knew he would never leave New York and would never leave the *Post*. Together they did the Sunday morning shows and late night and daytime. They did *CNN* and *FOX*. When they tried some interviews alone, it just didn't work. Like Hall without Oates, Simon without Garfunkel, or Dobie without Maynard, everyone wanted to hear and see them together.

Sweeney was sitting, having coffee and an apple crumb muffin, in Hedgehampton's Golden Plum Café, contemplating his good fortune. He loved Hedgehampton and the *Hedgehampton Press,* where he worked, but chances of another big story coming along were pretty slim. Sure the Hamptons were home for the rich and famous and a scandal or even an occasional murder could be counted on, but you can't put the genie back in the bottle. And Sweeney didn't want to live the rest of his life on the Dragon Lady Murders, as they were being called. His cell rang, and he answered, "Hello."

"What do you hear? What do you say?" asked Todd.

"What?" asked Sweeney.

"Never mind. It's an old Jimmy Cagney thing. How about, what's hot?"

"I was about to call you and ask the same thing."

"Who's on first?"

"What?"

"Fuhgeddaboudit. This conversation is going nowhere. Listen, I was thinking that if you're finished doing background stuff on Kim Ly, why don't we go up to Moscow, and see if there is anything to those reports we had heard before we went to Washington? You know before we got the tip to go to Jackson."

"You know I had a feeling President Burk and FBI Director Riley knew something about that."

"Me too. I'll go check it out unless you want to join me?" asked Todd.

"Why don't you go yourself? I still have more sources here to check out," said Sweeney.

A black Range Rover, driving through Bingham then Moscow, at 4 p.m. will not go unnoticed. As far as Colburn was concerned, he didn't care. He had no intention of spending time in either town especially with Faith in tow. Although both towns would get a big kick out of having a celebrity in their midst, he had all the supplies he needed and planned to stay close to the cabin and hunker down for a couple of peaceful days.

Deputy Hinds was having coffee at Patrick's Pub in Bingham when he saw the Range Rover go by.

"Deputy Hinds to chief. Deputy Hinds to chief. Over."

"Go ahead," said Chief Pruitt.

"They're back!"

FBI Agent Ross of the Bangor office, after her earlier run-in with Chief Pruitt, had checked on his story of a supposed call to the Bangor FBI, reporting suspicious behavior at Colburn's cabin. The chief had told her that he called the FBI when she and SAC Ceretti were dispatched to Moscow to pick up Colburn. She did this and more, on her own, without confiding with her boss SAC Ceretti. She found that Chief Pruitt did, in fact, call the Bangor office reporting suspicious behavior at Colburn's cabin, including an unauthorized helicopter landing. She contacted all the regional airports, and no helicopter activity or flight plans were ever listed. That is, except her and Ceretti's flight to and from Bangor to pick up Colburn and his dog. The call from Chief Pruitt was never acted on. Someone from Washington squashed it, and then ADC Michael Hoar from the NYC office called with an order for them to pick up Colburn and escort him to the airport. Besides looking into Chief Pruitt's complaint, she also got more information on Colburn, and it was not good. She decided to ask her boss if she could drive up to Moscow and have a further talk with Chief Pruitt. To her surprise, he agreed but would accompany her on the 70-mile drive to Moscow.

When Colburn, Faith, and Natasha pulled up to the cabin, it was almost 4:30 p.m. It was still light out but getting colder, and it looked like snow. The weather in Moscow, although only 200 miles away from Cambridge, more resembled the real Moscow. Natasha jumped out first and performed her vedette by circling the cabin.

"What is Natasha doing and how did she get out the truck?"

"She is scouting the area, looking for anything out of the ordinary, and she lets herself out. It's what she does."

"She is amazing."

"Don't encourage her. She understands the word, and hears it quite often."

Faith bent down and called to Natasha. Natasha, finding no threats around the cabin, responded to Faith's summons. Natasha came over to Faith and sat down. Faith rubbed her head and neck. "Natasha you're a good girl. You're so amazing!"

Natasha looked over at her Da. He nodded and Natasha put the icing on the cake. She stood up and put her arms around Faith's neck and gave her a licky kiss.

"Hate to break up this love fest but how about we get our stuff inside. I'll give you the tour, and we'll still have time and light to take a short hike."

Chief Pruitt never did get called down to Bangor to assist in the Colburn investigation. He took a lot of needling from Moscow's town fathers for being snookered by a female FBI agent.

"She played you chief. She batted her eyelashes and told you how she likes men in uniforms. Then she hijacked Colburn, the wolf, and the Range Rover. Three for three," said Mayor Logan.

The chief was about to respond when a big black Suburban pulled up and stopped right in front of the mayor and the chief. SAC Ceretti and Agent Ross exited the Suburban and walked towards them.

"Chief Pruitt, this is Special Agent in Charge, Rob Ceretti," said Agent Ross. They shook hands and stood there until it dawned on the chief to introduce the mayor. He did.

"Chief, we wanted to apologize to you for not getting back to you, about the incident," said Agent Ross.

Isn't it a coincidence that the FBI come rolling into town right behind Colburn? What are the chances? thought the chief.

When the chief didn't respond, SAC Agent Ceretti said, "Chief, mayor, we want to update you on the incident. Mr. Colburn is not a person of interest nor is he a suspect of anything. He was cooperating with us on an operation, which has been completed and because of that we want you to extend him every professional courtesy."

Agent Ross was hearing this for the first time. SAC Ceretti made it clear, on the car ride up, that she should follow his lead.

"So we can expect more nighttime helicopter flights?" said the chief.

"I don't think that's going to happen chief, but I wanted to tell you in person that Mr. Colburn is on our side," said Agent Ceretti.

"Agent Ceretti, you work for the federal government, and your boss is the president. I work for the state government, and my boss is the governor. I will decide who is and who isn't breaking the local law, and isn't it convenient, you two pulling into town just minutes after Colburn arrived?"

SAC Ceretti and Agent Ross exchanged a quick glance. *This is a coincidence, but it sure won't look that way to them,* thought Ceretti. *He only received the call from ADC Hoar yesterday telling him to defuse the situation and make sure Colburn is not hassled again.*

"Chief. I just want to make sure you get the message. This story is over," said SAC Ceretti.

Just then a black Mustang pulled up, and a man got out and walked over to the group. *Probably he's lost,* thought the mayor. *But he does look familiar.*

"Excuse me. I'm looking for a Police Chief Pruitt."

SAC Ceretti looked like he was about to run this fellow off, but the face looked familiar to him too.

"I'm Chief Pruitt."

"Nice to finally meet you Chief. I'm Ron Todd of the *NY Post,* and I hear you got a story."

CHAPTER 33

HEDGEHAMPTON, NY

Tom Sweeney had wanted to go to Moscow with Todd, but for some reason, Todd seemed to want to go alone. Maybe Bernstein wants to try a solo album. Sweeney got up and left the Golden Plum café and sat on the bench outside. Main Street was starting to get crowded and strangers who would have said hi to one another minutes ago, now ignored each other as they jockeyed for parking and personal space. Parked in front of the hardware store, the bank, the café, and the real estate office, were: pick-up trucks, Ferraris, Porsches, Fords, and tons of SUV's. People were browsing the shops and walking their dogs. The heart of the village was starting to beat.

Less than a half mile from where Sweeney sat on the bench, Mustafa Fadhil, Mohammed Atef and Abdul Yasin, in Railroad Yard Park, laid their prayer rugs towards the northeast and Kaaba, the central shrine in Mecca's Great Mosque, Islam's holiest place. They had slept in their car, in Railroad Yard, after a night of driving for Uber to deliver and retrieve the weekenders to and from Hampton's restaurants and clubs.

But now it was time to pray.

Allahu Akbar, Allahu Akbar - Ashadu an la ilaha ill Allah, - Ashadu anna Muhammadan rasoolulla - Hayya'alas salah - Hayya'alal falah - Allahu Akbar, Allahu Akbar - La ilaha ill Allah.

When Fajr, sunrise prayer was finished, they rolled up their prayer rugs and went to their car trunk. Opening the trunk lid they removed three 5.45 mm Kalashnikov short assault rifles with folding stock and attached 30 round magazine. One extra magazine each and one Kirpan, a type of religious dagger, each. They put the extra magazine and Kirpan down into the small of their back of their blue jeans and let their cotton loose fitting shirt hide the bulge. They rolled their Kalashnikov's in their prayer rugs, closed the trunk, and waited an hour, before they headed to Beech Street, just 50 yards east.

Mustafa Fadhil, Mohammed Atef and Abdul Yasin, were soldiers in the American Muslim Brotherhood, and they didn't come to Hedgehampton just to chauffeur infidels. They had come to Hedgehampton on a mission. The three walked across the park and turned south on Beech Street. They didn't have to go far. The house they were looking for was in the middle of the block, a big Victorian with a black Range Rover parked outside.

They were here to kill a writer, the infidel Jay Fitzpatrick, the little Satan, who wrote the novel *Fear Itself.*

The book, although a novel, had predicted and divulged their organizations plans to cause terror in the United States. Unlike Tom Clancy's 1998 *Debt of Honor,* where Clancy imagines a scenario where a pilot flies his Boeing 747 into the U.S. Capitol, the U.S. government didn't read the novel and did not prevent 9/11. After that oversite all of the government agencies, CIA, FBI, NSA, and now Homeland Security all have people who do nothing but read political thrillers. Not just to see if there is something coming they didn't think of but because they knew terrorists were reading them for ideas. Fitzpatrick's *Fear itself* gave them both, what's coming and ideas. Fortunately, this time, the alphabet agencies and Homeland Security took precautions and foiled several terrorist attempts based on Fitzpatrick's book. But more than that, Fitzpatrick's *Fear Itself* insulted Islam, the Koran, and the American Muslim Brotherhood and for that, he would die.

On 7 January 2015 at about 11:30 local time, two brothers, Saïd and Chérif Kouachi, forced their way into the offices of the French satirical weekly newspaper *Charlie Hebdo* in Paris. Armed with assault rifles and other weapons, they killed 11 people and injured 11 others in the building. *Charlie Hebdo* is a French satirical weekly newspaper that features cartoons, reports, polemics, and jokes. The publication is irreverent and stridently non-conformist in tone, is strongly secularist, anti-religious, and left-wing, publishing, among other things, satirical cartoons of the prophet Muhammad.

Mustafa Fadhil, Mohammed Atef and Abdul Yasin were going to have their "Charlie" party here and now in Hedgehampton. They had cased the house last night and the little Satan, Jay Fitzpatrick, was home.

"Mohammed you go around to the back of the house. Abdul and I will go to the front door," said Mustafa, the leader.

As soon as they entered the driveway, they were completely hidden from the street. The privet that surrounded the house was 12 feet high and the property was very private. The prayer rugs were discarded, and the Kalashnikov's appeared.

Fitzpatrick was, in fact, home, in his 2nd-floor office, working on a new book. His wife left the day before, to go back into the city to run her business. He did, however, have the company of his one-eyed rescue cat, Bowie and his best buddy Lucy, a four-year-old Maltipoo, a cross between a Maltese and a Toy Poodle. Unfortunately for the three Muslims, Fitzpatrick had good security. First and foremost Lucy started to growl. Somebody was coming down the driveway. Lucy didn't alert for normal activities such as the mailman or everyday activities, but when she did, Fitzpatrick always responded. He turned and looked out the back window behind his desk and saw someone walking in his back yard past the pool. He was carrying an assault rifle. Not good. He got up and walked across the hall to look out the front bedroom window, but didn't see anyone. He rushed back to his computer and brought up his four exterior GoPro security cameras, and saw the person moving towards his back door and another man at the front door. Another man hiding around the corner was picked up by the side camera. That man held two AK 47's. This was not good, and Lucy's continued growling confirmed it. His front door bell rang.

Sweeney was about to head off early to work, at the *Hedgehampton Press*, a short walk down Nugent Street. Boom! Crack-Crack-Crack-Crack......... The sounds of weapons being fired in the village. Shotgun reports in the village during duck hunting season was not unusual, but this was not duck hunting season, and these were not the kind of gunshots he ever heard. This was close and ongoing and nothing like in the movies. Crack-Crack-Crack-Crack............. Boom! He pulled his portable police scanner out to see if there was anything on the air. Nothing. He crossed the street and started running towards the gunfire. This was big. He pulled out his cell, dialed 911 and reported shots fired vicinity of the Catholic school and the train station and continued running towards the shots. The village police emergency dispatch operator wanted more information, but Sweeney couldn't run and talk at the same time, so he just kept running with the cell in his hand, still connected.

I hope to god it's not the grade school, thought Sweeney as he rounded the corner.

He was at the school, and another shot erupted. Crack! He moved closer to where the shot came from. He heard some voices then more shots, but from a different type of gun. Pop-Pop-Pop-Pop.........

Much closer now and coming from Beech Street, 25 yards away. He yelled into the phone; Beech and Prospect Ave. Sirens were now coming down Beech Street from Hampton Road and from North Main Street. When he got to the corner, it was completely quiet. No one was around. It was as if nothing happened. He expected to see dead bodies but nothing. But it was real. He could smell the cordite and see smoke. It was coming from behind the hedges. Something bad has happened behind the privet of the corner house. A neighbor appeared from across the street with a cell phone in his ear. He was excitedly talking to the police.

The first patrol car pulled up and skidded to a stop right on the corner where Sweeney and the neighbor, whose name he found out was Charley, were standing. Patrol Officer Susanne Petty got out with her Glock pistol at the ready and motioned Sweeney and Charley to join her behind the patrol car.

"Did either of you see where the gunshots came from?" asked PO Petty.

"I think right in that house," said Sweeney, pointing to the big Victorian house right on the corner.

"Yes, the shots came from Jay's house," said Charley.

"Jay who?" asked PO Petty.

"Jay Fitzpatrick. He lives there. He's a writer and works from home," said Charley.

Sweeney remembered the name, and when Charley put the dots together for him, he said, "Yea. He wrote a book last year about terrorists. I read it. It was pretty good." He then added, "Oh shit."

PO Petty was calling this in when another patrol car pulled up across the street, and an unmarked detective car pulled up right behind Officer Petty's car.

Detective Sgt. Gregg Keghlian got out and got behind Officer Petty's car.

"I monitored your report Petty. Anything new?" asked Detective Keghlian.

"Nothing. But Charley here, and Tom say more than 40 shots were fired and from different weapons. All quiet now except a dog is barking from the house."

"Alright. Let's move in and do it slowly and by the book," said Detective Keghlian.

"Petty you go in through that back gate and I will go in the Beech Street driveway with Officer Cavone." He put it over the radio, so everyone knew what was going down. He didn't want himself and his first responders getting shot by the backup. More patrol cars were pulling up.

He and Officer Jim Cavone entered the front drive while Officer Petty went through the back gate. Sweeney, with his phone now in photo mode, followed Detective Keghlian down the driveway.

CHAPTER 34

HEDGEHAMPTON, NY

Fitzpatrick had gone into fast mode. He went to his bedroom and took out his 1911 Colt 45, from the night stand, chambered a round, clicked the safety on and slipped it into the small of his back. From the closet, he pulled a Mossberg Persuader 12 gauge shotgun w/ pistol grip and pumped in a round. He always kept the doors double locked, to his wife's consternation and admonishment. He told Lucy to sit, which Lucy understood as sit, stop, no barking. It was her 'stop dead' command. He was going to call 911 but didn't want to have a long conversation with a dispatcher right now. He checked the camera monitor once more then went down the back stairs to the kitchen where he could see the one man standing at the door. Fitzpatrick bent down and crawled over to the half glass, half wood kitchen door, positioned the shotgun forward and slowly stood up like he was in an elevator. When they came face to face with the figure on the other side of the door, the man hesitated but brought his weapon around towards Fitzpatrick. Boom! Fitzpatrick's shotgun blast exploded right through the door, blowing a big hole and throwing the door open. The man was gut shot full of lead and wood splinters. He was thrown backward over the porch rail and onto the stone driveway while his Kalashnikov spit out a 30 round blast. Crack-Crack-Crack-Crack..........
The man's finger was stuck on the trigger, and luckily the rounds went up into the portico soffit. Game on. Fitzpatrick went out the open door, off the porch and into the privet. He waited for what he knew was coming.

Mustafa, not knowing what occurred out back, assumed that the little Satan had fired at Mohammed and missed then Mohammed finished him off. That's what Mustafa hoped but couldn't be sure of.

"Go down the drive to the back and see if Mohammed killed him. Be careful but quick. I will go through the house and meet you," whispered Mustafa.

Abdul handed Mustafa the Kalashnikov he was holding for him, then started down the driveway to the back of the house. Mustafa used his Kirpan dagger and his shoulder to pry the front door then the foyer door. Pretty easy work. He stepped through the foyer into the front parlor, and carefully and quietly began to walk towards the back of the house.

Abdul turned the house corner and saw the prone body of Mohammed. He went over and checked for a pulse, assuming the Satan was still inside the house. No pulse. Mohammed was dead. Abdul turned and sprayed the back window and door with a full magazine. He turned away and released the empty magazine and inserted a new magazine and let the receiver fly home chambering a round. Something caught his attention out the corner of his eye. He turned slightly towards the hedgerow and looked directly into the end of Fitzpatrick's shotgun barrel. Boom! Abdul's head exploded.

Two down, thought Fitzpatrick, as he quickly moved from the privet to the side of the house.

Mustafa was now at the same kitchen door that Fitzpatrick had blown through. He surveyed the carnage in the driveway but saw only his dead friends.

Mustafa was prepared to die and even intended to, but not without taking the little Satan with him. He could not fail. He rushed out the open door and vaulted over the porch almost landing on Mohammed. He got up just in time to see the little Satan come from the side of the house. Mustafa fired. Crack! The shot hit Fitzpatrick's shotgun and blew it out of his hands. Mustafa smiled. There was the little Satan not ten feet away with nowhere to hide. "Allahu Akbar," said Mustafa as he pulled the trigger. Nothing. He tried again and still nothing. The magazine must have dislodged when he landed on the ground. Mustafa tossed his rifle to the ground and pulled out his

Kirpan dagger and moved so fast that Fitzpatrick couldn't react. He sliced up and caught Fitzpatrick in the chest, jaw and up the side of his face. Fitzpatrick was badly hurt, but the wound was not too deep. Blood, however, was pouring out of him like water. Mustafa stepped back to regain his balance before he could finish the little Satan off.

"You're good with your knife," said Fitzpatrick, wiping blood from his eye.

Mustafa began circling his prey. "I have been practicing with the holy Kirpan all my life, and today I will use it to cut off your head."

"Is it something I said?" asked Fitzpatrick sarcastically.

Mustafa stepped forward. Fitzpatrick wiped some more blood from his face and said, "You know you should never bring a knife to a gun fight" Mustafa, not quite understanding what the little Satan was saying, lunged forward as Fitzpatrick's left hand came from behind his back holding his Colt 45.

Pop-Pop-Pop-Pop.........

Fitzpatrick emptied the entire 7 round magazine into Mustafa. He was dead before he landed on top of Mohammed's body. Fitzpatrick walked to the portico plinth and leaned back on it. Lucy came running out and jumped up on his lap shaking, crying and licking her Dad's face.

Patrol Officer Susanne Petty with her Glock 19 pistol drawn and out in front, walked past the pool towards the porch and portico. Detective Sgt. Gregg Keghlian and Patrol Officer Jim Cavone similarly armed came down the drive and turned the corner. Detective Keghlian and Patrol Officer Petty were talking to each other, on their portable radios through Bluetooth wireless mics, as they converged simultaneously onto the carnage. By now more village police had arrived and set up a perimeter. Town, state police and ambulances soon filled the surrounding streets. Mayor Early and Police Chief Drumming had just arrived and were being brought up to date. Lt. Suzanne Hurt arrived and was right behind Detective Keghlian and the patrol officers and immediately started issuing orders.

"Secure that man Officer Petty. Officer Cavone, grab some help and thoroughly search the house and grounds. Every inch. What the fuck are you doing in my crime scene Sweeney?" asked Lt. Hurt.

Sweeney had been shooting pictures with his iPhone and had recorded the gunfire.

"I'm the guy who called it in lieutenant, and I was the first one here. This is my story," said Sweeney.

Ignoring Sweeney, Lt. Hurt said, "Jesus Christ, detective, what the fuck happened? Who are these guys? Who is this guy?" pointing to the now hand-cuffed and blood-soaked Fitzpatrick.

Several more patrol officers had made their way back and were now kneeling down and checking the pulses of the two of the downed men. Nobody bothered to check the pulse of the headless man. Everybody began filling everybody in when Officer Cavone came out and announced, "All secure."

Lt. Hurt then told Officer Cavone to let the medics in and to call the coroner's office.

There was blood, bodies, guns and knives all over the back porch and yard.

"They look like Arabs," said Lt. Hurt.

"They are terrorists. Islamic Muslin Terrorists," said Sweeney.

"How the fuck do you know?" asked the lieutenant.

Sweeney steered the medic directly to Fitzpatrick, and the medic got to work cleaning the wounds and stopping the bleeding.

"Uncuff him," said Sweeney.

"You're not on TV now, Mr. Sweeney, and you don't give orders around here," said Lt. Hurt.

"Jesus lieutenant. This is Jay Fitzpatrick. This is his house. He was de-fending himself, can't you see that?" asked Sweeney.

"That's what it looks like lieutenant," said Detective Keghlian. "They tried to take him out, and he fought back. They had the Kalashnikovs, and he had the shotgun and the Colt 45."

The mayor and police chief now came forward.

"I know this guy," said the mayor. "He lives here and complains a lot about the weekend noise."

Officer Cavone had donned evidence gloves and was carefully collecting the Kalashnikovs, and removing the magazines, and checking the chambers.

He then did the same for the smashed shotgun and Colt 45. Reluctantly Lt. Hurt said, "Uncuff him, but keep an eye on him. Detective, get his statement before the medics take him to the hospital. He better have a permit for that shotgun and Colt 45."

Sweeney and Detective Keghlian bent down to Fitzpatrick and started to get his statement. The medics had him stabilized, but he needed stitches. They wanted to get him to the hospital, but that would have to wait.

Sweeney thanked his lucky stars that Todd went to Moscow alone. He now had a huge story, and he was part of it. Hedgehampton was looking better. He pressed Todd's number on speed dial and waited for him to pick up.

Boy, will he be pissed, thought Sweeney.

CHAPTER 35

MOSCOW, ME

Colburn and Natasha gave Faith a tour of the cabin and a little more history about its origin and renovation.

"It's only 4 p.m., plenty of time for a hike. Why don't you freshen up and meet us outside when you're ready? Boots or running shoes would be a good idea."

Natasha and Colburn went outside. Colburn sat on a step and put on a pair of Timberland boots.

"What do you say, girl? Want to climb the mountain?"

Natasha just looked at him and slightly tilted her head.

"Yea, you're right. By the time we get to the top, it would be almost dark, and we would be stumbling back down. How about a short lake hike?"

Natasha's bark and animation confirmed the lake hike as the way to go.

The cabin door opened, and Faith came down the steps. Colburn thought she looked gorgeous in jeans, sweater and New Balance running shoes, someone you could take anywhere.

"OK! Where are we going? Oh, and one thing, I don't like snakes," said Faith.

"Nobody likes snakes but with Natasha as our vedette, scouting out in front, we won't have to worry. Besides, Maine doesn't have any venomous snakes. The Timber Rattlesnake hasn't been seen in years. I have yet to see any snakes," lied Colburn.

It was well into fall, and the leaves were colorful and beautiful. The path along the lake was pretty flat and would take then a little over an hour and a half to complete the 4-mile hike. Natasha led the way but sometimes disappeared onto the scent of something or another. When they got back to the cabin, it was nearly 6 p.m.

"That was a perfect hike after being in the car for four hours," said Faith.

"How about a glass of Champagne on the deck, before we start thinking about dinner?"

"Perfect."

Da happy, Faith happy, Natasha happy.

No story here, Mr. Todd. The chief and I were just agreeing on that," said SAC Ceretti.

"And you are?" asked Todd.

"SAC Ceretti and this is Agent Ross of the FBI."

Agent Ceretti looked like an FBI agent right out of central casting. Dark suit, dark tie, and dark sunglasses, thought Todd. *While Agent Ross looked like a movie star in a well fitted black suit and blue silk blouse. No sunglasses but beautiful hazel eyes.*

"Agent Ceretti. Agent Ross. If there is no story, why is the FBI up here in Moscow Maine telling me there's no story? There was no unauthorized helicopter landing out in the woods? No visit by President Burk? No wolves howling at night? The Bangor FBI didn't swoop in here, onto the school parking lot, and take a Mr. Israel Colburn and his dog off to an undisclosed location? Everything reported by that local TV news show is bogus? Is that what you want me to believe?" asked Todd.

"I'll give you the wolves Mr. Todd, but the rest just didn't happen. And my advice to you is to let it go," said Agent Ceretti.

With that, Chief Pruitt turned and walked away.

"Chief," said Todd, but the chief kept walking away. When Todd turned back, both the agents were walking back to their Suburban.

Todd was now standing there alone. He looked across the street, and there was a young boy looking at him. Boys sometimes know what they're there not supposed to know. Todd reacted the way any reporter would when you're told there is no story. He crossed the street to the boy, to try and find one.

"Hi. I'm Ron Todd with the *NY Post* newspaper."

"I know who you are. I watch television. You're the older, shorter one," said Timmy Logan.

"Yes that's right, and you are?"

"Timmy Logan. My dad's the mayor."

"I'm sure he is Timmy. Both the chief and the FBI said I'm barking up the wrong tree, cause there ain't no story here. Are they right Timmy?"

Chief Pruitt watched the encounter between the reporter and Timmy but didn't intervene. *Out of the mouth of babes…,* thought the chief.

Back in the cabin, Colburn and Faith had finished off the good part of a bottle of champagne and were back in the kitchen prepping for dinner. Colburn would be the chef and Faith would be the sous-chef de cuisine – under chef. They would start with the Caesar salad, then the main course of Colburn's creation, spicy blackened tuna.

In an aluminum foil pouch, the tuna steak is dipped in olive oil and marinated in Cholula Hot Sauce. Before it goes on the grill, Chef Paul's Blackened Redfish Magic is amply applied on both sides. The tuna is quickly seared on both sides for two minutes each side, then put back in the aluminum pouch, and closed off, at the top, like a cone. The tuna and sauce continue to cook for another five minutes. What comes out is a delicious spicy blackened tuna steak, seared on the outside and pink inside, with a tasty sauce poured on top.

They also had to make home fries, from the Palm Restaurant recipe, so they had their work cut out for them. Colburn lit the fire, and the preparation and fun began. They were starting to get to know each other, really like each other, and feeling more comfortable together. As the night progressed, they booth hoped it would end in bed, together.

Moscow, Maine is a small town, a very small town. So when you see a grown man and a 12-year-old boy sitting in the schoolyard, on opposite sides of a picnic table, it is a teacher and a student, or it's something else. Chief Pruitt

had told the mayor, who was also Timmy's father, what had transpired between himself, the FBI and Mr. Todd. He said that Mr. Todd was now talking to Timmy and that that may be a good idea. The FBI wouldn't go after a
12-year-old, would they?

"Timmy, that's a remarkable story," said Todd.

Todd had his tape recorder on the table top and recorded the whole story
as Timmy told it. He told of his meeting with Colburn and Natasha. How
they were both really nice, not the mercenary and wolf everyone thought.
How they hiked the mountain together and found the wolf's lair. About the
helicopter, the President, and the howling at the moon. How the FBI came
in in a helicopter and swooped Mr. Colburn and Natasha away, and about the
chief's argument with the lady FBI Agent. Timmy told him everything. The
same as he told the TV reporter last week.

"Will Chief Pruitt and your dad back your story up?"

"They will if they're allowed, but I listened to the conversation between
the FBI agents and Chief Pruitt before you got here. The agent told Chief
Pruitt that Mr. Colburn was cooperating with the FBI on an operation, and
he wanted to make sure that the chief got the message."

I should hire this kid as a cub reporter. Smart kid. What could he be, 12? thought
Todd.

"And what was that message?" asked Todd.

"Just what he told you. There is no story, but if there were, it's now over."

"I heard the chief say that Colburn is in town. How do I get to his house?
Can you show me?"

Just then Todd's phone rang. It was Sweeney. *Boy is he gonna be pissed when I
tell him that the Dragon Lady story is not over and that we might have a roadshow revival,
right here in Moscow Maine,* thought Todd.

CHAPTER 36

MOSCOW, ME

Colburn was awake early and stood above his bed looking down at her. She was still sleeping but was beginning to stir. *Faith looked beautiful*, he thought. Her head, shoulders and one leg, almost up to her hip, were all that was exposed from under the cover. Her skin color and long golden hair complimented the silver bed cover. It looked like a posed photo shoot for *Vanity Fair.*

Natasha had slept, the night before, by the fireplace while her Da and the women made love in the bedroom. It was now morning, and she was again next to her Da, staring at the women in the bed.

Colburn began to turn away.

"Good morning," she whispered.

He turned back. "Did I wake you?"

"No. I've been awake for a few minutes but just didn't want to open my eyes."

She turned and pulled the cover up to above her shoulder and propped herself up on her elbows.

"I didn't want it to end," she continued. "Last night was the most wonderful night of my life. It was three stars."

"The dinner was that good?"

"The dinner was fabulous. The Caesar salad surpassed that of the restaurant. The hot spicy tuna recipe, well, I intend to have it published. The three stars were for the dinner and the sex. I have never thought it possible for a man to make love to a woman like that. You were amazing."

"Only three stars?" asked Colburn.

"Yes silly. Michelin only gives out three stars."

"One star: is a good place to stop on your journey, Two stars: is worth a detour, Three Stars: is worth a special journey, and that's what this was. The dinner and you were worth that special journey."

"I hope you don't intend to publish that part."

"No, but if *Harlequin* comes knocking someday, I'll be ready."

"I better put some coffee on, or we may never leave the bedroom," said Colburn as he leaned over and kissed her.

She grabbed him and pulled him down into the bed. Faith pulled him close and embraced him, and they began rolling around on the bed. Natasha, not sure how to react, decided her Da was not in trouble and left the bedroom for the kitchen. Close enough if her instincts were wrong.

Ron Todd put Tom Sweeney's call on speaker, and neither could get a word in edgewise as they both thought the other's story could wait. Finally, Todd said, "OK, OK, Tom. Go ahead; it's your nickel."

Tom Sweeney told the unbelievable story about the terrorists and their assassination attempt on Fitzpatrick, a local Hedgehampton author.

"When did this happen?"

"Just an hour or so ago. I'm the only one on it. *CNN* and *FOX* are on the way out. My paper put it out on the wire, and they are getting swamped with calls from all over, including Paris. This is going to be another *Charlie Hebdo*. You've got to get back here."

Todd knew Sweeney's story trumped his, but what is happening in Moscow, Maine ain't chicken liver.

"You've got a big story there kid, but I can't come back now. Something big is happening here, and my gut says to stick with it. You file your story with the *Hedgehampton Press* and then send it to the *Post* as a bi-line. I'll tell them to expect it, and don't talk to anyone, not newspaper reporters or *Le Monde*. Not *CNN* or *FOX*. Let them go to the police, but get your contact, what's his name, Detective Keghlian to stonewall. This is your story. You not only got it, you're in it. Don't let it go. I'll be back tomorrow morning," said Todd as he touched off.

Todd turned back to Timmy, who had been standing there listening to Mr. Todd's unbelievable conversation.

"So where's this Colburn guy live?" asked Todd.

Not sure yet about Mr. Todd's motives or loyalties, Timmy was not going to help him find his friend Colburn. He knew Mr. Todd, being a big city reporter, would eventually find Mr. Colburn, but it won't be with his help.

Timmy pointed north and said, "By the lake. I only know how to get there through the woods, but my dad doesn't want me going into the woods." *Kind of true*, thought Timmy. *But his dad had not forbidden him to go in the woods.*

"There's only one road north. How far could it be?" asked Todd.

"Never drove sir, but the last time I hiked through the woods, it took me almost 4 hours." *Not quite a lie, nor exactly the truth*, thought Timmy.

It was still early when Colburn and Faith made it out of the bedroom and into the kitchen. Faith walked out on the deck and joined Natasha, who was looking down towards the lake.

"What do you see Natasha?" asked Faith.

"She's focused on that tall tree over there. See the Red-Tailed Hawk at the top?" said Colburn as he joined them.

"I think I see the hawk."

He handed her the binoculars, and she began to focus.

"Listen."

As if on cue, the hawk screamed, catapulted out of the tree, and swooped down to the lake at an amazing speed.

Natasha, Faith, and Colburn followed its flight as the hawk gripped a snake in its talon's then flew skyward towards its nest. In less than ten seconds the hawk and the snake were gone.

"That was impressive. It's like watching *Wild Kingdom* live from your deck, but I thought you said there were no snakes," said Faith.

"I said there were no venomous snakes," said Colburn.

"That looked like a rattlesnake to me," said Faith.

"Well, we'll just have to take your word for it. You have the binoculars, but if you're right, then we should thank that hawk for ridding Maine of the last rattlesnake."

"Hmmm," said Faith.

"Let's have breakfast, then we'll hike to the top of Wolf Mountain," said Colburn.

On hearing that, Natasha excitedly started wagging her tail and shaking her bottom.

"Well one of my girls is excited about going," said Colburn.

Faith started shaking her bottom, emulating Natasha.

"I think both your girls want to go," said Faith.

CHAPTER 37

WASHINGTON, DC

*B*eing President of *the United States was like being in combat,* thought President Burk. *Hours of endless tedious meetings interrupted by moments of sheer terror.*

Today was a perfect example of a typical day running the nation. He started out with security briefings, staff meetings, and then cabinet meetings, phone calls with world leaders, meetings with congressmen, lobbyist, and governors. And countless other responsibilities, he dreaded, throughout the day. Until....

Until he saw the look on Kelly's face when she entered the Oval Office.

"Turn on *CNN*," said Kelly.

He did, and they both stood there speechless as a reporter was describing events unfolding in Hedgehampton, NY. Crawling across the screen's bottom, the text told the story. Islamic Terrorist bring French *Charlie Hebdo* terror to the Hamptons.

FBI Director Riley, followed by Chief of Staff, Bill Nicholas, and Secretary of Defense, Ed Stanton, entered the office and fell in behind the President and Press Secretary Kelly Sullivan.

They listened as the *CNN* reporter described the scene and the carnage. Reporting was sketchy at best, but what was known is that three alleged terrorists tried to assassinate a Hedgehampton writer. Then the camera man panned, and there was Tom Sweeney, on the other side of the yellow crime scene tape, talking with the police.

"Oh shit," said FBI Director Riley.

"You know I'm getting tired of hearing that. I thought things would quiet down here after the Dragon Lady sang," said President Burk.

"You think this is Vova?" asked Secretary of Defense, Ed Stanton.

"Hell, Sweeney's there. He and Todd have been 'First Reporters' since the VP's murder. And based on Colburn's call. Yea, I think it's Vova. Colburn said this Vova character was still in the game, but instead of killing bad people, he would now start killing good people. He said he even had a list. This writer could have been the first name on the list," said the President.

"Yea, but they didn't get him. That's not like Vova. That's not his style. Sending in a bunch of amateurs and fucking it up," said FBI Director Riley. "I've got ADC Hoar and his team on the way and expect a report any minute."

The *CNN* reporter was now holding the mic over the yellow police tape yelling a question at Sweeney. Sweeney came over and said, "All I can tell you now is the FBI has taken over, and they're treating this as a terrorist attack. Everything from here on out will go through them. I can say that the intended victim was a writer who lives here in Hedgehampton."

"Can you give us the writer's name?"

"Jay Fitzpatrick, and that's all I'm going to say for now."

"Fitzpatrick! That's got to be the guy who wrote the novel about us and the NYC bombings," said Riley.

Kelly was Googling Fitzpatrick, and when she got something she said. "He's the writer for God's sake. That's him. He lives in Hedgehampton, and he's the guy that wrote *Fear Itself*."

"That's the guy? Fitzpatrick? Now it's starting to make sense. I read the novel. Hell, it was loosely based on what happened to us, and the terrorist attack on NYC, and the dirty bombs," said FBI Director Riley. "It was about fake dirty bombs in NYC and terrorists setting fires in our national forest, trying to burn down the country. It was the American Muslim Brotherhood. This could be an isolated lone wolf pack attack by the AMB and not Vova at all."

CHAPTER 38

MOSCOW, ME

Faith, Colburn, and Natasha started up the west side of Wolf Mountain. As before the hike up and back down Wolf Mountain was about 14.5 K or 9 miles. Colburn packed some snacks, water, and his Colt 45 into his backpack, and off they went. It would take about 2 hours up, an hour exploring then another hour plus down.

Ron Todd was determined to get a story, especially after hearing the sensational scoop, Sweeney fell into back in Hedgehampton. Maybe people were getting tired of the Dragon Lady, but Todd felt a big encore coming. After a late breakfast at a local café, he drove north and saw a small white church, with a typical steeple. Its bones looked late 18th century but its skin a bit younger. He parked out front and went inside. He needed a form of guidance, and where better to get it than a church. By the pulpit, he found his source.

"Good morning reverend," said Todd.

"It's pastor, but good morning to you," said Pastor Buffer.

Todd walked forward, past the white wood pews that looked like they were original. He offered his hand and introduced himself.

"I know who you are Mr. Todd. I am Pastor Buffer, and I know why you're here," said the pastor.

"And why would that be, pastor?"

"You're here to find someone. Either the Savior or Mr. Colburn. I suspect it's Mr. Colburn for whom you search."

"Very good pastor. You either had divine intervention, or the chief has you on speed dial.

"Touché, Mr. Todd."

"I have GPS, so if you can give me his address, I can find him," said Todd.

"Are you sure, Mr. Todd?"

"Yes, I'm sure. It came with the rental. I used it to get here to Podunk."

"Well, in that case, his address is, 'The Old Colburn Cabin'," said the pastor as he walked away.

That's what you get for being a smartass, thought Todd.

Todd got back in his car and drove out of town heading north. With the town behind him, the road became very curvy with the forest coming right up to the road. Soon he started to descend and about 1.5 miles out from the town he saw a lake on his left. He slowed down and started looking for driveways or access roads on the left. After another mile of curves and ups and downs, he came to a driveway and turned into it.

Immediately after Todd left, Timmy hightailed it into the woods towards Mr. Colburn's cabin. He had to warn him that a reporter was on to what had happened and that the reporter knew about the President and the helicopters from the TV news report and his telling. He had to warn him that the reporter was coming to get a story. Luckily he made it to the cabin in less than an hour, but it was too late. They were gone. Not gone gone, because Mr. Colburn's black Range Rover was still there, but gone out for a walk or a hike. Timmy guessed they went on a hike, and he knew where. He started running east up the west slope of Wolf Mountain.

Todd pulled down the long gravel driveway that seemed to go on forever. But then he turned the corner saw a big black Range Rover. *Bingo*, he thought. Aside from the Range Rover the cabin was deserted. He looked inside and saw signs of life, but nobody was home. He decided to take a walk down by the lake, and if he couldn't find Colburn there, he would just sit on the stoop till he showed up.

Colburn, Faith, and Natasha were almost to the top of Wolf Mountain. Faith never lagged behind but kept up, and even pushed ahead, disregarding Colburn's suggestion to take a break. They came to a deer carcass that was only a few days old. They smelled it first. It was not pleasant. It was a large buck. Only four animals could bring this guy down: a mountain lion, bear, wolf, or man. Since the rack was still attached, and a six-pointer, that ruled out man. Men like trophies. Probably wolves. They continued up the mountain with Natasha on the flank and sometimes way up ahead.

"Where's Natasha?" asked Faith.

"She's out in front on the scent of something; I should think."

"What if she gets separated from us? Could she get lost?"

"I don't think we have to worry about Natasha getting lost. This is her environment. She instinctively knows where we are, and her senses are so that she can hear us and smell us miles away."

When they got to the top of Wolf Mountain Natasha was sitting there waiting for them. Colburn showed Faith the wolves' lair that he Natasha and Timmy found and explored the last time on the mountain. It had been recently used, and Colburn suspected Natasha had run ahead to pay her respects before the pack would flee at the sound of humans fumbling up the mountain.

"Did you see them, girl? Did they remember you?"

Natasha just looked at her Da and tilted her head.

"Of course, you did girl; that's why you ran ahead. You wanted to see your kinsfolks before we spooked them.

Natasha alerted, and Colburn turned expecting to see a pack of wolves circling. To his surprise, it was Timmy, and he was running up the clearing and seemed in a hurry and distressed.

"Whoa, Timmy. Slow down. Where's the fire?"

This must be the little boy Israel was telling me about, thought Faith.

Timmy seemed, for a second, a bit taken back at seeing a woman on the top of the mountain. He recovered quickly and said, "Mr. Colburn, I'm sorry to bother you again, but there's a reporter in town asking questions about you. He's headed for the cabin."

Colburn's brain registered instant comprehension. No need to ask clarification or more detail from Timmy, and he didn't want to upset Faith.

"Thanks for the heads up Timmy. It's Mr. Todd from the *New York Post,* and I have been expecting him," said Colburn.

Colburn introduced Timmy to Faith and then Timmy made a fuss over Natasha, which she returned in spades.

After Colburn, Faith, Timmy and Natasha had explored the mountain top and the wolves' lair, at a distance, Colburn picked up his pack, and they started their decent back to the cabin. Timmy had been checking Faith out and said, "You're someone famous aren't you?"

"I'm a singer, and I've been on TV. You may have seen me there."

"Yea. I know who you are, but you're more famous than that. My dad has several of your cd's, and we listen to them in the car. You're pretty good, and you're beautiful in person."

"Well thank you, Timmy. You're a charmer."

A little over an hour and they were down the mountain. Always faster going down than up. Natasha, way ahead, was barking wildly as Colburn and company turned the corner, saw Todd's car, and saw that Natasha had Todd cornered on the porch.

"Natasha nein! Out!" yelled Colburn.

Natasha backed away; then Colburn told her to sit.

Faith and Timmy stood behind Colburn watching.

Todd slipped his iPhone into his pocket as Colburn approached.

"Where's Woodward?" asked Colburn.

"And good afternoon to you. Mr. Colburn." He looked past Colburn, to Timmy and said, "Et tu Brutus." Timmy looked a bit sheepish and moved behind Faith.

Todd moved forward but was stopped by Natasha, who was now up and growling. This time, Colburn did not stop her.

"Mr. Todd, Natasha doesn't like fast moves or fast movers, so I recommend you ask her permission and not think you can beg her forgiveness."

"Yes. Well, I just happened to be in the neighborhood and thought I would pay a visit."

"Very neighborly of you Mr. Todd." Colburn turned back to Faith and Timmy and said, "Why don't the both of you go inside and make some ice tea while I finish up with Mr. Todd?"

After they went inside, Colburn could see them both peeking back out the windows. Natasha remained by Colburn's side, on alert.

"OK, Mr. Todd. You've got five minutes. What do you want?"

"Was that Faith Knoll?"

"Four minutes said," Colburn.

"OK. OK," said Todd, holding his palms up in surrender. "Perhaps we started off on the wrong foot. I'm following up a lead on the Dragon Lady murders, and it leads here to you and Moscow, Maine. Would you like to comment?"

"No."

Your voice sounds very familiar Mr. Colburn. Have we met before? I usually don't forget a face or a voice."

"We have never met. Three minutes."

"Mr. Colburn. There are reports from a local TV station, and from the police chief that a helicopter landed here at your cabin recently, and its passenger was POTUS. Further reports state that the next day, the FBI choppered into town and swooped you and your dog away. I smell a story."

"There is no story, Mr. Todd."

"Funny you say that. I have been told there's no story so many times today I'm starting to believe it. Not! Look, two FBI agents, Agents Ceretti, and Ross told me earlier today that there's no story, and now you tell me there is no story. Why am I having a hard time believing you guys?"

"Two minutes."

Todd's cell rang. He took out his phone and saw it was an unlisted number. He answered it anyway. That's how reporters stumble onto tips. "Hello, this is Todd." A pause then, "OK I'll be there in 30 minutes."

"One minute," said Colburn.

"OK, Mr. Colburn, I get it. I'll let you go for now. There is a story here, and you're up to your eyeballs in it. If you know me, you know I won't let it go until I get the story. And by the way, since you asked about my partner, Woodward, aka Sweeney, he's a bit busy now. He is, like you, up to his eyeballs in a big story. Only his is in Hedgehampton. You might want turn on your TV."

Todd got in his car and headed out the driveway and back towards town. When he got to the main road, he pulled over and stopped. He pulled out his iPhone, turned it on, unlocked it, and touched his photo icon. He got the shot. Actually, he got three shots. One of the dog snarling at him. One of Colburn and one with Colburn, the woman, the kid and the dog. A family portrait.

His voice is so familiar, thought Todd.

He drove to the post office in Bingham, the big town just about a mile south of Moscow. The caller, who would not give her name, said an envelope would be waiting for him at the Bingham Post Office. He entered the post office, and as he expected it was a one man, one window show.

"Good afternoon. Do you have a letter for a Mr. Todd?"

The clerk didn't ask for any identification he just reached over to the side shelf picked up a letter and handed it to Todd.

"By the way, do you remember who dropped the letter off?"

"I do," said the postal clerk.

Todd waited, but nothing more came.

"Can you tell me who it was?"

"No. I don't know who it was."

"I thought you said you knew who dropped the letter off."

"No. You asked me if I remembered who dropped the letter off, and I said yes."

"Can you tell me who you remember?"

"I can. It was a woman."

That much Todd knew from the phone call.

"Anything special about the woman that you can remember?"

"She was black and blue," said the clerk.

"Black and blue?"

"Black suit. Blue blouse. Black skin. Bluish eyes. She was definitely black and blue," said the clerk.

Todd thanked the clerk and went over to the counter and opened the letter and read it. It was printed and not signed.

Mr. Todd,

I followed your *Post* stories on the Dragon Lady and admired your reporting persistence and tenacity. I'm not sure how Mr. Colburn fits into that puzzle or if he fits at all, but the man you saw today, once lived in the shadows and may still live there. You will not find him in any newspaper archive, Goggle, or on Wikipedia, but his nom de guerre is Icy. Keep looking. I think you have a big story here in Moscow.

His nom de guerre is Icy. An assumed name under which a person engages in combat or some other nefarious activity or enterprise. Humm, thought Todd. *I thought it was Agent Ross's voice on the phone. Could that be where I recognize Colburn's aka Icy's voice? From a phone call? And the beautiful Agent Ross is my Deep Throat. What a lovely optic.*

CHAPTER 39

MOSCOW, ME

Faith and Natasha were out on the deck searching for pesky squirrels. Inside the cabin, Colburn asked Timmy to stay for dinner.

"Thank you, Mr. Colburn, but my dad will be looking for me. I better get going."

Timmy. Can I ask a big favor?"

"Sure, Mr. Colburn."

"Don't tell anyone who Faith is or that she was here. She's pretty famous, and if word gets out that she was here with me, I may not be able to ask her up here again."

"Her identity is safe with me."

"Thanks, Timmy. Now go out and say goodbye to Faith and Natasha. We'll be leaving early tomorrow for Boston."

While Timmy, Faith, and Natasha were saying goodbye, Colburn got on his satellite phone and touched onto *FOX News*. Sure enough, there was background tape showing Sweeney and an FBI Agent, walking through what looked like a crime scene. The studio anchorman was providing narrative which sounded unbelievable. American Muslim Brotherhood assassins in Hedgehampton, NY going after a writer. Drawing comparisons with the Paris *Charlie Hebdo* terror.

The reporter said "If you haven't seen it, we have an exclusive interview, originally aired earlier today, between the author of *Fear Itself,* Jay Fitzpatrick, the intended target of the Islamic terrorist assassins, and our own *NY Post* contributing reporter, Tom Sweeney."

They were sitting on a front porch in a pair of wicker chairs facing each other, a table in-between. On the table were a bottle of water and a copy of Fitzpatrick's book, *Fear Itself*. The porch had a blue-grey stained wood deck, a white bead & board soffit, white wood picket railing, and a red cedar shake wall as background. A typical Hampton porch. Fitzpatrick's face had stitches from his jaw up to his forehead, now covered with gauze, and his right hand was bandaged. Other than that he looked like typical Hamptonian. Blue blazer with white pocket square. White button down shirt, khakis, and Top-Siders. No story here folks.

"Mr. Fitzpatrick, thank you for letting us into your home today. The damage to your home and person is extensive. How are you holding up?" asked Sweeney.

"Still in a bit of a shock, but keeping calm and carrying on."

"What do you think about the comparisons being made between what happened here and in Paris, with *Charlie Hebdo?*"

"The comparison is fair and eerily similar. On January 2015, two Islamist gunmen forced their way into the Paris headquarters of *Charlie Hebdo* and opened fire, killing eleven, including two police officers and wounding another eleven. In my case, there were three Islamist gunmen, and they died. I'm still standing. During both attacks, the gunmen shouted *"Allahu akbar"*. In Paris, they were French Muslim brothers and were professionals. Here they were part of the American Muslim Brotherhood and were amateurs. *Charlie Hebdo* published a cartoon about Mohamad and Saïd Kouachi and Chérif Kouachi couldn't take a joke. I wrote a novel loosely based on a real terrorist attack against NYC and America, by Muslim terrorists. Even thought it was a novel, most of it was based on true events. It happened. My "Three Stooges" couldn't handle the truth."

"Aren't you worried that inflammatory comments like that will only incite additional attacks against you?"

"It works both ways. They burn our flag, cut off Christian's heads, denigrate our spiritual leaders, yet they can't take the bounce back. If they come, they come. We all have to die sometime."

"Do you think they will come again?"

"After the release of my next book, *Best Served Icy*, they just might."

"Is that more of the same? A sequel to *Fear Itself*?"

"Yes and also based on current events with a horrific ending."

"Can you give us a clue?"

"Let's just say that when the President of the United States is faced with no alternative and makes the call "Cry 'Havoc!', and let slip the dogs of war," there will be no turning back. What happens next will shake the world. The Great Satan, America, will shock and put the Fear of God into ISIS and Islamic Terrorists throughout the world."

"Can't wait to read it. How's *Fear Itself* doing?"

"As Lao Tzu once said, "New beginnings are often disguised as painful endings." *Fear itself* is, because of what happened here, flying off the shelves. Number one on *Amazon*."

Colburn couldn't take anymore. He heard enough. Was this Fitzpatrick character writing about him? Icy? Where did he get this? He touched the hang-up icon, then touched the Presidents speed dial number and waited. Faith came back in and said, "Is everything all right? Why don't you come on out on the deck with us?"

"Got to make a call. I'll be out in a minute. Why don't you start thinking about dinner?"

The President took the call.

"Icy. What's up?"

"Did you see Sweeney's interview with this Fitzpatrick guy?"

"Yea, do you think Vova's involved with this attack?"

"No. But did you catch the name of his next book?"

"I did."

"*Best Served Icy*? Do you think it's about me?"

"The thought crossed my mind, but how could this Fitzpatrick guy know?"

"Sweeney and Todd. That's how. Todd tracked me down at the cabin, and I think he recognized my voice from the phone tips I gave him."

"I think we need to have a barber chair discussion with Sweeney Todd. Let me sort this out and get back to you."

Colburn lit the fire and took a seat by the brass fender. Faith came over with two glasses of champagne and Natasha joined them. As they watched the fire, each knew that it would all soon come to an end, and each knew something was bothering the other.

"Israel. I received an email from my agent. They want me in Los Angeles tomorrow. They will have a jet waiting for me at Hanscom Airport outside of Bedford. Do you know it?"

"It's right off 95 and on the way back to Boston. What time?"

"They want to leave by 11 a.m. Is that alright?"

"Sure. We'll leave here tomorrow morning at 7 a.m. and get there in plenty of time, but tonight let's enjoy our last night. Champagne, a good dinner, and we'll make love and have great s….."

He let it trail off, but Faith understood and couldn't resist the needle.

"Can't say the 'S' word in front of Natasha?"

Natasha looked at her Da and tilted her head. She had been getting along with Faith like they were old friends. *Would she accept Faith into the pack*, thought Colburn.

Da safe, Faith safe, Natasha safe, Pack safe, thought Natasha.

The night went according to script, fire, drinks, music, dinner and then to bed. Natasha wanted to hunt so Colburn let her out. Faith and Colburn made wonderful love and stayed up long into the night. Around midnight just as they were starting to fall asleep they heard the wolves howling. Faith set up on her elbows and said, "Is that the wolf pack?"

"Yes."

"Is Natasha safe?"

Just then howling came from close to the cabin and chorused in with the howling coming from the mountain.

"Yea. She's home."

The next morning they were up by 6 a.m. and packing. Faith finished first and hit the shower. Colburn let Natasha out to do her business and put the coffee on. After Colburn had showered, they had toasted bagels with butter and cream cheese. Natasha had left over surf and turf - tuna and steak.

They drove non-stop through Moscow and Bingham, keeping well within the speed limits. One pit stop for fuel right off 95 then straight down to Hanscom Airport, in Medford, MA. Hanscom is mainly a general aviation airport, the largest in New England. Both runways can accommodate jets, and that's what was waiting for Faith, a silver Gulfstream V. Colburn drove right up to the VIP terminal. All three got out, and a flight attendant came over and took Faith's overnight bag to load on the jet. Faith would not be flying alone. Her administrative assistant, introduced as Kathy Rand, came over and informed Faith that her travel suitcase was previously picked up and was already on board, and all her paperwork was in order. She handed Faith a piece of paper which appeared to be an itinerary and said, "We're ready when you are."

Faith said a warm goodbye to Natasha, and Colburn could tell that Natasha didn't want her to go. Colburn and Faith said their goodbyes and sealed it with a kiss. She told Colburn what a wonderful time she had and was looking forward to more visits. He missed her already. She walked up the jets steps and turned to wave and said, "I'll call you guys in a couple of days. Stay out of trouble."

He watched her jet take off, then he and Natasha got back in the Range Rover, turned east, and headed home to Cambridge.

CHAPTER 40

Moscow, RUSSIA

Colonel Dmitri Vova thought long and hard about this alliance. Even he was nervous and disgusted in their individual presences and to have them all together in one room terrified him. They were throwbacks to another time of tents, camels, robes and daggers. With his and their bodyguards relegated to Vova's outer office, the three men, and three interpreters sat on pillows placed on the floor while Vova sat on a stool facing them.

Abu Bakr al-Baghdadi, a Sunni Iraqi and leader of ISIL, the Islamic militant organization known as the Islamic State of Iraq and the Lavant, located in western Iraq, Libya, northeast Nigeria, and Syria. He controls all of ISIL and he refers to his organization as 'The Islamic State.'

Ayman Mohammed Rabie al-Zawahiri, an Egyptian and leader of al-Qaeda which had orchestrated and carried out attacks in North America, Asia, Africa, and the Middle East. In 2012, he called on Muslims to kidnap Western tourists in Muslim countries.

Mullah Akhtar Mohammad Mansour, leader of the Taliban. The Taliban is an Islamic fundamentalist political movement in Afghanistan currently waging war within that country. The Taliban has been condemned internationally for their enforcement of Islamic Sharia law.

The meeting was secret, and only a handful of Vova's trusted staff and President Vladimir Vladimirovich Putin knew who was here and why. No phone calls or emails were used to set up the meeting. Everything was communicated by word of mouth and by trusted couriers. Each leader was flown to Moscow in an unmarked Russian military transport, separately with a minimum of personal security and would return home the same way. If the Americans knew all four men were meeting in one room at the same time, in Moscow, Russia, they would drop their newest and largest 30,000-pound Massive Ordnance Penetrator Bomb. Then beg forgiveness.

Tea was served, and smoking was permitted. Luckily, the cigarette smoke disguised the three leaders' horrible body odors. The meeting only lasted an hour. *Thank God,* thought Vova. The tension in the room was as thick as the smoke, and Vova prayed he could hold it together until he got what he wanted. These three were sociopaths without a shred of conscience. He did get what he wanted, but it cost him a lot in, armament and munitions, money in their private accounts in Switzerland, and money in their terrorist coffers. Each deal was proposed and accepted separately but all for the common good - destroy the great American Satan. A win-win for all four players.

Smart and ideology driven, they were also just men, and all men are just boys at heart. Boys will be boys when no one is watching. After the meeting all three would be tempted, separately of course, to the finest Mother Russia had to offer, gorgeous women, young girls or young boys, gambling and booze. Vova, after all his years fighting them in Afghanistan, knew how these holy men like to play. All their dalliances would be recorded and filed away for a rainy day.

After they had left, Vova had the offices, bathrooms and hallways fumigated and scrubbed clean. He had the interpreters killed. He then left the building, refusing to return for a week. He first went to Putin to tell him personally what transpired, what to expect, and when to expect it. Putin, skeptical, but supportive, decided to give Vova this last chance to amaze, or he would be replaced. In Russia that meant early retirement to Black Dauphin Prison, where prisoners are kept bent over at the waist, their handcuffed hands stretched up behind their back, higher than their hips. This stress position allows for maximum control over the inmate while depriving the inmate a view of their surroundings as well as preventing them from escaping and attacking prison staff. While there have been rumors of inmate abuse and misconduct at Black Dolphin Prison, there are no confirmed reports or complaints.

It took Vova several weeks to get over losing Kim Ly. She was one of his favorites, and Colburn killed her and tried to cover it up as a suicide. Vova was now circling looking for Colburn's weak link. He would find it, of course. He always did. For now, Vova and his new lady friend decided to spend a few days at his dacha in Yeysk on the Sea of Azov. His new lady, Hoàng Thùy Linh, is a beautiful Vietnamese actress and singer. She was well-known for her sex scandals, for which she has been compared to Paris Hilton. Vova could always spot talent. He didn't know yet if Hoang could become an operative on the level of Kim Ly, but for this weekend, that's not the kind of operative he needed.

CHAPTER 41

NEW YORK, NY

New York Post front page headline read:

Je suis Fitzy
by Ron Todd and Tom Sweeney

On 7 January 2015 at about 11:30 local time, two brothers, Saïd and Chérif Kouachi, forced their way into the offices of the French satirical weekly newspaper *Charlie Hebdo* in Paris. Armed with assault rifles and other weapons, they killed 11 people and injured 11 others in the building. After leaving, they killed a French National Police officer outside the building. The gunmen identified themselves as belonging to the Islamist terrorist group Al-Qaeda's branch in Yemen, who took responsibility for the attack.

On 17 October 2016 at about 8 a.m. local time, three Islamist terrorists, Mustafa Fadhil, Mohammed Atef and Abdul Yasin, soldiers in the American Muslim Brotherhood, forced their way into the home-offices of an American novelist in Hedgehampton NY. Armed with assault rifles and other weapons, they were there to kill a writer, the infidel Jay Fitzpatrick, the little Satan, who wrote the novel *Fear Itself.*

The book, although a novel, had predicted and divulged their plans to cause terror in the United States. Unlike Tom Clancy's 1998 *Debt of Honor*, where Clancy imagines a scenario where a pilot flies his Boeing 747 into the U.S. Capitol, the U.S. government didn't read the novel and did not prevent 9/11. After that oversite all of the government agencies, CIA, FBI, NSA, and now Homeland Security all have people who do nothing but read political thrillers. Not just to see if there is something coming they didn't think of but because they knew terrorists were reading them for ideas. Fitzpatrick's *Fear Itself* gave them both, what's coming and ideas. Fortunately, this time, the alphabet agencies and Homeland Security took precautions and foiled several terrorist attempts based on Fitzpatrick's book. That's where the similarities end...

CHAPTER 42

CAMBRIDGE, MA

Colburn was back in his Cambridge office. He just finished showering after his 10k morning run, while Natasha, who accompanied him, was by her bowl slurping water.

"Hot girl? Want to take a cold shower? Cool off?"

Natasha looked up at her Da and just tilted her head. She didn't understand the word shower, but her Da had that teasing look on his face. She knew he was expecting her to respond. She tried moaning to see if that was the reaction her Da wanted.

"Don't worry girl. I won't make you take a shower. You'd be all clean and smell good, and that big white poodle you've been fancying might make his move," said Colburn as he bent down and grabbed Natasha's neck scruff and shook her playfully.

It worked, Da happy, thought Natasha.

He was in his chair putting on his shoes when his cell rang. It's not Mary Weeks, his administrative assistant. She's in her office right outside his. So that leaves Sarge, Vova or Faith. He hoped it was Faith.

"Hello," said Colburn.

"Are we on speaker?" asked Faith.

"We are," responded Colburn.

"In that case. Hello, beautiful." She paused a second, then added, "And hello Israel."

There was a bit of static, and the call had a slight delay.

"Very funny. I think Natasha knew you were referring to her. Where are you?" asked Colburn.

"It's a surprise. Are you sitting down?"

"I am."

"I'm in Afghanistan," said Faith.

It was as if someone tasered him. His heart seemed to stop.

"I'm at Bagram Air Base lifting the spirits of America's troops. Israel are you still there?"

"Yes, I'm still here. I just didn't expect this," said Colburn.

"My recording label set it up, and it was all hush hush until I arrived. I just got here just a few hours ago and couldn't wait to call and tell you."

Colburn knew Bagram all too well. Bagram Air Base is the largest U.S. military base in Afghanistan. It is located next to the ancient city of Bagram, 11k southeast of Charikar in the Parwan Province of Afghanistan. The base is mainly occupied by Government contractors, the International Security Assistance Force (ISAF) and minimally by the United States Armed Forces. Bagram Airfield is currently maintained by the Combined Joint Task Force 10th Mountain Division and also maintained by 82nd Combat Aviation Brigade and Task Force Phoenix of the U.S. Army, with the 455th Air Expeditionary Wing of the U.S. Air Force and other U.S. Army, U.S. Navy, U.S. Marine Corps, U.S. Coast Guard, and ISAF units having sizable tenant populations. In addition, the U.S. government regional platform for the east is at the base, staffed by civilians.

During the 1980s Soviet war in Afghanistan, Bagram played a key role, serving as a base of operations for Soviet troops and supplies. Bagram was also the initial staging point for the invading Soviet forces at the beginning of the conflict, with elements of two Soviet Airborne Troops' divisions being deployed there. Aircraft based at Bagram, including the 368th Assault Aviation Regiment flying Su-25s, provided close air support for Soviet and Afghan troops in the field. The 368th Assault Aviation Regiment was stationed at Bagram from October 1986 to November 1987. This is where Icy landed with Colonel Vova after the prisoner swap during the Soviet–Afghan War.

Recovering, Colburn said, "That's wonderful Faith. When did all this happen?"

"I'm so happy you approve. After I had got to California, they told me I would be going. I always wanted to do something for the troops and my country, and when this opportunity came up, I couldn't say no. A couple other acts and I will be putting on two shows a day. I'll only be here a few days, and then I am off to Kandahar Airbase. After that a couple of smaller bases then I'll be back home with two weeks off, and I want to spend them with you."

This is bad, getting worse. He didn't want to say anything to upset her, and he hoped she was calling on a secure phone.

"They're going to love you Faith. That's so good of you to do this, and I know they are going to enjoy your show."

"Listen, darling, they're telling me I have to go, but I will call again as soon as I can. I love you Israel."

The line went dead.

Colburn couldn't move his fingers fast enough. He hit the speed dial for the President and waited.

Da upset, Faith happy, Natasha confused, thought Natasha.

"Icy, what's up?"

"Tell me you didn't know about it."

"Know what?"

"Faith is in Afghanistan."

"Afghanistan? What the fuck is she doing in Afghanistan?"

"You sent her. You tell me."

"Hold on a second."

The phone went quiet for a few minutes then the President came back on.

"Not sure yet. Could be the USO show. I just checked with Kelly and she's getting a hold of SecDef Stanton. I'll have an answer in a few minutes. Icy, discussions and decisions on who gets asked to perform in USO shows doesn't reach this high. Besides, it's strictly voluntary. If - hold on a second let me patch them thru. I got Kelly and Ed Stanton on the line. Go ahead Ed; I have Colburn on the line."

"Mr. Colburn, The United Service Organizations Inc. (USO Show) is a nonprofit organization and not part of the Defense or any other government agency. I just got off the phone with Jack Dyer, the president, and CEO, here in Arlington, and he confirmed that Faith Knoll's people said she would be glad to perform if the right opportunity came along and fit her schedule. A few weeks ago Bagram Base's, MWR (Morale, Welfare and Recreation) representative contacted us and said they could use a big show. We called Faith's people, and they agreed it fit her schedule. They worked it out with our Department of Defense liaison and that's as high as it went and how it works. It's been working like that since 1941."

"So they didn't ask for her specifically?" asked Colburn.

"No. Bagram asked for a show, and the USO then put it together. They take what they get."

"Any other questions for Ed, Israel?" asked the President.

"No. Thank you, Ed," said Colburn.

"Thanks, Ed. I'll get back to you later," said the President. The SecDef hung up.

"What's bothering you, Icy?" asked the President.

"Come on Sarge. She's over there in Afghanistan. It's gonna be in all the papers, on TV, and the internet. What's bothering me?"

"No one has put you two together. Is that's what's bothering you?" asked FBI Director Riley.

"Captain. I hope it starts bothering you and Secretary of Defense Stanton, so it doesn't start bothering me," said Colburn as he hung up.

Kelly also hung up and walked from her office into her husband's office and sat down next to Director Riley. All three sat introspectively for a moment until President Burk broke the ice. He pressed the intercom button "Noreen, Get me Ed Stanton back on the phone." He said no more. All three knew what was coming, and there was no need to discuss it.

"I have the Secretary, Mr. President."

"Ed, I'll give you the back story later but for now, just trust me. Get the Bagram commander, what's his name?"

"General Rainey," replied Stanton.

"Get General Rainey on the horn right now, and have him put his best security team 24/7 on Faith Knoll. Then have him put his next best on them. Don't scare her, but this is not an accommodation. It's an order. I am not prepared to order you to pull her out yet, but be ready. This is a need to know only. This could be really big Ed or nothing at all. I'll let you know. But for now, button her up tight until I tell you to stand down. Do it, and call me back when it's done," said President Burk.

"OK, guys. That's it for now. Let's get together a little later, before Sweeney and Todd get here."

After they had left, the President said, "Noreen. Please get me Mr. Colburn back on the phone."

"Icy, I'm sorry we dropped the ball. Faith will be buttoned up tight. I haven't ordered her home. That's your call. If your instincts are right, and I don't doubt them, we should pull her now."

"You got that Todd guy coming in, so make sure he doesn't connect the dots to me, you and Faith. He saw me with Faith, and as long as he keeps his mouth shut and keeps it off the record, we should be alright. Have Bagram get Faith in touch with me ASAP on a secure phone. Here's my black phone number. And Sarge, please don't give the number out to anyone else."

"Done. Anything else?"

"Yea. Just one little point. Let's hope Vova doesn't subscribe to *Billboard*. He's a smart guy and doesn't miss a trick. He has an information network as good, if not better, than ours. He's out to get me, and he's just looking for an opening. He won't stop until he finds one."

CHAPTER 43

WASHINGTON, DC

Sweeney and Todd had been unceremoniously summoned to Washington. It seemed that President Burk had a bone to pick with both of them about something or other. Sweeney thought it was about his Hedgehampton terrorist attack story while Todd was betting it had to do with his newest best friend, Icy. The flight down, as before, was on Jet Blue, and they were met, as before, by two black Suburbans and a team of Secret Service agents. Todd was feeling a bit uneasy, speculating the Secret Service may take them to an undisclosed location or worse – Bethesda Naval Hospital where they would both undergo, for national security reasons, lobotomies.

President Burk, FBI Director Riley and Press Secretary Kelly Sullivan were waiting in the Oval Office, for their arrival.

Secret Service Director Christin Bounty had, with his boss's permission, his agents take a capricious route from Dulles International Airport, in Fairfax, Virginia, to the White House. The route would take them east on the Dulles Toll Road, through Tysons Corner, then turned off onto the Dolly Madison Blvd., east to the George Washington Memorial Parkway, then south to Washington and the Theodor Roosevelt Bridge into Washington and the White House. But just after they turned into the GWMP, the two Secret Service black Suburbans turned off into Fort Marcy Park. They stopped, and the agents got out and walked out of sight into the woods, leaving Todd and Sweeney sitting alone in the back seat of the second Suburban.

"What the fuck?" asked Sweeney.

"Shut up and listen. Do you know where we are?"

"We're in the woods; I'm guessing Camp David?"

"Very funny. This is not a joke, Sweeney. This is Fort Marcy Park; this is where they killed him."

"Killed who?"

"Vince Foster that's who. Deputy White House Counsel Foster was found dead right here in this park in '93. They ruled his death a suicide, but I was a reporter at the time with the *Chattanooga Times*. I found out that Foster and former President Hilton were involved in an affair that led to Foster's death. There were Foster's Swiss bank accounts, possible espionage, and a cover-up. These agents are delivering us a message."

"Oh shit," said Sweeney.

"Yea. Oh shit," said Todd.

Todd, took out a business card, and wrote something on the back, and handed it to Sweeney.

Sweeney read it. *"Keep quiet. The cars probably bugged. Let me do the talking from here on out."*

The two Secret Service Suburbans carrying Todd and Sweeney came down Pennsylvania Avenue and turned into the N.W. Gate, down the drive, and right up to the West Wing. They were escorted into the West Wing, through the security checkpoint, and into the Oval Office by Secret Service Agent Bill Wells.

"Mr. President, Mr. Sweeney and Mr. Todd are here," said Noreen Ward.

"Bring them in and have some fresh coffee and a Diet Coke brought in," said the President.

When they came in they looked like the odd couple, Sweeney so tall and Todd so short. If their moniker of Sweeney Todd had not been perfect, they might have been tagged as Mutt and Jeff.

"Mr. Sweeney. Mr. Todd. So glad you could join us. How was your trip?" asked FBI Director Riley.

Todd, before he answered, acknowledged the President and First Lady.

"Wonderful Director Riley. I'm sorry we're late. On our way here, the Secret Service detail took us on a side trip to Fort Marcy Park. You know, the place where Vince Foster was killed. I wonder why?" asked Todd.

"Perhaps they were taking you for a trip down memory lane, Mr. Todd," said Riley.

"Perhaps," said Todd.

"Gentlemen, you're here now, and that's what counts. Have a seat, and we'll get you some coffee or tea and get down to why we asked you here," said President Burk.

After they were seated, the steward served tea and coffee and Diet Coke to the President. When everyone was settled, the President said. "Mr. Sweeney. Great reporting job on the Hedgehampton terrorist story. Can't believe they tried to go after that writer and with you right down the street. Well, that's bad luck for him, and good luck for you."

Why do I always get the feeling I'm in the Godfather movie when I'm talking to Burk and Riley, thought Sweeney.

"Aside from looking like Frankenstein and patching up some bullet holes in his house, Fitz came out of it pretty good. His book is doing well, and he just got a big book deal for his next couple of books," said Sweeney.

"You know that novel was loosely based on the three of us, the Manhattan dirty bombs and the aftermath," said the President.

"Yes, I know. I read the book when it first came out, and of course, I followed the actual events when they were occurring," said Sweeney.

"His new book, *Best Served Icy*, what's that about?" asked Kelly.

"More of the same I suspect. Murder, terrorists, and fear," said Sweeney.

"No I mean the title, *Best Served Icy?* Is that a play on the saying, *"Revenge is a dish best served cold?"* asked Kelly.

"Sounds like it, but I really don't know. Why don't you ask Fitzpatrick?" asked Sweeney.

"Do you think it has any connection to the revenge murders?" asked FBI Director Riley.

"I really don't know," said Sweeney.

As all three now turned their attention to Todd. He could only think of Jimmy Page's haunting lyrics from Kashmir; *"All will be revealed."* Todd had given a lot of thought to his Moscow visit: the chief, the FBI, Timmy, Colburn, Faith Knoll, helicopters, the President and the Agent Ross letter outing Colburn as Icy.

"Mr. Todd, what do you think his new book, *Best Served Icy* is about?" asked the President.

Todd was still connecting the dots but pretty much had the story in his head, knew where it was going, and he knew his three interrogators also did.

"Mr. President. The story he's writing is about us. He's writing his new novel about everything that has happened since the Vice President's murder. He's writing about you and me. He's writing about all the revenge murders and the cover-up. Hell, he's probably writing right now about this meeting," said Todd.

"Are you and Mr. Sweeney his source, Mr. Todd?" asked the President.

"In a way, yes, but we all are. He's just following events and chronicling them into a novel. It's all out there. He'll mirror the story and embellish the characters, no doubt to make them more interesting and likable, but it's all going to come out just like it did in *Fear Itself,*" said Todd.

"What's your story in Moscow about?" asked Director Riley.

"I'm having a hard time getting people to talk to me in Moscow. It seems someone put the word out that there is no story. Know anything about that Director Riley?" asked Todd.

Todd had sent an email of his Moscow notes and iPhone photos, to his editor as attachments. His message simply read, "Notes from Moscow and photos from Colburn's cabin. Summoned to Washington again. The story soon."

Riley didn't like Todd at all. He thought the President was too soft on him. *If it were up to me, I would cut out his tongue, lop off his fingers, poke out his eyes, and puncture his ear drums. A reporter that can't report. A reporter that can't communicate* thought Riley. But now was not the time to express his feelings. He had to internalize them.

"The story is this, Mr. Todd. We have helped you and you us, but we can't throw Colburn under the bus so that you can have another banner headline. That's not going to happen. You have no idea how important he has been and can be to us," said Director Riley.

"Look. If you want to know what's going on and about his new book, why don't you just ask him? Ask Fitzpatrick. After all, you guys have been giving him a lot of business for the last couple of years, so to speak. Here's his number," said Sweeney.

President Burk, Riley, and Kelly looked at each other, and all shrugged their shoulders and tilted their heads with a why not look. The President nodded to Riley, and he got up and placed a call to FBI SAC Howard Shaw, who was still in Hedgehampton. "Are you at the house? Is he there? OK. Tell him we want to have a secure conversation with him, and dial us back on a secure line. Use Runner's number."

The President looked at Riley and mouthed, *"Runner?"*

"Gentlemen you can stay, but this call is off the record," said Kelly. They nodded yes in agreement.

Less than three minutes later, Noreen opened the door and said, "Mr. Fitzpatrick on Runners line."

The President looked at Noreen and mouthed, *"Runner?"*

The Secret Service decided to change the President's call sign every two weeks but forgot to inform him.

The phone rang, and Kelly answered, "Mr. Fitzpatrick. Kelly Sullivan, White House Press Secretary. I have you on speaker phone with President Burk, Director Riley, Mr. Sweeney and Mr. Todd. Everything we say is off the record. Understood?"

"Mr. President, Press Secretary Sullivan, Director Riley, gentlemen. Understood," said Fitzpatrick.

"Mr. Fitzpatrick, President Burk here. I think we all read your book *Fear Itself*. Pretty accurate and not bad for your first time out."

"Thank you! Mr. President, but it was fiction."

"Yes, of course, it was, Mr. Fitzpatrick. Is your new book, *Best Served Icy* also fiction and what is it about?" asked the President.

"It is. It's is a sequel to *Fear Itself.*"

"Based on the title, it's about revenge?"

"It is, and more."

"The more is what I'm interested in. Why Icy? Why not chilly or chilled or cold?"

"Because Icy is Colburn's nom de guerre. His war name."

The office couldn't get quieter, but it did.

"How did you arrive at that assumption?"

"Oh, it's not an assumption, Mr. President. It's a fact. I got it from a pretty reliable source."

Sweeney found all eyes, including Todd's, on him. He just shrugged and shook his head no.

"Care to enlighten us?" asked the President.

"In this case, I believe I can, and will, because my source is dead. Kim Ly told me. Well not exactly, but this is what happened. I was in the Jackson International Airport on a stopover to San Francisco, having a cup of coffee when a very attractive Asian woman sat next to me. I was on my way to San Francisco to do some research on my current book. Talk about a coincidence. We chatted as stranded strangers do, and she told me she worked for a Boston firm, Beston Servienti and Colburn, and was on her way to Atlanta when her cell rang. She excused herself and said it was her boss. She answered, "Hello Icy." Nothing had yet been reported about the assassin's being Kim Ly, aka the Dragon Lady or Miss Saigon. Later when I saw the photos on TV, it didn't take long to connect the dots. I guess I'm pretty lucky she didn't ask me what I was working on. Had she, she might not have thought our meeting coincidental, and I may have been the first novelist to die in his own novel. Is that even possible?"

"Mr. Fitzpatrick. That is an amazing story. Are we still talking fiction here?"

"I am afraid not, Mr. President."

"We can't let you use our Mr. Colburn in your book, Mr. Fitzpatrick, but I would like to propose a deal. Are you game?"

"Mr. President. Your administration is the proverbial hand that feeds. I'll bite."

"We'll give you complete access to relevant events, and you continue to write your book. You can even keep the title, but Colburn, his legend, and his association to this office must be redacted. You merely replace a name, a legend, and a government."

"I can live with that, but with one caveat."

"Being?"

"If Colburn dies before publication, he, his legend, and his government will be unredacted.

"I don't think that's going to happen, so it looks like we have a deal."

The line was disconnected, and Director Riley turned to Sweeney and Todd and said, "That deal also goes for both of you, or you'll be going on a one-way trip back to Fort Marcy Park."

As they were leaving the office for the airport, the President said, "How do you think it ends Mr. Todd?"

"Not good I'm afraid. Not good at all," said Todd.

After everyone had left the office, President Burk called Colburn to tell him his identity was safe.

CHAPTER 44

WASHINGTON, DC

Two days after Sweeny and Todd visited the White House things seemed to be getting back to normal in the Oval Office. The President had just finished a series of Cabinet and staff meetings and was preparing for an upcoming Official State Visit by China's President. Tomorrow morning, President Burk will welcome His Excellency Xi Jinping, President of the People's Republic of China, to the White House for an official State Visit. This reciprocates President Burk's State Visit to China last year, making it the third state affair of the Burk Administration. The visit will be an opportunity for the two leaders to discuss a range of global, regional, and bilateral issues of interest to both countries, and to outline a joint vision for an international agreement on climate change that builds upon last year's historic announcement.

Chief of Staff Bill Nicholas was just finishing up with the President and was about to leave when Press Secretary Kelly Sullivan came in with a look of concern and anger on her face. The President caught her entrance out of the corner of his eye and felt relieved she was in the room until he saw the look on her face and the *New York Post* in her hand.

"That will be all, Bill," said President Burk. When Nicholas was out of the office, and the door closed, he turned to Kelly and said, "Don't tell me that son of a bitch released the story?"

"Worse," said Kelly, as she held the paper in front of him to see. Right there on Page Six, the *Post* infamous scandal and gossip page was a picture of Colburn and Faith Knoll, the one taken by Todd at the cabin and emailed to his editor.

The caption read, "Faith Knoll's new Boston Boy." It gave Colburn's name but did not mention his nom de guerre.

President Burk now had the same expression on his face as did Kelly.

"Noreen, get Director Riley in here now, and if he's not around get him on the phone, then get Mr. Todd conferenced in."

Director Riley was in his office, at FBI Headquarters on Pennsylvania Avenue when Noreen found him. Noreen put him through to the President, and the President filled him on what had occurred.

With FBI Director Riley on speaker, waiting for Todd to be patched in, the President asked where Kelly got the paper, "It is dated yesterday, and it was brought to me by one of the wives who attended the White House party for Faith. She thought I would be thrilled that they were together and mentioned in Page Six."

"I have Mr. Todd," said Noreen.

"Patch him into the Director Riley's line, please."

They heard a click on the speaker indicating Todd was on the line.

"Todd. Burk here. I thought we had an agreement."

"Whoa, Mr. President. We did. I mean we do. I just got wind of this photo myself. It's my photo, but I didn't authorize nor know that it was going to be published. I sent my story notes and some photos to my editor before coming down to Washington the other day and told him to hold them till I got back and could submit the story. Someone somehow got a hold of the photos and gave them to Page Six. This is the kind of gossip they live for, but they didn't out him as Icy."

Director Riley, unable to control himself jumped in, "You have no idea of the potential damage you did Mr. Todd. If this goes south, I will personally cut your balls off."

The President disconnected Todd and asked Noreen to get Colburn.

Colburn was sitting in his office in Cambridge when Mary Weeks, his administrative assistant, came in and placed a fax on his desk. It was Page Six showing the photo of him and Faith with a written note.

Icy my friend, so good to see you finally met someone nice. I look forward to meeting her.
Allahu Akbar,
Vova

Coburn sat there frozen. Mary knew when to leave, and she did so quickly. Colburn felt cold, Icy cold. His mind was like a computer, and it was churning the information he just received, what he knew, and what he suspected. He knew immediately what was going to happen. His black phone rang. He checked the caller and answered.

"Icy, we have a problem," said the President.

"No. We had a problem a week ago and now we have a situation. Vova just sent me a fax. I thought you had this under control. What the fuck happened?"

"What did Vova send you?" asked Riley.

"An invitation to the show."

They filled each other in then Colburn said, "Pull her. Pull her out now!" He hung up and started to warm up; then Icy got hot.

Noreen had been standing by the Oval Office door at the ready. She knew something serious was happening, and she had her assistant keep everyone away from the Oval Office.

President Burk said to Noreen, "Please get me Secretary of Defense Stanton on Director Riley's line."

She turned to go back to her desk when her phone rang. It was Secretary of Defense Ed Stanton. Noreen got up and stuck her head back in and said, "Mr. President, Secretary of Defense Stanton is calling you," and then she put him through.

"Mr. President, I just jot off the horn with General Rainey in Bagram. We have a problem."

CHAPTER 45

KANDAHAR, AF

The Bagram USO show, including Faith Knoll, her security, management, fellow performers, band members and roadies, had just finished their last show in Kandahar and were packing up to do one last show at Camp Leatherneck, then back to Kandahar air base, and home.

Camp Leatherneck is a 443-acre, United States Marine Corps base located in the Helmand Province. 156k, 96 miles west of Kandahar along AH1, Afghan Highway 1. It is currently home to the 2nd Marine Expeditionary Brigade, now referred to as MEB-Afghanistan, (nickname: Task Force Leatherneck). Located in the middle of the desert, Camp Leatherneck is divided into four areas and is still undergoing construction as troop levels continue to rise in support of NATO's, International Security Assistance Force in Afghanistan.

Camp Leatherneck was desperate for entertainment, and the USO was determined to provide it.

Faith Knoll had round the clock security. A team of eight Alpha Security contractors would protect her while in Afghanistan. Her own PSD (Personal Security Detail) Alpha Security is a private military/mercenary company providing armed combat, combat support, security or security advisory services to officials, diplomats, and celebrities. Four men for each 12-hour shift. Each was young, rugged, and combat tested veteran. Three former Marines, three former Army Rangers, a former Navy Seal, Joe 'Buco' Sambuco leading 2nd squad and former Airforce Air Commando, SSgt. Jeff Matthews, leading 1st squad. Jeff was the overall team leader. A smart, no-nonsense, combat controller, Jeff earned 2 Silver Stars for Valor in Afghanistan. The team call sign for today's mission was Petrified. Matthews call sign was Petrified 1-6, and Buco's was Petrified 2-6.

Each operator, as each man was called, carried identical armament:

One HK416 A5 assault rifle in 5.56 x 45 mm NATO caliber, one Glock 17 side arm, one Indy Hammered knife, frag, stun and smoke grenades, body armor vest, 782 vest and tan desert battle dress with tan baseball caps. Most had beards and wore Wiley X Guard sunglasses. Some wore shemag (scarves), and all chewed Grinds chewing tobacco. They communicated using TRI PRC 152 radios with Nexus microphones. They had NVG's (night vision goggles), suppressors, Airtronic USA Inc.'s RPG 7- Soviet style RPG 7 anti-armor rocket launcher, and M249 light machine guns (LMG). They had access to a motor pool of up-armored Humvees and gunships. They were a dangerous team that could call on their parent company for reinforcements if things got out of hand. They were better armed and supplied than regular troops and better paid. The operators averaged about $22,000 per month vs. Army pay of $2,500 per month.

Their mission was to keep Faith Knoll safe and sound while not making her feel like a prisoner. Difficult, but not impossible.

In addition to Faith's PSD, the USO show had its own security provided by a reinforced company of the 10th Mountain Division.

The biggest threat to the USO show were IED's. An improvised explosive device is a bomb constructed and deployed in ways other than in conventional military action. It may be constructed of conventional military explosives, such as an artillery round, attached to a detonating mechanism. IEDs are commonly used as roadside bombs. Usually followed up by an enemy assault with automatic weapons, rockets, and mortars. But the worst fear the operators had to deal with was the threat of kidnapping of their charge, their responsibility. In this case their Faith.

Jeff Matthews knew this first hand. An attempted kidnapping on a previous assignment was foiled but only after much blood. If they, the bad guys, the rag heads, decide to kidnap someone, they usually do or die trying.

Matthews had just received a call from his office that they were hearing a lot of enemy chatter. Not good. The good news-bad news was that things, up to now, had been quiet around Kandahar. Too quiet.

Jeff Matthews assembled his team for what Marines call a skull session, tell the team the what, when, where and how it was all going down.

"All right, listen up," said Matthews to his assembled team. "For this afternoon's convoy to Camp Leatherneck, both squads will go active. This is the 10th Mountain's convoy, and as far as they're concerned, we're just along for the ride. The convoy's call sign is Country Road, and the convoy leader is Lt. Rhea. He will be in the third Humvee, and his call sign is Country Road 3-6. The 10th has six up-armored Humvees including machine guns and TOW anti-armor missile launchers. The Marines, from Camp Leatherneck, sent over two 6x's for the band, staff, roadies, and extra security, and three Frankenstein's (monster trucks) for the roadies' gear. The 10th also has gunship support and an unarmed drone with a live feed to Kandahar. They have five unarmed transport Humvees for the performers and senior staff, H-1 thru H-5. My team and I will be Petrified 1, and I will be Petrified 1-6. We will be directly in front of H-3, Faith's ride. Petrified 2, with Buco as 6, will be directly behind H-3 in his truck. Besides the driver and shotgun, there will be one other entertainer in H-3 with Faith. Our AOR (area of responsibility) is H-3 and only one person inside of H-3. Understood?"

"Oorah."

"S-2 (Army intelligence shop) says this highway is deadly and that the Marines get hit often, especially with IEDs. I want us in full battle rattle (loaded with gear) ready to leave the green zone at 15 hundred hours.

It's 156k to Leatherneck, so figure three hours. That means we should be pulling to Camp Leatherneck by 18 hundred. No need for MRE's. The jarheads will feed us good left over Navy chow after we get secured. Understood?"

"Oorah."

After we leave the green zone, any local or ragheads wanting an autograph are dead. Any drive by's, by other than friendlies are dead. Understood?"

"Oorah."

"Go get your shit together and be back here at 14:30, ready to rumble."

"Oorah."

The mission the Russian Vova had given the ISIL, al-Qaeda, and the Taliban leaders, while in Russia, was to coordinate, prepare and execute large attacks on major US bases in Afghanistan and to kidnap VIP's. The decision as to the actual hard and soft targets would be forthcoming. Never in a million years could he have guessed how profound that mission set-up would become.

One of Vova's intelligence department heads, tasked with nothing but combing all intel on Colburn, brought him a newspaper clipping of a 'Page Six' showing Colburn and a beautiful woman by the name of Faith Knoll. All of Vova's FSB, Federal Security Service, headquartered in Lubyanka Square, Moscow's center, went to work to find anything and everything about this woman. In less than an hour, that same department head was back in Vova's office with more information, and it was unbelievable.

The Russian had finally given them a target, an exact target. They were to kidnap a woman, an infidel, named Faith Knoll. The name meant nothing to them, but the Russian made it absolutely clear that she was to be taken regardless of the cost. If they failed, they would suffer consequence so enormous that Islam would be set back a hundred years. That threat did not seem to register. The Russian did threaten that all funds would be clawed back or frozen from both their personal and organization's accounts. That they understood. He didn't need to mention that certain video of all three, taken in Russia, doing things no good Muslim would ever do, would be released on YouTube. Failure was not an option.

At about the same time Jeff Matthews was talking to his troops, and not too far distant, al-Baghdadi's Commander for Afghan Operations, Abu Suja, was giving detailed instructions to his fighters, for two simultaneous diversion attacks on Bagram and Kandahar.

Mohammad Mansour's operational commander, Mohamed Fazil, one of the Taliban 5 released in trade for Army deserter Bergdahl, would attack Camp Leatherneck and ambush any relief column sent out to rescue the American convoy.

Al-Zawahiri's operational commander, Ahmed al-Masri, son of slain leader Abu al-Masri, would attack the convoy and capture the woman known as Faith, whose name in Farsi translated to Iman.

Afghani civilian workers inside Kandahar and there were many of them, had been to the show and taken press release folders which included the performer's biographies, and glossy headshots. They knew how many vehicles were in the convoy, when it would leave, the level of security and most importantly, they would find out which vehicle contained the woman, Iman.

By 1400 hours the convoy was in place, and the worker-spies counted eighteen vehicles. They just had to wait until the performers were assigned to vehicles, but it was safe to guess it would be somewhere in the middle of the pack. They would wait patiently, observe, and then send runners out of the base, to a small store which acted as the operation center. The information would be sent by radio, in code, to all three force commanders: ISIL, al-Qaeda, and the Taliban.

Arjomand (beautiful boy in Persian) was a ten-year-old Afghan boy. He was so beautiful and delicate, he could easily pass for a girl, and often did. He was also a spy. His job was to get close to Iman, and give her his best smile, and a bunch of fresh flowers he just picked. If she accepted the flowers, they would be checked by her security. This was told him by his handler. He was also given a small, self-powered, magnetic modified LoJack transmitter, about the size of a half-dollar coin that, if possible, he would drop into the vehicle or attach to the vehicle's exterior metal skin anywhere he could.

It was imperative that the attacks on Bagram, Kandahar, and Camp Leatherneck did not proceed until after the convoy was ambushed. When the U.S. operational command in Kandahar heard of the ambush of the USO convoy, it would react swiftly, but when they found themselves, Bagram and Camp Leatherneck all under attack, well, helping the convoy would just have to wait.

The operation was now being called 'al-Iman qowa' (Faith is strength), by ISIL, al-Qaeda, and the Taliban commanders. Out of this attack and the capture of Iman, they would gain much: money, strength, and global publicity, and most importantly, respect.

By 14:00 hours Country Road was lined up with all eighteen vehicles. Many 10th mountain troopers were already beginning to congregate. By 14:30 everyone, but the USO staff and performers were on board and saddled up. Lt. Rhea, his two platoon leaders and Matthews met off to the side to finalize call signs, support, back-up, procedure, fall back and contingency plans. They would go out fast and hard. Lt. Rhea would have one Humvee, one half-klick out front, scouting and running interference. Lt. Rhea will be third in line. If there is a pressure detonated IED the lead Humvee would get it first. If it were an on command detonated IED, Rhea would luck out, but the Humvee in front of him wouldn't be so lucky. If an ambush were sprung, IED's would hit the front of the convoy then the back. They would bottle the convoy up. Country Road wouldn't be able to go forward or back, only off the road and into the sand, a possibility, but if it comes to going camel, the convoy would be in a world of shit. He had eighteen vehicles with a security force of 42 including 18 drivers and the 8 PSD's. The USO contingent contained 10 performers, 5 staff, 6 band members and 6 roadies, 69 souls in all.

At exactly 14:40 the USO performers and staff came out of their air conditioned metal Quonset hut and made their way, fifty yards, to the convoy. The senior staff director and her assistant made sure everyone was directed to the correct vehicle. When Faith and another performer, Johnny Jones, a Tom Jones impersonator and tribute singer, reached their assigned Humvee, Arjomand, with his flowers and transmitter in hand, made his move. He was known to the USO performers and considered a sweet young boy, so seeing him come towards Faith, carrying flowers, was not alarming. He wore a thigh-length, long-sleeved white linen shirt, belted at the waist with a skirt effect to the lower half, a blue sleeveless waistcoat worn over the shirt, and loose fitting white trousers. Buco, had one of his operators, Bush, intercept the boy and hold him at bay. Faith interceded, and Buco relented after having Bush pat down the boy. Bush did a quick but thorough pat down and found nothing suspicious. Bush took the flowers and checked them carefully, the transmitter was cupped in Arjomand's palm, then allowed the boy to approach Faith. Faith was seated in the back of the Humvee with the window down. She waved him forward.

"Aren't you sweet," said Faith, as she accepted the flowers. "What is your name?"

"Arjomand."

"Arjomand, did you see the show?" asked Faith.

Arjomand, like many Afghan boys, spoke very good English. "Oh yes, Miss. Your singing is wonderful. I want to be like you some day," said Arjomand, with his brightest smile, his red lips forming a heart around his white teeth. His beautiful green eyes, with long eyelashes, made him irresistible.

"Can I take him with me?" asked Faith half kidding, half serious.

"Not an option, mam," said Buco.

She put her hand out and pulled Arjomand closer and gave him a kiss on the cheek.

A loud yell went out from Lt. Rhea, "Saddle up!"

"Move the kid back," said Matthews, as he walked past Faith's Humvee towards his own truck.

Bear guided the boy away then joined his squad in the forward truck. The engines were all started, and the command from the LT sounded, "Move out!" All eighteen vehicles of Country Road came roaring to life. Lt. Rhea hit the audio switch and John Denver's voice singing *Country Road*, came blaring out from the LT's Humvee's speakers. The gates were opened, and they rolled out of Kandahar's green zone and into Indian Territory.

"Almost heaven, West Virginia, Blue ridge mountains, Shenandoah river. Life is old there, older than the trees. Younger than the mountains, growin' like a breeze. Country roads, take me home to the place I belong, West Virginia, mountain momma. Take me home, country roads."

Arjomand watched and listened as the convoy went out the gate and the dust and music dissipated. When the woman gave him a kiss and the man yelled "Saddle Up" he dropped the transmitter into the space behind the woman's seat. He was not sure why they wanted it done. They just did. *She is a very kind and beautiful woman. I hope she will be safe and return soon,* thought Arjomand.

CHAPTER 46

KANDAHAR, AF

The convoy drove northwest on A75 to the Aino Road, then west through the city of Kandahar, through the Kandahar gates, past the arches, and onto AH1. The LT turned the music off, and Country Road got real quiet and deadly serious.

ISIL Operational Commander Abu Suja was giving last minute instructions to his fighters for two simultaneous diversion attacks on Bagram and Kandahar. Their attack would focus on the airstrip and would include mortars, rockets, and snipers with Barrett M82A1-50 caliber sniper rifles, with an effective range of 1,800m, well over a mile. The mortars and rockets would prevent any aircraft from taking off to assist the convoy, and the snipers would concentrate on putting 50 caliber rounds through helicopter and fixed wing aircraft's windscreens, rendering them inoperable. When they received word that the primary ambush was sprung they would attack then withdraw into each city and disappear.

Taliban Operational Commander Mohamed Fazil was also giving last minute instructions to his fighters for their diversion attacks on Camp Leatherneck and the ambush of a probable relief column sent to help the convoy. Their attack would also focus on the airstrip and would also include mortars, rockets, and snipers. Their ambush of any relief column would involve blowing up the two bridges across the Gareshk city canal, 25 miles to the east of the camp. Once the relief column was stopped at the canal, a truck imbedded IED would be detonated behind the column, and pre-registered mortars would decimate the stranded vehicles. Snipers on rooftops on either side of the highway would pick off any survivors. When their mission was complete, they would move deep into the mountains surrounding Camp Leatherneck or disappear within the city of Gereshk.

72k (45miles) from Kandahar, almost half-way to Camp Leatherneck, on Highway AH1, was the small town of Maiwand. Either side of the highway was filled with two-story houses and haji marts (small stores). A valley runs north of the town into the Khakriz Mountains.

Al-Qaeda Operational Commander Ahmed al-Masri received word that the convoy had left Kandahar, how many vehicles there were, and which one contained the Iman. Some basic math was done, and an ETA was established. He would turn his tracker-receiver on soon, the one his son Arjomand placed in the Iman's vehicle. Hidden behind the houses and haji marts were a dozen Technicals, a type of improvised fighting vehicle, mostly Toyotas, modified to provide an offensive capability similar to a military gun truck. They were all open-backed pickup trucks, mounted with machine guns, light anti-aircraft guns, or anti-tank weapons. His fighters were with the Technicals and on the roofs and in the windows on both sides of the highway. They were armed with AK's, RPG's and RPK Kalashnikov light machine guns.

To fight against any Apache gunships, formidable fighting machines with speed, mobility, chain gun, and two rocket pod, that were sure to accompany the convoy, he had four SAM, surface to air missiles, located in the adjacent hills, along with two "Zikuyak" Soviet-designed 14.5-mm anti-aircraft guns strategically placed in the mountains above the hills. If there were a drone, they wouldn't know it unless it was armed and fired on them, and that would not be good. But if it came in low then they could take it out with a SAM.

Al-Masri had a special grab team to capture Iman, consisting of armed Humvees and Technicals, each designated to take out Iman's front and rear personal security details and capture the Iman. This special grab team was led by his fearless cousin, Saddam al-Jamal. Al-Masri turned on his transmitter-receiver, noted its location, and alerted his lieutenants that the convoy was ten minutes out.

In total, al-Masri had 141 fighters to take out a convoy with its security force of just 42, which included drivers. His orders were clear: close in fast, and close in tight. The Apache gunships are useless when his fighters are mixed in close with the infidels. If the Apache gunship fired the M230 chain gun or the rockets, everyone would die, and Americans don't fight like that.

Country Road was having a hard time of it. The highway was clogged with the LN's, local nationals, and they were in no mood to be subservient to the ugly Anglos and their war machines. These poor people have been fighting for their survival as long as their fathers, and their fathers, fathers could remember.

The First Anglo-Afghan War (also known as Auckland's Folly) was fought between the British East India Company and Afghanistan from 1839 to 1842 and ended in an overall Afghan victory.

The Second Anglo–Afghan War was fought between the United Kingdom and the Emirate of Afghanistan from 1878 to 1880 when the latter was ruled by Sher Ali Khan of the Barakzai dynasty, the son of former Emir Dost Mohammad Khan. This was the second time British East India Company invaded Afghanistan. The war ended after the British emerged victorious against the Afghan rebels, and the Afghans agreed to let the British attain all of their geopolitical objectives from the Treaty of Gandamak.

The Third Anglo-Afghan War also referred to as the Third Afghan War, began on 6 May 1919 and ended with an armistice on 8 August 1919, an Afghan victory.

The Fourth Anglo-Afghan War (or the American War in Afghanistan) is the period in which the United States invaded Afghanistan after the September 11 attacks and never left. The fact that 15 of the hijackers were from Saudi Arabia, 2 were from the United Arab Emirates, 1 was from Egypt, 1 was from Lebanon, and none was from Afghanistan, did not escape these poor, proud people.

Now, their enemies were the Americans, but the crazy religious fighters from Iran, Syria, and Iraq were also here killing Afghans, but today the people knew that these crazy religious fighters were going to kill Americans. They did not like the crazy religious fighters, but they hated the Americans more. Today both their enemies would die. No, they would not move out of the way for the Americans. Today would be a good day.

Moving hard and fast on AH1 was not the same as on I-95. There are only two lanes, and both were often crowded with people, carts, cars, and trucks. An occasional sheep crossing was to be expected. Even with Country Road's lead Humvee out ahead clearing the way, the convoy was reduced to 25mph. So much for fast and hard.

Matthews looked at his watch and realized, that at this rate, they would be lucky to get to Camp Leatherneck before dark. They just passed Mahajerin a small village to the south of AH1 and would have nothing but desert and mountains for the next 26k (16miles), until the next town of Maiwand, half-way to Camp Leatherneck. He wanted to tell Lt. Rhea to try and pick up the pace, but that would have been out of line. Instead, he just monitored the LT and listened to his frustrations about trying to maneuver thru the crowded highway, but he could try a different approach.

"County Road 3-6 this is Petrified 1-6. Over."

"Go ahead Petrified; this is Country Road 3-6."

"Country Road, there's one good thing about having with all these cars, trucks and cattle on the road."

"What's that Petrified?"

"They wouldn't be here if there were any IED's in the road."

"You got that right Petrified. When we don't see anybody, we're in trouble. Let's get this show on the road and move out," said Lt. Rhea.

"Roger that County Road. Out," said Matthews.

CHAPTER 47

THE AMBUSH

From his cave headquarters in the hill just above the town, al-Masri could watch and direct the ambush, and assist if necessary. He had direct communications with Saddam al-Jamal, his grab team leader, with the Technical, and AA team leaders, and had a clear view of the highway and the town below. He turned on the receiver again, but this time linked it to his laptop through a LoJack App. called, Absolute Software. Google Earth appeared on the screen with a small red light moving towards his position. The convoy was about 26k (16miles) away. Suddenly two Apache Gunships materialized out of thin air. They hovered just 25 meters above the highway. One turned and pointed its nose directly towards him as if they knew he was there. He saw his entire operation disintegrate before his very eyes. If they spotted him or if his SAM or anti-aircraft batteries opened up, the convoy would stop and return to Kandahar, but as quickly as they came, they lifted up and headed back towards the town of Gereshk. He contacted his AA units and commended them for their fire discipline and reinforced his direction to free fire immediately after the ambush was sprung.

The convoy was now tracking less than 10k (6miles) from the ambush site, and al-Masri gave the grab team a heads up and a 5-minute warning.

Closing in on the halfway point to Camp Leatherneck, the convoy slowed its approach into the town of Maiwand. The gunships were now about 40k (24 miles) out front toward Gereshk, and the convoy's lead Humvee was already on its way out of town. A heavily decorated Afghan truck, featuring floral patterns and poetic calligraphy and known by the slang term jingle truck, was directly in front of the convoy, moving slowly and taking up both lanes. It was as big as an American dump truck but not as well built or as powerful. It was loaded, overflowing actually, with huge bundles of woven material.

Lt. Rhea, in the third forward Humvee got on the horn to his forward blocker, "Country Road 2 this is Country Road 3-6, over."

"Go ahead 3-6."

"Push that sum bitch off the road, and do it now."

"Roger that 3-6."

Country Road 2, sped up and came along side of the jingle truck. The spec 4 in the open roof turret, swiveled his 50 caliber machine gun directly towards the truck and at the driver. With one hand on the gun hand grip and trigger, he used his other to strongly express his desire for the truck to pull to the side, and let the convoy pass. Reluctantly the driver obeyed, slowed and pulled to the side of the road allowing the convoy to pass by.

They were now close to the center of town when Lt. Rhea said, "Well done Country Road 2." Expecting a reply from Country Road 2, Lt. Rhea in his Humvee, about 20 meters behind, waited for a response. What he got was an audio-visual mind freeze. A deafening tremendous explosion and a blinding optic of a Humvee being tossed up in the air, wrapped in a cloud of black smoke and fire. Rhea's driver slammed on his brakes and skidded to a stop no more than 5 meters short of the horrific site of what was Country Road 2 settling in a crater of smoke, fire, and death. Every vehicle in the convoy similarly braked, some not as fast, and they slammed into the vehicle in front of them.

A collective murmur of "Oh shit" came from all the soldiers, as they knew what would come next. The USO troupe knew something had happened but had no clue how bad it was about to get. The jingle truck that was now behind the convoy's rear end Humvee picked up speed and rammed into him and exploded, completely engulfing both vehicles in smoke and flames, effectively sealing the convoy's fate. Lt. Rhea, his team, Matthews, and his team, knew that the back door had just closed and braced for what was coming next. A split second after it closed, Lt. Rhea with the mic still in his hand, hit the speaker call button, "10-2-2 this is Country Road 3-6, 10- 2-2 this is Country Road 3-6. We are in contact; 30degrees 36N latitude x65degrees 05E longitude, the town of Maiwand, casualties. Send help quick. Out."

Kandahar Operations Command, controlling and monitoring the drone over the convoy watched the live feed of the ambush while simultaneously hearing Lt. Rhea's desperate call for help. 2nd Battalion 2nd Infantry was also monitoring Country Road and were about to mount a rescue team when the eerie sound of mortars exiting tubes could be heard. These were incoming sounds not outgoing. A few seconds later a loud shattering ka-rump sound of exploding rounds shook the base. The distant whoosh of firing rockets and their freight train approach sent everyone for cover. Dozens of 81mm mortar and 140mm rocket rounds were landing all over the base but mainly on the airfield. The base battle station siren sounded, and all thoughts of mounting a rescue mission for Country Road were shifted to the back burner.

Bagram and Camp Leatherneck were also under similar attack, and all hope to mount a rescue attempts were on hold until they could silence the mortars, rockets and 50Cal snipers hidden in and behind the hills surrounding the bases.

Lt. Rhea knew Country Road 2 was gone and suspected the same of Country Road 6 in the rear end Charley slot. Nothing he could do for them now. He had to get his remaining convoy out of the kill zone and fast. He still had 15 vehicles with him and one more somewhere out front, and he had to get them moving now. On his convoy net Lt. Rhea gave the order. "This is Country Road 3-6, all vehicles turn south into the town, plow through to the end, and then turn east back to Kandahar."

"This is Petrified 1-6. Negative Country Road 3-6 on going through town. Turn right into the desert then we'll head west to Leatherneck."

"This is Country Road 3-6, Petrified. We're heading back to Kandahar. Join in or you're on your own."

Matthews didn't want to argue and didn't have time. He jumped out of his truck and got into the driver's seat of H-3, Faith's Humvee, roughly pulling the driver, a private, out and into the back with Faith and Johnny. On his prc-152 team radio, he yelled, "Petrified 1, move north around this cluster-fuck. I will follow, and Petrified 2 will bring up my rear. I am now Petrified 3-6, and this is now convoy Petrified."

Ant, Mathew's shotgun, assumed command of Petrified 1 and was out and off the road before Mathews finished speaking. Simultaneously the rest of convoy Country Road turned left into the town, and that's when Lt. Rhea saw the trap and realized his mistake.

A dozen Technicals came pouring out of the town directly towards them, effectively blocking their retreat. Just then both Apaches came roaring up the highway with their chain guns murderously spitting hundreds of rounds into two of the closest Technicals, tearing them and the onboard fighters to shreds. When the Apaches completed their run and turned back for another, the Technicals and Humvees were intertwined and banging it out, side by side, with machine guns, light anti-aircraft guns, or anti-tank weapons. It was a near run thing, and the Apaches could only watch and wait for a target, less they end up firing and taking out their own.

In the hills north of the town the anti-aircraft guns and the four SAM sites opened up a horrendous barrage onto the two stationary Apaches. The 14.5-mm anti-aircraft gun shells, 3x the size of a 50cal. rounds, riddled the Apaches until one SAM each hit home. Both Apaches were gone. Disintegrated. From his cave headquarters, al-Masri watched his fighters decimate the convoy and the infidels, but that was just a side show. The three Humvees that pulled out and away from the convoy had his attention. That they did so, was proof that the Iman, in the center vehicle, whom he was tracking on his computer, was protected by a special group of men. Men that don't follow the rules.

The Americans are performing just as expected, thought al-Masri.

Convoy Petrified with two armed Humvees and one transport Humvee drove through the sand and around the carcass of Country Road 2 and back onto the highway heading west towards Camp Leatherneck. All the enemy's firepower was directed towards the main column and nothing towards them.

It's as if they were destined to escape or allowed to, thought Matthews.

Rushing towards Petrified was Country Road 1, the scout Humvee that Lt. Rhea had placed in front of the main convoy, running interference. Matthews was monitoring radio traffic still coming from Country Road, but it wasn't good. The chatter was becoming desperate, then very quiet. Country Road 1 was heading to his death if he joined them, and Matthews got him on the horn.

"Country Road 1- this is Petrified 3-6. Country Road can't be helped. Fall in behind me, we are making a run for Leatherneck."

"Petrified 3-6, Country Road 1-6 that is not an option. Copy?"

"Copy that - Country Road 1-6."

Country Road 1-6, being the tough, loyal soldier he was, was going to the aid of his team even if that meant his and his squad's death. He did, and it did. As he got closer the AA guns in the hill lit him up. Country Road 1 never knew what hit them.

The sole survivors of convoy Country Road barreled down AH1 seemingly immune to attack. *Why us? Why did my team survive and the others didn't,* thought Matthews.

"We got company," said Ant, into his helmet mic.

"What do you got?" asked Matthews.

"Looks like the cavalry from Camp Leatherneck is coming to rescue us."

"See if you can raise them on Country Road's net."

"Leatherneck patrol this is Petrified 1 repeat-Leatherneck scout team this is Petrified 1 at your 12-over."

"Petrified 1 this is Blue Team 1-6, 8th Marines out of Camp Leatherneck here to escort you back to camp. Kandahar has a column coming to assist Country Road."

"Roger that Blue Team."

The Blue Team circled around, and Petrified fell in behind. Petrified followed them towards Camp Leatherneck and safety. One of the Blue Team Humvees fell back to provide rear security and Matthews made eye contact with the Marine riding shotgun. It was fleeting but weird. The Marine gave no thumbs up, no smile, or other typical jarhead euphemisms, just empty brown eyes. Matthews was not sure about a lot of things. Not sure how they escaped the ambush unscathed, not sure how they lucked onto the Marine Blue Team, and not sure where they were heading. But Matthews was sure of one thing. That that Marine was not a Marine. He pulled out his cell phone, and speed-dialed Alpha Security, his parent company based in Bagram and when they answered said, "This is Petrified 6, you got me?"

CHAPTER 48

WASHINGTON, DC

The doors of the Situation Room opened, and four Secret Service agents entered and took up positions by the door and around the room. The President walked in behind them followed by FBI Director Ray Riley, Chief of Staff Bill Nicholas and Press Secretary Kelly Sullivan. The room was full, and he held up his hand to indicate not to stand. Present were: The Chairman of the Joint Chief of Staff General Joe Dunnford, Army Chief of Staff General Mark Miller and Commandant of the Marine Corps General Joe Wheeler Jr., Secretary of Defense Ed Stanton, Secretary of State Matt Walsh, CIA Director John Bader, NSA Director Admiral Roger Michaels, and dozens of staff.

The President sat in his chair at the head of the table and looked at each of his advisors seated around him. "We all know why we're here," he said. "Bagram, Kandahar, and Camp Leatherneck attacked and virtually put out of commission. An entire convoy including a USO troupe decimated. Over one hundred killed and three hundred wounded. Dozens of aircraft are destroyed or disabled, and nearly two billion dollars' worth of damage. Thanks to the drone, before it was shot down, we know we have six Humvees, with somewhere between 18-20 poor souls still missing and unaccounted for, including a famous recording star, Faith Knoll." He was about to add, and girlfriend of one of the most dangerous men in the world, but didn't. The President was turning red as he tried to control his building anger. "I want answers. I know what happened, and we will deal with that in a second. What I want to know now is where are Faith Knoll, her personal security detail, and the Marine scout team that were last seen escorting them back to Camp Leatherneck?"

Except the President, CIA and the FBI, almost everyone else in the room reported to Secretary of Defense Stanton, and all heads turned towards him.

Secretary of Defense Ed Stanton, feeling all eyes upon him, including the President's, said, "We think that the Bagram, Kandahar, and Camp Leatherneck attacks were distractions. All three were hit moments after Country Road, the convoy's call sign was ambushed. The three bases were hit to prevent the bases from sending support and rescue to the convoy. The attacks on all three bases ceased immediately after the convoys…," he was about to say elimination, but chose instead, "last radio transmission."

"But the drone shows a Marine rescue team, from Camp Leatherneck, joining with the three Humvees that escaped the ambush. One of which, we presume, contained Faith Knoll, and escorting them back to Camp Leatherneck," said the President.

"That's correct Mr. President, and Camp Leathernecks 2nd BN/8th Marines did send a rescue column out, but it was stopped and ambushed at the blown canal bridge west of Gereshk."

"Then who were the Marines that hooked up with Petrified, the call sign of Faith's personal security detail?" asked the President.

"That's the million dollar question. 2/8 and 2 shop intelligence say they had no one out in that AO, and no one is missing."

"Could they have been with another unit?"

The Secretary of Defense turned to look at the Marine Corps Commandant General Joe Wheeler Jr.,

"We're working on finding out if that possibility exists, but the drone tape shows the three Marine Humvees had 2nd BN/8th Marine markings and badges. They say it's not theirs, and that leaves two possibilities."

"Which are?" asked the President.

"The first is that 2/8 has their heads up their asses and need to take a new roll call. The second is, the Marine unit was not a Marine unit, but a spider luring the fly into its web."

With that, everyone around the table closed their eyes and slowly shook their heads at what that suggested.

"General Wheeler. Who is the regimental commander of the 8th Maries in Camp Leatherneck?"

"Major General Jeff Banks."

"I want everyone in here to put all their assets; Human Intelligence, Hint Intelligence, Geospatial Intelligence and all those other acronym assets we're paying for: MANSIT, OSINT, SIGINT, CYBINT/DNINT, FININT and TECHINT, whatever the hell they are, and find that girl," said the President with a cold stare delivered to everyone around the table.

With that said, he got up and left the Situation Room.

Walking back to the Oval Office, the President turned to Secretary Stanton and said,

"Please tell General Wheeler for me, that Major General Jeff Banks better find the missing Petrified convoy and Faith Knoll or he and his 8th Marines are going to go from living in hot tents and fucking goats in Afghanistan to living in igloos and fucking polar bears in the Antarctic. And that General in charge of Bagram, General Rainey. Get rid of him."

"Understood, Mr. President, but what is it you're not telling me about Faith Knoll? ISIL, al-Qaeda or whoever did this, sure went to a lot of trouble for one singer. They had to have used a lot of capital to pull this off and for what?" asked the Secretary of Defense.

"Ed, I have a feeling we're about to find out, and it isn't going to be pretty."

Back in the Oval Office with FBI Director Riley and Press Secretary Sullivan, President Burk had a big decision to make. Call Colburn or wait till he found out and called them.

"Has any of this hit the news wire or has our Woodward and Bernstein gotten wind of it yet?" asked the President.

The Attacks of Bagram, Kandahar, and Camp Leatherneck are all over the wire, but we have been able to put a lid on the USO convoy and the ambush for the moment. If ISIL or al-Qaeda or whoever did this, takes credit, or worse, we're busted."

"What's 'or worse'?"

"Video of the USO Convoy ambush on YouTube."

"We have to call Colburn and level with him, then get Sweeney and Todd on the line so we can get them working with us not against us."

CHAPTER 49

Gereshk, AF

Alpha Security had been monitoring all radio traffic and knew Country Road was ambushed and the approximate location. They knew Petrified was intact, and that they hooked up with a Marine unit that was guiding them back to Camp Leatherneck.

"Affirmative Petrified 6. Got you now that you turned your phone on. We have Romeo Tangos (rescue teams) in the air and on wheels heading your way. ETA 20 mikes."

"Were heading to Camp Leatherneck and..."

Alpha Security broke in, "That's a negative Petrified. The bridges over the Gereshk canal have been blown. You're not going to Camp Leatherneck anytime soon. Surprised your escort doesn't know this."

"Get some of our guys here fast, partner. I think we're being led into another ambush."

Matthews hung up and Faith, in the back seat, who has been fearful but quiet finally spoke up, "Sergeant Matthews. We're not going to make it are we?"

Matthews didn't have time to answer, and what could he say anyway. Instead, he clicked his helmet mic and said, "Petrified 2 this is 3. You trust me."

"With my life."

"On my three count you take out the Blue Team truck in your rear. Our escorts are bad guys. Turn around and lead us back to Kandahar.

Petrified 1 you take out the Blue Team in your front then turn and fall in behind me. Understood?"

Neither hesitated. Both answered, "Affirmative."

Buco was in the shotgun position but Jackson, a former Ranger, in the 50 cal. gun turret had also monitored the call, turned to the rear and pointed to the three o'clock position to the right of the Blue Team. The Blue team turret gunner hesitated and looked right as Jackson swiveled his 50 towards the Blue Team turret.

"One, two, three."

Boom, Boom, Boom, Boom. Boom.......

Jackson's 50 tore up the turret gunner. Then he moved the 50 lower and took out the Blue Team truck while Buco's driver, Bear, slammed on the breaks and turned the wheel hard, and the Humvee turned completely around like you would see a professional driver do, and Matthews followed suit. Petrified 1's turret gunner opened up his 50 on the Blue Team in his front, but the Blue Team Humvee, an M1046 model, fired a TOW Missile for a direct hit, pulverizing Petrified 1. Matthews in Petrified 3 heard the tremendous explosion behind him, knew it was not good but couldn't do anything about it. Petrified 2 and Petrified 3 pressed on east towards the Country Road ambush and Kandahar, hoping to meet the alpha rescue team sooner than later. Directly to their front, two Technicals suddenly appeared on the highway blocking their way. Two more were off each side of the highway forming an arc. Behind him, the two remaining Blue Team Humvees skidded to a stop.

Petrified 2 tried to shoot its way through but one of the off road Technicals opened up with an AA gun and tore him to pieces. Their run was over. Aside from his A5 assault rifle, Glock, and the two lightly armed 10th. Mountain troops, they were an unarmed transport Humvee. All four Technicals had their big guns pointing at him as well as the Blue Teams guns behind him. They weren't firing; they were just watching. Matthews's responsibility was the girl and her safety. There was nothing more he could do that wouldn't endanger her life more that it was. He turned his cell on and pressed the speed dial for Alpha Security and pressed his mic button and left it open. He may not be able to talk much longer, but his shop and the Romeo Tangos could listen. He gave his location and situation and said, "This is Petrified. If anyone is out there and can help, now would be a good time."

To Faith and the others in his vehicle, and those listening on the phone and radio he said, "OK. This is what we're going to do. Everybody stay calm, and let them tell us what they want. If they were going to kill us they would have done so. They want something." *Or someone*, thought Matthews.

Saddam al-Jamal, dressed as a Marine Lieutenant, and four of his men, similarly attired as enlisted Marines, got out of the Blue Team Humvees and approached Matthews's vehicle from behind. Matthews watched them approach in the side view mirrors, three on his side and two on the other side. They were all armed with A5 Automatic rifles, and most were pointed at Matthews. He walked up to Matthews's door and said, "Petrified 6. May I congratulate you? You made a good effort. We only want the woman. You and the rest stay in the vehicle. You will be taken hostage and redeemed."

One of his men opened the back door and grabbed Faith by the arm and pulled her out. Matthews started to resist and was rifle-butted in the side of his head.

When the two gunships and four armed Humvees of Romeo Tango, from Alpha Security, finally arrived, all that was left was the burned out carcass of Petrified 2 and Matthews transport Humvee. A team approached the Humvee expecting the worst, but it was empty. There was blood all over the inside, but Matthews, the two 10th soldiers, and Johnny Jones, the tribute singer, were gone. They knew Faith Knoll wouldn't be there because they were monitoring both Matthews's cell and radio, which were now, along with some flowers, the only things left in the Humvee.

This abduction would not go well for Alpha Security. They lost their team, vehicles, and most importantly their charge, the person they were hired to protect. Hopefully, they could find Matthews, Faith, and the others before the unimaginable happened. But if they didn't, they would also lose their reputation and their honor.

CHAPTER 50

WASHINGTON, DC

With Press Secretary Kelly Sullivan and FBI Director Riley joining President Burk in the Oval Office, President Burk asked Noreen to call Colburn. As expected, it didn't go very well, in fact, it almost didn't go at all. Colburn was up on everything and seemed to know more than them. From his contacts, Colburn found out who was providing Faith's security. He knew the outfit, and they were good. He had spoken to Faith, just yesterday, and knew she was going to Camp Leatherneck for one more show before she would return home. Then the news reports started breaking about the attacks. *CNN* was reporting on the attacks at Bagram, Kandahar, and Camp Leatherneck, Colburn knew what had happened, and he blamed himself, and the President. President Burk took responsibility and vowed to get her back.

Colburn took over the conversation, "Listen, Sarge, I don't know how current your intelligence is, but I just got off the horn with a buddy from Alpha Security in Afghanistan, and he told me that they lost them. They lost Petrified, Faith's PSD's call sign, and they lost Faith. Faith is gone. Nobody from Bagram, Kandahar or Camp Leatherneck sent anyone to help Country Road or Petrified. They were on their own. You and I know why, and we didn't stop it."

"We'll find her, and we'll get her back," said President Burk.

"Don't say that. Your clowns over there wouldn't lift a finger when it was going down. Too dangerous they said, too dangerous to send out rescue columns. Back when we were in, you, the captain and I, before all these armchair political correct generals took over, that was our job. We lived for danger, and that's why we got the big bucks. You're not going to find her. She could be anywhere by now, and they didn't go to all this effort to let you send in Seal Team Six and take her back. You'll hear. We'll all hear soon, and it won't be pretty," said Colburn.

"How do you want to play this?" asked the Captain.

"Get that Admiral Michaels with the NSA. He said he was monitoring the terrorist's, ISIL, al-Qaeda, and the Taliban's family's right? Have him ready to round up all their mothers, fathers, sons and daughters, brothers and sisters, uncles, nephews and fucking cousins. When the terrorists make their demands, we'll be ready to move," said Colburn.

"Ready to move? What does that mean?" asked President Burk.

"Look. I know you will try your best to get her back, but you've got to find her first. She could be anywhere by now. Just do what I told you to do. I know you, Sarge. You'll look for her, and you'll even negotiate under the table to get her back. If that doesn't work, call me. But if you call me you better be ready, because I will get her back and it won't be pretty. I've got a call to make to our Russian friend, and then I'll know more," said Colburn. Then he disconnected.

"What is Icy going to do, and why monitor the terrorist families?" asked Kelly.

The President and Riley looked at each other, and then the President said, "He's not going to do anything. He's going to wait on us, but he wants the terrorist leaders families located. I assume because he feels that sooner or later they will make contact, and we will then grab them," said the President.

"And if we don't find her?" asked Kelly.

"Then we call Icy back."

CHAPTER 51

CAMBRIDGE, MA

Colburn sat at his desk in his office on Harvard Street. Natasha was, as always, under the desk, watching, listening, protecting, dreaming, and doing what dogs have always done, waiting for their Alpha to make a move.

"It's time girl. Can't put if off any longer."

He reached over to the credenza and took one of the leather gloves Vova had given him years ago while in Afghanistan, and tossed it to Natasha. She growled and twisted it around like a rag doll. Colburn grabbed one end and a tug of war ensued. Natasha won.

He took out his cell and dialed Vova.

"Salam Icy. To what do I owe this pleasure?" asked Vova.

Salam, my ass, thought Colburn.

"Cut the shit, Vova. I'm not going to ask you why you did what you did; I know why. You exercised your warped mind and jumped to conclusion that I killed Kim Ly. I would have, but she was a woman of honor who took her own life. I know this is about revenge. It's about hurting me by taking Faith, but return her back now safe and unharmed, and I will let you live."

"You know nothing, my friend. Even if I could help you, it's too late. I'm afraid the men who have your sweetheart have wills of their own and their own agenda. Quite frankly, I think they're animals. Have they made their demands known yet?"

Natasha was growling and baring her teeth.

"You know they haven't."

"Oh, but they will and soon, I suspect. All your President has to do is comply, and you get her back. That's not so bad is it?"

Natasha was growling louder. She dropped the glove and was staring intently at it.

"So that's the game you're going to play, is it. Go through the motions. Play or get played, isn't that what you said? If she dies Vova, you die."

"It's out of my hands, Icy. Just make the deal and you two love birds will be back in your sugar shack in the woods before you know it. One more thing. When you come for me, Icy, do bring your bitch wolf with you. I would like to teach her some table manners."

"She's looking forward to dining with you," said Colburn, and touched off.

Da mad, Sarge gone, Max gone, Faith gone, Pack not safe.

CHAPTER 52

WASHINGTON, DC

The White House Situation Room is a 5,525-square-foot (513.3 m2) conference room and intelligence management center in the basement of the West Wing of the White House. It is run by the National Security Council staff for the use of the President of the United States and his advisors to monitor and deal with crises at home and abroad and to conduct secure communications with outside (often overseas) persons. The Situation Room is equipped with secure, advanced communications equipment for the President to maintain command and control of U.S. forces around the world.

The President sits with his back to the entrance wall and doorway. The window openings at the left side of this space, visible from the exterior for historical appearance are blocked inside for security. FBI Director Ray Riley, Chief of Staff Bill Nicholas and Press Secretary Kelly Sullivan, and another thirteen deputy directors, adjutants, and staff fill all the seats on either wall paralleling the table. All additional twelve seats around the table were occupied by: Vice President Hilton, Chairman of the Joint Chief of Staff General Joe Dunnford, Army Chief of Staff General Mark Miller, Commandant of the Marine Corps General Joe Wheeler Jr., Secretary of Defense Ed Stanton, Secretary of State Matt Walsh, CIA Director John Bader, NSA Director Admiral Roger Michaels, Director of National Intelligence James Dapper, Director for Counterterrorism for the National Security Council Audrey Tomaso, Commander of the Joint Special Operations Group, General Webb

Marshal, and U.S. Army General John F. Camp, Commander, International Security Assistance Force and United States Forces-Afghanistan.

There were four large recessed side wall monitors, usually airing *CNN, FOX, Al Jazeera,* and *CNBC,* and one complete interactive wall directly facing the President, for video conferencing or MSPIP (Multi-Screen, Picture-in-Picture). Currently, a live feed from Afghanistan had on Lieutenant General Cyrus, Deputy Commanding General, United States Forces – Afghanistan and Eric Duke, former Navy Seal and founder of Alpha Security.

The President, from his seat at the head of the table, looked around the room at the most powerful assembled group of people in the world and said, "Gentlemen. Ladies. It's been two days since the attacks on Bagram, Kandahar, Camp Leatherneck, and the ambush of the USO convoy Country Road, and destruction of convoy Petrified, the abduction of its team leader Jeff Matthews, two 10th mountain troops, and two USO performers. One of which is Faith Knoll. Some of us suspect that all these events were orchestrated for one purpose, to abduct Faith Knoll. Since no one has whispered in my ear that she has been located you can assume that we're not here to discuss a rescue plan. We can't rescue her until we find her. Is that a fair assessment?"

No one acknowledged the President's condescending remarks.

The President continued, "We have the world's finest military operators, Delta Force, standing by, ready to go in and get her, and they are determined not to return without her. But we can't send in Delta Force because we can't find her. We have satellites that can read the words in a book from a hundred miles up in space. We have drones that can fly inside a house or tent or up a camel's ass if so ordered, but we can't find a blond in a desert of brunettes. Does anyone have one solid piece of evidence that suggest where she might be?"

"Mr. President," said Lieutenant General Cyrus, Deputy Commanding General, United States Forces – Afghanistan. "Mr. Duke, in charge of Alpha Security over here, and I have had all our assets looking. We may have caught a break. I'll let Mr. Duke take over.

"Mr. President, we require all our contractors to have GPS trackers imbedded. We have just started receiving a signal from Jeff Matthews's tracker.

He is the team leader of Petrified. We, General Cyrus and I, have a joint recon team on the way, as we speak."

"Gentlemen that's the best news I have heard since this whole thing started. General Marshal, have your Delta Force ready to go in," said the President.

"Mr. President," interrupted General Cyrus. "These terrorist are not stupid, and we have been tricked before. We need to be careful. We could find Miss Knoll and Petrified, or we could find Matthews leg with the imbedded tracker. Whoever did this planned it well, and I don't think they would go through all this trouble and leave a trail as easy as this to follow."

"Then why imbed the tracker in the first place if the terrorists are expecting it?"

"Sir. It's standard procedure for all our operators. An insurance policy requirement, I'm afraid. We usually use them to locate the bodies so that we can bring them home. Sometimes the tracker is the only identifier left. The terrorists do not like private contractors. They call them the al Sharmutas, the Whores, and they do not treat them kindly when captured."

"When will we know general?"

"Soon."

The President turned, from the screen image of General Cyrus to his left, towards NSA Director Admiral Roger Michaels, and said, "Admiral, has your team located the families?"

Several of those around the table who had not been fully briefed on this portion of the operation looked perplexed and seemed to wonder why the NSA was searching for families of the five missing Americans. Surely, they must have thought the U.S. Post Office or Google could find them with less drama.

"Mr. President, we have located, have eyes on, and appropriation teams ready," said Admiral Michaels.

"For all three families?"

"Yes, sir." Looking down at a list he began reading, "For Mullah Akhtar Mohammad Mansour, Leader of the Taliban, we have his mother and father.

His wife and two children were killed in an air strike. We have a brother, several cousins, aunts, and uncles.

For Ayman Mohammed Rabie al-Zawahiri, the Egyptian leader of al-Qaeda, we have his father, his mother and wife are deceased, four young children, brothers and a sister, several cousins, aunts, and uncles.

For Abu Bakr al-Baghdadi, the Sunni Iraqi and leader of ISIL, we have both mother and father, wife, two kids, a brother, and two sisters and a bunch of aunts, uncles, and cousins."

Hearing this for the first time produced an inaudible murmur throughout the room. Even the President stopped, as an icy chill went up his spine. *How profound*, he thought.

"We're waiting on you order to move, sir," added Admiral Michaels.

Everyone seemed to know where this might be going, but no one dared vocalize it.

The President feeling the contained outrage around the table attempted to quiet the tension by telling a white lie with the hoped of reducing their guilt.

"We are locating the families of these three terrorist leaders for the expressed purpose of sending in appropriation teams to capture, interrogate, and obtain information, from one, or all three leaders should an attempt at family contact be made. If we cannot locate Miss Knoll, they might provide us with crucial information needed to bring her, and the others home safely. It goes without saying everything discussed here stays here. The public is still not aware of Faith's abduction, and I want to keep it that way as long as we can. Hopefully, we will find and rescue her before anyone knows she was gone."

Some around the table suspected the real truth but never imagined the fruition of Michael's List, as it was to become known, including First Lady Kelly Sullivan Burk. She knew her husband as a man of honor, but she also knew what he, Riley and Colburn were capable of.

CHAPTER 53

WASHINGTON, DC

The Situation Room meeting had taken longer than anticipated and produced less than desired. General Cyrus's recon team had arrived at the tracker location and found his bloody GPS tracker, sitting on the front seat of an abandoned vehicle outside Kabul. Matthews might still be alive, but he was hurting.

Back in the Oval Office, President Burk and Press Secretary Sullivan sat on one couch and FBI Director Riley on the opposite couch.

"We are getting hundreds of calls and social media is all a buzz about these attacks. Why didn't we see them coming? Who is in charge over there? Who's in charge here? There are rumors starting to appear about kidnappings. We can't keep Faith's abduction under wraps much longer, and I don't think we should. There are thousands of soldiers over there who know what's going on. They have cell phones and access to the internet. It's going to get out, and we need to get out in front of it. I have something prepared, and I think we should release it immediately," said Kelly.

The President took the press release and read it. It was brief but said that several American including two soldiers and three civilians were missing and presumed captured. Everything possible was being done to find and rescue them. He handed it back to Kelly.

Just then Noreen Ward came in and said Mr. Todd and Sweeney were on the line.

The President motioned for Kelly to give the press release to Noreen.

"Noreen, please release this immediately," said Kelly, "then put Sweeney and Todd through."

Five minutes later Noreen buzzed the President.

"The press release is out, and I have Mr. Todd and Mr. Sweeney on the line."

"Thank you, Noreen, Put them through."

"Mr. Todd. Mr. Sweeney. I am here, on speaker, with Director Riley and Press Secretary Sullivan. Thank you for holding on. It's been a little hectic here this morning."

Both Todd and Sweeney acknowledged everyone. It was the Presidents dime, so Todd and Sweeney deferred and waited for the President to begin.

"Tell me where you are on your stories. Hedgehampton and Moscow?"

"Sweeney here Mr. President. Doing some follow-up on Hedgehampton, but it seems to be a one off. Got a lot of interest. Got Hedgehampton all in a tizzy, but it's a one off."

"Todd?"

"I have plenty on Moscow. Unlike Hedgehampton, it's got legs, but I can't seem to make the story work without outing our friend."

"I think that's a good observation and decision, and we appreciate your cooperation. Where are you guys now?"

"In the News Corp Building in Manhattan, but I'm sure you know that. We appreciate your time, considering everything happening in Afghanistan, but I don't believe we have done anything, recently, to rate another call to the carpet."

"I am going to tell you something. I just sent out a press release that tells the American people that there are five Americans missing in Afghanistan and presumed captured."

"We received it a moment ago."

"Then I am going to tell you something that's not in that press release Mr. Todd. One of the captured Americans is Faith Knoll."

"Oh shit! Wait a minute. What's she doing in Afghanistan? I didn't hear anything about that."

"Oh shit is right. She was entertaining the troops, and when we found out, we tried to keep it quiet."

"Look Mr. President. I kept my end of the deal. I didn't do the Moscow story."

"It was your photograph on Page Six that got her captured."

"Don't pin this on me Mr. President. If you were so concerned why did you let her go to Afghanistan?"

"I warned you of the potential damage of that photo, Mr. Todd. I told you that if this goes south, I would personally cut your balls off. You better hope we find her and soon," said Riley.

Suddenly the conversation got very quiet. Then, President Burk, Riley, and Kelly heard commotion and excited background chatter over the speaker. Then they heard Todd come back on.

"Jesus Christ, Jesus Christ this is so bad…"

"What? What's happening?" asked the President.

Noreen came in the room all excited just as the other door flew opened and Chief of Staff Bill Nicholas exploded into the Oval Office yelling for the President to come to the Cabinet Room immediately. President Burk, Director Riley, and Press Secretary Sullivan all jumped up and ran out of the Oval Office to the Cabinet Room just next door. As they left the office they could hear Todd's voice, over the speaker, "I'm so, so sorry…."

CHAPTER 54

WASHINGTON, DC

It took them less than five seconds to reach the Cabinet Room when they entered there were already several people gathered around a large wall mounted TV. Everyone parted and let the President through to the front. There on the screen was a *CNN* reporter, Christie Frank with "Breaking News" flashing over her left shoulder and a picture of Faith Knoll, kneeling in an orange jumpsuit next to a man completely encased in black.

The reporter was talking, "….. and this just in from *Al Jazeera*, Doha, Qatar. I have been told to tell you that viewer discretion is advised and that we can't authenticate, at this time, the video you are about to see." The reported faded, and a video came up on the screen. The video was like the picture. Faith, in an orange jumpsuit, kneeling with her hands tied behind her back. Her blond hair was pulled back and tied with a string, and her face held an expression of strength and resolve. The man was dressed entirely in black, wearing a black three-hole balaclava, completely covering his face, except for his eyes and mouth. He had a brown leather shoulder holster, containing an automatic pistol. In his left hand was a large knife, while his right hand held the back of Faiths orange jumpsuit. Behind him were the three flags of ISIL, Taliban, and al-Qaeda. They were in the desert with nothing but sand and more sand. His accent, as he began to speak in English, was British,

"I am Maharib Allah, Warrior of God. This infidel, you call Faith Knoll, is an American whore, who has come here to service the crusader army. As a government, you have been at the forefront of aggression towards the Islamic State. You have plotted against us, and gone far out of your way to find reasons to interfere in our affairs. Today, your military air force is attacking us daily in Iraq, Syria, and Afghanistan. Your strikes have caused casualties amongst thousands of innocent Muslims. You're no longer fighting an insurgency. We are an Islamic army and a State that has been accepted by a large number of Muslims worldwide, so effectively, any aggression towards the Islamic State is an aggression towards Muslims from all walks of life who have accepted the Islamic Caliphate as their leadership. We are now united as one force against you. Any attempt by you, Satan Burk, to deny the Muslims their rights of living in safety under the Islamic Caliphate will result in the bloodshed of your people.

We demand your crusading armies leave our countries immediately. You will pay $20 billion dollars restitution for the lives and property you have destroyed, and you will release the ten remaining Guantanamo Islamic prisoners. You have 48 hours to accept our terms. If you accept, she will be released. If you do not, she will pay for your mistakes with her life. I will slice her throat and cut off her head, and you and the world will watch her die a slow and painful death. You will see her infidel blood drain from her body the way it drains from ours.

Allāhu Akbar."

The video then focused on Faith's face, and while she attempted to appear strong you could see her captor's words had their effect. She closed her eyes, and a tear appeared and started to run down her cheek. She started to tremble and finally to hide her shame, she bowed her head so you couldn't see her cry.

The President and everyone in the room stood there in silent shock. Some were in tears.

"Why on god's earth would they want to hurt her? She was only over there to bring joy to our soldiers," said one of the staffers.

President Burk, Riley, and Kelly knew differently but weren't about to tell. President Burk looked at Director Riley, and you could see in their eyes that either would give anything for just one minute with that man.

The TV reporter reappeared on screen with the still picture of Faith and her captor back up again. The reporter was blond and attractive and might have been taken for Faith's twin sister, but she was visibly shaken. She tried to compose herself and finally said,

"I apologize for what you have just witnessed. I had not seen the video beforehand. It is shocking, and truthfully I don't think I can continue. I think I am about to be sick. You can't do this to this woman, not to America's Sweetheart."

With that, she got up from behind the anchor chair, pulled off her earpiece and mic, and left the set. *CNN* went to commercial.

The Secretary of Defense had been watching the breaking news, in another room, and came into the Cabinet Room looking for the President.

"Ed, get anybody that's around, into the Situation Room now. If they're not here, get them on live feed or Skype. Ten Minutes," said the President.

When the President, FBI Director, and Press Secretary Sullivan made it down to the Situation Room, most the same characters, from earlier, were still there and either seated or on one of the PIP screens. *CNN, FOX* and *AL Jazeera* were all airing on different monitors.

"Thank you for getting together again on such short notice. I'm sure you have all seen the video and appreciate that we have a real bad situation here that I don't see getting better anytime soon. Ed, can you bring us all up to date with what you have?"

"We have a lot of assets all over the world, and we're expecting feedback soon, but here's what we have right now. The video was hand delivered to *AL Jazeera*, headquarters in Doha, Qatar, a little over an hour ago, 10:05 a.m. our time, 5:05 p.m. in Qatar. They won't give us the package it came in or access to the video, but we have a team on the way there now to convince them otherwise. We also have our ambassador putting pressure on Sheikh Hamad bin Khalifa al Thani, *AL Jazeera* owner, and a member of the ruling al Thani Qatari royal family. He's on our side, for the moment, so we can expect results.

Britain's Secret Intelligence Service, aka MI6, has taken voice prints from the video and got a match. His name is Saddam al-Jamal, cousin of al-Qaeda operational commander Ahmed al-Masri, son of slain leader Abu al-Masri.

He reports directly to Ayman Mohammed Rabie al-Zawahiri, the Egyptian-born leader of al-Qaeda.

We're going over the video and the flags in the background tell a story, but it's not giving us anything on location.

From the video, we know that ISIL, the Taliban, and al-Qaeda have joined together to pull this off. They couldn't have come up with that themselves. They must have a common goal or sponsor. I'm thinking sponsor. If Zawahiri is involved, you can bet al-Baghdadi of ISIL and Mansour with the Taliban are thick as thieves in this. That's where we are now."

"Thanks, Ed. Your team has made some good progress, but we're on the clock and still have no idea where she is. They think we can't find her, and they know we can't negotiate with terrorists, especially with the time frame and demands they're making. But what they don't know is I will drop nuclear bombs on every fucking Muslim country before I will allow them to executive Faith Knoll on TV."

If the President was serious, the implication was obvious. Faith would die as collateral damage, and the world might go black.

"If we don't want to start WWIII, we have to find her and rescue her. We have less than 47 hours to do it," said the President, as he got up and walked out.

CHAPTER 55

WASHINGTON, DC

Walking back to the Oval Office, Press Secretary Kelly Sullivan and Chief of Staff Bill Nicholas, walking behind the President and Director Riley, were both still in shock after seeing the video. They both realized the President needed to address the American people and fast. Bill spoke up first.

"Mr. President. We think people around the world are going to be shocked, and sickened by what they just witnessed. The American people more so because she is America's Sweetheart. Kelly and I feel you need to get out in front of this and fast. Reassure the world and our country that you're not going to let it happen, that we have a plan. Something, anything, but you need to do it now. Tonight."

The President had stopped, in the corridor, to listen to Bill.

"I agree Bill. But as I stand here now, I really don't know if we can stop them. If we can't find her, how can we prevent it from happening?" The President thought for a moment and said, "Go ahead and set it up for tonight; by then we will either have her or a have a plan."

Back in the Oval Office, President Burk and FBI Director Riley discussed the situation and the options.

"I don't see us finding her and mounting a successful rescue within their time schedule. We don't even have a clue as to where she may be. They clammed up. There is absolutely no chatter, nothing but the video. We can try and get more time by pretending to agree to their demands, start mobilizing troops to leave the country, set time schedules, and start mustering Gitmo detainees. Go through the motions, but we need to call him," said Riley.

Kelly and Secretary of Defense Ed Stanton came in. Kelly sat on the couch next to her husband, and Stanton took a seat next to Riley.

"Let's shelve for a moment, any pretext for agreeing to their demands. As far as calling him, I know we should, but I am afraid if we do, there will be no turning back. We won't be able to stop him, and what scares me is I might not want to. If we call him, we release hell, and we will become worse than them. The world and our own country will condemn us. If we don't call him, she will die. We have yet to accept that we can't beat ISIL and the other terrorists with conventional armies and bombs. To beat them, we have to fight them on their terms. We have to get down in the gutter."

"You're talking about Colburn aren't you? You said he had a plan to get these terrorist leaders. How can that hurt? We need to do something," said Kelly.

"Kelly you may think you know Colburn, but you only know the Colburn he wants you to see. I know him when he turns into Icy. Colburn is strong, smart, and honorable. He can even be charming when he works at it, but when he becomes Icy, he becomes a predator. He is an apex predator, alpha predator, super predator. He resides at the top of the food chain upon which no other creatures prey. There's no right and no wrong. Only his absolute obsession with getting what he wants, and he won't stop till he gets it," said Riley.

"Ed, there are some things you will hear for the first time, but trust me and stick with it. Whatever happens, it is better you hear it first hand," said the President.

The Secretary of Defense nodded.

The President got up and walked to Noreen's office and asked her to get Colburn on the phone. She put her hand over the phone mouthpiece and mouthed, "It's Mr. Colburn calling for you."

The President nodded and walked back to the couch next to Kelly and pushed the speaker button, "Icy, just about to call. The Captain, Kelly, and SecDef Ed Stanton are on speaker with us. Listen..."

"Sarge, I know what you're going to say, so let's make this quick and easy. Your Admiral Michaels has everyone accounted for. His teams have eyes on all the family members of Mansour, of the Taliban, al-Zawahiri, of al-Qaeda, and Abu Bakr al-Baghdadi, of ISIL. Right?

Being a little taken back by Icy's assertiveness, President Burk let him have control. He looked at Stanton and Stanton nodded.

"Right."

"You have mothers and fathers, wives, kids, brothers, sisters, aunts, uncles and cousins. By my count, you have eyes on about forty family members in total."

"Right."

"OK. Write this down."

Everyone but the President grabbed a pad and pen from the coffee table.

"I want you to move on them now. Snatch and grab. Get your 3 Delta teams to pick them all up now. Everyone at the same time. It's got to be simultaneous. No tip-offs, no leaks, no locals involved. Get them all, in complete secrecy to Bagram, and stash them in a hanger. No locals see them coming in, and no locals get near them. They stay and sleep in the hanger. Build a separate room of about 1000 sf with a chain fence cutting the space in half. In the front half, I want a TV studio with redundant high-quality A/V systems linked for a live feed to *AL-Jazeera* in Qatar and feeds to *CNN* and *FOX*. I want the best geeks and treks, you have, to run it. I want a director and a real TV production crew. I want all the family members in orange jumpsuits, men, women, and kids. I want Army interpreters on site. I want someone in charge there who will follow my orders to the letter. That person will get that order directly from you, to report to, and obey only me. Understood?"

"Understood."

"I am in Cambridge. Get me and two of my mates to Bagram now, and send someone to get Natasha."

SOD Stanton was writing but thinking, *who the hell are these people? Captain, Sarge, Natasha? Is he talking to Putin? Is Putin Icy?*

"Got it. The Captain will arrange your trip. Anything else?"

"Yea. Lock up Sweeney and Todd before they get wind of this, and I read about it in the Afghan addition of the *NY Post* tomorrow. While you're at it put a sock in Fitzpatrick's mouth. We have less than 46 hours left, and I want my TV special to go live noon your time tomorrow."

The line went dead.

The President looked at SOD Stanton and said, "I'll explain later. Now, just trust me, but make sure you get your best people to make this happen. The Captain, excuse me, Director Riley and I have worked with this man many times. He doesn't fail, and he likes to be in charge, as you may have noticed. If we don't find and rescue Faith and the other four Americans by tomorrow morning, 'It's Show Time'."

Stanton shook his head in disbelief, but he was a loyal soldier, got up, pulled out his phone, and started issuing orders. Riley got out his phone to order an FBI jet to get Colburn and company from Logan to Bagram and get Natasha back to the White House. Kelly left to make sure everything was set for the President's Address to the Nation tonight at 9 p.m.

President Burk alone on the couch wondered, *where it will all end. If we can't find and rescue Faith will it all come down to Icy? I know what he's up too, but do they? The Captain knows, I saw it in his eyes. I just hope when the shows over, it's Porky the Pig who has the last word. "Th-th-th-that's all folks!"*

CHAPTER 56

BAGRAM, AFGHANISTAN

Bagram Air Base is the largest U.S. military base in Afghanistan. It is located next to the ancient city of Bagram in the Parwan Province of Afghanistan. Bagram is currently maintained by the Combined Joint Task Force 10th Mountain Division. It is also maintained by the 82nd Combat Aviation Brigade (Task Force Pale Horse) and 3-10 GSAB (Task Force Phoenix) of the U.S. Army, with the 455th Air Expeditionary Wing of the U.S. Air Force and other U.S. Army, U.S. Navy, U.S. Marine Corps, U.S. Coast Guard, and ISAF units having sizable tenant populations. The airfield features a dual runway capable of handling any size military aircraft including the Lockheed Martin C-5 Galaxy military transport, one of which just landed carrying The 1st Special Forces Operational Detachment-Delta (1st SFOD-D), popularly known as Delta Force.

Secretary of Defense Ed Stanton, after speaking with many of his top generals and advisors, including his Director for Counterterrorism for the National Security Council Audrey Tomaso, Commander of the Joint Special Operations Group General Webb Marshal, and U.S. Army General John F. Camp, Commander, International Security Assistance Force and United States Forces-Afghanistan, placed a secure phone call to Lieutenant General Ken Troy. General Troy was their man in Afghanistan, running the Eyes-ON phase of the operation, now assigned the code name Loro Famiglia (Their Family), heretofore referred to as Lima Foxtrot. General Troy was combat tested as a young company commander during Operation Enduring Freedom and every major operation since. His appropriation teams were ready for the snatch and grab.

"General Troy, I have our Commander-in-Chief on the line, and he would like a word," said Secretary Stanton on a secure phone from Washington.

"General, President Burk here. Secretary Stanton has given you your marching orders. Can I count on you to follow those orders?"

"Understood and affirmative sir."

"Do you have everything you need, and are your appropriation teams in place?"

"Affirmative on both counts sir."

"You will report to Mr. Colburn, who will arrive shortly, and who has my complete faith and confidence. You and your men, and the technicians assigned to you will follow his orders unflinchingly. Do you understand?"

"Understood, and if I may sir, we studied Mr. Colburn at West Point. His exploits and his ice cold reputation proceed him."

"Yes, well, I didn't realize he was old enough to make it into the history books, but I will be sure to inform him. General, just be prepared to go where you may have never thought possible. Be prepared to 'Cross into the Abyss'. You have your orders. Deploy your appropriation teams now."

"Affirmative sir."

The 1st Special Forces Operational Detachment-Delta (1st SFOD-D), popularly known as Delta Force, is a U.S. Army unit used for hostage rescue and counter-terrorism as well as direct action and reconnaissance against high-value targets. Delta Force is one of the United States military's primary counter-terrorism units and falls under the operational control of the Joint Special Operations Command.

Lt. General Troy had his Headquarters Company with him in Bagram, and his appropriation teams, 'snatch and grab', throughout the Mideast, Europe, and Africa. He had one Squadron hunting each family plus reserves and support.

A Squadron (Alpha) hunting al-Baghdadi's family.
B Squadron (Bravo) hunting al-Zawahiri's family.

C Squadron (Charley) hunting Mansour's family.

D Squadron (Delta) Reserve.

E Squadron (Echo SEASPRAY) Aviation.

G Squadron (Golf) Operational Support Troop and advanced force operations, reconnaissance and surveillance.

Combat Support Troop (Charley Sierra) contains WMD experts, breachers, and other specialists.

C Squadron, Charley Squadron, typical of the four appropriation squadrons, including the reserve, was commanded by Captain Mitch Beck and consisted of 36 operatives divided into 9 four man teams. Each team leader was a staff sergeant and in some cases a lieutenant. The size and amount of teams would vary depending on the location and density of designated family members, but Alpha, Bravo, and Delta were similarly staffed. Charley Squadron was hunting Taliban leader Mullah Akhtar Mohammad Mansour's family. Mansour's family was pretty centralized in two locations.

The first is the town of Karate, Kandahar Province, Afghanistan, near the border with Iran, where his mother, father, one aunt, one brother and his two children, and three cousins live. The second location is Quetta, Pakistan, just 100 miles from Kandahar, where another brother, his three children, and six cousins live. An eleven-year-old son thought to have been killed in an earlier attract, surfaced outside London, in Abbotsfield School, located in Hillingdon. MI5, the United Kingdom's domestic counterintelligence agency was requested by President Burk, through Prime Minister Tony Wilson, to handle his appropriation.

Captain Beck received his go order from Colonel Robert Axelrod, General Troy's operations director in Bagram.

With the support of Echo-Aviation and Golf-Reconnaissance and Surveillance, Captain Beck's teams moved in on the families. Five teams moved hard and fast into Karize, at the same time four teams moved into Quetta. Alpha hunting al-Baghdadi's family, and Bravo hunting al-Zawahiri's family, simultaneously moved in on their respective targets.

Beck with his Team Karize aboard eight Apache helicopters, and Sergeant Bell's Team Quetta's aboard eight Apache helicopters descended into both towns, disembarked and followed the GPS direction and laser pointers to each family member, whose location was provided by Golf-Reconnaissance and Surveillance, already in place on the ground. Family members were identified, corralled, bound with plastic ties, and boarded into the waiting Apaches. Neighbors looked on as the crying and scared family members were abducted, but did not try to interfere. They knew the family members and knew to whom they belonged. Whether they were intimidated or just too surprised to react, they just hid and watched. The Charley snatch and grab teams, the captured family members and the Golf- Reconnaissance and Surveillance team all boarded the Apaches and lifted off. In less than 15 minutes they were here and gone and headed directly for Bagram.

Alpha hunting al-Baghdadi's family, and Bravo hunting al-Zawahiri's family performed similarly and also headed towards Bagram.

General Troy's construction team, made up of the Navy's Construction Battalion, aka Seabees, were finishing construction of the hanger modifications, including living quarters for the captured families and the A/V studio for the live broadcast.

At 2 p.m. Colburn left Boston's Logan Airport, aboard an FBI commandeered Bombardier's Global 8000, one of the longest range private jets on the market, which got 7,900 nautical miles on a single tank of gas flying at Mach 0.85 with a crew of three and three passengers. It would make the 5,800 miles from Boston to Bagram with fuel to spare.

Just as the President was about to address the nation on TV, military helicopters and transport aircraft, containing captured terrorist families and Delta Force teams, began arriving at Bagram.

Colburn was in Afghan airspace and expected to touch down in 30 minutes, at 2 a.m. EST, 9 p.m. local, after a 12-hour flight. Time was winding down to meet the terrorist demand deadline, and Colburn's plan was coming together. He thought to himself as he looked out the jets porthole, *Everything is going too well. The hangers are secure, and the terrorist families are arriving on schedule and without incident. It doesn't feel right. What am I missing?*

CHAPTER 57

WASHINGTON, DC

It was 9 p.m., and President Burk was sitting behind his desk, in the Oval Office, waiting for his cue. 5,4,3,2...

"Good evening. Last Wednesday, our bases in Afghanistan were attacked. Americans soldiers and civilians were killed, wounded, and captured as they came together to celebrate freedom in a far off country. They were taken from family and friends who loved them deeply. They were white and black, Latino, Asian, and Muslims, immigrants and American-born, moms and dads, daughters and sons, brothers and sisters. Each of them served their fellow citizens, and all of them were part of our American family.

Tonight, I want to talk with you about this tragedy, the broader threat of terrorism, and how we can keep our country safe.

Our Intelligence Agencies are still gathering the facts about what happened in Afghanistan, but here is what we know. Our bases were attacked. Our soldiers, civilian contractors and USO entertainers and support staff were brutally murdered, injured, and some were captured and taken prisoner by the Islamic terrorist factions, ISIL, al-Qaeda and the Taliban. So far we have evidence that these killers were directed by a terrorist organization overseas and part of a broader conspiracy. It is clear that the three factions have gone down the dark path of radicalization, embracing a perverted interpretation of Islam that calls for war against America and the West. They had stockpiled assault weapons, ammunition, rockets, mortars, anti-aircraft weapons, and SAM missiles. This was an act of terrorism, designed to kill American soldiers, Marines, and innocent civilians, who were in Afghanistan at the request of Afghanistan's duly elected government. Our nation has been at war with terrorists since al-Qaeda, and the Taliban killed nearly 3,000 Americans on 9/11. In the process, we've hardened our defenses from airports to financial centers, to other critical infrastructure. Intelligence and law enforcement agencies have disrupted countless plots here and overseas and worked around the clock to keep us safe. Our military and counterterrorism profession-als have relentlessly pursued terrorist networks overseas disrupting safe havens in several different countries, killing Osama bin Laden, and decimating al Qaeda and Taliban leadership.

We are not at war with Islam. There are many more good Muslims than bad, but they seem to get caught up in the terrorist propaganda and get swept away with the movement like the German people did with the Nazis. As long as you think your guys are winning you drink the Cool Aid and go with the flow. When their guys start to lose, they have a change of heart, but by then it may be too late. Good Muslims are following the Muslin Reform Movement and standing up against Islamic Terrorism.

Over the last few years, however, the terrorist threat has evolved into a new phase, gotten stronger, and introduced a new player ISIL, the Islamic State of Iraq and the Levant. As we've become better at preventing complex, multifaceted attacks like 9/11, terrorists turned to less complicated acts of violence like the fear and mass shootings that are all too common in our society. It is this type of attack that we saw in New York, Chicago, and Los Angeles as well as in Fort Hood in 2009, in Chattanooga earlier this year, and recently in San Bernardino. And as groups like ISIL grow stronger amidst the chaos of war in Iraq and Syria, and as the Internet erases the distance between countries, we see growing efforts by terrorists to poison the minds of people like the Boston Marathon bombers and the San Bernardino killers.

For almost two years, I've confronted this evolving threat each morning in my intelligence briefing, and now they are attacking our bases and innocent civilians abroad. They are making unreasonable demands and have sunken to a new low by threatening to execute an innocent American hero, Faith Knoll.

So tonight I am sending them a message. If you target Americans, you will have no safe haven. Let me make this crystal clear. We will never give in to your demands, but we will get all the prisoners back safe and sound. When the President of the United States is faced with no alternative but to, "Cry Havoc, and let slip the dogs of war," there will be no turning back. What happens next will shake the world. America is being forced into the gutter with the terrorists, and we will now fight them on their level. May God help them. We will shock and put the fear of God into ISIS, al-Qaeda, the Taliban, their sponsors and Islamic terrorists throughout the world.

God help us and God bless America."

The President had kept the address short and sweet, but that did now stop the White House switchboard from lighting up. Social media was all abuzz trying to decipher and opine on the President's final remark. # Cry Havoc. (A remark he borrowed from Fitzpatrick's interview with *FOX*.) It was being tweeted by everyone everywhere. Everywhere there were photos and music videos playing Faith Knoll songs. There were candlelight vigils and *CNN* Specials. The other side of the aisle was calling for his resignation, and his own party was looking at a one term president.

President Burk had considered having FBI Director Riley accompany Colburn to Afghanistan, but decided against it. Colburn didn't play well with others, even his best friends. President Burk would have to rely on General Troy to be his eyes and ears.

America was running out of time to find America's Sweetheart or they would watch her die live on TV. Impossible! He would not let it happen. He called Lieutenant General Cyrus, Deputy Commanding General, United States Forces, Afghanistan and Duke, the head of Alpha Security, but they were nowhere with their search. He called Admiral Michaels, the NSA Director, and even with all their satellites and computer intercepts they were finding nothing but silence.

"The terrorists have stopped communicating, at least by phone and the internet. They have gone to the deep web. To the dark space," said Admiral Michaels.

The President ordered the continued illusion of accepting the terrorist demands by having funds transferred, asking the terrorist community for account information, and by moving troops and terrorist prisoners here and there. Just going through the motions.

Everything is falling apart according to plan, thought President Burk.

CHAPTER 58

BAGRAM, AFGHANISTAN

Colburn and his two mates, operators actually from his past life, jumped out of the Humvee in front of Hanger 22, now dubbed *Catch 22*. The hanger was pretty typical, in that it was a prefab metal structure of about 6000 sf. with a gable roof and skylights. The hanger was located in an isolated area of the base and well protected from prying eyes. General Troy and Colonel Axelrod, met Colburn at the hanger entrance.

"Mr. Colburn. General Troy. Pleased to make your acquaintance. This is Colonel Axelrod, my operational commander."

"General, Colonel. These are my two mates, Smith, and Wesson. They will be working with me."

General Troy did not at all seem upset with the fake names, especially after he noticed what was in the shoulder holsters all three wore; Smith & Wesson M&P 11 shot 357 Cal. Sig. Pistols. Unlike Colburn, neither man, Smith, 6'-3" and black, or Wesson 6'-2" and Chinese, shook hands with the general or colonel.

"General, what's the status?" asked Colburn.

"All three appropriation teams are back. No incidents. No casualties. All identified family members of Mullah Akhtar Mohammad Mansour, of the Taliban, Ayman Mohammed Rabie al-Zawahiri, of al-Qaeda, and Abu Bakr al-Baghdadi, of ISIL, are accounted for. We have several family members in route now, from Europe and Africa. Their ETA is 1 hour."

He handed Colburn the guest list and continued, "We have everyone settled in their quarters, which include areas for sleeping, toilets, showers, and dining. The chain link fence has been installed between the guest quarters and the studio, and between families."

"I want eyes on everyone all the time, even in the bathrooms. No private stalls, no belts, no razors, no meds. Just like a prison. Understood?" asked Colburn.

"We assumed as much, and it has been is done," said Colonel Axelrod.

"The TV recording studio is complete and being tested now. Everything is hooked up and working properly. The technicians are good and know their stuff. We have established live feed links with *AL- Jazeera, CNN, FOX,* and we also added *BBC* just in case. We have press releases and Breaking News Bulletins ready for pre-release to all the major TV stations, and to go out onto social media, including *Dabiq*, ISIL's magazine, via #dabiq. *Twitter* is their platform of choice. Everyone everywhere will know something big is coming and at what time it's coming," said General Troy.

"Good. I want to proof the releases; then you can send them out. Any luck with General Cyrus, and Alpha Security locating Ms. Knoll and the others?"

"Negative."

"OK. I asked that a curtain, like in a theater, be put on our side of the chain link fence between the families and the studio. Done?"

"Affirmative."

"OK. We have less than 30 hours left of their deadline. Let's head in, I want to review the releases, see the studio, and then I want to meet the families."

Just 196 klicks, 122 miles, east of Bagram, sits the town of Torkham. What is unique about Torkham is that the town spans the border between Afghanistan and Pakistan and sits within the historical and treacherous Khyber Pass. The hills and mountains surrounding Torkham are part of the Baba mountain chain and are honeycombed with caves. Some of the mountain peaks to the west reach as high as 5,000m, 17,000 feet. Mount Washington in New

Hampshire, as a comparison, is a mere 6,288 feet high. What else is unique about Torkham is that five very special prisoners are being held in a cave compound that, like the town, spans both Afghanistan and Pakistan, allowing the captors to move captives instantly between countries, should the need arise.

Three of the five prisoners were badly beaten and still in their tattered, smelly uniforms. Beyond name rank and serial numbers, they gave nothing, and for that, they were tortured. Nothing as civilized as waterboarding, or sleep deprivation, more in the kneecapping, foot roasting, and tooth and nail extraction genre. Despite popular opinion, torture, as performed by a professional sadist, does work, and little by little they gave up what little secrets they had. Nothing, however, the terrorists didn't already know.

Jeff Matthews, Petrified 6, attempted an escape and rescue of Faith, but it failed. His leg wound, where they removed, more like ripped, the GPS tracker out of his calf, had not healed and held him back. The wound had become infected and only began to heal itself when maggots appeared and began eating the infection. *Thank god for small favors*, he thought.

One of the prisoners, the USO tribute singer, was left unharmed as long as he provided entertainment for the captors. Who knew Tom Jones and *What's New Pussycat* had such a diverse and lasting audience. He was not a soldier and would do whatever they wanted as long as they didn't hurt him.

The final prisoner was keep separated, and treated with care. If not being tortured could be considered caring. Faith Knoll sat on her metal bed with a threadbare wool blanket over her orange jumpsuit. The temperature in the cave at this altitude was just under 5 degrees Celsius. She was not bound, but access out of her cul-de-sac was blocked by guards. She was constantly watched by gaunt, hard men with beards and guns.

She didn't know why she had been singled out but realized after the video and by what the man said that her days were numbered. By her reckoning, she had only one day left to live. She knew she was a considered a famous person, but realized the demands that the terrorists made, could never be accepted. She may have been an "A" list celebrity, but she was under no illusions of her worth. Her government would search for her. She did know the President after all, but she was not worth the ransom and would soon die horribly. She had never seen an execution, but she had seen news reports and was familiar with the photograph of men in orange jumpsuits and what became of them. Could she die with honor? Everyone, her family, her mother, everyone would see her die. She had to be brave. She wanted to be brave, but she knew when the time came, she would tremble, plead, and cry.

She got down on her knees and prayed to God for strength. She had stopped praying for a rescue days ago. When she finished, she got up and sat on the bed and began to cry. She thought of the man she believed could help her, if only he could hear her. *"Israel, my dear Israel. I love you and miss you so much. If you can hear me, I need you. You're so far away, but if anyone on this earth can save me, I believe it would be you. I asked God for strength, but I'm asking you for salvation. Save me from this horrible place, and certain death. Although you never said so, I believe you and God have a special relationship and know each other well. I think you may have sent him many wicked souls.*

CHAPTER 59

WASHINGTON, DC

President Burk, the White House, Congress, America and the rest of the world waited. Everyone knew something was going to happen. Faith Knoll would be rescued, or she would die, or something else would happen. According to President Burk, that something "Was going to shake the world."

Down in the Situation Room, most of the twelve seats around the table were empty. Everyone was crowded at one end of the table studying Marine Corp Commandant General Joe Wheeler Jr.'s laptop. They included most of the National Security Team, Secretary of State Matt Walsh, CIA Director John Bader, NSA Director Admiral Roger Michaels, Director of National Intelligence James Dapper, and Director for Counterterrorism for the National Security Council Audrey Tomaso. The monitors were all on but with the sound muted. A staff assistant in the adjacent room was monitoring the news stations and would un-mute if something important broke. They were watching a live feed, on General Joe Wheeler's laptop, of the events unfolding in Catch 22, the name now assigned to Hanger 22, not just because it's the abducted families' new home but unfortunately because of the absurdity of it all.

By now the terrorist leaders, Mansour, al-Baghdadi, and al-Zawahiri, had all gotten word that most, if not all, of their families, had been taken prisoner by the Americans. For now, each leader thought it was only his family taken, but as more information became available, it became apparent that all three families had been taken prisoners. Initially, all three leaders thought Colonel Vova had abducted their family as an insurance policy, but now they feared the worst. The three were not permitted to communicate with each other, as previously instructed by Vova, but he was now the least of their worries. Chatter between all three became loud, and it soon concluded, from witnesses' reports and the American Satan's speech, that the American Delta Forces had taken their families. To hell with Vova and Russia. Blood is thicker than Vodka.

Colburn had given instructions that until Faith and the other four prisoners were returned safely, the US, and its allies would take absolutely no actions against the terrorists. Complete stand down against terrorist leaders, soldiers, training bases, car and truck caravans. Nothing gets hit, or taken out, lest they risk accidently killing the five Americans.

Kelly knew the President was upset and had never seen him so worried. She tried to stay close as First Lady, press secretary, and friend.

It was just after 5 a.m. when Secretary of Defense Stanton stuck his head in the Oval Office and said, "I'm ready when you are Mr. President."

President Burk, Kelly, Director Riley and Chief of Staff Nicholas all got up and followed the Secretary of Defense down to the Situation Room. Although they would be a bit early, it was 'Show Time'.

CHAPTER 60

BAGRAM, AFGHANISTAN

It was just after 2 p.m. in Bagram, 7 a.m. in Washington, when the Breaking News Report was released to the TV stations, print and social media.

Breaking News.

World Prosecutors Charge 3, and Their Families with Terror in Connection to Afghanistan Attacks and Kidnapping of Americans, Including Country Music Star, Faith Knoll.

World prosecutors charged three men and their families with terrorism-related offenses Saturday: Mullah Akhtar Mohammad Mansour, Leader of the Taliban, Ayman Mohammed Rabie al-Zawahiri, the Egyptian leader of al-Qaeda, and Abu Bakr al-Baghdadi, the Sunni Iraqi and leader of ISIL, all believed to have participated in this week's attacks on American bases, and kidnapping of Americans, including country music star, Faith Knoll.

The World prosecutor's office said an investigating judge formally handed down a death warrant for all three terrorists and their families. AL Jazeera has confirmed it will carry a live feed today at 5 p.m. Afghanistan IRDT time, noon EST, where the sentencing will be handed down. The terrorists are being charged with taking part in terrorist activities, terrorist murder, and attempted terrorist murder, kidnapping of American citizens, death threats against American citizens. Family members are being charged with aiding, abetting, and acting as an accessory to terrorist crimes.

A condensed 140 character version for Twitter was also tweeted.

Who exactly the World Prosecutor was, or where his authority came from, was not explained. The Breaking New Report did, however, have its desired effect. The world was on fire. Every world power, news agency, social media site, blogger and person in the street, heard about the scheduled live feed and would be watching. It was being estimated that the Breaking News Report reached over 3 billion people in less than 15 minutes. Colburn was only concerned in reaching four men, and that those four men would be watching *AL Jazeera* at 5 p.m.

Colburn checked and double checked all the systems to make sure there would be no mistakes. Backup generators, cameras, technicians, and interpreters were all in place. He ran through with General Troy's team, including the TV crew, exactly what was going to happen and how he wanted it staged. He would bring several family members out, in a similar fashion to what the terrorist had done with Ms. Knoll, threaten them and then make demands. They did several rehearsals with stand-ins, and when he felt they had it down he said,

"When we go live at 5 p.m., less than 2 hours from now. We are going to change the way America fights terror, and you are going to be part of history. We are going to fight evil with evil, and we will see which devil blinks first. We will only have one shot at this, so I need you to be strong and give me your best work."

To General Troy and Colonel Axelrod, he said, "Make sure you have your best men behind the cameras and on the link up with *AL Jazeera*. I don't want anyone to trip on a plug, and we end up going to black."

Everything that transpired, Breaking News Report, conversations, rehearsals, everything, since Coburn's arrival, was being live fed back to the Situation Room in Washington. The assembled National Security Team, including recently arrived President Burk, Press Secretary Sullivan, and FBI Director Riley, watched, on a large monitor, and listened with complete fascination.

"Well, it looks like Coburn's plan is to go tit for tat with the terrorists. Threaten their family members the way they threatened Ms. Knoll. But World

Prosecutor? As soon as Colburn opens his mouth, they will know it's us. I'm not sure the American public is ready for it, but it's a good plan, by God. I hope it works," said Secretary of Defense Stanton.

President Burk and Director Riley turned from the screen and made eye contact. Kelly saw it because she was watching for it. It was one of those quick hard looks men give each other when they know something no one else knows.

On the monitor, they watched Colburn and Smith walk through the gate door into the room that held the families. The fence curtain was down, and Wesson closed the gate and blocked access to the General and Colonel Axelrod. "He just needs some private time with the family," said Wesson.

Colonel Axelrod was about to push through, when General Troy held up his hand, "I believe we can give Mr. Colburn a moment alone."

At 4:45 p.m., Afghan time, 11: 45 a.m. EST, the Catch 22 studio director, co-incidentally named, Captain Major, cued up the camera, sound, and lighting crews. In his glass-enclosed control room, Captain Major stood behind his seated technicians who were live streaming an empty stage to the *AL Jazeera* studio in Doha Qatar. Monitoring *AL Jazeera* in the Catch 22 studio, Captain Major could see *AL Jazeera's* anchor personality preparing to go live with the Breaking News graphics, then an introduction. As soon as Captain Major received his cue from his other half in Qatar, he would start taping Colburn and send the feed to *AL Jazeera*, where they would show it live to the world. General Troy, had received a final private call from President Burk, ordering him to stay with the director, and make sure the live feed goes out exactly as Colburn wants.

Everyone in the Catch 22 studio, including General Troy, Captain Axelrod, and Captain Major were expecting something exciting. A video filled with just enough shock and drama to get them Emmys had they been a commercial agency broadcasting from Los Angeles. But when the gate opened at 4:50 p.m., and three men completely dressed in black from head to toe came out pushing three older men dressed in orange jumpsuits, the reality set in.

The curtain, painted to resemble the dessert, separating the family from the studio remained down, forming a background and contrasts for the six men in orange and black. Colburn, Smith, and Wesson were dressed almost identically to Saddam al-Jamal, Faith Knoll's captor. Each with a brown leather shoulder holster, black pistol, black three-hole balaclava hood, and a large Rambo type knife stuck in their tunic belt. The knife was actually a black Russian Special Forces "Falcon" Combat Knife with an 12" serrated blade.

They formed a triangle with Colburn and Abu Du'a al-Zawahiri, al-Zawahiri's father, in the forefront. Each of the three fathers had their hands tied behind their backs and were made to kneel in front of, but to the side of his captor. As the previous rehearsals established, the whole show should take no more than 5 minutes and would end up with Colburn and company threatening to kill the three fathers of Mansour, al-Zawahiri, and al-Baghdadi, if Coburn's demand for the immediate release of the five hostages, including Faith Knoll, was not accepted within a proposed time limit. The whole concept was bold and unprecedented, at least by American standards.

With the Breaking News Bulletin flashing on the screen in English and Arabic, the *AL Jazeera* anchor in Qatar, read from his Teleprompter the earlier press release, and finished by announcing in Arabic then in English the following warning, "We now must inform our viewers, that what you are about to see may be graphic, and is being presented to you live and uncensored. The source is reliable, but the location of origin is unavailable. We take you now live to…"

The floor director, in the Catch 22 Studio, got his cue from Captain Major and said 5,4,3,2…

The man in all black, the one in the center, began speaking in Arabic.

"Ana almuddaei aleamm aldduli. Ana aittaham thlatht rijal w 'asrahum biartikab jarayim tataeallaq bial'iirhab……

This was not the way it was rehearsed. Colburn did the rehearsals in English, and everyone was taken a bit back, but translators in the studio and the

Situation Room quickly began translating from Arabic to English, and the cameras keep rolling.

Colburn continued in Arabic with a translator translating into English,

> *I am the World Prosecutor. I charged three men and their families with terrorism-related offenses, Mullah Akhtar Mohammad Mansour, Leader of the Taliban; Ayman Mohammed Rabie al-Zawahiri, the Egyptian leader of al-Qaeda; and Abu Bakr al-Baghdadi, the Sunni Iraqi and leader of ISIL, are all believed to have participated in this week's Afghanistan Attacks and kidnapping of Americans, including American country music star, Faith Knoll. The World Prosecutor's office investigating judge formally handed down a death warrant for all three terrorists and their families. They are being charged with taking part in terrorist activities, terrorist murder, and attempted terrorist murder, kidnapping of American citizens, death threats against American citizens, aiding, abetting, and acting as an accessory to terrorist crimes.*
>
> *These three men kneeling before you are the three fathers of Mansour, al-Zawahiri, and al-Baghdadi, and they will pay the ultimate price. You gave America 48 hours to accept and conclude your demands in order for you to release Faith Knoll and the four other Americans. They have 24 hours left.*
>
> *We now propose to you a counter offer. You have 6 hours to deliver, to an American base, the five healthy prisoners, including Faith Knoll. If they are not received safe and sound to an American base within the six hours, at exactly 11 p.m. tonight, one member of each of your families will die every hour until they are returned or until your seed is gone. Then we will come for you. You have 6 hours to accept our terms or your mothers, wives, children, sisters, brothers, uncles, aunts, cousins and all their children, will pay for your errors with their lives. I will slice their throats and cut off their heads, and you and the world will watch them die a slow and painful death. You will see their infidel blood drain from their bodies the way it drains from all the innocents you have executed."*

So far so good, outstanding drama and pretty much as rehearsed, except for the Arabic, thought Captain Major. All Colburn had to do now was praise God, and then they would fade to black and wait to see if the terrorists comply with their counter offer.

The camera pulled back for the final wide shot of Coburn's sign off, but Colburn went off script. Way off script. Simultaneously all three men stepped behind their captives and wedged their kneeling captives bodies between their knees. They then placed their palm on each captive's forehead and with their fingers gouged into their captive's eyes, pulled the old men's heads back, and pulled out their knives.

Colburn looked into the camera and said, *"I condemn you to die."*

Before the Catch 22 studio, the Situation Room in Washington, and the world, Colburn, Smith, and Wesson sliced open the three father's throats. Blood spurted out all over the floor, onto the camera lenses and poured down their necks, onto their clothes and onto the floor. The fathers struggled and screamed as the men in black cut and sawed through their necks. Their screams turned to gurgles, the struggling to twitching, and the dark red blood turned to pink bubbles, as their severed windpipes sucked blood and air into their lungs. The twitching stopped, but the men in black kept cutting. It was horrible to watch, but only a few watching turned away.

Screams and banging on the fence from family members behind the curtain increased in volume as the bodies were released and slid to the floor. Their severed heads were placed upon their prone bodies.

General Troy, like everyone else in the studio, was in shock. They had all just watched an execution, but did they just participate in murder? Some were silent. Some were crying. Some were barely heard over the screams from the families, exclaiming "Damn," "Oh shit" or "Fuck me." Before he became sick to his stomach, General Troy gave one final non-rehearsed order to the stage crew. The curtain was raised revealing to the studio and the world, the crying and screaming families. Colburn walked back to the chain link fence, separating the studio from the families and with his knife still dripping blood, pointed it at the screaming, crying and panicked men, women, and children, all dressed in orange jumpsuits. Smith went through the gate and grabbed a young boy and brought him out into the studio.

Colburn walked over to Smith and the boy. The cameras followed. It was Arjomand, the boy who had planted the tracker in Faith's Humvee. He was so beautiful and delicate he could pass as a girl. He was also the son of al-Qaeda Operational Commander Ahmed al-Masri. Colonel Axelrod, at Colburn's suggestion, took the boy as an added precaution. Colburn wiped the blood from his knife onto his pants then placed the knife tip against the boy's delicate cheek and with little pressure drew blood. A tear dripped from the boy's eye and pooled with the blood on his cheek. The camera went in for a close up, and Colburn said in English,

> "Saddam al-Jamal, Warrior of God, We know who you are. If you put the knife to the woman Iman, I will put the knife to the son of your Commander Ahmed al-Masri. Before 11 o'clock tonight you will deliver the American woman and the four Americans, or by 11:01, your sons and daughters will be the next to feel the knife.
> Allāhu Akbar."

The camera went wide again to capture the full horror. No more words were necessary. The carnage, the screaming, and the crying, like the three fathers moments before, faded to black.

CHAPTER 61

WASHINGTON, DC

"The National Security Council members around the Situation Room table, President Burk, Kelly Sullivan, Bill Nicholas, and Director Riley stood all gaping at the monitor.

"Oh shit. Oh my God, what have we done?" said Secretary of Defense Stanton.

Several members, including Kelly, excused themselves and bolted for the bathrooms.

Colburn's face appeared on the secure live feed monitor, from the Catch 22 studio. He removed his balaclava and appeared, to those watching, a terrorist, a Jihadi warrior. He stood there wiping blood off his hands and looking fatalistic.

President Burk and Director Riley appeared to recover quicker. They knew where Colburn would take this. They both knew the terrorist leaders would just consider a threat an idol threat. They knew Colburn had to take it all the way. There would be no turning back now. *The dogs have been let loose,* thought Riley.

Colburn ignored everyone he saw in the room, except for the President and Riley.

"When they bring her in tonight, we're both going to leave right away. The jet that brought me is still here and standing by," said Colburn.

Ignoring what Colburn had said, Secretary of Defense Stanton said, "I can't condone what you have done here sir. I certainly didn't authorize it, and God only knows what damage you did today."

The Secretary of Defense wanted it on record that he had no beforehand knowledge of Colburn's actions in case everything went to hell. Colburn ignored Stanton and said,

"Mr. President, I know you will stand fast as weak links tremble. They will come. They know now that we have plunged into the abyss. They know if the five prisoners are not here by 11 p.m. tonight, less than 6 hours from now, I will kill their children and then the rest.

"How can you be so cold, sir?" said Stanton.

"Under your watch, Mr. Secretary, you have indiscriminately bombed cities and towns in Iraq, Syria, and Afghanistan. Your policies have killed thousands of innocent women and children. Collateral damage, I believe you call it. And yet you have accomplished nothing but more terrorism. If it were up to you alone, and thank God it's not, you would send in the army, navy, and air force to fight small bands of jihadist ideologists. Tens of thousands to kill hundreds. They will just hide in plain sight, and you will continue to kill thousands of women and kids to kill a few terrorists. You issue orders to kill. I, and others like me, had to carry your orders out. Don't lecture me, sir."

NSA Admiral Michaels finished reading a report just handed him. "Mr. Colburn, if you are correct, and the captives are returned tonight, and I hope they are, we can then release the families, and we can order an immediate strike on Mansour, al-Zawahiri, and al-Baghdadi. I was just handed a report that verifies considerable increase in chatter, from and between all three, and we have been able to lock on to each location. We can, in effect, eliminate their top management tonight."

"No Admiral. That's not an option. Before Faith is delivered tonight, those three will be long gone from their lairs. They read your book and know your capabilities. We keep the families, and they stay in our custody. We don't take out Mansour, al-Zawahiri or al-Baghdadi. As long as we have their families, we have them by the balls, and they will behave, at least towards us. The rest of the world powers will have to follow our lead, or they will become the targets."

"Soon we will know if you are right Mr. Colburn, and if you are, and I think you are, we will owe you a great deal of thanks. We will abide by your direction pertaining to the three terrorists and their families. Keep your friends close and your enemies closer," said President Burk.

"I know what I did tonight is difficult to swallow, but I know what I did was necessary and right. The world will soon know I'm right. They may not like what I did, but they will come to respect what I had to do and come to understand its effect."

Later, alone in the Oval Office, the President was at peace with his decision to let Colburn loose. It was now almost 2 p.m., 9 p.m., Afghan time and still nothing. As he waited for news, under the desk, Natasha with Max, curled up beside her, waited for her Da. "Soon girl. Your Da will be here soon."

Sarge safe, Max safe, Da and Faith gone, Natasha worried.

Half the world might agree with what we did but the other half, the Muslims, and their panderers, how will they react? Christians beheaded and burned was the will of Allah, but what of their own? Will they understand and accept the old Arabic proverb, 'Curses are like young chickens: they always come home to roost', thought President Burk.

CHAPTER 62

MOSCOW, ME

Colburn put another split piece of apple wood on the fire, then returned to his chair beside the brass fender. The fire smelled wonderful, like fresh vanilla. Natasha sat by his side, with her head buried in his lap. She had been very clingy since his return from Afghanistan a little over a month ago. He glanced left through the open doors, leading to the deck, and watched her standing there with the snow falling down on her hair and shoulders. She had on a navy Ralph Lauren shawl collar robe with white piping. It came to just above her knees, and the contrast between the snow, navy robe and her blond hair was striking. He got up and walked out onto the deck to join her. He came up behind, put his arms around her waist, and gently kissed the back of her neck. He felt a slight shudder. What happened in Afghanistan would never be completely forgotten, but they were trying their best to bury it deep into their dark subconsciousness. They had been at the cabin only two days, but everything seemed to be returning to normal. At least to what could be considered the new normal. The snow was starting to come down a bit harder now, sticking to the pine and fir tree branches, and starting to weigh them down like a Currier and Ives Christmas print.

It seemed so long ago and so far away, but the view from the cabin of the woods, filled with pine trees was not all that different from looking out of her cave in Afghanistan. They came for her sooner than she thought. She was not ready. The cave was dark, and someone threw something onto the bed.

"Get dressed now. We are leaving," said Saddam al-Jamal.

She recognized the voice and fear and panic enveloped her. She started shaking and crying. She didn't want to die. Not here. Not now. Not at night. She wanted, she deserved one more sunrise.

"Stop it. Get dressed now. If I were going to kill you, I wouldn't have you change your clothes. We are taking you home. You are free. Get dressed woman. We have no more time to waste."

She was loaded onto a truck with other Americans. The back of the truck was dark and smelled terrible, but she was able to talk. Three of the men were in bad shape, but one could talk, she recognized him as Johnny Jones, the singer, and he told her what he thought had happened. They drove for less than an hour to a big military airport she later found out was Jalalabad. Their truck, waving a white flag was stopped outside the perimeter of the base and searched. When security discovered the significant cargo, American army personnel from the 3rd Brigade Combat Team, 101st Airborne Division were called out, the transfer was made, and she and the other Americans were brought inside the base.

Jalalabad like all American bases was on alert for the return of Faith Knoll and the four other Americans. General Troy, at Bagram, 121 k, 75 miles away was notified, and Colburn boarded an Apache helicopter to retrieve Faith back to Bagram. Everything for Faith became a whirlwind of emotions. Two hours ago she thought she was going to die, and now she was on a secure line with her savior Israel Colburn, who was in the air, just minutes away. She knew he would come. She prayed he would come, and he heard her. She didn't know how he did it, but here he was.

After a cursory checkup at Bagram, Faith and Colburn wasted no time boarding their jet and leaving Afghanistan forever. Smith and Wesson headed out on a military transport to God knows where. The four other Americans were admitted to the army hospital for treatment and observation.

Colburn got off in Washington and said goodbye to Faith as she continued home to her family in Alabama. Faith needed some time with her family, and they would not see each other again until later when he came to take her to the cabin.

In Washington, Colburn reunited with Natasha and spent the night with the President. After dinner, around the dining room table with Director Riley and Kelly, the President said,

"Thank you for what you did. For a while there we were on pins and needles."

"Why?"

"Why? What if it didn't work? What if some Grand Mullah or Grand Ayatollah overruled their decision to release Faith, and they went through with her execution?"

"Then I would still be there, wouldn't I?"

"What did you say to the families when you went through the gate and spoke with them?"

"I told them exactly what I was going to do and why. I recognized one of the older men. He was someone I fought with against the Russians many years ago. Mohammed al-Zawahiri, the father of the terrorist al-Zawahiri. He was the Mujahedeen commander who wanted to kill the Russian Vova during a prisoner swap gone bad. In hindsight, I should have let him. I told him the story about the Russian's deal with his son, and he became visibly shaken. The thought that his son was working with the Russian, who decimated his Mujahedeen fighters so many years ago, was something he could not accept. I told them they had to decide who would be the three to die. Mohammed stood, followed immediately by the other two fathers. It seems the elders hate the Russians more than they do the Americans. This didn't go down well with the other family members, but the three fathers, as the family patriarchs and leaders, silenced them and told them it was their time to die. I promised them that no one else would die."

"You were that sure?"

"Yes."

"You couldn't have just threatened to kill them?"

"I've never threaten."

"The Mujahedeen taught you Arabic?"

"And Pashto."

Later that night Icy, Sarge, and the Captain, with Natasha and Max at their feet, told war stories around the fire and shared in the ritual begun just months before. They didn't expect to be together again soon but were happy they were. As they were getting up to leave all three tossed their whiskey tumblers into the fire. "To survivors," said Sarge.

The next morning Marine Two flew Colburn and Natasha back to Cambridge. This time, they were the only two passengers.

World condemnation flooded the White House and the Capitol, but with the safe return of Faith Knoll and her fellow captives, it changed to vindication and solidarity. Everyone loves a winner, and America had won. The loudest proponents, China, and Russia, reluctantly jumped on board. America had given the world a new way to fight and win against Islamic Terrorism. Just the threat of hitting them where it hurt, their families and their loved ones, seemed to reduce tensions and reprisals. The terrorists accepted that the world changed and would now play by a different set of rules. Rules that they didn't write, and rules they didn't like.

CHAPTER 63

MOSCOW, ME

Faith, Colburn, and Natasha took a walk down by the lake. The snow was still falling, although lightly now, and had accumulated about two inches. Natasha was off to the right, up the embankment, barking. They hiked up towards the barking, and as they got closer, she stopped barking and went into alert. Colburn stopped short when he saw why. He called Natasha off alert and to heel, which she did reluctantly. He led Faith and Natasha back to the cabin. Once inside Colburn stoked the fire, added a log and moved over to the bookcase near where Faith was standing. He turned a pilaster sconce, and a three-foot section of the bookcase slid away revealing a narrow stairway.

"Faith, I have something I want to show you."

The three of them walked down the stairs into a part of the cabin that didn't exist or at least didn't look like it should exist. They came to a small foyer with a metal door which opened when Colburn put his eye against the electronic scanner. They entered a self-contained 12'x12' panic room, complete with its own supplies, including; water, food, heat, lighting, fresh air system, and an ample supply of guns and ammunition.

"Israel, what's wrong?"

"I'm going to ask you to trust me. I want you to stay here and keep quiet. I have to go out for a while, but you'll be safe here."

It's not over, is it?"

"No, it isn't."

"I'm going to lock you in, and call for help. Stay quiet and don't open the door for anyone unless you know and trust them. There is a camera and a monitor." He pointed to a shotgun and said, "You're from Alabama, so I assume your Daddy taught you how to shoot."

She nodded.

He grabbed a Spec Ops M4A1 automatic rifle with red dot sight, and silencer, along with an ECWCS, (extended cold weather clothing system) and harness which included a Glock G-41, 13 round 45 cal. pistol, and extra magazines for both. He put on the uniform, boots, and harness and showed Faith a trap door that opened to a tunnel. He kissed her, opened the trap door and said, "Use this tunnel as an escape of last resort. It leads to the lake." He handed her a small tracker, the size of a vitamin capsule and told her to swallow it. Colburn and Natasha headed to the lake through the tunnel.

I'm in a cave again, and I am going to die this time. They are going to get me and the only person that can save me just left me alone, thought Faith.

Outside by the lake, Colburn took out his Sat Blackphone and called the President,

"Icy, good to hear from you."

"Sarge he's here. I have Faith tucked away and trackable, but I don't know how many bad guys are out there. I'm going now to deal with it. Send the cavalry, and send them fast."

What had spooked him, while outside was what Natasha alerted to. Boot tracks in the snow. Not just any boots, Russian Spetsnaz boots.

The President, who helped Colburn build the cabin and security systems, knew exactly what he meant by "tucked away and trackable." He got ahold of FBI Director Riley, and Riley got ADC NY Hoar to get a field SWAT team up to Moscow ASAP. He then called SAC Ceretti in Bangor to get whatever assets available over to Colburn's cabin. He told him why and to secure the cabin and Ms. Knoll, and to notify the locals in Moscow and Bingham to secure the roads and make noise.

From a clearing halfway up Wolf Mountain, Colonel Vova, and his five-man Special Forces Spetsnaz unit, had a telescope focused on the cabin.

"Where are they?" asked Vova.

"Something spooked them by the lake. They headed back to the cabin. No one's come out," said Lieutenant Nikolai Alekhin.

"He knows we're here."

Colburn and Natasha exited the tunnel to the lake embankment, completely hidden from view. They followed the embankment until they came to where Natasha found the boot prints and followed them up the mountain. Natasha was eager to rush ahead but unlike Maggie, she was no war dog, and would have to learn on the job.

Vova and his team were equally equipped as Colburn. They all carried suppressed 9 mm SR-3 Vikhr compact automatic assault rifles and 17 round, 9mm Strizh pistols, and a few other goodies.

Natasha heard them first and alerted. Men, soldiers, moving down the mountain towards the cabin. Vova, Sergeant Georgy Zhukov, and Corporal Ivan Kolosov stayed up in the clearing monitoring the house and communicating by Motorola T460 2-way radios with Lt. Alekhin and his two man assault team, heading down the mountain towards the cabin.

Colburn was in great shape for an older man, but he was no spring chicken, and he, like other older men, knew they just didn't have the power and stamina they had when they wore a younger man's uniform. He knew he had to move fast and could not get in hand to hand with these young soldiers. He wouldn't last but a few seconds. From his blind, he and Natasha watched the three soldiers coming down the hill 50 meters away. Colburn put his hand on Natasha's snout and whispered, "Quiet girl. Please." He placed the rifle stock into his shoulder and looked through the site, armed the laser and placed the red dot on the forehead of the third man, just below his khaki watch cap, and squeezed the trigger. A low cough sounded and at the other end, a puff of red, pink, and white erupted from the back of the man's head. He quietly dropped into the snow, and because of the military interval maintained between them, the two in front didn't hear a thing. Colburn took aim on the next man in line, but suddenly the leader held up his hand indicating a halt, and took out his radio and listened. As he did, he turned to look behind him. He saw one man down and for a split second saw a red dot on his corporal's forehead before it exploded. He had one second to bring his rifle around or try to warn Colonel Vova. He didn't get to make the decision. Lt. Alekhin watched the red lazar dot climb the front of his tunic and knew it was over. The dot stopped on his head. He could almost feel it; then he couldn't.

Colburn and Natasha sprinted to the leader's prone body and souvenired his radio, then dashed back towards their blind, passed it, made a loop around into another dense blind and waited to see if anyone would follow. An old Vietnam RON (remain overnight) ambush tactic. Colburn listened, to the radio, as Vova was trying to contact Lt. Alekhin while Natasha growled at Vova's voice. Colburn waited ten minutes to see if their original blind was discovered then he pressed the talk button.

"Your assault team is down Vova. Will you come to me or shall I come to you?"

Colonel Vova feared only two men, Putin, and Icy. Putin feared only Icy and had given Vova one last chance to clean up his mess, and if he didn't kill Icy he couldn't come back to Russia. Icy, Vova knew, was getting old like himself, but even old, Icy was still an Alpha Predator.

"Come to me Icy. I believe I am your elder, and a bit slower, but do bring your bitch, would you?"

"I'm a bit slower myself, but just wait there, we'll be along shortly."

Vova signaled Sergeant Zhukov and Corporal Kolosov, to set up for an ambush. Vova knew he would probably die here today, and that was OK, as long as he could take Icy and his bitch with him.

It was just after 4 p.m. The sun was starting to set on the other side of the mountain. The trees were casting shadows and darkness was settling in. The snow was still falling, and about four inches had accumulated, but with his snow uniform on, Icy was warm and almost invisible. Natasha was never cold with her silver and black fur coat. Icy changed magazines, just to be safe, and he and Natasha started up the mountain.

Icy spotted Vova standing alone between a large felled tree and an earthen rise. From his higher vantage point, Icy could see, to Vovas left, a cliff that introduced a deep gorge. Vova, he knew, was baiting himself and would have a sniper, maybe two, hidden away. He had to take the snipers out first. He found two possible blinds and put a round into the first and got movement. A slight reaction to the crack of a supersonic projectile as it passed close by. He studied the blind and saw the tip of a sniper's barrel and walked his laser dot up the barrel to where he thought the head would be and fired. A soft cough from his M4 and the snipers barrel dropped an inch. He would take that as a hit. He searched for another sniper, but if there was one, he was very good and well concealed.

Vova was getting cold and tired of standing in the open. He had earlier changed channels on his radio and broke squelch. He had only one squelch reply, and it was Sergeant Zhukov. That meant Corporal Kolosov was down. He turned back around and came face to face with Icy and his wolf.

"You're like a ghost, Icy."

Natasha growled and snarled at Vova. Up until now she had only heard his voice, but his scent was unmistakable. Stronger than the glove her Da would let her tear apart whenever Vova called. Icy stayed behind the tree and out of the sightline from where another sniper if there were one, would probably be hiding.

Natasha was brave, but she was no war dog. She had the protective instinct that most German Shepherds have, but she was not Maggie and moved forward towards Vova. Vova had his pistol holstered, and Icy reached down to stop her, and that was their undoing. As he reached out, a shot rang out, and Icy was hit in the chest and went down. Natasha saw her Da go down and turned back to Vova. But now Vova had his pistol out and had it aimed directly at her.

Helicopters and sirens could be heard coming from below the mountain and from the highway, and Vova knew he had to move fast.

Icy, and now his wolf bitch, thought Vova.

Vova was about to fire when a foul odor and deep guttural growl enveloped him from behind. He turned slightly towards the fallen tree trunk, and there sat a huge Timber Wolf inches from his head, lips pulled back, fangs bared, eyes wide and threatening. Distracted, he failed to see Natasha come flying through the air, jaws apart, gums bared revealing her fangs. In less than a millisecond Natasha had Vova by the throat clamping down with such tremendous pressure that he was lifted off the ground. Vova's face was only inches from Natasha's, and he could see the pleasure in her eyes, the same look he had in his own eyes when he was about to end someone's life. He tried to scream, but nothing came out but blood and gurgling sounds. It was over soon, and as Natasha backed off, her mouth still contained most of Vova's throat tissue, muscle, and carotid artery. She turned to look for her Da, but he was gone. She went crazy. She couldn't even find his scent because her mouth and face were full of Vova's blood. She disgorged what was left in her mouth, rubbed her face in the snow and removed most of the blood. She was able to find her Da's scent, but it led to the cliff edge and into the gorge and then it was gone. Her cry was primal.

Down in the clearing by the cabin, they heard it. FBI SAC Ceretti, Agent Ross, and three other agents arrived by helicopter, just minutes before from Bangor, to secure the cabin. As they would attest to later the sound of the cry was something so sad and haunting they would remember it forever. The FBI SWAT team from NY was still ten minutes out, as was Marine One with the President, First Lady, Max, and FBI Director Riley.

It was close to 5 p.m. by the time the SWAT team touched down, cleared and secured the area. They found Vova's body, and Natasha sitting by the cliff ledge focused on the deep gorge. They found one sniper, head shot and another mauled, and half eaten by what appeared to be wolves. They found three more with head shots further down the hill. What they did not find was Colburn, but they had a good idea where he was.

The state police found a sea plane abandoned in Wyman Lake about three miles north of Colburn's cabin. They suspected the Russians came in on the seaplane and intended to leave the same way.

President Burk and Kelly Sullivan were in the cabin trying to console Faith. She was in shock after being locked in the safe room and left alone by Colburn. She wanted to go home. They didn't tell her anything about what happened to Colburn. They didn't really know themselves.

When Riley came back in with an all clear, he, President Burk, and a couple of Secret Service agents struggled up the mountain. It was almost 6 p.m. and would soon be dark, but the snow had stopped, and they had plenty of flashlights and torches to light the way. When they arrived at the killing site, they found Natasha still sitting and intently staring into the gorge. She acknowledged Sarge but seemed inconsolable and very anxious. They looked towards the gorge and with the help of the SWAT team commander were able to piece together what happened. They went over to the gorge and looked down. It was deep, jagged, and foreboding. They yelled Coburn's name, both names, but expected no response and got none. They would have climbers go down tomorrow, first light. Natasha was circling now and crying.

Da gone, Pack gone, Natasha sad, Da needs Natasha, Natasha needs her Da.

President Burk and Director Riley turned to look at the instigator of all their problems. Vova looked like a man lying on a white snow sheet with his head upon a red pillow. Aside from a missing throat, he looked too serene for a man of such scheming and violence. They turned back to Natasha, but she was gone. "Oh God," said President Burk, "No girl please, you didn't."

CHAPTER 64

MOSCOW, ME

The snow started again effectively grounding the President in the cabin for the night. Faith would have Colburn's room, President Burk, Kelly and Max could use the guest bedroom, and FBI Director Riley would get the couch. The other FBI agents and Secret Service who weren't on duty could bunk out on Marine One or in town. Tomorrow morning, the President, Kelly, Max, and Faith would head back to Washington and home while Director Riley and his agents continued the search and investigation.

It was close to midnight, and the girls were in their rooms asleep, and the guys, Sarge, the Captain and Max sat around the fire. On the mantel, the Captain noticed something he missed earlier. Three Waterford Diamond 7oz straight sided crystal tumblers, three Montecristo Cuban cigars, a wedge cutter and Icy's old Zippo lighter. On the sideboard were a bottle each, of Jameson Limited Reserve and Bushmill Old Single Malt.

"Do you think he knew this was going to happen? Could he have known Vova would come for him?" asked the Captain.

"I would never second guess Icy, but here it is, isn't it."

The Captain got up and poured some Jameson and Bushmill into the three crystal tumblers and handed one to Sarge, kept one himself and placed Icy's on the table between them.

As before, in the White House, Sarge said, "To God."

The Captain, replied, "To the Queen."

They both gave a little sigh, swirled the glass, sniffed, then drank.

The Captain reached for the cigars, as Sarge and Max got up and turned towards the glass doors leading to the deck. The Captain hesitated and said, "How does this end?"

"I guess we'll find out tomorrow."

"No. I mean now. How does this end," the Captain was looking at Icy's crystal tumbler.

Sarge thought a moment then said, "Just place it on the mantel."

"To survivors," said Sarge.

"And to absent friends," added the Captain.

Sarge took one last sip from his glass and tossed his crystal tumbler into the fire, as they had done at the White House. The Captain followed suit. The little alcohol left in the glass caused the fire to jump. The Captain picked up Icy's crystal tumbler, careful not to spill any, and placed it on the mantel.

They then headed out on the deck to smoke their cigars.

EPILOGUE

The town of Moscow was mostly all asleep except for the some of the SWAT team, local and state police, and a few townies. The Moscow Elementary School had been commandeered by Mayor Logan as the 'Go To' place for news and reporters. Bunks were set up in the gym, and it already had a small kitchen, dining area, and facilities. Timmy was still awake, making notes, and recording the day's events. His new hero, Tom Sweeney, was in town, and talking to him about becoming an investigative reporter. Todd was also in town, and he and Agent Ross had a delightful dinner and were now squeezed into student size desks talking about things.

The day had been a horror for some, a job for others, and a boon for the news stations and reporters that filled the town. Sweeney and Todd seemed to know more than anyone else about what happened, but were being very guarded and stingy releasing information. But the reporters and news stations, now flooding in from around the country and the world, were falling all over themselves interviewing anyone who could walk and talk. Todd and Sweeney had finished their breaking front page story for tomorrow's *NY Post,* which Todd had just sent it in. The headline read, "Russians Invade Moscow." You can imagine where it went from there.

The snow was ending, and it was less than a minute till midnight when Timmy shushed everyone and ran to the school's front door and pushed it open to the outside. Todd, Sweeney, Agent Ross, Pastor Buffer, Mayor Logan and Chief Pruitt all followed. Everyone knew that Timmy had the "ins" about everything in the town, and were expecting to see Russians stumbling out of the woods or two competing TV news reporters fighting over a background set up, but nothing of the sort. Timmy was just staring north with his hand up indicating quiet. Then they all heard it. From the top of Wolf Mounting came the spine-tingling howls of a pack in chorus, the "bark-howling" cries of chorusing wolves. The Wolf Mountain wolf pack had been growing in size. From the base of the mountain, where the cabin stood, they heard the return call of a wolf, which Timmy explained to everyone, was not a wolf but President Burk's German Shepherd Max. The conversation continued between animals while the humans remained quiet and transfixed.

Somewhere deep in the middle of the mountain came a lonesome call of a solitary wolf. Max attempted to jump off the deck but was restrained by the President. The wolves on the mountain, however, made their way down the mountain and soon the chorusing became one. Like a sad, haunting, echo.

Dawn came early, and things started to stir in the cabin. Coffee was brewing, and stuff was being packed and taken out to the helicopter. In the clearing, behind the cabin, Kelly and Faith said goodbye to Riley and with the assistance of several Secret Service agents made their way to Marine One. Kelly would tell Faith about Colburn after they were in the air.

The President and Riley had a moment together before he had to board.

"I have climber's now getting ready to repel into the gorge," said Riley.

"Keep me posted," said the President.

"Is it finally over?" asked Director Riley.

"Yea, I think it's over."

"But how does it end?" asked Riley.

"That depends on what you find, or we can just read about it in today's NY Post. Or...."

"Or what?" asked Riley.

"Or we can wait for Fitzy to finish his book."

The President followed by Max, walked out of the cabin to board Marine One. Director Riley walked past the couch he slept on last night, over to the fireplace and began spreading out the ashes, pieces of broken glass, and extinguished any burning embers. He placed the iron poker back in the stand and walked to the door. His thoughts were on all the sadness he would find today, and he failed to notice the Icy's crystal tumbler, which he placed on the mantel the night before, was empty.

ACKNOWLEDGEMENTS

As an Architect, I would design a project in my mind then have a team help me bring it to life. We would finish the design and present it to the client and then it was 'frozen', no more changes permitted. It would then get built. When the project opened, I would go and watch to see if the people interacted within the space as I intended. If so it was a success. I never knew otherwise.

As a writer, I wrote this book in my mind but not completely. It was never 'frozen'. I enjoyed having the opportunity to change and add ideas up until the end and then some. Writing is a more solitary profession and a sad day when it comes to the end.

I am dyslexic, and I can't imagine two more difficult professions to attempt, than architect and writer.

For Linda Lamm who knew me as an architect and now as a writer. She was with me through the entire process giving me well needed advice and encouragement.

To my wife Patricia who put up with me, but was always there to help.

For Robert Crais and Maggie, who gave Natasha a voice.

For Tommy Dean who served as a composite model for Tommy Burk. Tommy and I left for Vietnam together as young Marines. Had he lived he would have achieved greatness, of that I am certain. I hope I was able to shine a little light on what might have been.